CRITICAL ACCLAIM FOR SONYA BIRMINGHAM

Winner Of The Colorado Romance Writers Award Of Excellence.

FROST FLOWER

"*Frost Flower* is sure to steal your heart!"

—*Romantic Times*

ALMOST A LADY

"It took a fine stroke of genius to create such wonderful characters and bring them to life!"

—*Rendezvous*

RENEGADE LADY

"Sonya Birmingham captures the backwoods flavor with absolute perfection!"

—*Affaire de Coeur*

"Sonya Birmingham is talented in the clever use of contrast. Her love scenes are tender, passionate, and sometimes exotic, teasing, and tantalizing!"

—*Rendezvous*

SPITFIRE

"Sonya Birmingham is a winning new talent!"

—*Romantic Times*

Other *Leisure Books* by Sonya Birmingham:
FROST FLOWER

"A Brilliant story! 4+"
—Rendezvous

A BITTERSWEET KISS

Soft, tender feelings overcame Silky, and like a rose being torn apart by the wind, she almost surrendered to Taggart. But gradually her rational mind gained control of her desire and she realized her curiosity had gotten her into this predicament. She'd bargained for a kiss, but was getting much more—more than she could handle and still look him in the eye. Surely he would think she was an easy conquest if she didn't put a stop to the lovemaking right now. With fluttering lashes, she opened her eyes and eased away from Taggart, her skin still glowing from his hands.

Her fingers quaking, she pulled her gown into place and met his searching gaze, realizing she'd almost lost control of herself. Now standing at arm's length from him, she surveyed his tense face, which seemed all harsh planes and angles. For a moment she glimpsed the fire within him; then she sensed he was also reining in his emotions.

This time she'd managed to dredge up enough discipline to save her virginity, but truth be told, she still hungered desperately for his touch. She'd saved herself this time, she realized, still light-headed from the fiery kiss...but what about next time?

A LEISURE BOOK®

October 1996

Published by

Dorchester Publishing Co., Inc.
276 Fifth Avenue
New York, NY 10001

Printed in the United States of America.

Sonya Birmingham

Scarlet Leaves

LEISURE BOOKS  NEW YORK CITY

Scarlet Leaves is dedicated to my husband, Milt Birmingham, who patiently listened to me talk almost nonstop about the Civil War as I wrote the book. A gallant Southern gentleman, he has given me immeasurable love and support while I lived through the years from Fort Sumter to Appomattox Courthouse. Exhibiting the chivalry of Robert E. Lee, the tenacity of Stonewall Jackson, and the raw nerve of John Singleton Mosby, he stood up under an unrelenting barrage of adjectives, adverbs, and superlatives. Like Silky Shanahan, his war is now over and a blessed peace has settled upon the land, not to mention his battered ears. As Nathan Bedford Forrest said, he will always be the "firstest with the mostest."

A heartfelt thanks to my amazing mother, Cordie Tucker, whose lively wit and colorful imagination are a constant source of inspiration.

Roses to the fantastic staff of the Burleson, Texas, Public Library, who for years have tracked down and obtained all those much needed historical research books, no matter how obscure.

SCARLET LEAVES

AUTHOR'S NOTE

By the end of the Civil War, Union spymaster General George H. Sharpe had placed two hundred intelligence agents throughout the South, sending them into service with small fortunes in bogus Confederate money to aid their work. Coded telegraphic messages routinely flew across the lines, often unknowingly keyed in by operators who had no idea what they really contained.

In *Scarlet Leaves*, the character of Caroline Willmott was suggested by the famous Union agent Elizabeth Van Lew, acknowledged to be one of the greatest female spies of all time. Before her death, she became destitute and was supported by the ex-slaves she had freed and educated, and by donations from Union soldiers she had helped.

Upon entering Richmond, the Union forces restored order and brought the fires under control. Lee and a remnant of his army rode west, hoping to unite with Johnston for a last stand. In a final burst of glory, the starving Southern forces made a lionhearted charge in an effort to cut through Grant's lines and reach the mountains of Virgina. The Union was partially driven back, but in the end, the North's superior numbers and firepower took the day.

Dignified and regal, and dressed in an immaculate gray uniform, Lee met Grant at Appomattox Courthouse on April 9, 1865, and received the generous terms of surrender that Lincoln wanted. Grant later reported that rather than rejoicing in Lee's surrender, he was disheartened at the defeat of a foe who had fought so long and valiantly and lost so much. After four bloody years, the battle flags were furled, the muskets were silenced, and peace once again reigned over a united America, just bursting into spring blossom.

Chapter One

The Blue Ridge Mountains
Early October, 1864

"Lordamercy," Silky Shanahan whispered to her cousin Charlie, pulling him down behind a clot of thick laurel bushes. "There's a buck-naked man over yonder taking a bath in old man Johnson's pond!"

Never in all of her nineteen years had Silky witnessed anything like the riveting sight before her, and she carefully peeked through the leaves at the handsome, black-haired stranger a mere fifteen yards distant. Hot blood stung her cheeks at her first glimpse of a nude male, and inside, a wild sensation flared up, thrilling and frightening at the same time.

Illuminated by the rosy sunset, the tall, well-built man whistled as he splashed water over his muscled arms, obviously unaware of his secret observers. His clothes were draped over a log at the side of the pond while his horse, one of the finest mares Silky had ever seen, cropped grass, her reins loosely tied to a sapling.

When Silky had set out squirrel hunting this pleasant October afternoon, she'd never expected *this*. She and Charlie had just called it a day when she'd spotted the man. Now, dry leaves crackling beneath her, she scrunched on her stomach so the stranger wouldn't see her.

Fourteen-year-old Charlie, his freckled face alight with curiosity, pulled down his Confederate cap and scooted to her side. "Do you think he's ours or theirs?" he asked, echoing Silky's own thoughts.

"I don't know. That's what I'm trying to find out."

With the war raging, every able-bodied male in Sweet Gum Hollow had joined the Confederacy, leaving only feeble grandfathers and skinny boys like Charlie in this part of Virginia, so she hadn't seen such a fine specimen of manhood in years.

His broad, thickly haired chest lathered, the stranger turned about, presenting a view of his firm backside and slim hips. Letting her gaze move upward, Silky considered his haircut, then swallowed hard. This wasn't just any stranger, she suddenly decided—this good-looking man was the enemy!

With a soft chuckle, she elbowed her cousin in the ribs. "I think the good Lord has just given us the opportunity to participate in the war," she murmured, clutching the stock of her long-barreled rifle. "I'd bet my last Confederate dollar that's a Yankee we're looking at."

The redheaded boy squinted at the man. "Lordy . . . you can tell he's a Yankee buzzard by just lookin' at his backside?"

Silky pulled in a breath of pine-scented air, thinking that sometimes Charlie stretched the bonds of kinship to the limits. "No, of course not."

The stranger turned around, facing them as he lathered his legs.

"Look at his hair," she advised in a low voice. "Most of our soldiers lop off their own. That's a high-dollar barbershop haircut if I ever saw one." She nodded in the man's direction. "And that fancy mustache of his has a peculiar droop to it."

"That ain't all that's droopin'," Charlie replied with a

dry chuckle. "That water must be a mite chilly, but not as cold as it's gonna be a couple of weeks from now when the weather starts turnin'."

Silky, knowing a haircut wasn't enough to go on, studied the man's mare. "Take a gander at that fine piece of horseflesh," she ordered, surveying the grazing animal. "If I'm not mistaken, that's a U.S. Army saddle on that mare."

With a thoughtful frown, her cousin obeyed, then glanced at the stranger's discarded clothes. "Maybe so, but I don't see no Yankee uniform on that log."

"The man's probably a Union scout. Sometimes they don't wear uniforms."

"He might be just another drummer up from the flatlands," the boy proposed hopefully.

Silky considered the stranger's fine, high boots that he'd discarded near the log. "I don't think so. A drummer hasn't been through this neck of the woods since the war started. And I never saw a drummer wearing boots like that." She refocused on the man's magnificent body. No, this was no drummer, not this man, who positively radiated an air of vitality and confidence. She gave her floppy mountain hat a decisive tug. "I expect he's a Yankee, all right, and we're going to capture him."

"Capture him?" Charlie blurted out a little too loudly.

The soft wind had been covering their voices, but the stranger stopped bathing and, instantly alert, scanned the bushes.

"Now you've done it." Silky groaned, clasping the boy's arm. "We'll have to do something right away or he'll be moving on quicker than a snake through a hollow log."

Charlie widened his eyes. "I don't know about this. I—"

She clapped her hand over his mouth. "Are we going lay here jabbering, or get up and capture the rascal like the good Confederates we are?"

He pushed her hand away. "Land o' livin' "—he moaned—"what'll we do with him if we catch him?"

Silky knew there was a home guard in the hollow, but most of the men were so old and feeble they might let him get away, while the others were mean as striped snakes and would kill him before he could be properly questioned. "We'll put him up in the smokehouse," she answered easily. "We'll keep him locked up until a regular Confederate column comes through, then turn him in."

Charlie's lips trembled. "I-I've never taken a prisoner of war before."

"When I holler 'now,' " Silky commanded, giving his shoulder a little shake, "just stand up, point your rifle at him, and follow me. You can do that, can't you?"

For a moment her own courage wilted; then she remembered her brother, Daniel, soldiering with one of General Joe Johnston's regiments. With all he'd given to the Cause, how could she flinch from capturing one Yankee—especially when she'd literally caught him with his pants down? Why, it was her honor-bound duty to take the rogue in!

Her heart slamming against her ribs, she rose, cried "Now!" and started running. At the same time Charlie shot up and, making a great thrashing sound against the bushes, trailed her flying heels.

The startled bather dropped his soap in astonishment as Silky rushed toward him. An oath tumbling from the man's mouth, he moved toward dry land, but she cried, "Freeze, stranger, or you'll be shaking hands with eternity." She zinged a shot over his head to stop him. "Get your hands up and keep 'em up. I'm taking you prisoner of war!"

The man turned and raised his hands, his rakish grin saying he couldn't believe what had just happened. "Oh, you are?" he replied in a low, raspy voice. "Would you mind telling me why?"

Surprisingly flushed and weak kneed, Silky gazed at his sapphire eyes and flashing smile. Besides an abundance of crisp, black hair, he'd been blessed with a chiseled nose, high cheekbones, and a strong chin. Lord, Yankee or not, he was the handsomest devil she'd ever clapped eyes on, and for some strange reason, every nerve in her body tingled with anticipation. "Because you're a Yankee, that's why," she answered loud and clear. "If you aren't aware of it, there's a war going on and you're the enemy."

The words *you're the enemy* lingered in the air as Major Matt Taggart of the Army of the Potomac surveyed the unlikely pair. A cool breeze played against his wet skin, and he repressed an urge to groan and laugh at the same time. After slipping into Virginia by way of the Blue Ridge to avoid detection, the Union intelligence officer had just reached what he'd thought was a totally isolated area where he could rest and bathe. Now, ironically, he'd been abducted by a feisty mountain girl and a gangly boy with a cowlick poking from beneath his cap.

Over his first shock, Taggart let his gaze skip over the girl once more, and decided he'd never seen a more tempting example of Southern womanhood. Garbed in boots and snug buckskins, her soft curves had snagged his attention at first glance, but it was her creamy skin, sparkling green eyes, and cloud of auburn hair under a battered hat that now held his attention.

"Look here, Fancy Pants," he said expansively, noticing the dangling fringe on her buckskin breeches. "You've got it all wrong. Why, I was born and bred in the South."

"You don't sound like any Southerner I ever heard."

"Good God Almighty, woman," he said, realizing she was nobody's fool. "Who in the blue blazes are you, anyway?"

Silky lifted her chin a bit higher. "My first name is Silky and my last name is Shanahan." Her eyes on Taggart, she tilted her head toward her cousin, who clenched his rifle so tightly his knuckles had turned white. "This is my cousin, Charles Lynchfield McIntire, but the home folks just call him Charlie."

Taggart noticed the cool, slick pond bottom against the soles of his feet as he eased into the deeper water, covering up his vital areas. "If you'll permit me?" he asked, purposefully sending her his best smile. "I've always felt even a prisoner of war should be accorded some measure of dignity. You being a lady and all . . ."

Silky gave him a measured glance. "Don't be thinking you can smooth-talk your way out of this situation because I'm a girl, Yankee. There aren't any womanly curves on my trigger finger."

Taggart edged toward his clothes, only to hear two bullets whiz past his ear and explode into the log. With an astonished blink, he saw the log had been splintered and his belongings bounced on the grass. Jerking about, he noticed a mischievous grin race over Silky's lips.

"Seems we're not speaking the same language, stranger. I think I'll let this Henry repeating rifle do the talking for me," she said saucily. "I can load it on Sunday and shoot all week."

"I thought I'd put on my clothes. I—"

"I'll tell you when you can put on your clothes, Yankee."

Irritation raced through Taggart's veins like wildfire. At first the situation had surprised him, then amused him—but Lord Almighty, no woman told him when he could put on his own pants, no matter how fetching she was. "Now look here, you spitfire," he announced, narrowing his eyes at her. "I'm coming out of this pond, I'm putting on my pants, and I'm riding out of here." He jabbed a finger at her. "Do you understand that?"

Silky blasted three more shots into the pond, spewing water over him. "Move again and you'll be pumping thunder in hell at three cents a clap," she promised evenly.

Damn, the little heller was crazy. Crazy as a Confederate bedbug and determined to take him in! Stealing a swift glance at the boy who'd calmed down enough to hold the rifle without shaking, he realized that he wouldn't get any help from him either. No, this pair wouldn't be bullied into letting him out of the pond, so he'd have to change his battle plan. The only way through this situation was brazen charm—something all the ladies in Ohio told him he possessed in abundance.

Silky, her demeanor all business, studied him like a suspicious hawk. "What's your name and what's your company, Yankee?"

"My name is Matt Taggart," he answered in a warm, charming voice, "but I'm not a Yankee. I'm a Confederate—a lieutenant in the Forty-third Virginia Cavalry," he announced, making up the first thing that came to his mind. "I'm on extended compassionate leave. I've been taking care of my widowed aunt in the Shenandoah."

"The Shenandoah? That devil Sheridan is burning the Valley."

Taggart held a forced grin. "That's why I was there. The Union fired my aunt's farmhouse and I've been helping her relocate. I'm just taking a shortcut through this gap to get back to my company on the Rappahannock River."

She glanced at his clothes, then back at him. "Where's your uniform, then?"

He smiled, relieved he had a good answer for her. "As you know, the Yankees make frequent raids on the Shenandoah," he explained with a chuckle, "so I thought it might be a good idea not to wear one." To his dismay, Taggart noted that her suspicious gleam hadn't wavered one iota.

"How do you explain that saddle your mare is wearing?" She sniffed loftily. "It looks like U.S. government issue."

"It is," Taggart replied, realizing it had been a mistake to use his own saddle, no matter how comfortable it was. "I confiscated it after the Battle of Shiloh."

She aimed her rifle at a spot between his eyes. "You don't say? That still doesn't explain your Yankeefied way of talking, does it?"

"Well," he replied good-naturedly, feeling secure enough to put down his hands and laugh a bit, "I went to college up North, and their way of talking kind of wore off on me." He rubbed the back of his neck, wondering if she would let him out of the pond now. "Yes sir, my loyalty is to old Jeff Davis and the bonnie blue flag."

Silky nodded wisely. "It is, huh? Well, Charlie and I are going to give you a little test and see how much of a Southerner you really are."

"Fine," he replied, understanding that his only hope was to play along with her. "Go right ahead."

She studied him thoughtfully. "All right . . . tell me what goes into homemade soap?"

Taggart rubbed his chin. Being raised in one of the finest homes in Cleveland, he'd always used hard-milled French soap, and had never given a second thought to its components. But dredging up information from his West Point chemistry classes, he took a wild stab and, speaking up confidently, answered, "Alkali, some kind of fatty acid, and—"

"Wrong," Silky came back, abruptly cutting him off. "Around here we make soap from water, lye, and bacon drippings."

Taggart shrugged negligently. "Well, anybody can miss one question, you know."

Charlie shot him a lopsided grin. "How long do you let whiskey work afore runnin' it off?"

Taggart sighed, having no idea. "A week?" he guessed, frowning at the boy.

Charlie hooted with laughter. "That whiskey would taste like a hog died in it, mister. You run white lightnin' on the fifth day."

Not giving Taggart a chance to recover, Silky pinned him with a keen gaze. "What kind of wood do you use for a crow call?"

He chuckled, knowing he would get this question right. "Pine or ash, of course."

She shook her head. "Every true Southerner knows crow calls are made from green dogwood branches."

Taggart's temper rose higher. He hadn't come on an intelligence-gathering mission for General Grant to stand in a pond of cooling water at sunset and be interrogated by this wildcat. If he couldn't unearth the number of General Joe Johnston's troops and relay the information to his contact by November 15th, hundreds of Federal soldiers could lose their lives, and the Union Information Bureau would be humiliated. But at this particular moment Silky Shanahan and her repeating rifle were in control of the situation, and there wasn't a damn thing he could do about it.

"I'm going give you one more chance," Silky announced in an ominous tone. "In what phase of the moon does a person set fence posts?"

Taggart almost laughed at the ridiculous question, then remembered at the last second that he was on trial. "In the full of the moon," he answered boldly, thinking his chances one in four.

Silky laughed deeply. "Every child," she began with a smug smile, "knows that fence posts are set during the waning of the moon. You set 'em any other time and they'll wobble around like loose teeth."

Seeing Silky sight on him again, Taggart put out his spread hands, wondering if she was going to blow him to smithereens. "Come on, now. You can't be serious about this. I'm a Reb through and through!"

"Funny, but somehow I don't believe a word you're saying." She waved the rifle at him. "Now get out of the water. I'm arresting you in the name of the Confederate States of America." She cocked the weapon with a chilling click. "And I'm taking you to the smokehouse and keeping you there until I can turn you in."

With two rifles bearing down on him, Taggart could only climb from the pond, water dripping from his body. What a hell of a predicament this had turned out to be. Cold steel nudging his back, he grabbed his clothes and boots, realizing he'd get precious little information about General Johnston if he were locked in a smokehouse.

With feisty Silky Shanahan as his jailer he had a prodigious problem indeed, but at this particular moment he had no idea on God's green earth how to solve it.

Hearing a rooster crow, Taggart woke up in the earthy-smelling smokehouse, light filtering between the weather-beaten boards and streaming over the hard-packed dirt floor. A few hams and slabs of side meat dangled overhead, emitting their own tangy aroma. Still groggy, he stretched his stiff muscles, thinking he'd never had a worse night of sleep in his life. With a weary sigh, he recalled everything that had transpired since he'd been taken prisoner of war, as Silky had called the ridiculous abduction.

While Charlie had stabled his horse, Silky had marched him to the little shack and locked him inside, saying he could sleep on a pile of empty sacks heaped on the ground. She'd warned him that the smokehouse was "bull strong and hog tight," and after she'd left, he'd found that she was right, for all his efforts to break down the door or pull out a plank had met with defeat.

Depression spread through him as he thought of his surprising capture, knowing how his fellow agents in the Information Bureau would laugh if they discovered he'd been abducted by a plucky woodland sprite. He only hoped Silky wouldn't discover the hefty bankroll of counterfeit bills and coded cipher hidden under the false bottom of his saddlebag—both meant to smooth his spying expedition into the South. Somehow, he thought, hardening his resolve, he had to convince her he was a Reb or all would be lost.

Although Taggart had never known anyone in the Shenandoah Valley, he actually did have an aunt Clara who, when she was alive, had lived in Norfolk. Pacing about the near-empty smokehouse, he racked his brain, trying to recall his childhood visits to her home. Quickly he flipped through his memories, sorting out everything that had impressed him as being particularly Southern—everything from pecan pralines to mint juleps.

Just then the sound of footsteps crunching over gravel reached his ears, and he knew that someone was nearing the smokehouse. Within seconds, the door flew open, letting in a rush of cool, fresh air, and revealing Silky, standing with the dawn blush to her back. She was bareheaded this morning, but still wore her buckskins and still clasped a rifle in one hand—a rifle he knew she wouldn't hesitate to use. In the other hand she clutched a tin plate, supporting a piece of corn bread and a fruit jar filled with buttermilk.

"I brought you some breakfast, Yankee," she announced bluntly, shoving the food at him. "It doesn't seem right to let a man starve—even a Yankee."

Taggart accepted the tin plate and, noticing that her hand shook a bit, gave her a wide smile before scanning the area outside the smokehouse. "Where's your cousin?" he inquired, his voice threaded with light amusement.

Her eyes darkened. "Charlie? He's home with his granddaddy. That's the only menfolks that's left in the Blue Ridge now—boys and graybeards."

Although Silky had made no attempt to be provocative, there was something soft and vulnerable about her that made Taggart's blood run a little faster even as she held the rifle on him. In fact, meeting her reminded him of drinking his first glass of champagne: a heady, once-in-a-lifetime experience, full of potential for dire consequences. From the restless look in her lovely eyes, he was happy to note his presence was having a potent effect on her as well. Purposefully, he let his gaze travel from her blushing face to her luscious cleavage, then back to her smoldering eyes.

He set the plate on top of a barrel. "I was wondering," he asked casually, "if you had any watermelon-rind preserves to go with this corn bread?"

Her heavy lashes flew upward. "How does a Yankee come to know about watermelon-rind preserves?"

He laughed lightly. "Why, I grew up eating them. But I haven't had any in a coon's age, and lately I've worked up a real hankering for them."

She slid him a suspicious glance. "You're not still trying to convince me that you're a Reb, are you?"

"But I am," he answered passionately.

Her questioning eyes roamed over him. "Then how come you're so ignorant about Southern things?"

"Because you asked me about *country* things," he replied, being so bold as to lightly clasp her arm.

Silky, feeling warmth flush her skin where the Yankee had touched her, moved back a step, disturbed by the pleasant feelings swirling within her. Lordamercy, she never knew fighting Yankees could be so stimulating. Excitement trickled down her spine as Taggart made another inspection of her figure. She'd never gone calf-eyed over a Southerner, much less a Yankee, and she deeply resented the reaction of her own body.

She inched back a bit farther, but the rapscallion went on, his beautiful eyes boring into her, his husky voice filled with warmth and confidence. "I was raised in Norfolk," he said, smiling and showing strong white teeth, made even whiter by his dark mustache. "No one there talks about making moonshine or setting fence posts," he explained in a reasonable tone. "Ask me about the city, the great houses, the shops, the balls."

Doubt welled inside of her. "I-I don't know about those things," she replied slowly. His comment about the watermelon-rind preserves had made her doubt her own judgment, and as he plunged ahead, rattling on about the glories of Norfolk, she could feel her confidence eroding.

"Here, let me give *you* a little test," he suggested, his face suffused with amusement. "What does it mean if the left corner of a gentleman's card is bent down and returned to him?"

She stared at him, having no idea.

"At a formal dinner, who's served first, and where is the dessert spoon placed?" he quizzed, disarming her with another smile. "What time does the theater usually begin?" he continued, overwhelming her with the rush of questions. "What length gloves does a lady wear to the opera and how soon should thank-you notes be written? How long—"

"Stop," she interrupted, laying a hand over her heaving bosom. "I don't know the answer to any of those questions."

Soft laughter tumbled from his lips. "No, you wouldn't have need for such knowledge here in the mountains . . . but that doesn't mean you're not a true Southerner, does it?" He gestured at himself. "I may have failed your test on country things, but that doesn't mean I'm not a Reb the same as you."

Silky grudgingly held his gaze.

"Why, I love everything Southern, especially Southern food," he vowed, brushing a callused palm over her cheek. "I was raised on it. Sweet-potato pie, grits, collard greens, black-eyed peas, corn bread . . ."

Her heart did a somersault at the touch of his hand, and, trying to ignore the weak feeling sweeping through her, she suddenly blurted out, "What's the name of General Lee's horse?"

He looked at her with surprise; then a satisfied smile crept over his lips. "Traveller."

"What does J. E. B. stand for in Jeb Stuart?" she asked, her composure now seriously ruffled.

With crossed arms, he leaned against the doorjamb, his eyes sparkling. "James Ewell Brown," he answered confidently, now so near she felt the warmth of his body engulfing her.

"Where was Jefferson Davis born?" she inquired, her heart beating faster.

His sensuous lips curved upward. "Christian County, Kentucky."

Still holding his gaze, she picked up the tin plate, realizing he'd taken advantage of her with his charming ways and suggestive glances. She had no intention of returning his subtle advances, but at the same time, for some unexplainable reason, she knew she was going to give him another chance—a chance he probably didn't deserve.

"Come with me," she ordered, nodding at her log cabin that nestled in a close of dark pines. "I'm going to give you a final test."

Confident he was making progress, Taggart walked across the dew-jeweled landscape, well aware of the rifle pointed at his back and the baying of three vicious-looking hounds that raised their hackles as he passed. Squawking chickens flapping all about him, he spied a milk cow tied in front of a ramshackle barn that was in the process of being shingled. Sprinkled over the roof in a haphazard manner, the shingles sat at odd angles, telling him the workman wasn't acquainted with the finer aspects of the craft.

Once they were inside the cabin which smelled of warm biscuits and sausage, the cozy atmosphere wrapped itself around him. Furnished with a table and chairs and old bedsteads, and decorated with copper pots and strings of onions that hung from the rafters, the room was filled with items of daily living. Several rifles were placed across a deer-horn rack above the hearth, reminding him of an illustration he'd once seen in *The Last of the Mohicans.* After circling the interior with his gaze, he decided every item there had been produced when the Blue Ridge Mountains had lain on America's western frontier.

Silky plunked the tin plate on the table and gestured a slim finger at the chair, ordering him to sit down.

Taggart, feeling his stomach rumble with hunger, expected to be served flaky biscuits, but after she'd gone to a cupboard lined with shelves of home-canned vegetables in glass jars, she set a bowl of cold boiled okra before him. He stared down at the congealed contents, which reminded him of a stringy mass of green wallpaper paste, but which he knew wouldn't be as appetizing.

"Here you go," she announced, scooping some of the okra onto his plate. "This was left over from supper, but since you love Southern food so much," she added with a suspicious gleam in her eyes, "I thought you might like a little for breakfast." She handed him a fork along with a meaningful glance. "All true Southerners love okra, you know."

Taggart stared at the slimy mass again, wanting to tell her that no one, not even Robert E. Lee, ate okra for breakfast, but he realized the seemingly frivolous test was really a very clever maneuver on her part. Since okra was an exclusively Southern vegetable, and very much an acquired taste developed over many years, most Northerners would gag on their first bite of the boiled version. He only wished the vegetable had been fried, which was the way it was served at his aunt Clara's. That he could stomach—but cold boiled okra at this time of day was enough to turn even the strongest stomach.

Silky tossed back her flaming hair. "Well . . . Lieutenant Taggart?"

Taggart, finding it ironic that his whole future might depend on his ability to consume the dish before him, speared one of the okra pods. It drooped limply from his fork. Bravely he plunged the okra into his mouth, chewed, and swallowed, trying to forget it reminded him of a slimy grub.

When he caught his jailer's questioning gaze, he shook his head with relish. "My, this is really tasty," he mumbled with a full mouth. He swallowed hard and, forcing down another pod, gave her a wink. "If it was any better, I think I'd rub it in my hair."

With wondering eyes, she handed him the buttermilk. "Here's something to wash it down."

If there was anything Taggart hated worse than boiled okra it was lukewarm buttermilk, but, taking a deep breath, he clasped the fruit jar and drained its thick, sour contents, fighting back a strong urge to retch.

After he'd finished the bowl of okra, he set it aside and, marshaling every last ounce of strength within him, asked, "Do you have any more?"

Silky gave him an astonished look. "Who was Stonewall Jackson's chief of artillery?" she questioned, easing down in a straight-backed chair beside him.

"Colonel Stapleton Crutchfield."

"Why was he retired?"

"He lost a leg at Chancellorsville," he answered, recalling the instance from an intelligence briefing.

A soft expression on her face, Silky heaved a doleful sigh. "Lieutenant Taggart," she said in a thoughtful tone, "maybe I've made a mistake. There seems to be a fair-to-middling chance that you might be what you say you are."

Hope flickered within him.

Silky smiled gently, her eyes moist with emotion. "In fact, I've decided you're either a Reb or the best liar in the whole state of Virginia."

Taggart laughed at the backhanded compliment, amazed that her position had changed from adversary to friend so quickly.

"I'm sorry I detained you, Lieutenant," she went on, placing her rifle on the table, "and I apologize for your night in the smokehouse. You must have thought I was crazy, but with the war going on a person can never be too careful."

Now that the weapon was out of her hands, Taggart stood, thinking he'd finally extricated himself from the ridiculous situation. "I understand, miss," he replied, feeling strangely sad he'd be leaving his plucky adversary. "As you say, with the war raging a lady must be careful, indeed."

Silky rose beside him. "I know that's right. My brother, Daniel, is soldiering with Uncle Joe Johnston, and you'd be surprised the letters I get telling about Yankee rascals taking advantage of Southern womenfolk." She folded her arms under her bosom and walked about the table. "Some wounded men from Daniel's company," she added thoughtfully, "are coming back for sick leave in a couple of weeks."

"Oh? Why is that?"

"It seems the convalescent hospitals are so full, most of the soldiers that can walk are being sent home to recuperate." She gave him a slow smile. "The whole hollow will turn out to welcome them, and I'll bet those soldiers will have stories about Yankees that will curl your hair."

When Silky's words penetrated Taggart's brain, he captured her gaze, realizing that his abduction had been a godsend in disguise. Information about General Johnston's troops was just what he was looking for—but he'd thought he would have to ride into the heart of Virginia to find it. With a burst of insight, he realized that if he lingered in this cozy hollow the information would come to him. And besides that, now that Silky wasn't peering down the barrel of a rifle, she was more desirable than ever.

Once again using the smile that had melted half the feminine hearts in Ohio, he ambled to her. "I couldn't help but notice . . . you're shingling your barn, aren't you?"

She stared at him with parted lips. "Why, yes, Charlie and I have been trying, but—"

He clasped her soft shoulders, noting how small and shapely she was. "Why don't I stay a few days and smooth up that roof?" he asked, feeling her body trembling under his hands. "Right now it's letting in as much rain as it's keeping out. I can sleep in the loft close to my work."

His throaty proposal rushed pleasure through Silky, almost frightening her with its intensity. Even now sexual tension sizzled between them, and an inner voice told her it would be best if she refused the offer. But at the same time she was powerfully drawn to him, in spite of the dangerous risk that the attraction presented.

"After the way I treated you?" she murmured, flustered from his nearness. His seductive gaze swept over her and she felt herself blush hotly. "I can't let you shingle my barn roof—not a fine Southern gentleman like you!"

A slow smile curved one corner of his mouth, making him devastatingly attractive. "Think nothing of it. As a Southern gentleman, it's my duty to assist you." His eyes glinted with warmth. "And, I might say, my pleasure, too."

"Lordamercy, what about your company on the Rappahannock?" she asked, her pulse fluttering wildly.

"I overestimated the time it would take to relocate my aunt. I still have weeks before I need to report," he answered smoothly. "Certainly long enough to shingle your roof before the bad weather sets in."

Silky's heart lurched with excitement. The last thing she wanted to do was to become emotionally involved with a Yankee, but the handsome stranger had turned out to be a gallant Confederate lieutenant, and he would not only be sleeping in her own barn, but shingling it as well. Until this moment she hadn't known how strongly his masculinity had affected her, and she sighed, strange new emotions storming within her.

"A-All right," she stammered, a warm glow spreading through her like the sun's rays. "I could use some help on that roof. The weather will be hardening in a few weeks, and this high in the mountains we always have early snows, too." She smoothed back her hair, noticing her hand was none too steady. "Your horse and saddlebag are already in the barn, Lieutenant."

Taggart gazed at her radiant face for a moment. "Fine . . . I'll get to work right away." Guilt welling within him, he turned to go, surprised at how simple it had all been once she accepted him as a Southerner.

Trying to salve his conscience, he told himself his stay in the hollow could save the lives of hundreds of Union soldiers. And after all, no harm would come to the girl. When he had his information, he'd ride on to Charlottesville and report to his contact in the North, leaving her with some warm memories and a barn ready to face another mountain winter.

"Lieutenant?"

He turned about, struck with how young and vulnerable she looked with the morning light streaming over her. "Yes?"

"I just wanted you to know," she said, offering him an appealing smile, "I'll cook boiled okra three times a week while you're here."

"Can you imagine," Silky asked, looking across the table a week later with a beaming face, "what the folks in Washington thought last summer when they saw General Early marching on the city?" Taggart noticed her eyes glistening as she added, "Folks say Lincoln himself came out to the forts with bullets whizzing all around him, just to see what was going on."

"The fact is, though," he replied, lighting up a long cheroot, then shaking out his match, "that Early didn't have near enough men to take the capitol."

Silky seemed affronted that he should mention it. "Maybe

not, but I'll bet those folks were scared stiff as Sunday starched shirts when they spied Old Jube and his troops.'' She flicked a critical gaze over Taggart. ''Lordamercy, sometimes you talk more like a Yankee than a Confederate officer. What makes you take such a dim view of things?''

Taggart took a long draw from his brandy-scented cigar. Every evening for the last week, she'd predicted a Southern victory, when in both his heart and head, he knew the South was almost defeated. Despite Early's saber-rattling, most of the Confederate soldiers were without provisions, and as for the ragged civilians, they were living on little more than black-eyed peas and hope. ''Merely an observation,'' he stated with a smile. He tried to steer the subject to something less controversial. ''What do you hear from your brother?''

''I hear quite a bit.'' Luscious curves strained against her soft buckskins as she rose and walked to a rough-hewn chest of drawers. ''Just a minute,'' she said over her shoulder. ''I'll read you some of his letters.''

With a flicker of pain, Taggart watched her gather up the letters, thinking of his own brother, who was a victim of the war. At sixteen, Ned, a passionate abolitionist, had lied about his age and enlisted in the infantry, only to be quickly captured by the Confederates and sent to Andersonville. Several months later, he and seven other men had been shot in reprisal for a violent Northern raid on a small Virginia town.

The day Taggart found out about his brother's death, his whole outlook had changed, and his role in the war had suddenly become not a duty, but an intensely personal crusade. Moreover, when he'd realized that a single intelligence agent could often accomplish as much as a regiment of men, he immediately volunteered his services to General Sharpe, head of the Information Bureau, vowing to do everything within his power to see that the Union won the war.

Thinking of Ned always troubled Taggart, but as Silky walked back to the table with her bundle of letters, he reined in his emotions, making his face perfectly impassive.

''You can't imagine all that's in these letters,'' she commented, swinging her shining hair about her shoulders. With a tender expression, she sat down and spread the tattered envelopes over the table. ''Daniel tells a lot about Uncle

Joe," she explained, a trace of laughter in her voice. "He says he's a little half-bald fellow, but so full of fight that his eyes just sparkle."

Taggart listened to her lulling Southern drawl as she read, and he realized that her brother's comments were merely observations about the general's character and humorous anecdotes about camp life, not anything that would be useful to him.

After she'd finished reading, a silence fell between them, and as the wind moaned in the pines, he studied her delicate features, highlighted by the hearth's glow. Lord, was he staying because of his mission or because he wanted to take her in his arms? he wondered, noticing the spirit in her emerald eyes. He found no answer to his question, but felt his loins quicken just considering the situation. "I suppose your brother signed up right after Fort Sumter," he finally ventured, corraling his runaway thoughts.

Her eyes snapped with amusement. "Yes, Daniel was raring to get into the war. He said it was just going to be a breakfast spell, and he'd miss all the fun." She smiled at the memory. "He spent a few days fixing up things around here; then he and the Wilkerson boys tore off faster than greased lightning to Charlottesville to join the army." She sighed heavily. "I miss him terribly, but he's faithful to write, and his letters keep me going."

"Do you ever think about anything but the war?" he asked softly, wanting to enjoy a conversation with her that had nothing to do with generals or troop movements.

She sat back and straightened up. "Of course," she replied, rising once more to fetch a pile of Beade's dime novels from beneath her bed. At the table she plopped them down, then reseated herself, her expressive eyes shining with pleasure. "Pa taught me to read before he died and that's the best gift anyone ever gave me." She smoothed her white hands over the soft-bound books as if they were precious volumes. "I got these from a peddler who came through before the war. There's wonderful stories on these pages—stories about the frontier and life in California." She leaned forward, revealing the tops of her creamy breasts. "I read they found gold nuggets as big as goose eggs at Sutter's fort.'' Her face took on a dreamy look. ''I've always dreamed of going to California.''

Taggart was touched. What a shame she'd learned to read, but hadn't received the opportunity to go to school. She was so alive, so vibrant, so unlike the jaded debutantes he'd met at West Point balls and in Washington salons. And so brave, too, he thought dryly, knowing he'd never catch one of the perfumed socialites holding a rifle on him and making it stick.

''It sounds like you'd like to see the world.''

''Oh yes,'' she answered with eagerness. ''I've never had enough money to get out of the county, but even when I was a little girl I'd watch the sun slide behind the ridge and wonder what was fifty miles from here, and a hundred miles from here.'' Her eyes kindled with memories. ''I'd ask Pa what was over the far ridges and he'd say, 'More trees, child, just like the ones in Sweet Gum Hollow.' ''

They both laughed and he found himself clasping her slim fingers and wondering what she would do if she could see New York or Washington. He idly ran his thumb over her hand, fascinated with this soft, tender side of her, so different from the fiery personality she'd displayed at the pond.

''Mama died when I was only four and I can scarce remember her,'' she went on, a hint of pain darkening her eyes. ''She was taken away with the scarlet fever. Pa said it was her that nicknamed me Silky, for my shiny hair.'' She laughed self-consciously. ''My real name is Mary Kathleen, after some of my Irish kinfolks who lived way back there when the devil was just a pup, but I think Silky fits me better. Don't you?''

''Yes . . . I do,'' Taggart replied, thinking it not only described her wonderful hair, but her creamy skin, and even the graceful way she moved.

Silky rose and, crossing her arms, walked to the fire that sizzled pleasantly in the hearth. ''I can remember playing with Daniel as a child—he's five years older than me. Although he never had a lot of book learning, he always seemed to know what was really important in life.

''And I remember Pa tucking me into bed every night when I was a child and telling me wild mountain stories.''

Her face lit up. ''He told me about wolves and bears that could talk just like regular folks, and birds that laid square eggs.''

''Square eggs?'' Taggart laughed.

Silky's eyes twinkled. ''Yeah . . . they take three days to boil!''

She put her hand on an old rocking chair that sat nearby, giving it a soft shove, and setting it creaking over the floorboards. ''Pa had a beautiful voice, all rich and low, and after he told me the wild stories, he'd sing to me until I went to sleep.'' She ran her hands over her arms. ''I get a warm feeling inside right now just thinking about it.''

Her eyes danced as she moved about the cabin. ''Pa and Daniel taught me to shoot, and hunt, and even track,'' she explained in a low, smooth tone. ''Those are Daniel's hounds outside, and when he was here we went hunting three or four times a week.''

''You're a fine shot,'' Taggart commented with a chuckle. ''I'm only glad your lessons stopped when they did.''

She considered him, her expression sobering. ''Pa died when I was ten,'' she continued, her soft voice quavering with emotion. ''He took pneumonia one cold winter and there was nothing we could do to save him.''

Taggart sat there absorbing her every word, amazed she was revealing so much of her personal life.

Moisture gleamed in her eyes. ''We buried him on the top of a hill not far from here—just us and a handful of the folks. A person can see three days from that hill. In the spring there are clouds of sweet-smelling dogwood and red azaleas trailing down the hills like flame. And in the winter the ice makes the bare trees glisten like silver, and there's nothing but miles and miles of rolling ridges covered with snow and purple shadows.'' A tender expression welled in her eyes. ''When it rains up there, the drops are as soft as angel tears.''

Taggart rose and, moved by an impulse he didn't understand, walked to her and brushed a shiny curl from her cheek. Somehow impelled to comfort her, he held her lightly, marveling at how beautiful she really was.

She pulled herself up to her full height and raised her chin.

"Don't worry about me," she said in a steadier voice. "I've always had plenty to eat and this old cabin was always filled with lots of love." She laughed a little. "Daniel is a great one for cutting up, and he plays such a lively tune on his fiddle it would make a wooden Indian step out and dance."

She surveyed Taggart, exhaling a deep breath. "Lordamercy, I'm happy you're not a Yankee, because if you were, I just don't know what I'd do," she confessed, her voice vibrating with emotion.

She seemed to shake off her nostalgic mood, and with a teasing light in her eyes, suddenly announced, "I think you deserve a rest from all that shingling, Lieutenant. Tomorrow I'll show you a place on a hill where we can pick wild apples."

Outwardly Taggart grinned, but privately he wondered if he'd got himself in over his head by deciding to stay. "Fine, I'd enjoy that," he replied, suddenly realizing this would be the hardest mission he'd ever undertaken.

She went on talking about her plans, but the sighing wind and snapping flames worked their soft magic, and, caught up in the enchantment of the moment, he heard little of what she said. Her sweet Southern voice washed through him, making him want to pull her closer, delve his fingers into her hair, and devour her lips. Lord, he thought, this lovely girl before him might technically be his mortal foe, but tonight, with the firelight playing over her face and her lips curved in a tender smile, she looked the farthest thing in the world from an enemy, and new feelings stirred within him.

And at this particular moment Taggart would have given anything in the world to have been a farmer, or a horse trader, or even a peddler of dime novels—anything but what he was: a Federal intelligence officer whose bound duty it was to gather military information and move on.

For one flickering moment he experienced a wild impulse to leave and forget he'd ever met Silky; then in his mind's eye he saw Ned's young face, and knew he must stay.

Chapter Two

It was a luscious fall morning with sparkling sunshine, a light breeze, and a blue sky graced with majestic clouds—a morning made for apple picking. Silky and Taggart rode out after breakfast and, following a woodcutter's trail, were soon in the woods, where a flickering mixture of light and shadow enveloped them like a protecting hand.

Taggart, his senses saturated with the sound of birdsong and the pungent aroma of evergreens, studied the ripely curved beauty riding beside him, thinking she was as refreshing as sunlight after a storm. The little firebrand looked deliciously appealing this morning in a red flannel shirt molded to her womanly bosom and buckskin breeches covering her shapely legs. The sun struck fire in her long hair, and green eyes twinkled at him from the shadows of her battered hat, sending his temperature rising at least two degrees.

She'd been in high feather all morning, and with the reins slipping through her hand, she pointed down the trail, where scarlet maples and deeper-toned blackhaw stood out vividly in the morning light. "There's a little settlement about three miles on the other side of these woods—Bear Wallow. We've got a meetinghouse, a burying ground, a general store, and a tavern that does a booming business when the menfolk aren't off at war."

Taggart chuckled, suddenly feeling better than he had since the war began. "You know every foot of these woods, don't you?"

One hand on her hip, she sat tall in the saddle. "You bet. Folks say nothing has changed in this part of Virginia for a hundred years. My granddaddy Shanahan came up this very trail fifty years ago, straight off the boat from Ireland. He cleared the land I'm living on, then built him a good log cabin and started looking for a bride."

"And who did he find?"

"Little Nellie MacNaley from Snyder's Hollow. She was as pretty as sunup and sweet as a baby's kiss."

They rode on a few yards, their bridles jangling pleasantly. "And . . ." he prompted.

"And," she answered, cutting her gaze at him, "they got married on the eighth of January, 1817. Her daddy made whiskey and he set a quart of his best on his cabin doorstep. Fellows from miles around staged a horse race to get it."

Taggart had come to the mountains with secrets to unearth, and now found all he could think of was what it would be like to steal a kiss from her full, pouting lips. But how could any normal man look at her and not be affected? he asked himself, wondering if he might be lucky enough to steal that kiss today.

"The winner brought the whiskey to my granddaddy to give him the first swig," she continued, amusement snapping in her eyes.

"Being an Irishman," Taggart commented, "I'm sure he was happy to oblige."

A grin slid over her lips. "Michael Shanahan and Nellie MacNaley had eight children. Some of the old grannies say it was because they got married on the eighth of January."

"It sounds like Mr. Shanahan was a man of considerable virility."

She swung a direct gaze over him. "Don't forget Sweet

Nellie, Lieutenant. A rooster may crow, but it's always the hen that delivers the egg."

Taggart burst out laughing, but before he could reply, she challenged, "Come on, I'll race you to the apple trees." The words barely out of her mouth, she snapped her reins and thundered down the trail, glancing back at him with a teasing smile.

Taggart touched his heels to his horse's flanks and raced after her, only to see her veer from the woods and head out across a strip of rich meadowland. With a silvery laugh, she sailed over a split-rail fence; then the daring minx had the audacity to rein in her horse and actually whistle at him to follow.

Taggart tore after her and made the jump himself, feeling as lighthearted as a boy of sixteen. But as soon as he'd drawn his mount abreast of hers, she was off again, entering the forest on the other side of the meadow. Her hair streaming behind her, she urged her horse onto a winding trail that worked its way to the summit of a high wooded hill.

He followed her up the gradually ascending trail, and a quarter of a mile later they suddenly emerged into a clearing that looked down on all the hills about them. From their elevated position, the distant land spread below them in blue, mauve, and purple ridges, wrapped in haze. A river snaked between the undulating hills like a thread of silver, and, closer in, the full flush of autumn had painted the trees in bright hues that dazzled the eye. Never in his life had Taggart seen such a concentration of beauty, and, as he rested his winded horse, he stared at the breathtaking sight, glorying in the fall colors.

"Damn, if this isn't the prettiest place God ever made," he said, looking across the sweeping vista, "I don't know what is."

Silky dismounted and, after loosely twining her reins about a sapling, sauntered to him. "It's a wondrous sight to behold," she stated, her face glowing with pride as she surveyed the view herself. Then a contemplative expression stole over her features and she declared, "People have always felt happy and free here. It's a shame the Yankees are trying to change our ways."

Taggart knew that slaves were almost nonexistent in the high mountains, and Silky didn't understand the moral crusade fueling the fervor of the Northern forces. To her, the Yankees were intruders, bent on destroying a beloved way of life. "If I remember correctly," he said, swinging down from his mount, "South Carolina fired first at Fort Sumter."

She whirled about, her large eyes searching his face. "Lordamercy. I'll tell you straight out. Sometimes you worry me to death. Why do you keep bringing up things like that?"

"Just stating another fact," Taggart offered, casually looping his reins about the saddle horn.

Her solemn expression broke into a hint of a smile. "You have more facts in that handsome head of yours than a pickle has warts, but I'd be pleased if you kept the more depressing ones to yourself."

Her gaze took in the largest apple tree, whose great boughs drooped with the weight of their colorful burden, then settled back on him. "Come on, we'd better get to work," she advised with a forgiving grin.

Gunnysacks were drawn from her saddlebag, and after Taggart shook the tree limbs, they began gathering the shiny fruit. When pulled downward, the smaller boughs often recoiled and burst away, but not before showering the earth with fragrant apples, which were scooped into the rough sacks.

Silky, moving to another tree, spotted Taggart striding purposefully toward her, a roguish light in his eyes. His shirt and trim breeches strained over his huge form, telling her there was nothing but rock-hard muscle beneath the fabric. The man was as awesomely attractive in clothes as he was— No, don't think of that, she warned herself, trying to forget the way he'd looked in old man Johnson's pool, his body burnished with the sun's last rays.

Under the shade of the tree, he deposited his sack and took a bite of crisp apple. "Want a bite, Fancy Pants?" he inquired, holding the apple toward her in his big hand. His voice had a husky catch to it, and his lips curved upward in a devastating smile, adding heat to her already warm cheeks.

Had this ruggedly handsome man told her the truth about

himself? she wondered with a gnawing pang of doubt. Some of his comments troubled her deeply, but now that she'd accepted him as a Confederate, she didn't want to consider the alternative. That someone as charming as he was could be a Yankee was unthinkable. With a racing pulse, she accepted the piece of fruit, and he placed his hand over hers, its coiled strength pleasuring her. "Try it . . . it's good," he said, his resonant voice sending an aroused tingle through her veins.

Gently he traced the line of her cheek, and she steeled herself against the surge of desire sweeping over her. She studied his craggy features, amazed at how sure of himself he was with women. Oh, he was a gentleman, all right, but he was a ladies' man, too. You could see it in his eyes. Why, he was probably such a heartbreaker, it would take a ten-buggy prayer meeting just to *begin* saving him!

With a leaping heart, she met his searching gaze. Without waiting for permission, he gently took her in his arms. She trembled, acutely aware of his strength and vitality, and felt her pent-up longings clamoring for release. Slowly he bent his head, and his warm lips smoothed over her closed eyelids, ruffling her lashes, then brushed over her lips, soft as a butterfly's wing.

Almost immediately she noticed a pleasant ache between her legs, and her knees went weak beneath her. She'd never experienced such a feeling, and it thrilled and frightened her at the same time, sending her heart thudding as if it would burst from her rib cage. Lordamercy, he'd only brushed his lips against hers, but she couldn't let this continue—she had to show him this was one mountain girl whose will wouldn't crumble beneath his entrancing charm. Her heart still pounding with excitement, she eased back from him, trying to pretend the half-kiss had never happened. Still, even as she did so, she yearned for the golden warmth and security of his arms, and wondered if she'd ever be as happy as she was this very minute.

His eyes dancing, he towered over her, looking more amused than angry. "Aren't you going to try the apple?" he murmured in a caressing tone, sending fresh shivers down her spine.

She held his sparkling eyes, her body still pulsing with warmth from his touch. "Sure," she replied, biting into the juicy apple. "I already know they're good. I should, because I've eaten a jillion of them." Determined to repair her frazzled composure, she handed the apple back to him with a trembling hand. "You know," she remarked shakily, desperately trying to change the subject and put the last few minutes behind them, "sometimes I wish that General Grant would saunter right through the middle of Sweet Gum Hollow."

Surprise flared in Taggart's eyes.

"Him and his big cigar," she complained in an irritated tone, mightily relieved the intimate moment had passed.

Taggart scanned her blushing face. The Union might be winning the war, but he'd just lost his first battle with this sweet Reb. He realized she needed some time to understand the new feelings he'd aroused within her, so he'd best go slow for a while. "Why would you want to meet General Grant?" he asked, accepting the fact that he'd have to settle for apples and talk today instead of real kisses. "What would you say to him if you saw him?"

She picked up her sack and walked to another tree.

Amused at the direction the conversation had taken, he followed her, wondering what she'd say if she knew he was well acquainted with the general.

"I wouldn't *say* anything to him," she finally answered, pulling down a bough and giving it a shake, "but you know what I'd do with him?"

"I'm afraid to ask."

She fell to her knees and began tossing apples into her gunnysack. "I'd see that some of the home guard tarred and feathered him and rode him out of the hollow on a rail."

Taggart considered her words, sorry to hear there was a Confederate home guard in the vicinity. Although home guards were made up of older men and those unfit for regular service, it didn't take that much strength to pull a trigger. Their existence put a new light on his stay in the hollow.

She looked up with flashing eyes. "And I wouldn't care if the men included Sheridan and Sherman in that little operation."

Just imagining all those feathers made Taggart want to sneeze.

Her sack full, she rose with a jaunty air. "Yes, sir," she said, tossing back her shining curls. "If there's anything I hate worse than poison, it's a low-down, sorry, blue-bellied Yankee buzzard."

Taggart hoisted up his gunnysack, thinking this peppery Reb never let up. The last time he'd heard such a superb string of invective had been at a Virginia horse race over fifteen years ago. "Four-flushing," he calmly interjected.

She stared at him with big eyes. "What?"

"You forgot to say four-flushing. If there's anything you hate worse than poison, it's a low-down, sorry, four-flushing, blue-bellied Yankee buzzard."

Silky laughed. "Yes, how could I have forgotten that?" With a companionable air, she clasped his arm. "I tell you what," she proposed happily, "I've got some sugar saved back. Let's go home and I'll make some apple pies for supper tonight."

She tossed a shiny apple into the air, then caught it and polished it on her sleeve. "These apples will make fine applejack, too," she commented, critically inspecting the fruit before returning it to her sack. "I made a batch last year that I'll let you sample," she added as they carried their burdens to the horses. "It's smooth as a moonbeam."

Taggart knotted the top of his gunnysack on his saddle horn and swung into place, relieved that Silky still believed he was a Confederate officer, and thankful that he'd been invited back to her cabin for pie and applejack instead of the activity she'd described for the Union generals.

As they galloped down the trail, reentering the woods, one thought pounded through his head repeatedly, in time with the horses' thudding hooves. Despite the obvious sexual attraction between them, this fire-snorting secessionist would have a rifle at his back and a rope around his neck in a heartbeat if she only knew who he was.

"You mean to tell me," Charlie croaked in disbelief, staring across the table at Taggart, "that you went to school right up there amongst them Yankee buzzards?" Silky laughed to herself at the expression on the boy's face, thinking she'd never seen him look more stunned.

From his place beside her, Taggart lit up an after-dinner cheroot, and puffed on it until he could get it going. Outside, the wind had risen and a few raindrops pecked against the windowpanes, but inside the snug cabin, flames crackled in the hearth and the scent of apple pie permeated the air, creating a warm, cozy atmosphere. "That's right," he answered, rolling the cigar to the other side of his mouth and regarding the boy amiably. "A family connection helped me get an appointment to West Point. After graduation, I was posted out West for several years. Of course, after Jefferson Davis was elected president of the Confederacy, I resigned my commission and offered my services to the South."

Charlie eyed him with fascinated horror. "Is is true them Yankee buzzards have horns?"

The sound of Taggart's laughter in her ears, Silky rose from the table to deposit her plate in the dishpan. "Charlie," she drawled, slowly turning about, "that's the wildest thing I ever heard. Yankees are low-down varmints, but any sane human being knows they don't have horns."

The boy cast a hurt gaze over her. "Well, Wilbur Clingerman over in Snyder's Holler said he killed one the first year of the war, and the critter had little bitty horns on his head, kinda like a yearlin' deer."

"Wilbur Clingerman is a drunk. The only time he refused a drink he didn't understand the question. He probably saw horns on the Yankee, all right, and if you'd ask him, a tail and hooves, too."

Taggart combed a hand through his hair.

With an inward groan, Silky surveyed his droll expression. No doubt he believed all mountain people were as ill informed as her cousin, she decided, wanting him to think only the best of her. Gnawing her bottom lip, she wondered what embarrassing topic the boy would bring up next.

She didn't have to wait long, for Charlie turned a speculative eye to Taggart. "You got the itch on your head? I saw you scratchin'. A good dose of sulfur, lard, and gunpowder on your scalp will kill it right fast." He frowned at Taggart's cheroot. "Course you can't smoke 'cause it might set your hair afire, but I reckon it'd be all right to chew tobacco.''

The boy blinked thoughtfully. ''If you got anything else ailin' you, just ask Silky. She knows a heap about mixin' herbs. Reckon she's herb-doctored near ever'body in the holler. If you need a purgative, she'll fix you up quick as a minnow can swim a dipper.''

Lordamercy, Silky thought with alarm. Had some kind of spell come over the boy? She'd better send him on his way before he brought up something worse than he already had. ''Aren't you finished yet?'' she asked a little sharply. ''You better start for home.'' She hurriedly placed a clean towel over one of the pies she was cooling. ''It's fixin' to come a rainstorm.''

When she'd removed the boy's plate, he stood and snapped his suspenders. ''Guess I'll be moseyin' on now,'' he announced, slapping on his cap and studying Taggart with a satisfied expression. ''Think on what I told you about that itch of yours, now.''

With a relieved sigh, she caught the lad at the threshold and handed him a cooled pie. ''Take this to your granddaddy. He's always been real partial to apple pie.''

When the double-battened door had slammed shut after the boy, Silky and Taggart both burst out laughing. ''That boy,'' she exclaimed, shaking her head. ''Sometimes I think he could talk a gate off its hinges. And I know he can stay longer in an hour than most people can in a week.''

She removed a brown jug from its place on the shelf, then scanned Taggart's frankly sensual face, excitement rippling through her. ''Now . . . how about a smattering of this applejack?'' Near the table, she paused meaningfully. ''You won't be sorry,'' she teased playfully. ''It'll make your ears ring, your eyes water, and sweat pop out on your brow.''

Taggart's white teeth gleamed under his mustache. ''Sounds like just what the doctor ordered,'' he replied, holding out his empty cup with a twinkle in his eyes.

She began filling the cup with amber liquid, noticing that her hand was a little unsteady. Confound it, she thought, why was it suddenly so important to earn this man's respect and admiration? And why did just pouring him a cup of applejack made her feel all soft inside, like a silly schoolgirl? She'd been thinking of those brief moments he'd grazed his lips over hers all day. Even now, her pulse raced faster just recalling it. Why couldn't she get the disquieting memory out of her head? Not having time to analyze the troubling question, she served herself, then placed the jug aside, her heart quickening with unnamed emotions.

"You know," she remarked, sinking into her chair, "sometimes I'm about as curious as Charlie myself." Amazed at all Taggart knew and the many places he'd been, she lowered her voice. "Tell me . . . what does West Point look like? The Lord knows I'll never have a chance to see it."

Taggart studied Silky's inquisitive face, then leaned back and remembered the academy he'd attended so many years ago. "West Point," he began thoughtfully, "is situated above New York City in a beautiful setting where the Hudson River cuts a narrow channel through the Appalachian Mountains."

He looked at her and smiled, recalling the sound of a bugle's burst, and the symphony made by hundreds of boots marching over the parade ground. "The buildings are clustered on a steep hillside above the river. Sometimes on spring nights, I would lie in my bunk and, through an open window, smell greenery and hear the roar of the river." He leaned forward and took her smooth hand. "But I think the academy is prettiest in winter when there are sleigh bells on the nippy air." He ran his fingers over her hand, noticing color stain her cheeks.

"When I was a little girl," she said in a throaty voice, "Pa bought me a fairy-tale book about a castle on a hill. The things you say sound like they might have come from that book." A second later, her face lit up. "I just thought of something," she breathed, blinking her eyes in excitement. "You've probably met Jeb Stuart and Stonewall Jackson. Daniel said they went to West Point, too."

Taggart stood and walked toward the hearth, holding out his hands to warm them. He realized that these generals were heroes to Silky, and, knowing them both, he recalled them as men of principle who'd suffered agonies before casting their lot with the South. Why should he deny her a bit of pleasure because he disagreed with the cause they embraced? "Yes," he answered slowly. "Today Stuart wears a plumed hat and a red-lined cape, and sports gold spurs on his boots, but during his West Point days the other cadets dubbed him Beauty because he was so homely."

"And poor Jackson—what a shame he's dead," Silky commented sadly. "Can you remember anything about him?"

Taggart stared into the flames, recalling the great general who'd stood like a stone wall at Manassas and died at Chancellorsville a little over a year ago. He tossed the remainder of his cheroot into the fire, then turned, focusing his attention on her rapt face. "Jackson always wore a plain uniform and rode a common-looking mount, but he was a great man and a finer general," he answered with true conviction. "I believe, with his death, the Confederacy lost part of its fighting spirit."

Silent, Silky rose and walked toward him, her eyes taking on an almost worshipful look. "And Lee?" she inquired, her voice quavering a little. "Have you ever seen the great Robert E. Lee himself?"

Lee had been at West Point the year Taggart graduated, and he'd been privileged to hear him speak. Once again recalling the general's soulful eyes and genteel Virginia voice, he remembered how he'd always been awed by the man's powerful presence. "I've heard him lecture, and I think," he said softly, truly speaking from his heart, "that he represents all that is fine and noble about the South."

Silky let out a ragged breath, obviously impressed that he'd met the commander of the heralded Army of Northern Virginia. For a moment they stood quietly, a companionable silence gently settling over them; then she remarked, "This has been quite an evening for me—hearing about West Point and those gallant Southern generals."

Listening to the rain that now pounded against the cabin roof, Taggart studied her inviting lips and her remarkable green eyes that were flecked with gold and glinted beneath long, sooty lashes. Her face softening, she glanced at the ceiling, then back at him. "It would pleasure me if you slept in the cabin tonight,'' she suggested with a quiet smile. ''You can use Daniel's bed.''

Taggart felt a kick of emotion. ''But—''

She shook her head. ''You don't need to say another word. You don't need to worry what the neighbors will say, because I haven't got any.''

''Your brother—'' he began, knowing most Southern men would strongly object to the situation.

A gentle smile graced her mouth. ''The war has changed many things.'' Dimples formed in her cheeks. ''Why, Daniel would be proud to have a fine Southern gentleman here protecting me from the Yankees.''

Taggart's conscience twinged with every word she spoke.

''Besides,'' she continued in a sensible voice, ''how could I sleep in this warm cabin knowing you were getting wet as a drowned rat in that leaky barn?'' She eyed the rain-lashed window, then floated her gentle gaze over him. ''It's getting a little chillier each day. I know this old cabin doesn't look like much to a man like you, but it's better than the barn.'' Her eyes shone with happiness. ''After all you're doing for the South, providing a dry place for you to sleep is the least I can do.''

Taggart surveyed Daniel's tidy bed with its clean quilt, and it looked mighty appealing compared to the drafty, leaky barn. And how nice it would be to feel cool clean sheets against his skin after sleeping on a bedroll in the open for several weeks. Sending her a broad smile, he nodded his head. ''Very well, if you insist, I accept with gratitude.''

Back at the table they drank a little more applejack and talked about the war. Later they tacked a quilt from one of the rafters, separating Silky's bed from the rest of the room to give her some privacy. When she finally blew out the kerosene lamp, the room dissolved into darkness, smoke briefly scenting the air. Firelight alone now illuminated her willowy frame, and for a moment their eyes met and held.

She swept her gaze over him, her eyes looking, it seemed, all the way to his heart. ''I sure appreciate you roofing that barn. It's been needing it for a coon's age.''

''That's all right,'' he responded, touched by her open gratitude. ''I'm glad to do it.'' She stood silently for a moment and, more to break the tension than anything else, he added, "Sleep well."

She nodded and he watched her until she became one of the swaying shadows.

When she'd disappeared behind the quilt he sat before the fire, thinking of the events of the day. Silky's news about the home guard left him concerned, and he reminded himself he'd have to be especially careful to stay away from Bear Wallow, where he was sure the old men congregated until the day the wounded soldiers would come home. Their presence definitely presented a risk, but in his mind an acceptable one that he would have to take to gather his vital information. That risk would be mitigated by the fact that the woods were so scarcely populated and Silky's cabin was nestled so far back in the pines, he decided, feeling more secure at the thought.

He lit up another cheroot, his mind now turning to their conversation this evening. He watched the fire's glow flickering over the room's humble furnishings. In the shadows he saw the faces of the Confederate generals, then that of Grant, who, on the recommendation of General Sharpe, had personally dispatched him on the spying mission. Taggart smiled wryly. How surprised the general would be if he knew he was now successfully ensconced behind enemy lines, sleeping in a snug cabin with a flame-haired Reb whose loyalty to the Confederacy included a desire to tar and feather the general.

He chuckled and moved to Daniel's bed. Two boots hit the floor; then, stretching out, he listened to the popping of the fire and the soothing drum of rain on the roof. With a long sigh, he remembered the feel of her lips under his. He'd kissed her more as a game, just to see if he could, but the little game had shaken his sensibilities and fired his desire to the boiling point. Then, recalling the vow he'd made when Ned was killed, he warned himself he couldn't let his personal feelings interfere with his mission. Still, he realized that he and Silky had passed a new milestone, and his senses quickened at the thought of what lay ahead of them.

Tomorrow, he thought just before sliding into a comfortable sleep, he'd move his belongings into the cabin.

* * *

Late one afternoon a week later Silky took Daniel's hounds and started walking to her "thinking place," a beautiful spot in the woods where she'd always gone since she was a child to sort out her troubles. In the forest dark evergreens stood out against brilliant foliage, and sunlight, dancing with dust motes, slanted across a twisting path covered with pine needles that crunched under her feet.

Fifteen minutes after she'd entered the fragrant woods she arrived at a place she knew well, a boulder with a smooth top that overlooked a creek swirling over white pebbles. Climbing atop the boulder, she watched the hounds frolic along the creek's edge, the scent of moss and earth and moldering leaves enveloping her. In the distance she could hear the gurgling creek and the cheerful call of mocking birds—all old familiar sounds, but today her mind pondered a brand-new problem. Just how did she feel about this good-looking flatlander named Taggart who had burst into her life as unexpectedly as a sudden frost?

Since he'd been sleeping in the cabin a new closeness had developed between them, and she found it almost impossible to believe this was the same person she'd once locked in her smokehouse. He was more interesting than any man she'd ever met, and just being near him filled her with crackling passion. Still, the fact that she really didn't know that much about him hung in her mind like a thunderstorm ready to break. Was he all he claimed to be, or someone else, someone trying to deceive her? Oh, he had all the right answers, and a heap of charm to boot. There was no doubt about that, but at times she sensed there was something slightly amiss about him.

Silky's heart beat fast as she remembered his smoldering gaze that had melted her heart to something resembling a puddle of butter. He was so masculine, so devastating, she thought, hot blood singing through her veins like white lightning at just the memory of that ornery grin on his lips. And in that moment, she revised her opinion that it would take a ten-buggy prayer meeting to save him. Someone who'd had as much experience charming women as he obviously had would need a whole two-week revival with dinner on the church grounds thrown in.

Over the noise of the water, she heard the sharp sound of breaking twigs and, twisting about, saw Charlie emerge from the trees, spotty sunlight firing his shaggy red hair. As always, a battered Confederate cap shaded the expression in his eyes, but she couldn't miss that familiar smile she knew so well. "I reckoned I'd find you here," he drawled, scooping up a handful of pebbles, then strolling to the boulder and claiming a place beside her. "Thinkin' about *him?*" he inquired, chucking a few pebbles into the creek.

Silky regarded her younger cousin, for the moment wishing he hadn't intruded on her privacy; then she told herself he had as much right to be here as herself. "You know I am," she answered with a long sigh. "Who else would I be thinking about?"

Charlie sailed a few more pebbles into the creek. "You shouldn't have let him move into the cabin," he warned, using the tone Daniel always took when he advised her about something important.

"I couldn't let him keep sleeping in the barn," she retorted, irritated at the advice. "It's leaking rain."

"What do you think Daniel would say about him sleepin' in the cabin?"

"Daniel isn't here," she returned, aggravated to be lectured by someone she considered a child. "With the cold weather soon coming on, he'd freeze to death in the barn."

"Oh, I reckon he'd keep on livin' all right—a smart feller like him."

Silky considered her cousin's sly grin. "And what do you mean by that?" she asked, perturbed because she already knew what he meant.

"Do you reckon he's really what he says he is? I think you may be lettin' your heart get in the way of your head."

"You're fourteen years old!"

The boy's mouth slanted upward. "Yeah, I am—but I ain't blind. I see the way your eyes light up like a lamp every time he looks at you."

Silky turned her head. "Oh, I'm just trying to be friendly. I'm not serious or anything."

The boy chuckled. "You ain't? Well, you sure had me fooled. Just lookin' at your eyes when they're travelin' over him, I figured you was about as serious as a rattlesnake."

"Wipe that silly grin off your face," she ordered irritably. "You look like you got struck by lightning." Then knowing she really had no defense against his accusation, she simply ignored him and stared at the creek. After a long silent spell, she added, "I thought you liked him."

"I do like him. He's a heap of fun when he starts talkin' about them far-off places. I just don't trust him."

Charlie sat silently for five minutes, chucking the last of his pebbles into the water; then he slid from the boulder, a droll smile catching the corner of his mouth. "You took a real shine to him, didn't you? Do you love him?" he asked bluntly. "Are you fixin' to run away with him when he leaves the mountains?"

Silky let out her breath in an exasperated rush. "My lands-a-living, who's the grown-up here? You or me?"

He gave her an impish grin. "That's what I'm tryin' to find out."

"Sometimes," Silky vowed, leveling a hot glare at him, "I think you're the biggest granny woman in the whole hollow—either that or some kind of talking machine that never runs out of steam!"

The boy ambled away from the boulder, but at the edge of the trees, he glanced back over his shoulder. "You just think on what I'm tellin' you," he advised, tugging down his cap. "There's somethin' that just don't set plumb level about that feller. There are things he says I wouldn't believe unless God and the apostles swore to 'em and Jefferson Davis backed 'em up."

Silky watched the boy disappear into the forest, then turned and stared at the creek again, wondering why she was so upset. A moment later she decided it was because she'd secretly thought the same thing herself. Then she remembered the questions Taggart had asked her about city life, and gradually her better sense took control of her heart, advising caution where he was concerned.

Lordamercy, the places he'd been and the things he'd done: all those plays and operas and parties, and all that fancy living! Why, he was as far above her as the sun was above the earth. A Norfolk gentleman like himself who'd known scores of sophisticated women took pleasure where he found it and rode on, she sternly warned herself. She couldn't let herself be swept away on a tide of emotion, for an uneducated girl like herself could only be a light amusement to him. She dared not give this stranger her heart or he'd break it for sure, then ride away without a second thought.

Yet at the same time, she recalled the feel of his lips against hers, and went all soft and tender inside. Never had she felt so alive and totally happy as when he had held her in his arms. And to make matters worse, when he looked at her with those gorgeous eyes, oozing his charm all over her, she felt an exciting warmth in parts of her body she'd rarely considered before. And what a deep, totally overpowering sensation it was, too.

Silky had always found an answer when she went to her thinking place, but she found none today. Still struggling with her problem, she sat on the boulder until a cool, damp breeze blew through the woods, telling her evening was near. Slowly, she rose and called the hounds. Taggart would be coming down from the barn roof soon and would want his supper, the rightful due of every working man.

As she and the yapping dogs entered the woods for the walk back to her cabin she decided it would be best if she never let Taggart take her in his arms again. But even as she branded the promise into her brain, she realized it was a vow she'd be hard-pressed to keep.

Chapter Three

It was almost dusk, the time the mountain people called candlelight, when all nature stilled before slipping into darkness. From his position on the barn roof, Taggart started gathering up his tools, thinking he'd done enough work for the day. After putting them in a satchel, he stared through the dim light, studying Silky's rough-hewn log home, chinked with clay. Orange light glowed through its windows and a silvery wisp of smoke curled from the chimney, scenting the nippy air with the aroma of burning hickory.

With a tingle of anticipation, he thought of her stirring up corn bread or rolling out biscuits as she cooked dinner for them. The cabin would be warm and cozy and filled with rosy light, and in just minutes he would enter, prompting Silky to come up with an expression guaranteed to make him laugh. Just thinking about the scene conjured up a list of words: happiness, fulfillment, joy—all words he'd never applied to his life before.

For a heartbeat he wondered what it would be like to see those glowing windows every candlelight—to know her exquisite face was waiting for him in that sea of contentment.

Then like a cold, clammy hand, the growing pressure of his mission bore down on him. Was he going mad? The first few days of November had already passed and he still didn't have his information. As soon as he questioned the returning soldiers, he had to be on his way.

Even if he could stay, he and Silky would make a poor match. He'd come from a rich, privileged background in Ohio, and he could see his life laid out for him like an impeccably tailored suit upon a bed. Although it wasn't to his liking, there would be marriage to a well-born debutante, and after a career in the army he'd take over management of his father's brick factory, the largest in Ohio. Of course, he'd have membership in all the dull, but socially correct, institutions and clubs, and shoulder all the responsibility that came with a great fortune. Despite its stifling restrictions it was a life of privilege that most men would be thankful to have—but a life Silky would be totally unsuited for.

But even if she came from the finest family in Virginia, he realized, the political differences between them would create a chasm a thousand feet deep. She of the fiery Secessionist persuasion would never accept his views that the Union must stand, no matter what.

Hearing soft whimpering sounds, he noticed the hounds cautiously rising from their place in front of the cabin as they laid back their ears and looked in the direction of the woods. From his high position, Taggart gazed at the woods himself and spied flashes of horses and riders on the trail that led to Silky's cabin. To his dismay, he noted that the trio wore bits and pieces of Confederate uniforms. With a spurt of alarm, he guessed the older men were from the home guard and, spotting him in the woods, had come to investigate. As irregulars the shabby soldiers weren't as informed as the battlefield troops; still, if they realized he was a Union officer, they would take him to the nearest Confederate command post or shoot him on the spot, which they were within their right to do.

He knew the alternatives handed to him were to scramble for the woods, revealing who he was without a doubt, or face them down. Perhaps he had a chance, he decided, dropping his satchel and climbing down the ladder. Once on the ground, he strode toward the cabin so he could get a rifle to even up the odds. When he was halfway to the door there were sounds of neighing horses, and three bearded riders burst into the clearing, stirring up the scent of dust.

Armed with glinting muskets, the men wore scuffed brogans, buckskin breeches, and threadbare Confederate jackets missing half their brass buttons. The heaviest soldier, an unkempt sergeant, sported a faded kerchief and a battered kepi cap that covered most of his long, greasy hair. His face was seamed by wind and weather, and deep-set eyes glinted under grizzled brows. "Hold up there!" he yelled at Taggart, putting a hand on the butt of the pistol strapped to his side.

Over the din of the barking dogs, Taggart heard the cabin door slam. Turning, he saw Silky's long white apron flashing in the twilight as she ran toward him, clutching the repeating rifle in her hands. Instantly he read the worried look on her face, and when she paused at his side, he grabbed the weapon and stepped in front of her in a protective gesture.

The riders' mounts shied back from the snarling hounds, and the sergeant bellowed, "Call off your dogs afore they spook the horses!"

"Hush, you hounds," Silky called at the baying dogs. "Get now. Get!" With a long whimpering wail, the hounds dispersed and slunk of out sight behind the cabin.

Without a greeting, the slovenly man dismounted, leaving his frightened mare to toss her head. Taggart, meeting the sergeant's gaze, noticed an insolent look in his steely blue eyes. Gray stubble covered the woodsman's jowls, and the hard-bitten look on his features said he hadn't come to swap howdys.

The man spewed a stream of tobacco juice on the ground, then drew himself up importantly. "My name's Holt," he announced, a mountain drawl coloring his gruff voice. His focus moved to the other men, who sat astride their mounts with grim-faced obedience, then circled back to Taggart. "Word gets around real fast in the mountains. We heared there was stranger over here and since they ain't no menfolks in this neck of the woods but a young'un and his grandpappy, we decided we'd better take a look." With a loose-jointed stride he ambled forward, a slight limp to his step, and an almost tangible hostility shining from his hard eyes.

Taggart straightened his back, but quick as lightning, Silky sashayed in front of him, her hot eyes riveted on the soldier. "You could have saved yourself a long ride, Sergeant. There's no trouble over this way. This stranger you're staring at is named Taggart and he's a fine gentleman all the way from Norfolk." Her voice was low and quiet, but shot with firm resolution that revealed a will of iron.

Twilight had settled over the clearing, but through the blue haze, Taggart noticed she was shaking and he put his arm about her.

Silky scanned the sergeant and his friends, all from the roughest families in the hollow. Although two of the men were too old and feeble for regular military service, Holt had been exempted because of a bad leg that pained him constantly and did nothing to improve his vile disposition. She wondered if the men could see her trembling. The Lord knew she was quaking inside—quaking like a leaf in the wind at what these crazy wildcat whippers might do, now that they had a war to lend authority to their violence.

With the dogs silenced, a strained stillness had fallen over the clearing. Hot and sick inside, she scanned Taggart, who, his face hard as granite, held the rifle by his side, looking large and extremely intimidating. On the surface he seemed remote and icy calm, but she sensed tension boiling within him. Under his unwavering gaze, the ruffians eased back a bit, their slumped shoulders bearing evidence of their shrinking confidence.

"The lady's right," Taggart said coolly, the lines deepening about his mouth as he focused on the sergeant's face. "I'm a lieutenant from the Forty-third Virginia Cavalry on furlough. I'm on my way to the Rappahannock to meet my company."

The man grinned sourly, showing rotten teeth. "You got a strange twang in your voice, mister."

Fire flew through Silky, who'd temporarily forgotten she'd made the same comment herself when she'd first met Taggart. Pigs would be ice-skating in hell before she let this rabble trespass on her homestead and interfere again, she thought hotly. "That's 'cause he's a fine, educated gentleman who's gone to West Point with the likes of Jeb Stuart and Stonewall Jackson. Not all Southerners talk like ignorant peckerwoods, you know."

Holt eyed the older men, who grinned slyly, displaying the first spark of emotion since they'd arrived. Then the sergeant studied Taggart again. "What's your business with this gal, stranger?" he asked suspiciously. "Sounds to me like she's kinda sweet on you."

Taggart shifted his gaze to the barn, now only a dark silhouette against the twilight sky, then returned it to the soldier. "I'm helping her shingle her barn."

The sergeant rubbed a hand over his stubbled jaw. "That don't sound like somethin' a fine West Point gentleman would be doin' to me." He cut his gaze at the other riders and started reaching for his pistol, prompting Taggart to take aim.

Silky, understanding Holt would be less inclined to shoot a woman than a man, snatched the rifle from Taggart's grip and pointed it at the sergeant's head. She'd once held the same weapon on Taggart, but now that she knew the measure of him, it angered her that trash such as this would confront him. "I reckon that's 'cause you don't have a spark of gentlemanly feeling in your whole body, Sergeant Holt," she remarked, salty tears pricking her eyes. "Quality folks don't mind getting their hands dirty once in a while if it'll help somebody out."

Silky cocked the rifle. "You've done fried my patience," she asserted, her throat almost closing with emotion. "This is *my* place, and if there's going to be any shooting, *I'm* going to be the one doing it."

"You scare me," he scoffed, raking a mocking gaze over her.

She permitted herself a little smile. "You don't know what scared is yet. Funny thing about a repeating rifle—it'll kill you five times before you can blink once."

Holt widened his eyes in surprise.

"It's getting plumb dark already," she remarked, her voice a raspy whisper. "It would pleasure me greatly if you and your friends rode on home for supper."

She could see the man reaching for his pistol, but also realized the inhabitants of the hollow wouldn't tolerate him drawing on a woman who was standing on her own property asking him to leave.

With a scowl, the sergeant dropped his hand, then limped to his horse and slowly remounted. "You best be careful, missy, who you bring into your cabin," he growled, stabbing his finger at her. "This is war times and it ain't safe, nor smart either, to go takin' up with ever' stranger that comes traipsin' through the woods."

He moved a hard gaze over Taggart then, jerking his head in the direction of the forest, rode away, disappearing into the deepening shadows. Their faces stony masks, the old men followed, the sounds of their nickering horses gradually fading away.

Taggart watched Silky lower the rifle with trembling hands. Although fire still lingered in her eyes, her face had relaxed visibly. Knowing it wasn't the time to speak, he remained silent, impressed that she'd taken a stand to defend him. Thank God the irregulars hadn't stayed long enough to search his saddlebags, or they would have found enough evidence to shoot him on the spot. Whether the little spitfire knew it or not, she'd saved his life.

If she'd wanted to turn him in, if she'd had any doubts about his loyalty to the South, she could have easily given the word, and he'd now be a dead man. Without a doubt he'd completely deceived her with his story, he decided, wondering why that fact should make him a bit sad.

He'd made it through this confrontation, but there would be other encounters with Confederates, many of whom would be harder to back down. Could he keep up the charade until the wounded troops returned to the hollow and gave him the needed information? And more important, could he cut off his growing feelings for Silky and ride away without looking back?

Placing his hand on the small of her back, he escorted her to the cabin, thinking those were questions he'd be forced to live with every day he lingered here. "What are we having for supper tonight?" he asked quietly, suddenly realizing that the cabin's glowing lights had never looked prettier.

She looked up with smiling eyes. "Ham hocks and beans," she answered, tears of relief clinging to her lashes. "Let's eat before the corn bread gets cold."

The next morning Silky hurried toward her log home, carrying a bowl of freshly gathered eggs in her hands. The morning was nippy and the grass glistened with frost, but remembering the way Holt and his friends had beaten a path for the woods the evening before made her feel warm all over. Once inside the cabin, she smelled burning paper, then noticed Taggart suddenly turning from his place before the hearth, a surprised expression flashing on his face.

Her gaze traveled to the flames as they licked over a paper with close writing and numbers, then turned the page into gray ashes that dissolved into the fire. After placing the eggs on the table, she met Taggart's eyes, deciding she'd never seen them hold such a look as they did now. What did she see in their depths? she wondered: guilt, concern, regret, or a subtler emotion she wasn't acquainted with?

He stared at her for a moment. "I was just getting rid of an old letter," he stated, his tone rough and somewhat unsteady. He smiled brightly, a bit too confidently, she thought with a dart of misgiving. "I didn't know you would be coming back so soon," he added, his voice still uneven.

Silky regarded him, not knowing just how she should respond.

"Well," he finished briskly, reaching for a jacket, "I'd better be getting up on that roof. From what you say the first snow will be coming soon and I still have some work to do."

Silky stared at him, feeling her spirits sink, but not understanding just why. "I-I think I'll go into the woods this morning and pick some persimmons," she stammered. "Now that we've had a couple of hard frosts they should be good and ripe."

Taggart nodded, then shrugged on his jacket, moved past her, and left the cabin.

After washing a few dishes, Silky put on an old jacket

herself, picked up a basket, and departed for the forest. In the distance the Blue Ridge Mountains stretched as far as the eye could see, a misty haze floating over them, and closer in, dark evergreens towered upward like giant sentinels. But Silky's mind was so preoccupied with the burning paper, she scarcely noticed the beauty about her. For a while she searched for persimmon trees, plucking the orange-red fruit and dropping it into her basket. Before she knew it, she found herself back at her thinking place.

Her mind racing, she sat atop the flat boulder, the noise of the creek and trilling birdsong providing a pleasant background for her troubled thoughts. Why had Taggart waited until she'd gone to gather eggs to burn his letter? she wondered—and why had she felt that thick air of tension between them? There were still so many things about him that left her puzzled. She knew Charlie didn't trust him, but that didn't necessarily prove anything. He was just a boy, and surely jealous now that an outsider had come to pull her attention away from him.

Yes, Taggart projected an air of danger and toughness that was truly tantalizing, but in him she found none of the cold, rude qualities she'd always imagined Yankees to possess. She sensed that under his brooding good looks lurked a gentleman and a thoughtful, caring lover, even if he'd lost some of his Norfolk drawl up North.

Silky sat on the boulder pondering the situation for a good half hour; then, drawing in a long breath, she cast aside her doubts. She was wasting her time. She'd stood up for Taggart against the home guard, hadn't she? She should trust her own good judgment and let the matter rest. Holt and his friends could sulk all they liked, and the granny women could gossip about the good-looking stranger till they fell out of their rocking chairs. She'd accepted Taggart for what he said he was, and she'd stand by her decision.

Kneeling atop the barn roof, Charlie offered Taggart another shingle. "Reckon it'll snow soon?"

Ignoring the boy, Taggart inched forward, feeling the uneven roof against his knees. He slapped the shingle into place, took several nails from his clenched lips, and banged the rough square in place. Several days had passed since Sergeant Holt's visit, and although he hadn't seen the man or his friends again, he was glad he'd taken the precaution of memorizing the coded cipher and burning it, and also breaking the money into smaller bundles and secreting it in his clothing. Now if the men reappeared, he wouldn't be caught with the damning evidence.

His mind dwelled on Silky, who'd gone to Bear Wallow this morning to bring back a few provisions. With a flicker of anxiety, he remembered the questioning look on her face as she had watched the flames consume the cipher. Had she believed his story that the paper was a letter? That was something that only time would tell, he finally decided with a lingering sense of concern.

"Lieutenant, you ain't payin' a lick of attention to what I said," Charlie prodded, shaking Taggart's arm and steering his mind back to the present. "I asked you if you reckon it'll snow soon."

Taggart glanced up. After several hours of work he was only half listening to the boy who'd been rattling on all morning. He gave the fourth nail a last swat for good measure. "I suppose," he replied, tired of the lad's endless chatter.

Charlie balanced himself against the slanting roof. "I'll bet it does. Up here in the mountains the weather can change overnight, and when it starts snowin' sometimes it goes on for days." He chuckled. "Yessirreebob. I reckon this winter will be as cold as a cast-iron commode."

Taggart paused to wipe a handkerchief over his damp brow. The cold November breeze felt good against his skin. As he surveyed his work, he noticed the shingling was almost finished, and experienced a surprising pang of disappointment.

"When there's a real nip in the air like today it always reminds me that hog-killin' time is just around the corner," Charlie went on, a broad grin racing over his face. "What's your favorite part of the hog? Mine's souse. I'm right partial to liver paste, too."

Taggart hammered down another shingle.

"Silky always makes sausage at hog-killin' time and has

me take it to all the widder ladies in the holler.'' The boy seemingly never ran out of breath. He shook his head. ''I reckon if somethin' happened to that girl the whole dadgummed holler would fall to staves.'' For one blessed moment he was quiet; then he burst out with, ''You ever been married?''

Taggart studied him, wondering what had brought on the personal question. Although Charlie was always friendly, he knew he really didn't trust him. Then, understanding that, as Silky had once said, the boy was curious as a pet coon, he decided the question was totally innocuous. ''No, I've never been married,'' he answered matter-of-factly.

''Have you ever had a hound dog?''

Taggart snorted, thinking his father, who kept a kennel of registered spaniels, would be horrified at the thought of a hound dog lazing on his marble veranda. ''No, I've never had a hound dog, either.''

The boy leaned closer, filling Taggart's nostrils with the warm, tangy scent of chewing tobacco. ''How about a coon or a crow?'' he asked with exasperation. ''They're both real smart.''

Taggart tossed his hammer aside. ''No, I've never had a hound dog, a coon, a crow, a mouse, a tadpole, or even a one-legged grasshopper,'' he answered, trying to put an end to the conversation.

Charlie scratched his head. ''Lordy, your folks must have been poor as Job's turkey.''

Taggart laughed; then his curiosity go the best of him. He caught the boy's troubled gaze. ''You were going to say something?''

Charlie tugged his ear. ''Naw . . . I better not. Reckon it wouldn't be mannersome.''

Taggart sat back, really curious now. ''Go on,'' he commanded. ''Spit it out.''

A blush worked its way across the boy's freckled face.

''Well, I was just thinkin',' he finally stammered, ''th-that you've sure lived a dull life. No wife, no hound dog, no coon . . . or even a little bitty ol' crow,'' he said, picking up speed once he'd started talking. ''Life must be a pure disappointment to you.'' He gave him a keen look. ''Maybe you should do some long thinkin' about what you want to do in your declinin' years."

Declining years? thought Taggart. Of course it would do no good to tell the boy he was only thirty-three and a lifetime of exciting events stretched out before him like a golden road. Still, it seemed that never owning a hound dog or a coon made him a real failure. "Yeah, things have been pretty dull, all right," he sighed, deciding to join the game. "Duller than ditch water, sometimes."

"Duller than a widder woman's ax?" The boy chuckled.

"Oh, a heap duller than that," Taggart replied, realizing that much of his life had been dull because it was filled with meaningless rituals he'd been forced to carry out because of the family name. Wasn't that why he'd decided to go to West Point . . . to get away from a life of boring ease and predictability? "I reckon a lot of my life has been flatter than a mashed cat."

"Hey, you two," came a voice from the ground below. "Are you all working this morning or just making chin music?"

Taggart peered over the edge of the roof, and his spirits rose when he spotted Silky. A radiant smile on her lips, she led her mount toward the barn, the wind molding her clothes to her shapely body.

"I've got some good news," she announced, whipping a battered envelope from her pocket and waving it in the air. "The mail came in from Charlottesville yesterday. I got a letter from Daniel, and Uncle Joe's boys will be back in Bear Wallow day after tomorrow."

"That *is* good news," Taggart replied, as he realized his time with Silky—their shared jests and teasing chatter—was scheduled to end promptly. "I'll have the barn shingled by then, too," he added, the fact hitting him solidly in the gut.

Their gazes locked and he thought he detected a touch of sadness on her face—but he couldn't be sure. She looked at him for a moment; then, her voice full of forced cheerfulness, she lightly remarked, "Just wanted you to know." Her bosom rising and falling with emotion, she stared at him a moment longer, then led her horse through the open barn doors.

Taggart put down another shingle and hammered it hard. The soldiers would soon be home and he'd have his information, he thought with deep relief. There wouldn't be any excuse to linger in Sweet Gum Hollow any longer. He could get out of this Godforsaken backwater, ride to Charlottesville, and relay his information to the Union. Then, somewhere deep within him where truth dwelled, he realized this last month had been the best of his life.

Getting another shingle, he noticed a silly grin on Charlie's face. "Silky's real pretty, ain't she? And nice, too. If she weren't my cousin, I reckon I'd be sweet on her myself."

Taggart stared at the boy, amazed by his acuity. How did the lad know she'd worked her way under his skin like no woman before? How his friends in Washington would laugh if they knew that he, who'd squired the most fashionable women in the capitol, had gone soft over a mountain girl who'd never been twenty miles from the cabin where she was born.

Taggart pounded down another shingle, realizing he had to accept the situation at hand, or he'd end up leaving a piece of himself behind when it came time to ride away.

"You mad or somethin'?" Charlie asked point-blank.

Frustration filled Taggart's soul. "No, I'm not mad," he muttered, giving the nails several hard swats that reverberated over the roof. He gazed at the boy, irritated by his lopsided grin. "I'll tell you when I'm mad."

"That's funny," Charlie chirped, his grin now turning into a broad smile. "Just lookin' at you, I woulda sworn you was mad as a rained-on rooster."

That evening, Silky looked up from her work, her face alight with curiosity. "I still don't understand why so many men were killed."

Taggart watched her as, garbed in a scoop-necked dress of russet, she sat before the hearth slicing apples into a bowl. For the last ten minutes he'd been pacing about the cabin to burn off energy as he tried to reconstruct the Battle of Shiloh for her. Both harrowing days were vivid in his mind, for before going to work for General Sharpe, he'd fought there under Grant.

She stopped working and stared at him, the firelight crowning her auburn hair with a glowing halo. "We were winning at first, weren't we?"

He held her inquiring gaze, explaining the battle as if he'd fought with the Confederacy. "Yes, at first," he answered slowly, seeing the flashing guns in his mind's eye, "but a lot of the soldiers were new and didn't know much about keeping together in battle."

The ferocity of the hours stamped on his mind forever, he came to kneel by her chair. "In the smoke, little groups got separated and fought with the Union for a patch of woods or a hill. No one had ever seen such a battle. The trees were stripped of their very leaves by the bullets." He watched the play of emotion on her features. "Johnson was killed that bloody day and Grant had his horse shot from under him."

Her eyes brimmed with emotion. "I've always imagined what it would be like to go into battle," she remarked, wiping her hand on a dishcloth and placing her bowl on the hearth. "Sometimes I tremble for Daniel. It must be the awfulest thing on earth." Her soft hand clasped his. "What is it like . . . can you tell me?"

Taggart rose and studied her delicate face, knowing he must shield her from the worst of what he'd experienced. "As I think of it now," he answered, recalling the bitter scent of smoke-thick air and the rattle of musketry, "what I remember most vividly is the time directly prior to battle. How quiet and calm it is. It's as if nature herself were holding her breath."

He walked from the hearth and turned about, seeing her, but almost looking through her as his mind dwelled in the past. "It seems we were usually lying on the earth behind a fence with our rifles resting on the bottom rails. The men's faces were pale, their features set, their muscles strung like steel. Some major or captain would always cry, 'Steady men! They're coming! Get ready!' "

Silky's gaze was transfixed upon him.

"Then the warning click of hammers ran down the lines as the guns were cocked—and Lord, what a chilling sound that was, for at that moment everyone knew the shooting was ready to begin." He met her large, liquid eyes, knowing he dared not tell her more.

Silky searched his taut face, realizing how profoundly the battle still affected him two years after it had happened. "I've often wondered if Yankees feel like us," she slowly ventured, trying to understand a people who, in her perspective, were almost of another race.

His eyes lit with amusement. "I can assure you they do. They love, and marry, and have babies, and die, just like people in the Blue Ridge Mountains."

She rose and, smoothing back her hair, walked to him, grasping for words to express what she meant. "But from what I've heard about them, they seem so different," she insisted, noticing the corners of his eyes crinkle in a smile.

He clasped her shoulders. "As you would to them. Personal taste and beliefs may vary, but below the skin we're all alike. The big things, the important issues in life, are universal."

Battling her confusion, she looked at him for an answer. "This war has changed and upset everyone," she breathed with a worried sigh. "Do you believe in the Cause—really believe the South is doing the right thing?" she asked, finally voicing the question that had been pressing on her heart like a stone.

He expelled a harsh breath, and, as he began speaking, she heard the raw tension in his voice. "I love my country and I believe in doing my duty," he finally answered. He regarded her with a veiled gaze. "The right thing can be different for different people."

His answer failed to satisfy, but his restraint told her presently that she would get no others. Despair about the future suddenly swept through her like a chilling wind, leaving her desolate. "Lordamercy, when will all the fighting be over? When will this terrible war end? I'm so tired of it!"

An expression of tired sadness passed over his features. "I truly don't know," he answered, his hand rearranging one of her tresses, then moving to the small of her back. "Who can say? But I think it must be soon."

His raven hair draped appealingly over his brow; his jaw

was strong and set, and his lips sensuously inviting. His hand sent a pleasurable warmth over Silky's flesh. Before she knew it, his other arm was about her, and he held her so gently she could easily pull away, yet his nearness tugged at her heart, rooting her where she stood. Tenderness softened his expression, but the lines about his mouth revealed he was wrestling with his thoughts—focusing all his strength into solving some problem. Broken only by the sound of the flames and the wind, a poignant silence welled between them; then slowly, impulsively, as if he couldn't help himself, he pulled her toward him, his virile appeal shaking her heart.

Inky lashes framed his heavy-lidded eyes, which blazed with a passion that wore down her already crumbling resistance. What did it matter that she still secretly worried about the letter he'd burned? Surely one kiss wouldn't drastically change her life. Surely she could risk that, she reasoned, finally casting aside the caution she'd harbored for so long.

He trailed his lean fingers over her face and she trembled, for he roused some sleeping emotion buried deep within her that struggled for release. "I've wanted you from the first moment I saw you," he whispered, his steely arms tightening about her and making her forget everything but this glorious moment. When he pressed her more firmly against him, she felt the strength of his arms and the thud of his evenly beating heart.

She guessed that he was a practiced lover, but, putting aside her nagging regrets, she told herself that tonight she would enjoy just one kiss and discover what provoked the raging desire within her. In that moment some unspoken communication passed between them, not of the mind, but of the heart and the soul, and she relaxed in his warm embrace.

He brushed her long hair aside, then lowered his head, and she murmured contentedly as his moist mouth nuzzled her neck. His tangy scent sloughed over her, and his lips moved to the throbbing pulse in her throat, making her shudder at the fiery sensation they aroused. He cupped her chin in his large hand, and she boldly traced the warmth of his tanned face. Not satisfied, she caressed his corded neck and slipped her fingers into his partially open shirt, where dark springy hair coiled about them.

He fluttered kisses over her face. His breath was upon her while his teasing lips nibbled her ear, driving her to distraction. With a sigh, she raised herself a bit to loop her arms about his shoulders and run her hands over his back, hungry for the pleasure she'd been so long denied. When her fingers threaded themselves into his thick, glossy hair, he looked down at her with twinkling eyes. "Searching for little horns?" he asked, arching a questioning brow.

Surprised, she felt a blush warm her cheeks. "Why, no . . . I . . ." She burst out laughing and he laughed, too; then suddenly his mouth was upon hers and an unexpected sweetness shot through her. He smelled of the outdoors where he'd been working, and she caught the taste of tobacco on his lips. Trembling with the dark, delicious sensation he triggered within her, she found herself drowning in passion. Never before him had she enjoyed the thrill of a man's kiss, and, unaware of the emotions it could invoke, she reveled in its intensity. Her heart turned over in her bosom as she realized this was what she'd been secretly yearning for, but had been afraid she'd never know.

The kiss fueled a fire that fanned out from her belly and stole through her body, leaving her weak and trembling. His lips were fierce, demanding, insistent, and as his hard tongue plunged into her mouth, she surrendered to the moment. His hand kneaded her hips, holding her closer, and the proof of his aroused passion pressed against her abdomen, eliciting wild, almost frightening needs she'd never experienced.

Gently but firmly he ran his hand over her breast, and his touch burned her flesh through her gown, sweeping away the last of her defenses. Using his tongue expertly, he deepened the ravenous kiss, and a lulling sensation rose within her. At the same time her breasts strained against the gown, while her heart pounded crazily. When his tongue entwined with hers, a sharp pleasure throbbed between her thighs, leaving her limp and pliant. It was at this moment she decided without a shadow of a doubt that he wasn't a Yankee. No Yankee could kiss like this, with so much fire and spirit it took her very breath away.

Then she noticed the warmth of his hand through her gown once more, and as he tugged down the material and cupped her breast, smoothing his hard palm over it, she felt a delicious shock. When he rolled her aching nipple in his fingertips, ecstasy exploded within her, leaving her on the verge of swooning. As he teased and tantalized her with sure strokes, all the pent-up desire she'd known since setting eyes upon him rushed forward, demanding satisfaction.

Soft, tender feelings overcame her, and, like a rose being torn apart by the wind, she almost surrendered to Taggart. But gradually her rational mind gained control of her desire and she realized her curiosity had got her in this predicament. She'd bargained for a kiss, but was getting much more—more than she could handle. Surely he would think she was an easy conquest if she didn't put a stop to the lovemaking right now. With fluttering lashes, she opened her eyes and eased away from Taggart, her skin still glowing from his hands.

Her fingers quaking, she pulled her gown into place and met his searching gaze, realizing she'd almost lost control of herself. Now standing at arm's length from him, she surveyed his tense face, which seemed all harsh planes and angles. For a moment she glimpsed the fire within him; then she sensed he was also reining in his emotions.

This time she'd managed to dredge up enough discipline to save her virginity, but if the truth be told, she still hungered desperately for his touch. She'd saved herself this time, she realized, still light-headed from the fiery kiss . . . but what about the next time?

At that moment a log fell in the hearth, scattering embers and making popping sounds; then Taggart spoke, his voice threaded with a hint of regret. "I think we should call it a day," he suggested, tracing his warm fingers over her cheek.

He took in her thoughtful expression and heaved a deep sigh. He'd tried to kiss her on Apple Hill, and now on his second attempt he'd succeeded. But at what price? he thought, realizing the kiss had only whetted his appetite for more lovemaking. In fact, he'd never known such a savage need, and only moments before, he'd felt his good intentions not to touch her tear away from their moorings.

It seemed she'd mesmerized him in an almost magical way. Gazing at her soft face, he pondered the future with trepidation. Could he actually be falling in love with her? That was the last thing he wanted to do now, or at any other time, as a matter of fact. No, he wasn't falling in love with her, he sternly lectured himself. He'd just been caught in the trap of being marooned with a gorgeous woman full of life and fire.

Once he returned to Ohio women would be falling all over him, he advised himself. They always did, didn't they? He just had to settle down and wait out his emotions—put his priorities in order. With a rush of relief he decided his relationship with Silky presented no difficulty at all. Why, three months after he'd left the mountains, he probably wouldn't remember her name. But why was his heart still hammering like it might burst from his chest? He decided he needed to take some precautionary measures against this happening again.

"I think I'll go outside for a smoke," he announced softly. He gazed at her steadily, noticing a suspicious gleam of tears in her eyes. Then, knowing he had only one more day to spend with her before the wounded soldiers returned, he pulled up his courage. Surely he could keep himself in check for that long, he thought with firm resolve. His emotions knotted like a ball of twine, he turned and left the cabin, noticing that the first snowflakes had begun to fall.

Chapter Four

The next morning Silky and Taggart rode into Bear Wallow. Surrounded by scarlet-leafed maples powdered in white from the overnight snow, the village consisted of a blacksmith shop, a tavern, and a general store. Judging from the clustered wagons and horses, Taggart realized all the inhabitants of Sweet Gum Hollow had come to hail the returning soldiers as Confederate heroes.

But now as he swung from his mount, the curious highlanders meandered up, every eye riveted on him. A somber-faced group, they looked well acquainted with hardship as well as hard work. From their glinting eyes he could only imagine what they were thinking, but he felt uncomfortable being surrounded by such loyal Confederates who all had fathers, sons, and brothers fighting for the South.

Silky dismounted and claimed a spot on the porch of the general store. The fringe on her buckskins swaying in the chilly breeze, she tugged down her hat and announced, ''This stranger is named Taggart. He's a lieutenant in the Confederacy, so make him feel at home.''

As Taggart mingled with the mountaineers, he compared

them to the stolid citizens of Cleveland, knowing the stiff-collared businessmen would be amazed that such an array of colorful characters still existed in this country. Everyone was bundled up, for now that the hollow had received its first snow, it could become bitterly cold within a matter of hours. Smelling of tobacco and whiskey, some of the old men still wore coonskin caps and shoe packs made of animal hides, as their forefathers had. Many of the wizened grannies sat on wagon seats, their heads covered with thick shawls, and smoked clay pipes. A tired, undernourished look filled the eyes of the pale children, who, dressed in an odd assortment of oversize clothing, played tag and teased their barking puppies.

What were they thinking about him? Taggart wondered, studying their curious faces. Although they were outwardly friendly, he sensed their bluff camaraderie was underlaid with sly mountain suspicion. Surely if this group of ardent Secesh had a real inkling of his identity they would string him up on the spot, and afterward celebrate the hanging with a few swigs of white lightning.

A grandfather with a flowing white beard limped up and, pointing a walking stick at Taggart, assessed him with clouded eyes. "What town be ye from, stranger?"

"Norfolk."

"That's on the water, ain't it?" came another voice out of the crowd.

Several of the men eyed Taggart's mount. "That's a fine piece of horseflesh, mister. Bet you paid a considerable sum for that mare."

A shiny-eyed girl of courting age who'd been talking to Charlie at the general store's hitching post spied Taggart and edged toward him. "Lordamercy," she exclaimed, cutting her eyes at Silky, who now stood by his side, "that's the handsomest dark-headed man I ever saw in all my born days. Where in the world did you latch on to him?"

Taggart let his gaze glide over the group and noticed Sergeant Holt and his friends drinking moonshine while they stared at him with hatred in their eyes. More than ever, he understood his presence was putting Silky in danger, and he realized he needed to get his information, then ride out of the mountains forever. Once he was gone, she would be safe.

He was talking to some old men when a slim youth came galloping into the clearing waving a homemade Confederate flag. "The wagon is a-comin' from Wilson's Gap. The wagon is a-comin'!" he yelled, whipping the banner in the air.

A rumble could be heard; then a wagon, driven by a hillman, rolled into the clearing, filled with wounded men wearing slings and bloody bandages. The soldiers, big grins creasing their stubbled faces, waved and shouted at the cheering mountaineers, who surged forward, cheering loudly.

Tears in their eyes, women and children ran to be united with their loved ones before the teamster could pull the horses to a halt. Slowly and painfully, the soldiers came off the wagon, scattering hay that had been placed beneath them to cushion their ride from the tiny whistlestop of Wilson's Gap. With outstretched arms, their families received them, laughing and crying at the same time.

The team was unhitched and led to a watering trough while the wounded men, their arms about their sweethearts, limped away for a private embrace and a basket lunch, to be eaten on the spring seat of their own wagons. One soldier pulled a banjo from his pack and, his face splitting into a toothy smile, broke into a fiery rendition of "Dixie," to the delight of the clapping crowd. Families were reunited; giggling children chased each other about the clearing; hounds yapped; and jugs of white lightning were passed to every man, who each imbibed liberally. Surely it was a sight to gladden a heart of stone.

Taggart surveyed the reunion, realizing the more he lingered among the mountaineers the more he liked their unvarnished honesty and keen wit. Still, they were Southerners, and as such, part of the Confederacy that had snuffed out his brother's life at sixteen, he reminded himself.

Silky surveyed the noisy crowd, her face brightening into a smile as she clutched his arm. "Oh, there's Jimmy Wilkerson," she remarked, spotting a ragged youth with his arm in a sling. "He was one of my brother's best friends." She looked up at Taggart with large, hopeful eyes. "I think I'll talk to him and see if he has any fresh news about Daniel.'' So saying, she hurried across the snowy clearing, now filled with visiting family and friends.

Slowly, Taggart walked among the people, and at last he saw a grizzled sergeant who, between swigs of moonshine, leaned against a wagon regaling two old men with war stories. From his red face, glazed eyes, and loud voice Taggart decided he would be a good source of information. Already planning what he would say, he pasted a smile on his face and strolled in the sergeant's direction.

Fifteen minutes later, Silky finished her conversation with Jimmy Wilkerson, discovering Daniel had been transferred to another company that would see action soon—something he'd failed to mention in his letters, undoubtedly to save her worry. Searching for some of Daniel's other friends, she saw Taggart, a preoccupied expression on his handsome face, talking to Amos Evans. Lordamercy, why would he want to talk to Amos? Everyone in the hollow knew the man was a drunkard and a bigger gossip than any granny woman who ever lived.

Then, with a pang of sadness, she decided Taggart could do what he wanted. The barn roof was shingled, his furlough was almost over, and he would soon be leaving. Before she knew it, her cabin would be filled with lonely memories instead of joy and masculine laughter. How would she get through each day? she wondered, trying to forget the recent evening he'd taken her breath away with his fiery kisses. Then, with a spurt of defiance, she straightened her back. She wouldn't torture herself—wallowing in self-pity. She had to think of someone else for a change—someone like Daniel and the wounded soldiers who'd done so much for the Confederacy.

She took a large dipper of cool water from the common barrel at the general store and trailed from one wagon to the next, to any place a wounded soldier was visiting with his family. For half an hour she offered water to the wounded, always asking about Daniel and his new company. After a while the temperature dropped, and she glanced at the smooth gray sky, hoping it wouldn't snow until everyone had returned to the warmth of their own cabin.

Her mind still dwelling on her brother, she eventually came to Zeb Clingerman, who had signed up with Daniel what now seemed so long ago. His face ashen with pain from a shoulder wound, Zeb sat on the seat of his father's wagon, coughing and pulling a frayed quilt about his shoulders. For a while they talked about the war; then the boy studied Taggart squatted by Amos Evans, who was scratching something in the dirt with a stick. "Who's the tall stranger?" Zeb asked in a weak voice. "Some drummer?"

Silky answered his question, mentioning that Taggart was returning to the 43rd Virginia, now bivouacked along the Rappahannock.

At the words a strange look settled on the boy's face. "The Forty-third Virginia?" he whispered with disbelief.

"Yes, that right," she replied with an uneasy feeling that something was terribly wrong. "What of it?"

The youth blinked doubtful eyes. "Because," he insisted in a raspy breath, "that company is no place near the Rappahannock."

Pain squeezed about Silky's heart. "You must be mistaken," she said hurriedly, refusing to accept his words. "You're mixed up. You—"

"I *ain't* mixed up," the boy retorted, looking at her a little sharply.

She stared at him, her throat going dry with emotion. "A-Are you sure about this?" she stammered, beginning to tremble.

The boy nodded. "Yes, I'm sure . . . certain-sure. One of my duties was to tidy up General Johnston's tent. There was this big old map on the table with pins stickin' in it showin' the location of all the regiments and their companies. It got where I knew that map by heart." He nodded at Taggart, suspicion flooding his face. "If that feller there is tellin' folks the Forty-third Virginia is bivouacked along the Rappahannock, he's lyin', sure as God made little green apples. They've never been near there."

"Well, where are they, then?" she demanded, still hoping against hope he'd made a mistake.

A coughing fit seized the boy, and his father wrapped the

quilt tightly around him. "They're in Loudoun County," the boy wheezed between coughs. "That's miles from the Rappahannock."

Her heart pounding, Silky gazed at Taggart, watching him nod and smile at Amos, who continued to draw in the dirt, obviously showing off his knowledge about something important. Please Lord, don't let this be happening! she cried out in her mind, completely shattered by the fact that Taggart had been deceiving her. Feeling as if her world had just been turned upside down and smashed to bits, she clasped the side of the wagon seat, tears stinging her eyes.

Silky looked across the table at Taggart as he ate, a sick feeling coiled in the pit of her stomach. They'd shared a cold ride from Bear Wallow, and a silent one, too. At first the gray sky had spit grainy snow; then larger flakes began whirling down faster and faster, clinging to the tree limbs like feathers until the woods glistened white.

Fears and accusations had darted through her mind since she'd spoken to Zeb Clingerman, and she'd wanted to confront Taggart instantly. But the happy gathering at Bear Wallow wasn't the place to air such a scene, and all the way home she'd been so shocked, so hurt, she couldn't trust her voice. Once at the cabin, Taggart had groomed and fed the horses while she'd hidden her tears to go inside and cook an evening meal. A little light chatter—talk about the soldiers—had passed between them during dinner, but the rapport they usually shared was gone. She knew it, and by the look in his eyes, he knew it, too.

Taggart shoved back his plate and gazed at her with puzzled eyes. "What's wrong? I know something is wrong. Tell me what it is."

Silky had planned to be calm and dignified when she confronted him in the privacy of her cabin, but as it happened, she slammed her tin cup against the table and the words tumbled from her mouth like water gushing from a mountain spring. "Why did you lie to me?" she demanded, still so stunned by his deceit that she could hardly think. From the anguish flickering in his eyes, she knew it wasn't necessary to mention the location of the 43rd Virginia—he knew exactly what she was talking about.

Slowly he rose and walked to the hearth; then, turning his back and bowing his head, he braced his hand on the rough mantelpiece. When he faced her it seemed he carried the weight of the world on his shoulders. "I lied to protect you," he answered quietly, his voice threaded with pain. "I lied because it was necessary."

Silky rose and clenched the back of her chair. This smooth-talking city man had taken advantage of her, then used her for his own selfish purposes. She recalled how beguiling he'd been when she'd brought him food at the smokehouse, and she silently cursed herself for being the biggest fool in Virginia. Why, she'd even stood up for him against Holt, and the sergeant's hot warning about taking in a stranger resounded in her head this very minute.

Trembling with fury, she rushed to him and, balling her fists, buffeted him on the chest. "Zeb Clingerman said the Forty-third Virginia isn't at the Rappahannock and they never have been." Again she flailed at his chest, but he grabbed her wrists with both hands. "Why did you tell me that pack of lies?" she sobbed, trying to twist away. "You're a *Yankee,* aren't you?" she cried, her hair flying about her. "You're nothing but a blue-bellied Yankee!"

Taggart met her hot, glassy eyes, deeply regretting he hadn't ridden on when she took her rifle off him over a month ago. As he'd expected, Amos Evans had spouted off and he'd obtained the number and condition of Johnston's regiments. But at what price?

Anguish rising within him, he scanned Silky's pale, tear-streaked face, holding her still as she tried to pull away. She was quaking all over, and her eyes burned with a consuming fire. A knot of emotion gathered in his chest, and in that split second, he made a decision to do something utterly unbelievable. To ease her pain, he decided he must lie to her yet again.

What would it matter if he twisted the truth once more—this time to protect her innocence? It would be different if he were staying, but he had his information, and in the morning he'd be gone. It had never been his intention to hurt her, and now that he'd come to understand her innate goodness, the thought of crushing her pained him deeply.

"No," he murmured, attempting to hold her close and caress her hair. "You don't know what you're saying." He rained kisses over her stricken face, trying to soothe her as he would a panicked child. "It's true that I have no aunt in the Shenandoah, and my regiment isn't the Forty-third Virginia, but I am from Norfolk, as I told you." He thought swiftly, simply turning his life inside out as he had once before, about the Battle of Shiloh, to fashion an acceptable story.

Calmer now, she stared at him with huge eyes, and he held her at arm's length, searching her astonished face as he spoke. "I'm an intelligence officer," he explained in a warm, soft voice. "I'd been on an information-gathering trip to Maryland when you came upon me at the pond."

As his words sank in, he saw the despair and anger fade from her features, and he gave silent thanks, thinking any fabrication was worth the cost to take away the hurt he'd caused.

Thoughtfully, she blinked her eyes, staring at him as if she couldn't believe her ears. "A-Are you telling me that you're a *Confederate* agent?" she whispered, still trembling beneath his hands.

He swallowed hard, hoping all that was holy would forgive him for what he was about to say. His heart pounded evenly as he considered the next words out of his mouth. "Yes," he answered softly, a convincing story falling into place in his mind. "Soon after I crossed the Virginia line I met my contact and gave him the information. I was told to take some time off, then report to Charlottesville for my next assignment."

Her eyes widened in disbelief. "But you lingered here in the hollow, shingling my roof. Surely—"

"I can explain that," he interrupted with a laugh, caressing her tense shoulders as he spoke. "A major—I cannot mention his name—is to meet me in Charlottesville a few days from now and give me my next assignment. Since the major wasn't able to be there himself until the prearranged date, I had some time on my hands before the rendezvous." He gave her a big smile, hoping his words had soothed her troubled emotions. "I realized I could spend the time here in Sweet Gum Hollow just as easily as waiting for him in Charlottesville."

He knew she was quite intelligent and he could see she was evaluating every word he said. Would she believe him? he wondered, hoping against hope that she would, so her heart wouldn't be broken. Something inside of him violently recoiled from telling her more falsehoods, yet at the same time, another side realized he'd try to convince her that black was white, if he could leave her as innocent and full of life as the day they'd met.

"But I—" She broke off, confusion shadowing her glassy eyes.

He ran his hand down her back, trying to console her. "Forgive me for the pretense I was forced to offer you," he whispered, the falsehood burning his lips, "but I was instructed to tell no one my true mission." He clasped her shoulders. "I do it now only because I can't hold the facts back from you any longer."

He studied her softening expression and saw she was beginning to believe what he'd said. Thank God, she'd remember him as a Confederate lieutenant who'd helped her, rather than as a Yankee who'd deceived her. He would gladly bear the guilt of the lies to preserve her illusions, he decided with a growing sense of relief.

Taggart's words left Silky in a confused daze, but at the same time a sense of ease rose within her, dimming her anger. His story was rather dramatic and certainly far-fetched, but unheard-of things often happened during wars. And, sheltered in the remote Blue Ridge, how could she know all that was happening in the flatlands? Yes, the storm inside of her was quieting now, she thought, staring into a pair of sapphire eyes that willed her to believe him. And, God help her, she wanted to believe him so badly!

From deep within her, a nagging voice challenged his words one last time, but it was so much easier to believe him—to believe that someone who could set her mind and body aglow was one of her own kind. The thought that he could be a Yankee was so incomprehensible, so repulsive, that she simply pushed it aside, not ready to entertain it when another alternative, even a weak one, was available.

Of course, now that he'd explained things, she could see why he'd been forced to give her a falsehood. Everyone knew that scouts and spies were forbidden to speak of their missions, even to their families or sweethearts. Gradually her mind accepted what he'd told her, accepted all of it because she simply wanted to accept it. It was so much easier this way. To believe something else meant unbearable pain, while the bridge of faith required no effort and was supported with her cherished hopes and dreams.

The thought that he was a Confederate agent, possibly working for Robert E. Lee himself, left her shaken. "I . . . I didn't know," she said softly, surveying his concerned face. "I would have never guessed."

His eyes twinkled with warmth. "Well, I should hope not. A fine agent I'd be if I couldn't convince you of what I said."

She met his sympathetic gaze. "Why did you spend so much time talking to Amos Evans today?" she suddenly asked, still bothered by the incident.

"Why, I'm just interested in Johnston's troops like everyone else in the South. Old Amos has been with the general since the war began and seems to know everything about his regiments." He laughed lightly. "And he's a real colorful storyteller, too."

Still not completely satisfied, Silky knew she had to pose one more question. "That paper—the one I found you burning when I came in from gathering eggs—it wasn't really a letter, was it?"

Taggart caressed her hair. "No," he whispered. "The paper concerned some observations about my mission in Maryland, and since it was no longer needed I wanted to destroy it."

For some strange reason his confession served as a final confirmation that he was now telling the truth about being a Confederate agent. Perhaps it was because she'd harbored a strong feeling that the paper wasn't a letter all along, and he'd just proved her suspicions right. Serenity now overtook her as fears about him being a Yankee abated, and she enjoyed a renewed sense of hope and well-being.

Taggart experienced a surge of relief that he'd been able to conceal his identity, more for her sake than his own. For the moment the crisis was over, but now that he'd managed to calm Silky, he considered her statement about Zeb Clingerman and realized that another problem was brewing. If the lad spread the word that he'd deceived Silky about his company, a pack of angry men would arrive at the cabin, no doubt led by Sergeant Holt and Amos Evans.

He had no choice now. He had to move as soon as possible, not only to protect himself, but Silky as well. She'd told him that because of heavy drifts, the train stopped running to Wilson's Gap after the first big snowfall, so he was left with one option—to ride out at daybreak. Tonight he must say good-bye to the most charming female he'd ever met, knowing he'd never see her again.

Full of deep emotion, he surveyed her shiny unbound hair and noticed the outline of her full breasts under her buckskins. The little Reb prompted a wild flash of desire in his loins, and as the warmth of the fire and the music of the snapping flames surrounded them, he temporarily surrendered to an age-old law that paid no heed to political loyalties.

In the course of his life, he'd known many sophisticated women, but none so arousing as Silky Shanahan, country girl that she was. Just holding her in his arms refreshed his spirit and whetted his zest for life. Here in this quiet, isolated cabin, he didn't want to be Silky's enemy. He wanted to cherish her and love her, and protect her from war's harsh realities.

A nagging bit of conscience reminded him of his promise not to touch her, but his reckless nature finally won out over his better judgment. For several moments he regarded her silently; then as the wind wailed, blowing driving snow against the window, he pulled her close and tightened his arms about her. The clean scent of her hair fired his senses, and as he pressed her luscious curves against him, he knew her delicate beauty would tempt any man. "You're so lovely," he murmured huskily, desire exploding within him.

Silky looked into Taggart's hungry eyes, and the resonance of his deep voice sent her heart racing wildly. She sensed the almost palpable tension between them and her heart leaped with excitement. He lowered his head and, ever so gently, his lips feathered over hers, prompting her to melt against his hard chest, overwhelmed by the sensation of the moment.

Soft as a whisper, his lips skimmed over her cheeks, her eyelids, and the pulse in her throat—then they claimed her mouth, darting pleasure through her veins. His tangy scent assailed her nostrils, and when he traced her lips with his tongue, a sense of fierce expectation surged through her and she shivered with delight. Instinctively she reached up to encircle his wide shoulders, and as the kiss continued, her nipples hardened and tingled with a pleasant tenderness. Held so close to him, she felt the hard proof of his desire pressing against her, and she trembled with excitement.

When he ran his palm over her breast, she moaned in anticipation. At his skilled touch, her nipple ached with pleasure, and, light-headed with passion, she tightened her arms about his shoulders. He urged her lips apart with his questing tongue, and as the kiss grew deeper, a wild sensation quickened in her soul. Then just as she slipped into a rosy world of erotic desire, he gradually raised his head and ever so gently eased her away.

So stunned she could scarcely speak, she stared at him, noting his look of troubled resolve. She clasped his arms, wondering if she'd done something to displease him. Why had he kissed her so passionately one moment, then stopped suddenly without an explanation? "What's wrong?" she whispered. "Lordamercy, you look like your mind's a thousand miles away."

The color of his eyes changed subtly. "I'm leaving in the morning," he announced, his face set in firm lines. "At first light. It's best this way."

The words hit her full force, each one a bruising blow to her heart, for she'd supposed he'd stay until the snow cleared. "But the weather is getting worse," she gasped in a tumble of words, looking for any excuse to delay his departure. "You can't go now—not in all this snow. Stay until it stops."

His hands moved over her shoulders. "No," he replied

gently. "I must get to Charlottesville in time to meet my contact. I need to leave in the morning."

Silky stared at his tense face, worry and concern pressing on her bosom like an aching weight. Tears suddenly filled her eyes and she realized that what she'd been secretly dreading for so long was coming to pass at last.

Taggart was leaving Sweet Gum Hollow, never to return.

At dawn Taggart stood just inside the cabin door, ready to leave, while his saddled mount waited outside in the whirling snow. With a heavy sigh, he eyed Silky, who stood before the glowing hearth, her back to him, as she removed a skillet from the grate and placed it aside. She was dressed in a flannel shirt and her fringed buckskin britches, and her long reddish hair fell in loose curls down her back.

When he'd returned from the barn a few minutes ago, a bittersweet sense of expectation had rushed over him that he knew had nothing to do with the crackling flames or the scent of coffee and freshly baked biscuits permeating the air. The feeling was connected with Silky Shanahan, whom he'd soon be leaving.

When she turned about, moisture glistened in her green eyes and her ever-present smile had faded, to be replaced with a sad, wistful expression. "Your chances of getting to Charlottesville in this snowstorm are slim and none," she suddenly announced, her troubled gaze shimmering over him. "Why in God's name don't you wait until the weather clears?"

Taggart had no desire to ride into the howling storm, but he knew he must go. His superiors were depending on him. The fact that Holt and the homeguard might be soon visiting the cabin only added to the growing pressure he already felt. But not being able to tell Silky all this, he simply answered, "I need to meet my contact in Charlottesville. Don't you understand it's vitally important that I be there?"

"I understand you probably won't get there at all," she replied, her face tensing with worry.

In an effort to reassure her, he cleared a place on the table, then pulled a map of Virginia from his jacket and tossed it on the ring-marked boards. He ran his finger over a wavy line that worked its way from the mountains to Charlottesville. "I'll follow this road. It looks like I can make it in two or three days by this route."

Silky bent over the table and tapped her finger on the map. "I went to Charlottesville once with Daniel to sell furs. Don't expect this road to be anything but a logging trail, and to get through, you'll have to ford Nacachee Creek. Sometimes the water runs high, but if you ride up this way about a fourth of a mile"—she swerved her finger—"it shallows out to almost nothing."

Taggart noticed her pain-filled eyes and realized she was giving him the warning as one would to save a stubborn child from his own folly.

"And here," she said, jabbing at the map, "the trail is so steep and narrow you may have to lead your horse." Advice continued to flow from her lips after he'd folded up the map. "There's a little wide space in the road where two trails meet—Biglow's Crossing. Veer right there. If you press hard, you might be able to spend your second night at Snyder's Tavern."

She stared at him as he rolled the last of his clothing in an oilskin and lashed leather thongs about the bundle. "I think the only one who could make it to Charlottesville in a storm like this would be an Indian—and a crazy Indian at that."

Taggart scanned her face, searching his mind for words of comfort. Last night after he'd told her he was leaving, she'd retreated into herself, and from the smudges under her eyes this morning he guessed she'd hardly slept. For breakfast she'd brewed the last of her precious coffee—coffee she'd saved for Christmas Day—and she'd made gravy to go along with the bacon and biscuits in an effort to fortify him for the journey. They'd spoken hardly a word, but her eyes had communicated volumes.

"I expect you're right," he finally answered.

Thankfully, her mountain pride had sustained her, and they'd both been spared her tears. What had started out as a falsehood to protect Union lives had turned into a tale of personal sacrifice, and in his heart, he knew they'd both remember the encounter the rest of their lives. He sighed inwardly, hardening his courage. At least he'd left her with pride and hope, he told himself. At least he'd done that.

He watched her snatch a cloth from her cabinet and wrap biscuits and bacon for him to take with him. His interlude with her was now ending, to become only a memory. He tried to etch her image in his brain, never wanting to forget a single thing about her. This is the last picture I'll have of her, he thought, watching her purposeful movements and treasuring them in his heart. "That isn't necessary," he offered, noticing that her hands trembled ever so slightly while she worked.

In answer, she turned, a fiery glint in her eyes. "Here," she said roughly, offering him the bundle of food. "You'll need it."

Silky's throat tightened with emotion. Most of his belongings were already packed in his saddlebags and on his mount. She'd given him Daniel's heaviest jacket and muffler, and also a floppy mountain hat that was sprinkled with snow from his trip to the barn. The oilskin roll was over his shoulder, his hands were gloved, his feet were booted, and, although dim light only now pushed away the darkness, he was ready to go.

Suddenly a spate of memories tumbled through her brain. She recalled how surprised he'd been when he'd first seen her, the awed look on his face when he'd seen the view from Apple Hill, and how cool he'd been when Holt had come to challenge him. The vivid images sang with life and color and filled her with a thick, warm longing that made her weak. In a moment he would be gone, and there was nothing she could do about it. "The winter will seem long," she said woodenly, hardly trusting her voice. "Mountain winters are always lonely."

His face softened, and without a word, he tossed the food bundle on the table and put his arms about her, pulling her close. The roughness of his coat touched her cheek, and the sense-drenching scents of tobacco and damp wool sloughed over her, tearing at her heart.

He kissed her forehead and brushed his lips over hers. "Good-bye, Fancy Pants. Take care of yourself," he offered in a resonant voice, shot with emotion. A grin touched his lips. "Don't shoot too many Yankees with that remarkable rifle of yours."

"Good-bye, West Point Gentleman," she whispered brokenly.

He swept his gaze over her, then in a flash, picked up the bundle, and through her blurry vision she saw him leave.

The door stood open, letting in a chilly blast. At the threshold she stood immobilized, regarding him as he walked to his mount, snowflakes pouring over his shoulders. How she wished she had the nerve to go after him, throw her arms about him, and, like a child, beg him to stay with her always. She watched him add the food bundle to his saddlebag and lash the oilskin roll into place, big feathery flakes clinging to his hat and clothing.

Without warning tears stung her eyes and a lump swelled in her throat. Impulsively she left the cabin, the icy wind stinging her face. "Taggart," she yelled over the whining wind.

He turned about, and as their eyes met, he held out his arms and she ran to him. He pressed her hard against him in a last moment of rapture. "Silky," he said softly, cupping her face in his gloved hand. Then, his eyes glittering like fire, he kissed her with a devastating tenderness that made her heart pound crazily. The kiss was full of passion and desire, and as his mouth moved over hers a shudder passed through her. Her lips were still warm and moist when he lifted his head, prompting a rush of tears to her eyes.

Quickly he released her and swung into the saddle. Without looking back, he rode into the snow that soon obscured him behind a veil of white. For a moment she saw the smudgy outline of a rider—then nothing.

He was gone.

Chapter Five

A knitted shawl draped over her head, Silky sat in front of her hearth and stared at the flames dancing over the big logs. It was about five in the afternoon and shadows engulfed the cabin. The only light pooled from the fire's glow, an island of warmth in the drafty room.

With a long sigh, she recalled Taggart's parting that morning. It seemed so long ago—ages ago, in fact. She'd spent hours thinking about him. Truth be told, she'd worried about him all day. Where was he now? Was he all right? Was he hungry? Why hadn't she packed more food for him? She wondered if he'd taken the right turn at Biglow's Crossing. It was so easy to become disoriented with the heavy snow swirling down, obstructing all landmarks. The questions and possibilities raced through her mind like the flames darting over the logs, tormenting her.

She rose and paced about the little room. It all looked the same—a place of refuge and safety—but she was keenly aware that everything had changed. She paused to rub her hand over the back of the chair that Taggart had sat in at dinner. Drawn to the bed where he'd slept, she picked up his pillow and held it against her, his scent full and warm in her nostrils.

She envisioned him squatted down at the soldiers' homecoming, talking to Amos Evans. Taggart had passed the conversation off lightly, but something still bothered her about the picture. Why had he been so interested in Uncle Joe's soldiers? she wondered. Of course as a Confederate, he would be interested, but there was something else about the situation that troubled her—something she couldn't quite understand.

A gust of wind rattled the shingles, and she dropped the pillow and glanced outside. The light was almost gone. The weather was getting more violent by the minute, she thought nervously. At the window she drew back the curtain and frigid air seeped in about the poorly fitted frame, chilling her and telling her the storm was blowing up into a full blizzard.

She squeaked a circle on the frosted pane and peered into the twilight, seeing nothing but driving snow. With a fresh pang of worry, she leaned her forehead against the cold glass, praying with all her heart and soul that Taggart was all right. How could she have let him go out in such bitter cold? With the temperature falling at this rate he could easily freeze to death before dawn.

Wet and aching with cold, Taggart hunched his shoulders against the wind, giving his mount her head down the narrow trail. The forest was beautiful: dark evergreens, white-powdered maples, delicate hackberries, and wild plums. But the gale had whipped the day's snow into huge drifts, slowly but efficiently blotting out all landmarks, just as Silky had predicted. Now, as twilight settled in, Taggart's eyelashes and cheeks were covered with frost from his frozen breath, and his feet and hands were numb. Soon blackness would descend and the temperature would drop even more.

He'd followed Silky's suggestion and crossed the Nacachee at its lowest point. The swiftly moving water couldn't have been more than a foot deep, but it was bitterly cold and iced about the edges, and just remembering it made his teeth chatter. To make matters worse, after forcing his horse across the creek, he'd found the trail soon petered out.

A path had appeared once again, and he'd given silent thanks—but was it the same trail? He'd never found what Silky had described as Biglow's Crossing. Gloom now settled over the crusted snow, and flakes twirled down in gusts, burying everything under a blanket of white. There was no question about his riding on. He must find shelter and find it quickly.

His patient mount plodded ahead for a quarter of an hour, then whinnied and floundered in a huge drift. After the frightened animal had regained her footing, Taggart led her, slogging along one step at a time. The wind flapped his hat brim and whipped snow in his face, but he made himself keep going, knowing that stopping now would first mean exhausted sleep, then death.

Back in Sweet Gum Hollow it was dusk—candlelight—and Silky would be cooking supper, he told himself, his feet so numb he could scarcely feel them striking the frozen earth. The satisfying aroma of meat and biscuits would fill the cabin, and a cozy fire would be popping in the hearth. The memory prompted a keen loneliness, but he held it close, for he could picture her safe and warm. The vision sustained him, and he trudged forward, refusing to stop.

At last he came to a little clearing, and through the lacy snow he noticed boulders jutting all about him. It was then he realized that since his horse had floundered, he'd strayed from the main trail and been walking in a dry creek bed. Here in this draw, some ancient river had undercut the limestone, and at last he found what he was looking for: a natural shelter with a ledge over its top where he and his mount could take protection from the wind and snow. Partly shielded by a stand of trees, it was as good a place as he could have found in this icy wilderness.

Working quickly before the dim light faded, he tethered his horse, then gathered broken limbs from deadfalls and stacked the material on the exposed side of the undercut to make a windbreak. Before he was finished he'd constructed what the old-timers called a half-faced camp—a crude shelter that might see him through the night.

Just as blackness settled over the mountains, he piled together dry wood and crumbled bark atop it for kindling. By the time he reached for his matches, he could scarcely see his own hand. He shook with cold and dropped his first three matches, but with the fourth match sparks raced over the kindling.

Protected from the wind by the stacked limbs, the fire finally took hold and a small flame bloomed in the inky blackness, promising survival. Only after the fire was going well did he bring his mount into the shelter, take off her tack, and feed her a precious portion of the oats he'd brought along in the saddlebags. The horse nuzzled into the grain, her warmth a friendly comfort against the unyielding cold.

After Taggart fed the mare, he made a bed of evergreen boughs, spread blankets atop them then, squatting down, stripped off his gloves and held his hands over the struggling fire. His fingers stung with a thousand pinpricks as feeling returned, but he welcomed the pain, for it meant he might survive. Yes, for now he was alive, and since the windbreak reflected the heat's warmth back into the overhang, he would remain relatively warm. But outside the shelter the snow continued to fall steadily. Aided by the fire's glow, he could see the world had turned white and silver, the heavy snow bending the tree boughs and wiping out any trail he might have left.

In his heart he knew he was in trouble—deep trouble—but for the present, the only thing he could do was hang on.

Dawn broke cold, with clouds so low the darkness was almost like a second night. With aching limbs Taggart walked out to gather more branches from the deadfalls, which he stacked under the ledge along with a supply of bark for kindling. Afterward he brought the horse from under the ledge so she could paw at the snow and nibble the winter-burned grass that lay beneath the crusty blanket of white.

What he needed now was just a small bit of good luck, he thought as he hunkered down to eat some of his rations. With a firm resolve, he fought down a feeling that threatened to turn into useless panic. He needed to concentrate on today—on surviving the next twenty-four hours, then surviving another twenty-four hours. There was nothing to be done now except let the storm blow itself out. He needed to save his strength and think—think of a way to better his situation.

Three hours dragged past, and then another three. In the middle of the afternoon he cut a hole in one of the blankets to make himself a long poncho. Who knew how long he'd need to make his food last? he thought, realizing if he was warmer he'd need less to eat. After putting on the poncho, he looked at the sky, which seemed like a blanket of white. Only the Lord knew how long he'd have to stay holed up, and evidently the Lord wasn't talking today.

It had been dark and gloomy all day, but, studying the falling snow, he judged that it was abating a bit, and the fact bolstered his spirits. Before darkness fell, he fed the horse, then let his mind drift and dozed a while, dreaming of his boyhood, then of Ned.

At first the dream was pleasant. It seemed they were walking through a park, talking and laughing about some incident that had happened to Ned at school. Then the dream darkened and became the nightmare that Taggart was so well acquainted with. How often had he experienced the troubling dream? he wondered, aware that he was sleeping, but unable to awaken.

With a moan, he saw his brother taken away to his execution. Ned, a look of stark fear in his eyes, glanced over his shoulder and cried, "Help . . . for God's sake, help me!" In the dream, Taggart was always rooted to the ground where he stood, unable to move as Ned, a pleading look on his face, was shot by a Confederate firing squad, his cap tumbling from his head as he fell to the earth.

With a start, Taggart suddenly woke, his heart pounding. It was always the same, he thought, silently cursing the recurring dream that had tormented him since the boy's death. Upon waking, he would remind himself that in actuality he couldn't have prevented the tragedy; nevertheless, he always experienced a lingering sense of guilt and a righteous anger at the Rebs who committed the act. Feeling his heart slow, he promised himself yet again that he would do everything he could to see that the North won the war. Perhaps in this way he could honor Ned's memory and mitigate the deep sense of loss he still carried in his heart.

An hour after awakening from the disturbing dream, Taggart ate, and decided to make himself a little camp coffee, boiling a bit of ground beans in a tin cup. He was halfway through his coffee when the muffled sound of a horse's whinny caught his attention. Cautiously he put down the cup and stared in the direction of the noise. At first he saw nothing; then very faintly through the swirling snow, he spied the outline of a rider coming up the dry creek bed. Thank God he'd heard the noise, for visibility was so poor that otherwise he wouldn't have seen the figure.

Every nerve tingling with awareness, he peered at the blurry form that seemed no more than an apparition. Consisting of shades of white on white and shrouded in fog, the rider wore a hood over his head, and the vision reminded him of the Grim Reaper himself. For a moment Taggart wondered if he was hallucinating: then the sound of another whinny carried loud and clear and he realized the horse and rider were no specters.

But who would travel in weather like this? Only a desperate man like himself, or a man with his mind set on trouble—a man like Sergeant Holt, he thought, picking up his rifle. The phantom drifted closer, his hood shielding his features. Taggart knelt on one knee and, bracing the rifle on the limbs he'd stacked for a windbreak, put the icy stock against his cheek and took aim. If this vision had risen from a frozen hell, it was his intention to blow it back to its source.

The rider entered the line of fire, seemingly without fear. When the figure came into range, Taggart squeezed back on the trigger, needing to pull it only a hairbreadth to send the bullet ripping into the phantom's heart. Let him come three yards closer and he would be dead.

Suddenly the rider pulled his mount to a halt, and as the horse shied, the figure's hood slipped down, revealing a floppy hat and long hair. With a start of surprise, Taggart realized the figure was a woman with a blanket draped over her.

"Taggart, is that you?" the rider called over the moaning wind.

Taggart's heart nearly burst from his chest. Recognizing Silky's voice, he put down his rifle, thanking heaven he hadn't killed her. The horse slowly plodded forward, and Silky's gorgeous hair now glistened in the light of the flames while her face shone with a rosy glow. Stunned, he met her worried eyes, both thrilled and amazed that the feisty spitfire had trailed him from Sweet Gum Hollow. *Damn, what a woman this is.* A howling blizzard would have slowed down most females, but not Silky Shanahan.

Weak with exhaustion, Silky slid from her horse and, through the falling snow, saw Taggart running toward her. Within seconds, he was clutching her in his arms, pulling her against his hard, tough body. She'd finally found him! she thought, scarcely believing her own eyes. "Taggart," she rasped, trembling with excitement.

With his blanket poncho he looked like a wild mountain man, and beneath his battered hat his hair and mustache were matted with frost. But to her he'd never looked better, and she ran her hands over his wide shoulders, just to prove to herself that he was all in one piece.

Gently he cupped her face and his lips met hers. A moan burned her throat as he deepened the kiss, once again stirring a familiar fire within her. Talk was forgotten as she responded to the passionate kiss, letting the joy of being reunited with him sweep her along on a cresting wave of happiness. At last he fluttered little kisses over her forehead and cheeks, then gently eased back, holding her at arm's length. "You should have announced yourself sooner," he chided, his eyes tender with amusement. A wry grin curled his lips upward. "I came within an inch of blowing off your pretty head."

"I'm sorry," she apologized, trying to regain her breath after her long ride. "With the gloom and falling snow, I could hardly see. I finally caught a glimpse of your fire."

Taggart quickly tethered her mount, and she smiled as they entered the warm shelter, their arms about each other's waists. Relieved to be out of the wailing wind, Silky squatted by the flames. Thank God she'd found him, she thought, blinking away nervous tears. And how happy she was she'd made the decision to go after him. After worrying for hours, she'd finally decided it was her only choice. Lost in the storm herself, she'd almost given up hope, but something within her had made her forge ahead despite her fear. Let him believe it had been nothing, she advised herself, hoping he'd think the stinging wind had produced her watery eyes.

Taggart wrapped an extra blanket about her, then handed her his cup of coffee. "Lord, what possessed you to follow me?" he inquired, his eyes running over her in sheer disbelief. "It was a damn foolish thing to do."

She tilted her head and grinned, unable to resist the urge to tease him a bit. "I suppose it was. About as foolish as starting off to Charlottesville in a blizzard," she quipped, her mood rising now that she knew he was all right. "It'd take the biggest fool in Virginia to do something like that. Why, city folks might put a fellow away for something as crazy as that."

Taggart watched her hunching by the fire, sipping coffee, and chuckled at her peppery tongue and remarkable spirit. She'd looked so exhausted when she slid from her horse that he'd automatically taken her in his arms, marveling at how someone so small and delicate could be so full of courage. The kiss had happened just as naturally, and as he'd pressed her softness against him, passion had swirled through both his heart and mind.

Just looking at her lovely face prompted a wild joy that shook him profoundly. He'd never been this happy to see anyone in his life, and with a burst of insight, he knew it had nothing to do with his present circumstance. Digesting the frightening thought, he realized that he must send her back to the safety of her cabin as soon as possible. All that was decent told him it wasn't fair to the girl or himself to prolong a relationship that could only end in sorrow.

Resolving himself to this fact, he stooped beside her and adjusted the blanket about her slim shoulders. "How in the hell did you find me?" he questioned, truly awed at her remarkable abilities.

Silky noticed her body relaxing under his appreciative gaze. "I tracked you, of course," she replied lightly.

"But how?" he repeated, a deep frown plowing his brow. "The wind covered up my tracks."

"That's right, but a lot were protected by trees and bushes." She sipped the hot coffee, feeling it spread through her stomach and warm her insides. "Besides that, I found some broken brush." She gave him a grin. "By the way, you got off the trail after you crossed the Nacachee."

He wiped a hand over his face. "Yeah . . . I figured I did."

She surveyed his concerned features, deciding she wouldn't tell him she'd been lost for a while herself. "I found the place where your horse floundered, and from then on it was easy."

He widened his eyes. "Easy?"

"Sure, after I got a whiff of your fire I didn't need to do any tracking. The smoke blended in with the clouds and the snow, but it was my nose that led me to you. I just kept following the scent of that smoke." She stood, then looked down at him and smiled, anticipating his reaction with relish when he heard her next words. "Say . . . if it's all the same to you, why don't we go on over to Jake's cabin and wait for this storm to clear?"

Taggart slowly rose, his face stamped with disbelief. "I know how much you like a good yarn, but this is hardly the time for one of your wild mountain tales."

"I'm not joking," she said with a laugh.

His eyes traveled over the heavy forest appraisingly. "Are you saying someone actually lives in this frozen wilderness?"

Silky chuckled to herself, thinking she'd never seen such a surprised-looking man in all her life. "I sure am. There's an old trapper named Jake Coulter who lives about five miles"—she pointed at the woods—"thataway."

Taggart stared in the direction she'd pointed. "Thataway? I don't see anything *thataway* but a stand of timber so heavy a tick couldn't get through it."

She drank more coffee. "Oh, he lives over there all right," she replied, still savoring his reaction. "Daniel used to trap with him, and the old fellow came by our cabin for vittles a few times. He must be ninety if he's a day, but he's as independent as a hog on ice.'' She shrugged her shoulders, not missing an opportunity for a little fun, now that the crisis of finding him had passed. ''I would have mentioned him to you, but when you told me what trail you were taking, he wasn't in the vicinity.'' She smiled again. ''I didn't know you were gonna drift seven miles thisaway.''

Silky studied his face as he mulled over the information about Jake, thinking he looked as if she'd just told him the whole Army of Northern Virginia would arrive in five minutes. She let her gaze ripple over him. ''Well, what do you say, West Point Gentleman?'' she queried, deciding as a general rule flatlanders were a passel of trouble. ''Did they give you any classes in that fancy military college about navigating woods so heavy a tick couldn't get through them?''

Taggart stroked his jaw. ''No, not a damn one,'' he replied with a slow smile. ''But the way I see it, we don't have a hell of a lot of choices.'' He glanced skyward, and, peering up herself, she noticed the snow had lightened and a sliver of pale moon was peeking from the clouds. Turning his attention to the fire, Taggart shoved snow on the flames with the toe of his boot, then moved away and started folding blankets. ''If we hurry,'' he commented, glancing over his shoulder, ''we just might make it by midnight.''

Silky grinned and sloshed the remaining coffee on the ground, convinced it was going to be an interesting evening indeed.

Three hours later the exhausted pair walked into a large clearing. Through the falling snow, they crossed an open expanse, leading their horses toward a dilapidated cabin set back in a grove of cottonwood trees. A split-rail fence and a wood pile peeped through the mantle of white, but there was no welcoming light in the cabin's window, leaving it and the stable behind it with a lifeless, abandoned look.

''Jake must have already gone to bed,'' Silky rasped, pausing to catch her breath, ''but he'll wake up right enough when we beat on his door.''

When they arrived at the cabin, she pounded on the door with her fist and called his name—then her heart sank, for she noticed the door had been padlocked and boards covered the windows. For the first time in her memory, Jake's place was boarded up tighter than a drum.

After Taggart tried to remove a window board with no success, he strode to his horse, and from the mare's saddle, retrieved a rifle. "Step back," he ordered. He aimed at the lock and blasted it apart with a shot that tumbled snow from the cabin's eaves. Acrid-smelling smoke swirled from the rifle barrel as he kicked open the door and escorted Silky into the shack, whose well-chinked walls offered shelter from the storm. With a loud creak, the door blew closed behind them, muting the sound of the sharp wind, but leaving them in total darkness.

Taggart scratched a match on the door, then held it before him, revealing rough-hewn logs covered with fox and beaver pelts, and an open ceiling with exposed rafters. Finding a kerosene lamp in the center of a table, he lit the wick, and a flame spluttered momentarily before gaining brightness. Silky clicked a glass globe over the light, then slowly walked about the room, the musty aromas of stale tobacco, leather, and bacon grease hitting her nostrils. "Lordamercy, how glad I am to be in out of the weather," she confessed, stripping off her gloves and tossing them on the table. "My ears are numb and these wet boots are cutting into my feet like knife blades."

Rubbing her stiff fingers, she turned her gaze about the cluttered cabin. An iron skillet sat on the blackened hearth, still holding congealed bacon grease while clothing littered the homemade furniture, making it look as if Jake had decided to leave without much forethought. "Brrr, it's cold in here," she observed, briskly chafing her shivering arms.

Taggart moved to a mantel topped with a collection of snuff cans and shaving mugs. "Hold on a minute and I'll have this place warmed up," he advised, kneeling and rummaging through a battered kindling box. "Looks like Jake left a good supply of wood," he added thoughtfully, "and it's good and seasoned."

At a dry sink, Silky opened boxes, discovering flour and cornmeal in the larder. "This meal is still fresh," she said, tasting a pinch of it before putting a lid on the box. "So he couldn't have been gone for too long. He has a sister in Wilson's Gap. He probably got lonely and decided to winter with her.'' She chuckled and shook her head. ''Come spring he'll be right back here in his cabin, hollering about townfolk being the root of all evil.''

Flames soon whispered over the kindling, producing the comforting aroma of wood smoke. Taggart hung Silky's hat on a pair of deer antlers above the hearth, then removed her blanket and jacket and laid them near the fire, the scent of damp wool wafting from the sodden material. After the pair had lingered by the flames, warming their half-frozen bodies, he returned outside to feed and stable the horses while she prepared something to eat.

Silky put up food herself and was familiar with the jars of vegetables she found on the shelves, but she had to smile at the thought of an old bachelor canning his own food. On the counter by the wash pan there was rainwater in a stoneware crock, a small tin of coffee, and, on the shelf below, several jugs of moonshine. Prepared for a long winter, old Jake seemed to live in fine style.

She'd just finished cooking when Taggart reentered the cabin carrying the saddlebags, rifles, and other gear from their mounts. ''There's some corn in the crib,'' he reported, placing everything on the floor and taking off his damp outerwear. ''Seems like Jake's place is that piece of luck I've been needing.'' With pleased eyes, he looked at the pork and beans, hot corn pone, and spiced peaches she'd placed on the table, then sat down to eat. ''How about some beefsteak, woman?'' he teased good-naturedly. ''A man's got to keep up his strength.''

Silky shook her head. ''Jake left us pretty well supplied, but there's no meat at all.''

''Never mind,'' he commented, slathering a hunk of corn pone with wild plum jelly. ''If the weather lets up we'll find some game tomorrow.''

After they'd eaten, Taggart poured them a few fingers of moonshine in their emptied coffee cups. ''For medicinal purposes only, of course,'' he said, handing it to her with a mischievous grin that made him especially handsome.

The cabin was now warm and cozy. Silky's stomach was

full, and her head was light. Within a few minutes she was feeling fine. "Has the snow stopped?" she asked, feeling the liquor soothe her aching muscles.

A cheroot clenched between his teeth, Taggart went to the window, then turned about, answering her with a frown. "No, not yet, but it's slowing."

Silky smiled, her spirits rising. "Reminds me of the winter of thirty-eight," she drawled, watching his amused face as he recognized she'd begun one of her father's mountain tales. "Pa said it was so cold and snowy then that words froze in the air right while folks we were saying them. People had to use sign language like Indians all winter. Nobody knew what anybody was talking about until spring came and they got all those words thawed out. Lordamercy, what a babble it was then!"

Taggart chuckled, then slipped back into his chair, the muscles of his big shoulders rippling against his shirt. "Well, the winter of eighty-four may best thirty-eight. With all the deep drifts, I'm going to have a devil of a time getting to Charlottesville."

Silky ached to accompany him to the town that lay at the foot of the Blue Ridge. She knew that part of her motive was simply to enjoy his company a bit longer and help him get through the treacherous mountains. Then, facing the truth, she suspected she was in love with him, and just didn't want to let him go. "Don't worry," she remarked, lazily running a finger about the top of her coffee cup as she tried to slip the statement past him, "I'll guide you into Charlottesville."

Taggart studied her openly. "You'll do no such thing," he returned, a dangerous spark in his eyes. "As soon as it clears you'll go back to Sweet Gum Hollow. I won't have you risking your life to get me through the mountains."

Silky sighed, thinking that now that they'd dealt with the problem of freezing, another more personal problem had taken its place. She knew he was trying to protect her, but she also knew he wouldn't make it to civilization without her. Why, it was almost her duty to the Confederacy to help him, she told herself, building up her courage for the battle to come.

"I won't be risking my life, as you put it," she said forcefully, ignoring his displeased countenance. "I've traveled the Blue Ridge all my life and I know the way to Charlottesville." She permitted herself a sly grin. "Not like some people I know."

Taggart stood and took the cheroot from his mouth. "Your place would go to rack and ruin. Who would take care of your cow, and Daniel's hounds, and—"

"Charlie's taking care of them," she swiftly interrupted, trying to remain calm under his growing disapproval, "and he could just keep taking care of them a while longer. There's not a thing on that place that needs doing that he can't handle."

With catlike grace, Taggart paced about the cabin, then turned and shot her a hot glower. "You're not going," he announced, his voice ringing with authority, "so forget about it."

"I *am* going," she declared, the effects of the moonshine increasing her natural feistiness. She stood and shoved her hands on her hips. "You just don't know about it yet."

His eyes shot sparks. "Did anyone ever tell you that you're a damn hard-headed woman?" he said, jabbing his finger at her.

Silky tried to ignore his fiery gaze. "A few times . . . but it never kept me from doing anything I really wanted to do," she parried, promising herself she wouldn't let him intimidate her with his manly assurance. She realized he was about to explode, and, sensing she temporarily had the upper hand, she decided to go to bed before he could give her another lecture.

"Well, good night," she offered airily, sashaying to the bed. She sank to the mattress, pulled off her boots, and tossed them on the floor, watching the startled play of emotions on Taggart's face.

"Good night?" he echoed, striding to the bed with a blank, amazed expression. "You're going to end this conversation with, 'Well, Good night'?"

She slipped under a soft fur throw, feeling the feather mattress give under her weight as she stretched out. "Yes—good night. I've decided continuing this conversation would be wearisome and useless. I'm tired and I want to go to bed. I suggest you do the same. There's some quilts on that shelf over there you can spread before the fire."

An angry light flickered in the depths of his eyes. "If you think this is the last of this conversation, young lady, you're sadly mistaken. You're not going to Charlottesville. You're returning to Sweet Gum Hollow."

Silky observed the deep lines on his face, thinking she'd never seen him look so stern. His glare burned her skin, but before he could say anything else, she turned her face to the wall, pulling the covers far over her shoulder.

"You're not going to Charlottesville," he repeated in a commanding tone, "so get the idea out of your head. As soon as this storm blows over, you're going home."

Silky nestled into the mattress, then closed her eyes and pretended she was asleep, completely ignoring him.

There was the creak of floorboards, then the sound of Taggart plopping into a chair before the fire. As the mumbled words "Damn, if that woman isn't more stubborn than a two-headed mule!" reached her ears, Silky smiled to herself, knowing that come hell or high water she would accompany him to Charlottesville.

Chapter Six

The next morning Taggart and Silky rode out, looking for game. The snow had finally stopped and the woods glistened like silver, etched in sharp relief against the soaring mountains and a sparkling blue sky. Spotting a little creek snaking through a clearing like a bright ribbon, they dismounted and, leaving their rifles in the saddle holsters, walked to the rushing water to see if they could find deer sign.

They trailed along the creek, their boots crunching over the frozen vegetation as they looked for tracks. Bundled to the chin and wearing his blanket poncho, Taggart pointed at the snow at the water's edge. "There's bound to be deer around," he commented, clouded breath streaming from his nostrils. "Look at all those tracks."

Filled with curiosity, Silky noticed a dead tree had toppled across the creek and she decided to cross it and check the bank on the other side. Holding a limb to steady herself as she climbed on the tree, she looked over her shoulder at Taggart's frowning face.

"Be careful," he warned, tugging down his hat. "That trunk is probably slick."

"Why, I've crossed dozens of foot logs," she answered, edging out on the tree and gazing at the swirling water below her, "and this amounts to the same thing." She held out her arms under her blanket poncho, carefully balancing as she walked across the tree trunk. "See, I'm almost halfway across already and—"

Suddenly Silky's boot hit an icy spot and, her heart lurching, she tumbled into the creek, sucking in her breath as the icy water rushed over her. Losing her hat, she went under all the way, cold water pouring into her ears and nostrils and penetrating her clothing.

Sounds were garbled and magnified under the water, and she heard the rushing current and the noise of her own floundering body as she desperately tried to get her footing. Panic swept over her, but with a mighty effort she righted herself, and finally touched the creek bed with her boots. Coughing and spluttering, she realized the water came only to her bosom. Relieved, she struggled for the bank, her muscles aching with pure agony as the heavy poncho pulled her back. Wiping her eyes, she saw Taggart, a horrified look on his face, rushing into the shallow water, calling her name and holding out his gloved hand.

Silky scrambled toward him, and he clasped her hand and pulled her into his arms, half dragging her up the snowy bank.

"I-I almost drowned." She gasped as the wind hit her wet hair and clothing, producing a series of uncontrollable shivers.

He jerked off her wet poncho, then, after taking off his own, pulled his over her head. "You're completely soaked. We've got to get you back to the cabin so you can warm up," he announced, his voice rough with worry as he pushed his hat onto her head.

He hoisted her in his arms and hurried across the clearing to their horses, his powerful legs striding through the deep snow. "Can you ride?" he asked, lifting her to his saddle.

Silky managed to straighten in the saddle, but was still shaking so hard she could scarcely speak. "Y-yes, I think s-so," she answered, her voice hardly more than a whisper.

Taggart untied the horses, then looped her mount's reins

about his saddle horn. Snatching up his own reins, he swung up behind her and surrounded her with his strong arms. Colder and more frightened than she'd ever been in her life, Silky felt his warmth and his pounding heart. He kneed his mare and they started toward Jake's cabin, the two galloping horses churning up the snow in great plumes.

Taggart kicked the cabin door closed behind him, then carried Silky to the hearth and deposited her on a bearskin rug. There she crumpled into a kneeling position, feeling the blessed warmth of the flames wash over her as his hat tumbled from her head. Instantly he knelt beside her and pulled off the blanket poncho, then, with worried eyes, scanned her wet clothing. "You've got to take off your wet shirt and britches," he ordered, stripping off his gloves and unbuttoning her shirt before she could murmur a protest. He stood and swept the room with his eyes. "We've got to find something to use for toweling." As his back was turned, Silky managed to slip off her sodden shirt and, feeling icy water trickle down her back, covered her bare breasts with her crossed hands.

Taggart shrugged off his jacket and threw it aside. After inspecting the cabin's shelves, he came back with a collection of cotton flour sacks and ripped their seams, turning them into flat pieces of material. Kneeling again, he began to dry her face and arms. Still shivering uncontrollably, Silky could only moan as he wiped the material over her skin. He eased her to a sitting position, then took off her boots and placed them aside. "Do you think you can stand?" he asked, genuine concern flickering in his eyes.

Silky nodded and he helped her to her feet. At the bed, he tore off the fur throw, brought it back, and wrapped it about her. "Here, I'll hold this while you shed those wet britches. Can you do that?" he inquired, cupping her chin.

"Yes, I think so," she answered, thinking his fingers felt warm against her face. As he held the throw about her, she slowly undid her sodden breeches, them let them fall to the floor and stepped out of them.

"Come closer to the fire," he urged, putting his arm around her.

By now she could hold the throw about herself, and he brought more flour sacks and ripped them apart to dry her hair. As she sat before the flames, basking in their warmth, he tenderly rubbed the absorbent material over her locks. "I was so cold," she murmured, catching his eyes, "so cold and frozen I thought my ears might snap right off."

Taggart grinned as he examined both of her ears, shaking them a little. "Nope, they're still attached," he answered before tossing the soaked material away and stroking her back. They both laughed; then he eased back, his expression relaxing a bit. "Lord Almighty, Fancy Pants. What a scare you gave me when I saw you fall in that creek."

Silky studied Taggart's sympathetic face and suddenly realized this was the moment to push her case for going to Charlottesville. Of course he really couldn't stop her from accompanying him to the flatlands. She could follow behind like a dog, or gallop ahead and appear out of the bushes every so often to keep him on the right trail, but it would be so much more pleasant if she had his blessing.

"Let me guide you to Charlottesville," she whispered, watching a slow frown move over his features. She clutched his shoulder with one hand, pressing her fingers into his flesh to emphasize her point. "God saved me from drowning, and I think it was to help you get to the flatlands." She threaded her voice with passionate longing. "You've just got to let me go. You just have to."

For a moment Taggart looked stunned; then a low chuckle erupted from his massive chest. "You're a foxy little minx, aren't you? If you can't go in the front door, you come in the back, is that it?"

With great delight, she noticed a rakish smile tug at his mouth. Lord, please let him say yes! she prayed, her heart doing a somersault. Let him say yes, and she'd never ask for anything again.

Taggart watched her sitting there like a wet, bedraggled kitten, her eyes shining with pleading hope. How could anyone who looked so angelic and innocent be so single-minded and so downright ornery when it came to getting her own way? he wondered, letting out a resigned sigh. "All right," he finally conceded, knowing full well he was being manipulated but admiring her spirit and tenacity nonetheless. ''I might have been able to fight you alone, but now that you've enlisted divine providence on your side, I'll wave a flag of truce.''

Joy burst over Silky's features like floodwaters taking a dry riverbed. ''You won't be sorry, I promise you that,'' she vowed, a victorious smile flashing on her lips. ''I knew there must be some way to convince you,'' she added, her face wreathed in glowing happiness, ''but I didn't know I'd have to fall in the creek to do it!''

Like it or not, Taggart thought with wry amusement, it looked like the little cat would be traveling on to Charlottesville. Trying to cheer himself up, he realized she would be a great asset in crossing the treacherous mountains. Quickly his mind raced ahead, sketching out the future. After arriving, they'd put up in a hotel; then while she was doing whatever women did, he'd telegraph his information to the Union. Another assignment would be telegraphed back to him; then they'd say good-bye forever. Since money was no problem, he'd give her enough to pay her hotel bill until the weather cleared; then she could return to Sweet Gum Hollow.

Silky gazed at Taggart's thoughtful face, her heart pumping with pure, undiluted joy. ''I lost my hat in the creek,'' she commented with a little laugh as she threaded her fingers through her hair, ''and it was the best one I ever had.''

Taggart smiled indulgently. ''Well, I'm just glad you can speak again. I was beginning to think this might be the winter of thirty-eight all over again.'' She chuckled and he smoothed back her tangled locks, his big hand brushing over her face. ''Don't worry about your hat. We'll take one of Jake's floppy-eared caps, and leave him money for it and all his food as well. I'll board up the door, and when the old gent breaks in, he'll find a roll of bills on the table for his trouble.''

A blush warmed Silky's cheeks. ''I'm so ashamed,'' she admitted, ''so humiliated. I can't believe I actually fell in the creek like some city girl.''

Taggart rose and, from the dry sink, brought back a jug of moonshine and two tin cups. ''Believe me, I can.'' He laughed, sitting down and pouring a drink for her and one for himself as well. He put the cup in her hand, and noticed she'd stopped trembling enough to hold it. "When I saw you go under," he admitted with a worried smile, "my heart nearly stopped."

Silky took a sip of the fiery moonshine, then looked up at him. "Mine, too. I've never been colder in my life."

Taggart drank some liquor, then feathered his fingers through her slightly damp hair so it would dry completely. "Are you warming up?" he asked, tracing his hardened palm over her cheek.

"Yes," she whispered. "I'm feeling a lot better."

His hair had grown since he'd been in the mountains, and he looked so dashing it made her pulse race. The flames threw a flickering light over his face, and she thought she detected a glint of desire in his eyes. At the same time, her heart pounded crazily and she knew she was almost recovered from her tumble in the creek. No, this sweet, wild sensation was connected with the intensity of their present situation, and it imbued the moment with a magical quality.

Lordamercy, she didn't have to suspect that she loved him, she *did* love him with all her heart and soul, even if she didn't understand everything about him. It seemed that nothing else on the face of the earth mattered but the present, and she would trade anything for the feel of his arms about her. "Can I ask you something?" she continued in a soft voice. "Do . . . do you have anyone waiting for you at home?"

Taggart met her inquiring gaze. Lord, the girl had no idea how lovely she looked with her eyes sparkling, her cheeks flushed, and her auburn hair rioting over her shoulders in loose curls. What an original she was: amusing, intelligent, and ten times more intriguing than the debutantes he'd squired at the West Point balls. Her dewy lips were parted, and her breath came rapidly, her breasts rising and falling beneath the fur throw as she waited for the answer to her provocative question. "No," he answered at last, knowing he spoke the naked truth. "There is no one waiting for me at home. No one at all."

Taggart, who'd always taken women as the slightest of

diversions, noticed this girl brought out his deepest feelings. Her fall into the creek had shaken him and, in a strange sense, put everything into perspective, making him realize just how precious she really was to him. She was so soft, so delicious, so tempting. Deep within him, he realized that making love to her could only mean trouble and heartache. Hadn't he fought his attraction to her for weeks now? Hadn't he tried to leave her behind in Sweet Gum Hollow? But at this particular moment, with her safe and warm before him, he wanted her as he'd never wanted another woman, and some powerful, carnal emotion—a fiery life force—stormed within him, demanding he make her his.

Silky's pulse raced as Taggart lowered his head and brushed his lips over hers, his warm breath caressing her face. Like steely bands, his arms pulled her to him, and she felt his heart thudding against hers. Nothing in her experience could have prepared her for the sensations now streaking through her—still, some sane virginal part of herself cried out against this madness.

Then as his mouth seized hers in a fiery kiss, the floodgates of passion swung open within her, leaving her limp and compliant. Breathless, she relaxed against his hard chest and circled her arms about his shoulders, the fur throw falling from her shoulders as she surrendered to the fire within him.

At long last the barrier of pretense had crumbled between them, and sensual hunger flowed through her like a mighty river, sweeping away the remnants of her inhibitions. His warmth flowed over her, and the rhythm of his pounding heart spurred her own desire, frightening her with its fierceness. Gentle as a whisper, his lips nibbled over her cheeks and the throbbing pulse at her throat, making her shiver with delight.

"Relax, little one," he whispered in a resonant voice as he ran his warm fingers over her back. "I want to pleasure you." When his hand came forward to brush over her breast, she gasped, and her whole body took on a wild, sensual glow.

Her cheek was pressed against his rough shirt, and she felt his lips on her skin as he kissed her neck and nuzzled his way to her collarbone. Leaving her skin tingling, he settled his mouth on her swollen crest, which he suckled until she moaned with delight. Around and around his tongue swirled over the sensitive peak, flicking back and forth until an ache asserted itself at the apex of her femininity. Within seconds, her body fairly reeled with voluptuous sensation.

Her heart lurched when he rose on one knee, securely positioned her in his arms, and stood, lifting her from the floor. The intensity of the moment rushed over her like a tidal wave and turned her will to water. For a moment it seemed as if time had stopped and she was seeing his handsome face through a gauze veil. Who was this passionate stranger she'd given her heart to? Would he return her commitment of love? Seemingly sensing her fear, he slanted his mouth over hers, and the power and tenderness of the wild kiss stilled her pounding heart as he carried her to the bed. Gently he placed her on the mattress, and she lay before him, clothed only in the glory of her love.

He eased back and she met his searching eyes. "I didn't want this to happen," he murmured, his passionate tone spurring her anticipation, "but it seemed to be in the cards all along."

She let her gaze travel over his rugged features. "Some things were meant to be, and I have a feeling this is one of them."

He made no reply, but the spark of desire in his eyes darted fire through her veins. Why was she letting this happen? she asked herself one last time, her body already languid with desire. Everything in her warned caution, but it was as if fate itself had decreed the moment, and all the longings they'd both harbored for so long now surged forth, demanding their passionate due.

He sat on the mattress, and the expression of aching need on his face quickened her heart with excitement. When he pressed a kiss on her palm, a sweetness welled up within her that reminded her of rosebuds opening their petals to the morning dew. She vaguely knew their lovemaking was rash and ill-advised, but it was so precious, she just couldn't suppress the overpowering desire rushing over her. "Lie beside me," she whispered, her bosom tightening with emotion.

For a flickering moment her words hung in the air; then slowly he stood, and, his gaze never leaving hers, he unbuttoned his shirt. A shudder of pleasure passed through her as he finished undressing and cast his boots and garments aside. Diffuse light washing over his powerful body, he stood before her. She scanned his broad shoulders, well-defined chest, and lean stomach before letting her gaze drift downward to his hairy chest and aroused flesh. How wonderfully made he is—how stunningly perfect, she thought, the symmetry of his bronzed muscles touching her heart.

He stretched beside her and drew her close, his warmth and musky scent washing over her. Tenderly he brushed his lips over her face, then captured her mouth in a fiery kiss that left her weak with passion. His tongue flicked wet and bold against her lips, and a full, ripe sensation eddied through her as his questing tongue plunged deeper into her mouth. One hand moved to her breast and he caressed it until her skin glowed with a shimmery warmth. With practiced ease, his fingers toyed with her pebbly nipple, while rapture burst within her like a flight of birds taking wing.

He rained kisses over her forehead and her hair, then gently took her hand and placed it over his long hardness, eliciting a soft gasp from her lips. "Don't be afraid," he rasped, the deep resonance of his voice triggering a new audacity within her. With a shaky hand, she pleasured him, tentatively at first, then more boldly, luscious surprise racing through her bloodstream as his flesh became harder still under her questing fingertips.

He put his hand over hers, and as she continued her administrations, he moaned her name, sending a delicious shiver down her spine. With firm strokes, he tantalized her swollen nipples, and keen pleasure flamed within her, shaking her with its intensity. Exquisitely attuned to her passion, he branded her lips with an achingly tender kiss, foreshadowing breathtaking things to come.

A hot flush rose from her bosom as he moved his mouth to a rosy nipple and suckled first one sensitive peak, then the other. She felt herself writhing, heard herself moaning, as she surrendered to a wild carnal feeling she never knew existed. Her breath caught in her throat and she dug her fingers into his back, enjoying the incredible pleasure pouring through her.

She gasped with agonizing delight as his fingers seared a path to her feminine softness, then delved into it to tease her bud of desire. She thought she might faint with ecstasy before he could satisfy the sweet, tormenting ache he'd aroused within her. She caught her breath and shuddered with pent-up anticipation.

"Let me make love to you," he whispered as he raised his head, sexual excitement glinting in his heavy-lidded eyes.

"Yes, teach me—show me," she answered through trembling lips. She scanned his bronzed face, memorizing every line of his craggy features, and for a moment it was as if she were seeing him with her heart as well as her eyes, seeing his courage and tenderness, and everything she loved and cherished about him. Once again she thought of the consequences of their passion; then, lost in the lush atmosphere of the moment, she gave in to the overpowering need consuming her.

Taggart gazed down at her, considering the perfection of her sweet face. In the flickering light, her long lashes cast shadows on her cheeks, and her auburn hair fanned out on the pillow in a tangle of silken curls. As impossible as it seemed, this girl of the mountains excited him more than any woman he'd ever met, and the thought of awakening her to womanhood sent hot blood whipping through his veins.

He wanted to pleasure and cherish her, and with a soaring feeling he realized that lovemaking had never been like this for him before—so deep and rapturous. Giving way to his heart, he reveled in the glorious emotion, and a fresh, reborn sensation lifted his spirit. With her soft, trusting eyes and creamy skin she looked like an angel, and he gathered her luscious body close to his, her womanly aroma firing his desire to a white heat.

Silky felt his tongue leisurely swirl about her aching nipple, unleashing a pulsing sweetness between her legs. He reclaimed her mouth, and as his searching fingers slipped between the silken folds of her moist flesh, she quivered with desire. Never did she dream it would be this way—a pleasure so keen it bordered on pain. How she wanted him. Wanted to feel his powerful masculine strength making them one forever.

He nuzzled her ear, speaking endearments before his taut body slid over hers. She thrilled to the warmth and scent of him as he braced his arms, supporting his weight on either side of her shoulders. "I think you've bewitched me," he whispered roughly, gazing into her eyes. "I want you so badly."

For a second her rational mind cried out at what she was doing. Still, at the same time she couldn't deny herself the opportunity of tasting bliss.

He claimed her mouth in a sweet-hot kiss, then entered her with gentle power. There was a moment's pain, and then breathtaking pleasure leaped within her like a wild flame. He began to move and his matted chest brushed her bare breasts as she wrapped her arms tightly about him. With sure, slow movements, he thrust into her firmly and deeply, and she clung to him, lulling pleasure rising within her. Lost in rapture, she noticed a deep, languid satisfaction steal through her body as he increased his speed, teasing her sensibilities to a boiling point.

Fluttering little kisses over her face, he roughly whispered, "Open your legs a bit wider, my darling."

She did as he asked and felt his hard manhood plunging deeper into the recesses of her quivering body. Trembling, her legs clenched his slim hips, and he stroked faster, confidently building and deepening her passion. Overcome with excitement, she stifled a cry of pleasure as he tenderly labored her toward a breathless climax.

A new sensation welled within her like a rising tide. Beginning at the core of her being, it stole through every limb, leaving her flesh glowing with unspeakable pleasure. By now she was operating on raw instinct and she arched herself against his hard abdomen, total abandon overtaking her. Her heart thundered as she reached shuddering release, her body, mind, and spirit caught up in a blaze of ecstasy. With one last thrust, he spilled his hot seed inside of her and an all-consuming fire swept through her, snatching her breath away.

Time dissolved as they fell through starry space together, united in a splendor that emanated from the life force itself. For long moments, the pair glided through the heavens, then at last slowly floated earthward together, their spirits bound in glory. As her turbulent heartbeat slowed, he slumped against her, then turned to his side and held her in his arms, his hands worshiping her flesh. He caressed her breast, leaving it warm and glowing, and a gentle smile moved over her lips.

In her mind they were now handfasted, man and wife in the sight of God, but without the benefit of a marriage ceremony. The idea was not new to her. Sometimes mountain couples lived as common-law man and wife for years until some circuit-riding preacher came through to perform a legal ceremony. Hadn't her own parents, whose love had been as strong as that of any couple she'd ever known, been handfasted for months?

She'd given her heart and body to Taggart and she trusted he would do the right thing, although they'd never spoken of marriage. The most sacred bonds were made with the heart and not the tongue, she thought with reassuring certainty. He might not be able to marry her now, with his duties to the Confederacy, but later he would wed her in a church and take her home to meet his family. She knew he would.

Joy rose within her as she thought of their new relationship. Surely they'd become one flesh and spirit. What was a wedding or a marriage license when her own heart told her they should be together? Taggart was her man, and she was his woman, as long as they both lived, and no one could ever change that fact. As he cradled her in his arms, rapture touched her soul and a peaceful sensation settled over her, dissipating all her worries.

He was hers, hers forever, she thought, a tear of joy sliding down her cheek.

Chapter Seven

Three days later Taggart and Silky paused on a ridge overlooking a snowy mountain valley. "Well, there she is—there's Charlottesville," Silky exclaimed, shifting in the saddle as she pointed at the clustered buildings that, from their elevated position, looked like children's building blocks placed in a Christmas setting.

With a feeling of deep relief, Taggart surveyed the town, whose church spires glinted in the setting sun. After boarding up Jake's cabin, he and Silky had ridden on to spend a night at Snyder's Tavern. A night camped on the trail in another half-faced camp and a day of riding had put them here. The weather had been unpredictable, the snow periodically whirling down in fits and flurries, but Silky kept them on the right track. They'd made it to civilization in time for him to send his message to the Union with one day to spare, and he owed it all to her, he thought with warm admiration.

"Look," she remarked, the edge of her poncho fluttering in the icy wind. "I see rising smoke, and smoke means fire, something that's been pretty scarce for the last few days."

"I agree, Fancy Pants. We never did get that deer. What would you say to the biggest steak in Charlottesville, eaten in the finest hotel?"

He watched a slow grin spread over her surprised face. "I'd say, throw it on the fire."

Taggart snapped his reins. "Let's go, then."

The hill was steep and pocked with boulders and brush, but they negotiated their mounts down to the bottom, churning up flying snow behind them. At the foot of the slope, they raced across a field of white, then turned onto the thoroughfare leading into the town that, due to the efforts of Colonel John Singleton Mosby and his Partisan Rangers, was still in Confederate hands. The stinging wind at their faces, they hurried toward their first taste of civilization, thinking of a soft bed and a steaming bath to go along with the sizzling steaks.

While Charlottesville itself boasted many brick structures, its outlying buildings were ramshackle and flimsy, consisting of log cabins and shacks, some abandoned and others collapsing of decay. But it was here they were greeted with the first sounds of life: ringing hammers, barking dogs, and creaking carriage wheels.

Once in the town proper, they passed through nice residential districts, drawing the stares of homeward-bound businessmen, who eyed their heavily packed mounts and mountain garb. Taggart studied the feisty girl who'd guided him through some of the roughest country he'd ever seen and had done it with a smile on her face. Now sitting proudly astride her mount, her hair up under one of Jake's caps and a poncho concealing her feminine curves, she looked like a slim boy—the antithesis of what she was, he thought, his loins stirring at the memory of their blazing night of love in the trapper's cabin.

Even now his mind wrestled with what had happened and he realized the lovemaking had touched him more deeply than any encounter he'd ever had. Part of him rejoiced that they'd made love, while another part knew it had been a mistake, a mistake he'd failed to prevent. Whether she knew it or not, their lives were going in completely opposite directions. For now, he thought philosophically, all he could do was live his life one day at a time while he tried to sort out his tangled emotions.

In the heart of town, lights shone from a melange of businesses, so one might pass a fancy dress shop and a livery, jowl to jowl. A more consistent pattern of building emerged where the businesses were larger, but even the brick courthouse on the square and the false-fronted hotels had a raw atmosphere of newness, as if their planners had built them in haste.

At the Excelsior Hotel, a three-story establishment with brass lamps flanking the wide front doors, the pair dismounted and threw their saddlebags over their arms. Taggart, intending to walk to the livery stable later, pitched a gold coin to a waiting boy and asked him to take their mounts on ahead. When they entered the hotel, there was soft carpeting underfoot, and a wonderful warmth rushed over them, mingled with the sounds of clicking silverware and muffled conversation that drifted from the adjoining dining room.

"Lordamercy, I've never been in such a fine place," Silky marveled, casting her gaze at the red-striped settees and velvet draperies.

The clerk, a middle-aged man with an amiable face, glanced at Taggart, then opened his registration book and shoved it across the counter. "Yes, sir. How can I help you and your son?"

Taggart laughed to himself and, not taking the time to correct the mistake, scribbled his name in the book. "My son and I need a room for the night. Your best."

"Yes, sir," the man replied in a nervous tone, "but our best is the bridal suite, and I'm afraid it's quite expensive."

Taggart pulled a wad of Confederate notes from his saddlebag and slapped them on the counter. "That won't be a problem."

The man picked up the currency, his eyes widening in surprise. "Y-Yes, very well, sir," he stammered, fanning out the big bills.

While the clerk made change, Taggart scanned the diners, some of whom were craning their necks to get a better look at Silky and himself. "Have dinner sent to our room," he ordered. "Two of your finest steaks with all the trimmings." He started to walk away, then paused and looked back at the bewildered man. "Send up a bottle of wine, too."

The clerk came from behind the counter and handed him a large brass key on which the number *14* was inscribed. "Wine? I'm not sure we have any, but I'll check. The suite is on the third floor," he mumbled, nodding at the carpeted stairs. "The first room to your right."

A thrill of anticipation ran through Silky as they went up the stairs. When she and Daniel had visited Charlottesville to sell furs they'd stayed in a run-down boardinghouse on the edge of town. Never had she been in such a fine establishment.

As they entered the spacious room, she placed her burdens aside, delighted with what she saw. Furnished with an old-fashioned curtained bed flanked with marble-topped tables, the slightly chilly suite also boasted overstuffed chairs and a large wardrobe. When she lit the china lamps, light spilled over the chamber, revealing a symphony of delicate color. Rose chintz curtained the windows while a like-colored sofa and mahogany tea table stood in front of the fireplace, whose mantel was decorated with china bric-a-brac.

With a cry of joy, Silky tossed off her poncho, spread out her arms, and sank onto the bed, testing its softness. "Why, it's like resting on a cloud!" she exclaimed, running her hands over the slippery taffeta counterpane. Excitedly, she rose to inspect the dressing room, and discovered a vanity and chair, a cheval glass, and, on a bureau, a basin with scented soap and soft damask towels. She glanced at Taggart, who was lighting kindling he had placed over the neatly laid logs. "This place is as pretty as sunup," she murmured like a pleased child.

She was lightly tracing her fingertips over the bureau, when on the wall above it she saw a painting of a centaur chasing a maiden though the spring woods. She'd never even heard of the mythical creature, but the lascivious gleam in his eyes told her all she needed to know. She motioned at Taggart, and, amusement lighting his expression, he strode to her. "Take a look at this horse-critter," she breathed, pointing at the picture. "What kind of place are we staying in, anyway?"

"Don't forget," he reminded her, laying a hand on her shoulder, "we are sleeping in the honeymoon suite. I imagine the painting is for inspiration."

"Inspiration? Looking at something like that could warp a person for the rest of their natural life."

Ignoring his laughter, she was off again, inspecting the rest of the bedroom. When she spied a chamber pot peeking from beneath the hem of the counterpane, she gingerly pulled out the receptacle, finding it decorated with a cherub wreathed in roses.

"Lordamercy, look at this thing with the fat baby on it. Is it supposed to be a chamber pot? It's too nice to use. I'm surprised someone hasn't planted flowers in it." She turned it over and found an inscription on the bottom reading *Made in France*. "Imagine that," she whispered, so awed she could scarcely speak. She sank to the bed and gazed at Taggart as he removed his jacket, his face breaking into a smile. "This must be the finest room in all of Virginny. Why this place is so fancy, they send all the way to France just for their chamber pots!"

She'd just finished washing her face and hands and combing her hair, when a waiter knocked on the door, carrying a tray that held their dinner and a chilled bottle of wine. Taggart received the food at the threshold, then carried it to the tea table so they could eat in front of the cozy fire that had already warmed the room up nicely. Silky thought the savory steaks, buttery potatoes, and tender vegetables would almost melt in her mouth, and when she took her first bite of jelly roll, she leaned against the sofa with a sigh, saying, "Why, that's the best thing I ever ate."

"What do you think of the wine?" Taggart asked with dancing eyes, as he refilled her glass.

She took another taste of the light wine, comparing it to the applejack she distilled herself, and the moonshine she was so well acquainted with. "Not bad," she replied, not wanting to hurt his feelings. "It kind of reminds me of sour plum juice." Noticing the beginning of another smile on his lips, she decided she should really let him know her true feelings. "But if you paid two whole dollars for this bottle like you said, you got skinned good. Uncle Newby back in Bear Wallow makes a 'shine that's so powerful it'll take the hair off a cat, and he only charges a dollar for a half-gallon jug."

After they'd finished eating, Taggart announced he was going to the livery stable, and a few moments later bundled up and left. When the waiter came to get the dishes, he gaped at Silky's long hair and curvaceous body, and she smiled to herself, knowing he'd tell the clerk that during the course of dinner, Mr. Taggart's son had turned into a woman. Warm and satisfied, and slightly mellow from the wine, Silky ordered a hot bath, thinking that city life was certainly fine. After a tin bathtub and five tall cans of hot water had been brought to the room, she told the boy to put it on the bill, as she'd heard Taggart say when the food had arrived.

Once she was alone, she stripped off her clothing, pinned up her hair, and looked at herself in the tall cheval glass. It was the first time she'd ever seen all of her body, and she marveled at the wonderful looking glass that was so big it could reflect a person from head to toe all at once. A blush rode her cheeks as she considered her face and figure, wondering if she was as pretty as the city women Taggart had known before her, and for a moment a poignant sadness seeped through the wine's glow.

Surrendering her virginity to him had been a reckless thing to do, she thought, a little frightened at the step she'd taken, but even now she couldn't gainsay her decision, for she knew she loved him with all her heart. Never had she wanted anything more than to have him make love to her, and to deny that fact would be like denying the very life God had put in her body.

She dreaded tomorrow, for he'd already told her he would get his new assignment and be ordered to another part of the South, or even back to the North. She'd felt strangely timid about bringing up the subject of being handfasted, for she didn't want him to feel trapped. No doubt before he left, he'd broach the matter of their future himself—then she could talk about it, she thought, hope rippling through her like a sweet mountain melody.

They might be separated for a while, but one day he'd return to Sweet Gum Hollow with a ring and they'd be married. Then nothing could ever come between them again—even another war.

Silky had been relaxing in the warm, sudsy water for half an hour when she heard approaching footsteps and a key turning in the lock. With a great splashing sound, she sat up and crossed her hands over her slick breasts. A moment later Taggart entered, closed the door, and leaned against it, his eyes shining with wicked amusement.

"I didn't know you were coming back so soon," she exclaimed nervously. "I thought you were still at the livery stable. I—I—" Like a locomotive running out of steam, she ran out of words, knowing she was in trouble for the time she'd ambushed him at old man Johnson's pond.

After taking off his hat and jacket, he knelt by the tub and gently brushed back a lock of her damp hair. "One thing I've noticed in life is that what goes around, comes around," he remarked, an amused smile hovering on his lips. "Have you ever noticed that?"

Silky swallowed hard, realizing how vulnerable she was. "Y-Yeah . . . I suppose I have." Lordamercy, if the expression on his face—which resembled that of the horse-critter on the wall—was a reflection of what was going on in his head, she was in more trouble than she could shake a stick at.

He caressed the back of her neck, working his fingers in wonderful little circles. "Yes, sir, it isn't every day of the week that a man runs across a beautiful lady in the bathtub." With his other hand, he tilted her face to his. She couldn't miss the seductive gleam in his eyes as he lowered his head and rasped, "When he does, he just naturally feels challenged to do something about it."

His mouth, which tasted of wine, covered hers in a shivery kiss that sent her passion skyrocketing like sparkling fireworks. Gently he removed her crossed hands from her breasts, and as his fingers teased her wet nipples, a delicious sensation darted down her spine. Automatically she put her arms about his shoulders, yielding to his masterful touch. At last his lips moved away from hers, leaving them tingling with warmth. She looked into those smoky eyes that beckoned her to satisfy the sweet agony possessing her. "I think it's time to get out of the tub," she whispered, now tightening her arms about his neck.

A smile twitched the corner of his mouth. "Anything to help a lady," he replied, lightly kissing her forehead, her nose, her lips. "Here, stand up and I'll dry you off."

His playful manner and the intimacy in his voice made him almost irresistible. Oh, he was a master at the game of love, she thought, his masculinity overpowering her as he rose, bringing her to a standing position. "How many other helpless females have you ambushed while they were taking a bath?" she murmured, her body already aching for his touch.

Humor shining in his eyes, he peeled a towel from a chair and began drying her as gently as a nursemaid. "Actually this is a new experience for me"—he flashed a broad grin—"but if it works out well, I may begin haunting hotels, looking for other opportunities."

She smiled. Then, as he dropped the damp towel and took her in his arms, she laid her head against the hollow of his neck. "Make love to me again," she whispered. "This may be our last night together for a long while." She looked into his eyes, which gleamed with sharp longing. "Who knows when you'll return. I want this night to be special . . . something I can hold in my heart forever."

For an instant his eyes darkened and he sighed deeply.

"What's wrong?" she asked. "Did I—"

"No," he murmured, "don't talk." He slid an appreciative gaze over her. "Did you know you're the most desirable woman I've ever known? You're completely, absolutely irresistible," he admitted, his tone rough with a passion that fired her own.

Taggart looked down at Silky's delicate face, noticing her seductive eyes and soft lips. Lord, what a predicament she was putting him in, asking him to make love to her again. If only he could take her home with him after the war, he thought. But that was utterly impossible. Ohio was the home of antislavery newspapers, the Underground Railroad, and fiery abolitionists; Ohio was solidly Union, the belt buckle of federal feeling and sympathy, a state that had answered Lincoln's call for volunteers with 30,000 soldiers.

Silky was as Southern as Carolina jasmine and moonlight on the Mississippi—a fiery Reb, who hated Yankee buzzards worse than poison, as she often said. If she found out his true identity, she would loathe and despise him, and, if possible, put a bullet in his heart. If there was ever a star-crossed relationship it was theirs—yet she was the most delectable, enticing woman he'd ever met, and at this particular moment, he simply couldn't resist her.

Silky, scarcely knowing what she was doing, unbuttoned his shirt, revealing his broad, thickly haired chest. She boldly ran her fingers over his corded neck and muscled shoulders, finding the experience strangely exciting. She noticed a pulse in his throat as she stripped off his shirt, then unbuttoned his breeches. When she finished and he stood nude before her, a dizzying current of excitement tingled through her.

He took the pins from her hair, and it fell cool and soft about her shoulders. With warm eyes, he drew her close and his gaze melted over her, as tender as a benediction. She draped her arms about his neck, and he hungrily kissed her mouth before lowering his fingers and rolling her nipple between his fingertips. His palm slid over her rib cage to her stomach; then his hand feathered over her sensitive inner thigh, making her tremble. When his fingers invaded her damp curls and flicked over the flower of her femininity, a wild yearning flared up within her, and her desire spilled forth like water rushing over a high fall.

She traced her fingers over his back, aching for their union, but yearning for more than the feel of his hands upon her flesh. How she hungered to be one with him, not only in body, but it spirit and purpose, heart and soul. Soon the craving exploded into a fire that would not be denied.

Taggart swung her feet from the carpet and carried her to the bed, where soft light gleamed over the taffeta counterpane. The fire had died down a little and its gentle glow pooled over the room and flickered against the walls. He cradled her against him and with one hand pulled back the covers, then placed her on the cool sheet. Silky felt his warmth as he lay down beside her and gathered her into his arms.

She relaxed against his hard chest, noticing the rhythm of his beating heart. Tenderness welled within her as he reclaimed her lips and caressed her, seeking out the places that would bring her the most pleasure. Seemingly insatiable, he devoured her mouth, at the same time lavishing attention on her most intimate flesh until a languorous heat consumed her body like silken flames.

When his searching fingers slipped into her femininity again, passion jolted through her like sheet lightning. The emotions were so sweet, so sharp, she thought as pleasure pulsed between her thighs. With a moan, she dug her fingers into his back, feeling as if she were reliving every wonderful thing that had ever happened to her all at the same time.

Her mind fogging, she moved her lips from his, then clutched his questing hand. She met his passion-dark eyes, noting a spark of surprise. "Nobody gets this good without a lot of practice," she whispered, her breath catching in her throat. "I'll bet you've made love more than any man in the Confederacy. How long will it be before I know as much about lovemaking as you?"

He trailed feather-light kisses over her face, then held her gaze with mischievous eyes. "I don't know if that is even possible," he answered, his tone laced with self-mockery. "But being the generous soul I am, I'd be willing to try to teach you." A roguish grin touched his lips. "Now, be quiet, woman, and let me finish your lesson."

Chapter Eight

When Taggart opened his eyes the next morning, the first thing he saw was Silky sleeping beside him on her back, her lovely face wreathed in relaxed slumber. The counterpane had slipped from her during the night, revealing her shapely shoulder and one creamy breast, whose pink crest peeked provocatively from the sheet, reminding him of a delicately colored rose. With her shining hair spread out over the lace-edged pillow, she seemed younger and sweeter than ever, and he raised himself on an elbow and impulsively brushed his lips over hers. Sighing a bit, she fluttered her lashes, then sank into deep sleep once more, her bosom rising and falling rhythmically.

Resisting a keen urge to make love to her again, he slipped from the bed, telling himself the Union was depending on him. Pale light streaked over the carpet from a crack between the curtains as he hastily washed and dressed, his mind already stirring with the business of the day. Afterward he sat down at a table and wrote a message to his contact in Maryland, all in cipher. At first he struggled a bit to recall certain key words, but the cipher had been so well drilled into him before leaving for the South, he managed to compose the message in a relatively short time.

When he'd finished, he rose and placed some large Confederate bills on the bureau, then dashed off a note and placed it beside the money.

Fancy Pants:
I've gone out to meet my contact. Buy yourself an outfit from one of the shops we saw coming into town. I'm tired of wartime concessions to fashion. Surprise me with something luscious, and buy the prettiest bonnet in Charlottesville to replace that hat you lost in the creek. Meet me at the hotel at one for lunch. A roast this time—with more sour plum juice, if you like.

With a last glance at the lovely vision she made, he left and softly closed the door behind him. On the way through the hotel lobby, his rough garb caused people to stare, and he decided that now that he was back in civilization he, too, should buy some new clothes.

Outside, there was a blue sky for a change, but ruffles of snow lined the streets like dirty suds. Pedestrians passed by him on both sides: black laborers in shabby clothes and brogans, and clerks and merchants wearing overcoats and boots. At the telegraph office he met two young soldiers coming out the door. Although there was no military installation in Charlottesville, it was a crossroads for Southern companies marching to all points of the compass. Once again Taggart was struck with how young the recruits looked—hardly more than children, he thought, like some of the boyish Confederates he'd seen at Shiloh.

Inside the cramped office, a lamp glowed from a desk, casting light over a dried-up little man wearing a green visor and small spectacles perched low on his nose. "Yes sir," the clerk croaked in the whispery voice of the old. "How can I help you?" With a hint of suspicion, the oldster's rheumy eyes inched over Taggart's civilian garb, but at last the man's lined face relaxed visibly. No doubt the clerk assumed he was a plantation overseer, one of the few able-bodied men in the South holding a military exemption.

"I'd like to get in touch with my brother in Hagerstown, Maryland," Taggart explained nonchalantly, handing him the note he'd prepared. "Unfortunately, my father is ailing."

With a sigh, the old man began keying in the long message. When he reached the first stop, he cut his gaze at Taggart. "If you're waiting for a return message it may take a while." He nodded at a straight-backed chair. "Would you like to have a seat?"

"I think I'll walk out on the porch for a smoke," Taggart answered casually, already moving to the door. Meandering out of the office, he lit his cheroot. Lord, once an agent had a cipher in his hands or head, it was all so easy, he thought, relieved the information was on its way. He knew the operator in Maryland would have a boy deliver the telegram to his "brother," really another Union agent, who would send back instructions. Dozens of messages flew back and forth across the Mason-Dixon line, relayed this way. Some of the codes were more complicated than others, but to an untrained telegraph operator, they all appeared to be nothing more than everyday correspondence concerning business or family life.

Taggart smoked, studying the Charlottesville traffic for thirty minutes. Heavily loaded wagons jostled toward the railroad with timber and other goods for the Confederate war effort. Later he heard a stirring song and spied a company of Southern troops marching up the street, singing their hearts out as they put on a show of bravery for the local citizens. Unfortunately, he realized many of these young men would be dead in a few days, leaving only the memories of their brief lives behind.

"Mr. Taggart, I have your return message," came a cracked voice from the telegraph office.

Taggart entered the building and took a message from the old man's blue-veined hands, eagerly scanning the paper that appeared to be information about his father's health. Knowing he needed a place to decipher the code, he paid the operator and, with a sense of great anticipation, walked to a small eatery a block down the busy street.

Once there, he ordered coffee, but received a bitter chickory blend instead. Totally absorbed in the message, he sat down to study it, generally ignored by the workingmen who frequented the modest establishment. The cipher's key was given by a prearranged first word that informed the receiver in what sequence to restore the original message. Taggart turned over the paper and, pulling out a pencil, went to work deciphering his orders.

Thirty minutes later, he folded the message, put it away, and sat back, impressed with the importance of his new mission that would last for the duration of the war. He was to monitor the Petersburg line, a lengthy string of trenches and fortifications looping under Petersburg, Virginia, which lay twenty-five miles south of the Confederate capital of Richmond.

Grant and Lee had been faced off with opposing armies here for months, and for the Union, the key to winning the war was breaking through the well-entrenched Reb line. Once that was accomplished, Richmond would fall, and along with it, the South's last hope, the Army of Northern Virginia. Another agent would be involved—surprisingly an aristocratic lady named Caroline Willmott, who resided in Richmond. He'd been advised she could relay his messages to Grant. He was also warned not to approach her directly, but to make her acquaintance socially in order to shield her identity.

He knew Silky would question him about the assignment, but he would plead secrecy. He would buy her a fine meal at the Excelsior, then escort her to the room and begin the farewell process once again. A girl such as herself belonged in Sweet Gum Hollow, not traipsing around the South, believing he was a Confederate when the heartrending truth was sure to come out sooner or later.

Perhaps her innocence could still be preserved. Once she returned to the Blue Ridge, and the war was over, any of the local swains would be proud to take her as a wife. Undoubtedly she would refuse his offer to stay in the hotel until the weather got better, but he would force the issue, simply leaving the money as he had this morning.

For a moment his throat tightened, and a part of him wanted to wad up the message and throw it away. Hadn't he deceived the girl enough? Then he considered the hundreds, possibly thousands, of lives depending on his assignment. If he failed, Northern boys almost as young as Ned would die, never to see their families again.

The war was almost over. With his information, the Union would be able to deal the coup de grâce to the dying Confederacy; then the long process of healing could begin. Still, on this fine November day, it seemed being an intelligence agent had cost more than he'd ever imagined.

About that same time Silky returned to their room at the Excelsior Hotel, and tossed down a shopping bag containing her old clothes. At the cheval glass, she fingered the lush pile of her new burgundy velvet mantle and matching gown, amazed at how fine the garments looked. Having never worn anything but buckskins or plain calico gowns she'd cut and sewn herself, it was hard for her to believe the elegant reflection was her own. At the same time, she wondered how Taggart could buy her such a wonderful ensemble on a Confederate lieutenant's pay. He gave her the impression that his family was wealthy; still, the way he spent money took her breath away.

She'd been somewhat bewildered when she'd walked into the dress shop and the lady proprietor had gazed at her mountain garb in disdain. At first Silky had guessed at her size, then after trying on a few things, found what suited her best. When the shopkeeper saw the color of her plentiful Confederate bills, she readily came to her assistance, selling her a corset and a puffed horsehair crinoline, and even kid gloves and a reticule to go with the ensemble.

Now whirling before the mirror to make her skirt rise, Silky viewed her new shoes, which neatly buttoned up her ankles, making her feet look unbelievably small and dainty. She'd also purchased a burgundy-colored bonnet and, with trembling fingers, pinned her long locks atop her head, noticing the change it made in her.

Gently she opened the hatbox, eased the satin bonnet from its nest of tissue paper, then settled the exquisite creation upon her head. How different it was from the battered mountain hat she was used to wearing! Festooned with a little plume and decorated with moss-green ribbons that she tied under her chin, the chapeau not only brought out the luster in her hair, but the fire in her green eyes.

Suddenly remembering she hadn't spent all her money, she opened her reticule and saw she had enough cash to buy Taggart a muffler and some gloves. She recalled she'd seen a men's clothing store somewhere near the courthouse and, with a rush of happiness, hurried from the room, thinking how surprised he'd be with the purchases.

After leaving the hotel, she walked briskly in the direction of the courthouse, a fresh breeze lifting her spirits. She kept to the planked sidewalk, for the sun had come out enough to turn the street into a slushy gray mass cut with buggy wheels. In her new finery she felt like a queen, and many of the Confederate soldiers threw her admiring glances, one officer even lifting his hat as he passed.

When Silky's gaze fell on a fresh-faced soldier with bright red hair poking from beneath his cap, she thought of Charlie and the mountaineers she'd left behind in Sweet Gum Hollow. No doubt the boy had been asked about her whereabouts by now, and the fact that she'd ridden after Taggart would be the talk of the hollow. *Just a-ridin' after that flatlander in a blindin' blizzard!* she could imagine the granny women saying. Lost in her reverie she walked on, scarcely giving a thought to where she were going.

Near the courthouse, she passed an elderly man, but was so preoccupied she accidentally brushed against him. Dressed in a fine suit and carrying a brass-handled walking stick, the silver-haired gentleman raised his top hat, then stepped aside. "My pardon, miss. My fault altogether," he apologized, bowing gallantly. His genteel Virginia accent fell sweetly on her ears and immediately placed him as a landholder and man of some rank.

"No." Silky laughed, touching his arm. "I'm afraid I was daydreaming." She started to walk on, then noticed people milling up and down the courthouse steps, some crying and clutching the brass handrail running down the middle of the steps. A few of the ladies sobbed openly, pressing lacy handkerchiefs to their eyes. "Pardon me, sir," she ventured, catching the gentleman's attention again, "but what is the sad occasion at the courthouse today? A trial, perhaps?"

Tenderness gathered in the old man's moist eyes. "From your comment, I see you're a visitor to Charlottesville," he replied softly. He indicated the large courthouse doors with a gloved hand. "The new lists of the Confederate dead and wounded were posted on the courthouse doors this morning. Unfortunately, this sad situation is now a common occurrence in our city."

Silky's heart turned over in her bosom. "You mean the lists for the soldiers from Charlottesville are posted there?" she replied, shielding her eyes to stare at the long white sheets.

The old man gave a deep sigh. "No, my dear. The lists cover all the men in service for the whole western section of Virginia. They include seven counties, I believe."

Silky bit her lip. "My brother is in the service. We both come from a little place up in the Blue Ridge—that would be listed, too?"

The gentleman regarded her kindly. "Yes, I believe it would," he replied in a solicitous voice, his eyes holding hers. He glanced at the courthouse steps, then back at her. "If you would like to read the lists, permit me to accompany you."

Silky realized the courtly old man was prepared to escort her up the steps, but noted again his walking cane. "Thank you, sir," she answered, swallowing the lump in her throat, "but I'll go myself. I'm fine—really I am."

She moved toward the steps, then glanced over her shoulder, seeing he was still watching her with a worried gaze. "Are you sure, miss?" he called after her, raising his hat once more.

"Yes . . . thank you so much." She waved farewell before slowly turning to walk up the high steps, her anxiety mounting by the moment. The fact that Daniel had been moved to a company that was to see action resounded in her head like the blows of a ringing hammer. His name might be there now, just waiting for her to discover it, she thought, noticing a leaden feeling about her heart.

At the top of the steps, she stood patiently behind an older couple who'd just found their son's name on the list of those killed in action. Her heart ached for the sobbing lady and the grim-faced man as they walked away with heads bent in sorrow.

Her hand trembling, Silky placed a finger at the top of the list and traced downward until she found the names beginning with *S;* then, praying as she'd never prayed before, she inched her finger downward until she found the first name beginning with *T.*

She exhaled a deep breath. One more list, she thought, girding her courage. I must force myself to read one more list; then I'll know he's all right. She began at the top of the list of the wounded and worked downward, her heart thumping as she neared the letter *S.*

Then she saw it.

The name *Daniel Shanahan* jumped out at her with the force of a sharp blow, snatching her breath away. Tears stung her eyes. Daniel had been wounded and was in Chimborazo Military Hospital in Richmond. Through a thick mist of emotion she read his name several times, and even traced her finger over it in an attempt to verify it. If there was any mistake about there being two Daniel Shanahans in the Confederacy, his home was neatly listed to the right of his name as Sweet Gum Hollow.

For a moment the courthouse steps, the people walking up them, and Charlottesville itself seemed distant and far away, and in her mind's eye she saw her brother's smiling face as he kissed her good-bye before leaving for the war. Then she pictured them as they played together as children, laughing and running in the woods. What she'd silently feared for over three years had finally come to pass—Daniel had been cut down by a Yankee bullet.

She walked down the steps, an otherworldly feeling closing in about her. Her brother was hurt and she didn't know how badly. He was lying in a hospital in Richmond, alone and undoubtedly racked with pain. What if he died? she asked herself, her vision misting at the thought. She'd never forgive herself for not making an effort to see him. For a moment the horrible thought came to her mind that he might have lost an arm or a leg, and she clutched the handrail, refusing to let herself even contemplate the possibility.

She remembered the wounded soldiers who'd returned to

Bear Wallow. Some of them had looked relatively well while others had seemed completely broken, not only in body but in spirit. She wouldn't let that happen to her brother, she vowed, recalling how his eyes had danced when he played his fiddle. Thank the Lord, she'd saved a little money and brought it with her! She must go to Daniel and find out if he needed special medicine or richer nourishment to recover.

At the bottom of the steps, she was vaguely aware of people walking around her as she stood in a state of shock, trying to absorb the horrible news she'd just received. Then gradually, a steely resolve rose to fortify and comfort her, and with a sense of hope she considered Taggart. Perhaps if his assignment took him someplace in Virginia he'd escort her to Richmond. She'd never bought a ticket, never ridden a train, never been a hundred miles away from home. If she was awed with Charlottesville what must Richmond be like with its sprawling hospitals and government offices? Her mountain skills, good as they were, would count for naught in the great city, and despite her resolve, she'd be virtually helpless.

Possibilities flying through her head, she numbly walked in the direction of the men's store. Today after lunch when Taggart was in a warm, pleasant mood, full of good food, and perhaps several glasses of that wine he liked so much, she'd inform him she was going to Richmond. Then after she was sure he was convinced of the fact, she'd ask him if he would escort her there.

Taggart regarded Silky as she sat on the little sofa before the fire. They'd just finished lunch and returned to their room for a private chat, and he thought how lovely she was in her new velvet ensemble, even with a hint of tears in her eyes. During the long meal she'd been sad and reserved—much too quiet for the mountain spitfire he knew so well. Something was troubling her deeply, and his intuition told him it had nothing to do with his upcoming departure. "Something happened today while I was gone, didn't it?" he asked, sitting beside her and taking her hand. "I can see it in your eyes. Won't you tell me what it is?"

Obviously trying to control her emotions, she met him with silence.

"Has someone insulted you? Said something about you?" he asked, a protective feeling rising within him at the thought of anyone hurting her.

Silky stared at Taggart, her heart lurching. The moment had arrived. It was time to tell him what was in her heart and ask for her favor. For a moment the words that she'd held back all through lunch faltered on her lips, but his insistent gaze demanded an answer.

Building up her courage, she lowered her eyes. "All right, but first tell me about your new assignment," she countered, looking up to find him watching her intently. "Will you be in Virginia? Will you have some type of deadline to meet?"

Taggart's expression clouded. "Yes, I'll be in Virginia," he admitted reluctantly. He sighed, his manner guarded. "And I'll have some freedom as far as time goes, but I can't reveal anything else." His jaw tensed and from his implacable countenance, she realized that he wouldn't give her more information about the assignment. His face slowly softening, he cupped her chin. "Now—tell me what happened while we were apart."

"I-I visited the courthouse this morning—before I bought you the gloves and muffler," she began softly. His face first registered shock, then sympathy and understanding, and she realized he knew about the lists on the doors.

"Daniel?"

She let out a tremulous breath. "Yes . . . he's been wounded and he's in Chimborazo Military Hospital in Richmond." Now that she'd broached the subject the words tumbled from her mouth in a rush, expressing all her pent-up emotions. "Who knows how badly he's hurt?" she added, panic tightening her throat. "He may be hanging on to life this very minute. I can't tell you how I felt when I saw his name—like all the breath had been knocked out of me."

Taggart's mouth curved with tenderness. "He probably isn't wounded as seriously as you think," he advised, his hand sliding to her shoulder in a reassuring caress. "Even if he's only slightly wounded, if he can't walk, he would be hospitalized."

She spread her fingers in frustration. "But I can't depend on that. I need to go there and see how he is. He'd do the same for me—I know he would. I'll write Charlie and tell him about Daniel, and mention he'll need to look after the place a while longer." She grasped his hand. "I don't know how much the ticket will be, but I can sell my horse and saddle—and my rifle, too. That Henry will fetch a fine price—I'm certain-sure of it!"

Taggart looked into her frightened eyes, feeling his gut tighten with emotion. From the reports he'd been given, Richmond was presently a city at hell's gate.

"I could scrape the fare together, I know I could," she went on with fierce determination. "I've never been farther than Charlottesville, and I have no idea where this hospital is, but the people in Richmond will probably help me."

Taggart listened to her in amazement. Although the Confederate command tried to keep Richmond patrolled, it had become a magnet for sharpers and opportunists and was exactly the type of place an inexperienced young woman like herself shouldn't visit. Once the capital fell to Grant, which was now a virtual certainty, Northern riffraff would also pour in like vultures, making the place even more treacherous.

She sat forward. "I'm going," she said decisively. "I've laid it out in my mind that I will," she vowed, her soft voice steeled with determination. Moisture glistened in her eyes. "Will you come with me?" she asked brokenly. "If your assignment is in that vicinity, will you help me get there?"

Taggart stood, trying to cut off her statement, trying to stop her pleading request that had obviously taken so much courage to verbalize. They must say good-bye today. Their relationship had to end. Already he'd foolishly let his headstrong heart bring them to this pass. Now was the time for discipline, no matter how much it hurt. "No," he firmly replied, feeling the words cut something inside of him as he spoke. "I cannot go with you. And you must not go yourself."

Her stricken expression pulled at his heart, but he kept speaking, trying to forestall her folly. "Richmond is a city coming apart, a large, dangerous city, filled with pitfalls for someone like yourself. You must not go there. I'll arrange for you to stay here, then when the weather—''

Silky stood, clutching his arms. ''You don't understand,'' she exclaimed, her voice laced with frustration. ''I must go. I must go, for my brother might be dying.'' Her voice gained strength and fire. ''And I will go, if I have to ride the train, or ride a horse, or even walk.'' Tears sparkled in her lovely eyes. ''I'm going to Richmond,'' she vowed passionately, ''and no one can stop me—not even you!'' For moments her determined gaze clung to his; then she crossed her arms and began restlessly pacing about the room.

Damn, Taggart thought, the little firebrand will go or die trying. That flinty mountain will of hers had asserted itself, and he knew that at this point, no one could stop her, short of binding her to a bedpost. Courage like that inspired his admiration even though it was misguided. How many people crept through life, not caring deeply about anyone, even their own kin? Plenty of people, most of them, in fact—but not Silky Shanahan.

He wanted to think of her safe in Sweet Gum Hollow or at least here in Charlottesville, in a regional town where people would be more sympathetic to her mountain ways. Once she was in Richmond—if she wasn't killed trying to get there—and the rascals heard her soft drawl and saw those clear green eyes, she would be as a sheep among wolves. The thought of what could happen to her there left a sick feeling in his stomach.

Then, as he studied Silky's stricken face, an idea exploded in his head—an idea that attracted and repulsed him at the same time with equal force. Since Richmond was only a short train ride north of the Petersburg line, it would be possible to live in Richmond and travel back and forth to Petersburg for his work. As an added bonus, if he were staying in Richmond for the rest of the war, instead of Petersburg, Caroline Willmott could introduce him into Confederate society, where he might glean some extra bits of information. That was the positive side of the situation—and it glittered with staggering potential. On the negative side, he would once again be using Silky without her knowledge to spy on her beloved South.

Silky walked to him and, grasping his shoulders, stared up at him with a pleading gaze that penetrated his heart. ''Well, what do you say, West Point Gentleman?'' she inquired through trembling lips. ''Will you take me to Richmond to see Daniel? Will you?'' she asked again, her expression shining with fierce longing.

Chapter Nine

Taggart watched Silky's eyes glisten with excitement as the single-gauge engine clickety-clacked over a switch crossing and chugged away from the Charlottesville railroad station. He couldn't help but chuckle, for her delight in the new experience reminded him of that of an excited child on Christmas morning.

"I feel like I'm flying," she announced, her face shining as she settled back against the seat. "I've never gone this fast in all my life!"

A Confederate corporal walked past them and nodded in greeting, then claimed a seat in the rear of the near-empty car along with a few other soldiers traveling to the Richmond area. Conversation now rippled among the men as they lit up pipes and, settling in for the long trip, began talking about their families.

Taggart scanned Silky's bright face as she looked from the window. That bubbling innocence was her real strength, he suddenly realized. From such a childlike view of life sprang her amazing will and her admirable courage—a courage that would provoke her into attempting a trip to Richmond, when a more sophisticated person would have declared it too difficult. He watched her staring back at the smudgy blotch that Charlottesville had now become, recalling the last twenty-four hours when he'd made the decision he was sure would affect them both for the rest of their lives.

After much agonized thought he'd decided the opportunity Silky's trip presented was simply too great to overlook. By accompanying her, he could continue to assume the identity of a Confederate lieutenant, now claiming he was on extended leave to travel with Silky as she visited Daniel.

Silky had suggested that since she might be in Richmond for months she should sell her horse instead of stabling in it Charlottesville. She'd also boxed up her repeating rifle and mailed it back to Charlie, along with a letter explaining that due to Daniel's condition he'd need to take care of her place indefinitely. Taggart had sold his rifle, horse, and tack along with Silky's mount, given her the money she'd earned, and purchased tickets for them both with his funds. Knowing she needed simpler clothes for traveling, he'd bought her a blue gown, mantle, and bonnet, and also a huge carpetbag in which she'd packed her other belongings.

With a pleased sigh, she now focused her attention on him and, adjusting the sashes of her bonnet, settled in for the trip. Despite her excitement, the concern he'd seen in her eyes at the depot this morning told him she was deeply worried about her brother. In one sense it seemed the wrong moment for a conversation, but at the same time, the soldiers were absorbed in their own talk, and there was a delicate subject he needed to broach—a subject he knew she might be quite sensitive about.

Silky regarded Taggart with a rush of affection, immensely thankful he'd agreed to her proposal. Lord, was all this really happening? she wondered, feeling as if she were in a dream. Could she, who had never ridden on a train, actually be on her way to Richmond? The vibration of the car and the click of the wheels under her feet answered her question. Although the musty-smelling car was poorly equipped, with torn seats and tacky little light fixtures, to her it was a magic carpet transporting her to see her brother.

With a flicker of apprehension, she noticed Taggart looked

at her as if he wanted to say something.

"I thought I'd talk to you about our plans for Richmond," he ventured, moving a speculative gaze over her.

"Good, I was wondering how we'd work things out when we got there," she answered. "How long will you be able to stay?"

A cautious expression settled on his face. "I'm not sure—probably quite some time. While there, I'll be presenting myself as a lieutenant attached to a regiment in the western theater of operations. It's a story we both need to stick to."

Silky nodded, willing to do anything to assist his secret work.

"I think," he continued slowly, his eyes roaming over her, "that it would be best if we claimed to be cousins."

"Cousins?" Silky echoed, feeling a prick of pain at his words. With all the tension in the air about Richmond, she had thought it best not to mention the subject of being handfasted—that little detail could wait until later. But she hadn't expected this and was somewhat disappointed that he expected her to disguise her relationship with him. He had a way of bending her to his will as he'd done since they first met, but what he was now proposing took some getting used to.

"Yes, that way we can get adjoining rooms, and move about Richmond very openly without causing any notice." His eyes seemed to send her a silent message. "It would be best for us personally—and also for the Confederacy, I think," he added meaningfully.

Silky's heart plummeted. She wanted the whole world to know she loved him in a distinctly uncousinly way; then, realizing how finicky most flatlanders were about marriage licenses and wedding rings, she gradually saw the wisdom of the plan. After all, he was only trying to protect her reputation and save her embarrassment when people asked questions about their relationship. Besides that, to protest a plan he'd devised not only to shield her, but to help him in his work, would at this point seem rather petty, she decided.

She had no idea how long he would be able to stay with her in Richmond, but she wanted their time together to be pleasant and go smoothly. In truth, she loved him so deeply and outrageously and unconditionally, she simply couldn't deny him anything. If this was what he required, she thought, pushing her own emotions aside and recreating herself to conform to an image that would please him, she would comply.

"All right, *cousin,*" she softly agreed, suddenly realizing that love made people do things they ordinarily wouldn't do in a hundred years. She noticed a pleased look in his eyes, and now that she'd agreed to the proposal, she began to feel much better about it herself. The fact that they were kissing cousins who would be married after the war was something the flatlanders didn't need to know. In her heart she clung as tenaciously to the belief that he would offer her marriage someday as she did to life itself.

They talked about Richmond and Daniel and several other subjects for a while; then, seeing him staring at the rolling landscape, she ventured, "Pretty country, isn't it?"

"Some of the prettiest I've ever seen," he answered with a smile.

"I hear there's lots of fine land out west."

His face darkened, leaving her to wonder why. "Yes, land like this." He nodded at the window. "That's what I'd really like to do with my life." His gaze moved over her. "Own a fine tract of land. Something I could put my sweat and dreams into. Something I could pass along to my sons."

Silky regarded him carefully. "I thought a fine West Point gentleman like you would want to own a factory or be a bank president when the war was over."

He shook his head. "I'd rather feel damp earth between my fingers, or catch the scent of rain as a thunderstorm comes rolling in."

This new side of Taggart surprised and pleased her, for she had been sure he wanted to live in a city. How much more did she need to learn about him? She knew which food he liked best, how he took his coffee, and dozens of other little things about him, but did she really know him, know the hidden things of his heart? Her mind flashed back to the picture of him squatting on the ground talking to Amos Evans.

Then, silently chiding herself for still harboring doubts

about him, she relaxed, suddenly understanding that beneath his air of danger and potent sexuality he had quite a poetic heart. He was like that, she thought—like the clouds scudding over the sky on a windy day. One moment they would be talking about something totally frivolous, and the next, they would be discussing something deep and profound. What an amazing man he was. Why, she was just beginning to realize she hardly knew him at all.

"Yes, that would be a wonderful dream," she responded, feeling a warm glow about her heart. "That's a fine dream. The best I've ever heard."

Three hours later Taggart reclaimed his seat, then bent forward to hand Silky a paper sack and bottle of lemonade. "I found a vendor and thought you might like something to eat," he said, sitting back to unwrap his own food.

Silky slipped a sausage biscuit from her sack and, holding it over a newspaper in her lap, began to eat. They'd made many stops during the morning and now at noon they waited at a small depot between Gordonville and Yellow Tavern. General confusion reigned outside as a grizzled sergeant shouted orders at soldiers lining up to enter the train. So many soldiers, thought Silky. At every stop more Confederates, their grim faces pale with fatigue, stepped on the train until it was now packed with men.

When she and Taggart had left Charlottesville that morning, everything had looked clean and untouched; then as the train emerged onto the Piedmont and started winding its way southeast to Richmond, rows and rows of slave cabins had caught her eye. In the summer they would be bright with honeysuckle and climbing jasmine, and the ground about them well swept, but now, at the beginning of winter, they looked bleak and depressing, with hungry-eyed children sitting near the doorsteps. And the host of charred chimneys from burned plantations left a sick feeling in the pit of her stomach. Standing black against the sky, they reminded her of the flames of violence that had ravaged the gently rolling land.

Everyone in Bear Wallow spoke of the Cause with great loyalty, but as she got her first look at the scarred land, reality crept through her like a deep illness, making her almost physically ill. And the soldiers. Lord, how weak and sick they all looked! The war was all so different than she'd thought, not fine and glorious as she'd expected. She felt her mind changing and growing, putting out fine little feelers as she desperately searched for an explanation that would explain the troubling things she'd seen today.

Her appetite at low ebb, she put her half-eaten biscuit away, and stared from the window, noticing a fine carriage pull up to the depot. Several high-ranking officers got out, the last one respectfully holding the door open for a handsome young man with a mustache and wavy brown hair. The gentleman sported a fine suit, a ruffled shirt, and a silk top hat. In his gloved hand he carried a soft leather portfolio. Taggart had already finished eating, and Silky caught his eye, then pointed out the man with a nod of her head. Evidently this was someone of importance, for the officers escorted him to the conductor, then doffed their hats as the young man entered the train.

In the aisle, soldiers trudged past, being directed to the back of the car by the conductor at the door. When the fine gentleman stepped aboard, the conductor swept a searching gaze about and let it come to rest on Silky. Personally escorting the man down the aisle, he paused within arm's reach, then looked at Taggart. "I was wondering if Mr. Harrison might sit next to the young lady for several hours?" he asked with an embarrassed smile. "At the next stop, I think I can arrange the passengers so he can occupy the car behind the engine and have a whole seat for himself."

Taggart rose and extended a hand of welcome to the distinguished gentleman. "Yes, of course. I'm Lieutenant Taggart"—he glanced at Silky—"and I'm escorting my cousin, Miss Shanahan, to Richmond."

Harrison shook hands with Taggart, took off his top hat and placed it on the rack above his head, and sat down by Silky. He laid his portfolio, emblazoned with the gold initials *B.H.,* on his lap, still holding a gloved hand upon it. "Thank you and the young lady for your kindness, sir," he offered in a cultured Southern voice.

Taggart reclaimed his seat, interest flashing on his face as he glanced at the portfolio, then back at the young man. "I'm acquainted with your last name, sir. Are you perhaps Burton Harrison, Jefferson Davis's personal secretary?"

The gentleman nodded. "Yes, his personal aide"—he smiled gently—"and on occasion his weary courier."

Silky swallowed back her surprise. She knew by the way the officers were treating him that he was someone of importance, but the fact that he was Davis's secretary amazed and astonished her. She noticed that the man's eyes were red-veined, as if he were short of sleep, and utter fatigue lined his finely chiseled face. "Do you work with President Davis every day?" she whispered, so impressed she couldn't hold back the impulsive words.

Harrison chuckled. "Yes, my dear," he replied, placing his hand over hers. "Monday through Friday I'm privileged to pass my time with the President of the Confederate States of America, and I often socialize with him on the weekend."

There were a few moments of tension; then as the train chugged away from the station, a more relaxed atmosphere filled the car. In the background, she heard the soldiers talking and laughing, and caught the scent of their tobacco. "We're going to see my brother in Chimborazo Hospital," she volunteered quietly, first surveying Taggart, then returning her attention to Harrison. "He's been wounded, but I don't know how badly."

A frown flickered over the young man's face. "I'm sorry to hear that," he replied, his brown eyes reflecting heartfelt sympathy. "I hope the wound isn't serious." He observed Taggart with concern. "I'm glad you're escorting the young lady. Richmond is in a deplorable state at this time."

Taggart studied the man, recalling from an intelligence briefing that he'd graduated from Yale and was a junior professor at Oxford, Mississippi, at the outbreak of the war. Intelligent and verbally gifted, he'd wanted to enlist as a common private, but Davis, who thought of him as a son, prevented it and made him his secretary. The thought that Harrison and Davis worked with each other daily fired Taggart's imagination with exciting possibilities. Only a few feet from him was the man who knew Davis's heart, as well as his military secrets.

Her face shining with interest, Silky caught Harrison's attention again. "Is President Davis really as grand as his pictures show him to be?"

The young man considered her for a moment, then seemingly passing her off as the innocent girl she was, began speaking in a tired voice, undoubtedly answering the question he'd been asked a hundred times. He first told her things that Taggart already knew: Davis had attended West Point, built a fine plantation in Mississippi, been elected to the House of Representatives, and finally secured a position as secretary of war.

Taggart studied Silky's face, wondering what was going on in her head as Harrison described Davis's kindness toward his slaves. Yes, sometimes men of integrity and commitment held differing views, but to him there was no way on earth that slavery could be made attractive.

Harrison patted Silky's hand. "Now, my dear, I must ask you to forgive me. If nature will allow, I shall take a short nap. My conversations with the officers ran most of the night and I find myself incredibly spent."

He laid his head back and closed his eyes, a wave of brown hair falling over his forehead. Silky winked at Taggart, and he had to grin, sharing her amusement that they were guarding Jefferson Davis's private secretary as he slept.

After a few moments Silky looked from the window, while Taggart's attention drifted to Harrison, who held both gloved hands over the portfolio in his lap. So near, yet so far, he thought. Perhaps there was nothing in the portfolio but scribbled papers—then again, maybe it contained the information he was seeking. Harrison's grasp, the car full of Confederates, and the speeding train made it irrelevant now.

A few moments later, Silky, who seemed exhausted herself, smiled at him, then also laid her head back to sleep. Deep in his heart Taggart acknowledged the commitment he'd made to get her safely to Richmond without incident, and with a surge of surprise, realized how terribly important she'd become to him. The sound of the clicking wheels engulfing him, he stared straight ahead, his mind full of deep, troubled thoughts.

* * *

Silky noticed a flurry of activity as the train crossed over the James River and, its whistle shrieking, pulled into Richmond only an hour before sunset. Burton Harrison had been moved to another car during their last stop, but the conductor's arrangements had only packed their own car more tightly. Light-headed with fatigue, she stood and waited as Taggart slid their carpetbags from the rack above the seats, then held back the flow of passengers until she could step into the aisle.

When they reached the platform, a porter took their baggage and she stared about in amazement, listening to the sound of the jolting boxcars and the chugging hiss of the departing trains. Smoke produced by the pine-burning engines and the depot's sickly gaslights made her cough. Glancing over her shoulder, she noted that some of the disembarking soldiers were happily reunited with their wives and sweethearts, while others had to be assisted to waiting ambulances, merely rough wagons with crude canvas covers.

Taggart put a hand on her back. "Let's see if we can find a hackney and get to a better part of town," he suggested, guiding her through the crowded depot. Placing a handkerchief to her nose to ward off the stifling smoke, she walked by his side until they emerged into a street filled with old victorias and other shabby carriages.

Once they were away from the depot, cool, fresh air flowed over her, clearing the cobwebs from her brain. An evening chill settled in, but the noon's warmth had melted most of the snow, except for scruffy spots in the shadows. The sinking sun now silhouetted bare-limbed trees along the street and touched fiery light atop the tall gray buildings whose mellow facades made them look as if they had been there forever.

Taggart paid the porter for carrying their bags, then hailed an open-sided victoria, driven by an old man who looked over sixty-five and therefore too old for military duty. She felt the steel in Taggart's arms as he lifted her up onto the torn leather seat, then placed the baggage at her feet and claimed a place beside her.

The driver raised his shabby top hat and regarded Taggart with dim eyes. "Where to, sir?"

"The Spotswood," he answered, settling back and putting his arm about Silky's shoulders.

Within seconds they were off, wheels rattling against the rough paving stones. The old man sat on an open box before them, and often called back over his shoulder, informing them where they were. "That's the Tredegar Iron Works," he wheezed, pointing at a sooty building that belched black smoke. "They manufacture right smart for the war, and remake rifles."

Since their heads were covered only by a leather hood that curved halfway over the carriage, Silky could see all that was going on in the street as they rumbled along. At one intersection, she noticed young recruits carrying remade flintlocks, which looked terribly crude compared to the repeating rifle she loved so well. How could the soldiers fight Yankees with old guns that might blow up in their faces? she wondered, shocked the men didn't have better weapons.

The clomp-clomp of the horse's hooves in her ears, she snuggled against Taggart, amazed at what she saw. "Look at all those people," she remarked in an awed tone. "Why, there's jillions of them. Where did they all come from?"

Taggart laughed. "Most of them were born here, and the war drew the rest."

To Silky, Richmond was a sea of color and movement. A hundred sights and sounds and pungent aromas enveloped her, vying for her attention. There were fancy shops and open markets with potatoes and turnips and deep red apples glistening in the sun's last rays. She saw elegantly dressed ladies and gentlemen, their servants trailing behind, the black women with kerchiefs wound about their heads. There were soldiers and officers everywhere, it seemed, and to the side of the street, brigades of slaves with shovels over their shoulders trudged toward the Petersburg trenches.

Taggart took her hand. "Well, what do you think?" he asked with twinkling eyes.

Silky heaved a perplexed sigh. Everyone was hurrying and rushing so, she thought, remembering the relaxed pace of the mountains. "Why, Richmond is nothing but a big anthill," she answered with amusement, wishing her friends in Sweet Gum Hollow could see it for themselves.

At first only the city's brilliance and intensity caught her eye; then she noticed its underlying air of desperation. RAGS WANTED signs and crudely written notices were plastered on the sides of buildings. Tattered children and beggars held out their hands for food and money. Despite the clatter and disorder, bright Confederate flags snapped atop almost every building, and theaters advertised plays and concerts as if nothing were amiss.

They passed towering St. Paul's Church and the elegant Davis mansion at Capitol Square; then the driver was forced to wait for a teamster to navigate his burden across the intersection. Like a swift blow, the sight of a wagon full of crude pine coffins met Silky's gaze. An old white man drove the wagon while a small black boy, garbed in scruffy clothes, sat atop the coffins, playing a harmonica.

"Them coffins are headed for Chimborazo," the driver called over his shoulder. "A heap die there every day." Silky clutched Taggart's hand more tightly and shivered at the words. This was the Paris of the South she had heard so much about—this dark, churning mass of humanity with its ever-present reminders of war and death?

At last the carriage stopped in front of the Spotswood, a great stone structure of five stories that displayed a Confederate flag fluttering against the ruddy sunset. A surge of weariness passed through Silky as Taggart lifted her from the victoria, then paid the driver. Moments later two porters in the fanciest suits Silky had ever seen emerged from the hotel to carry their luggage in. From Taggart's manner, she could tell he was giving her time to collect her emotions, and she sighed, trying to take it all in. At last, his hand at her back, she slowly walked to the hotel entrance, bolstering her courage before she entered the imposing building.

Once in the beautiful lobby, she noticed it had a fresh, clean smell, so different from the stuffy train that had transported them from Charlottesville. While Taggart registered, she glanced about in awe. The lobby itself was gorgeous: richly colored draperies covered the tall windows, flames glowed in a huge marble fireplace, and a chandelier sparkled from overhead, the first Silky had ever seen. Staring upward, she thought it was spectacular, like an explosion of stars, dripping shiny icicles.

Yes, this was a fine place, a fine place indeed. She swept her gaze over the beautifully gowned ladies who meandered about the lobby with their military escorts. Why, it was all like something out of a fairy-tale book, she finally decided, scarcely believing a place like this even existed.

Taggart returned from the registration desk to escort her up the curving staircase. They had adjoining rooms, both filled with gleaming dark furniture: wardrobes, dressers, velvet-upholstered sitting chairs, huge canopied beds, and gold-leafed mirrors. They inspected her room first, and she realized servants had preceded them as they were checking in, for her luggage was already there. Lights glowed in the delicate china lamps and logs crackled in the fireplace, sending forth a warm, welcoming aroma.

Silky traced her fingers over the dark, polished furniture and caressed the cool satin draperies. Walking from her room into Taggart's, she found it contained a brass-trimmed writing desk that supported a softly glowing reading lamp. How different all this was from her humble cabin, she thought, feeling as if she were moving in a dream. If she'd thought the room in Charlottesville was pretty, these rooms were marvelous, and she told herself the Spotswood must be the best hotel in Richmond.

Hearing footsteps behind her, she turned about, realizing Taggart had been watching her since they entered the suite of rooms. "Will it do?" he asked, his eyes gleaming with amusement.

"Will it do?" she echoed, letting her gaze travel over the gorgeous chamber, then back to him. "I-It looks like a place God might live if he had the money."

Laughing, Taggart crossed the room and took her in his arms.

Yes, it was all more than she could have dreamed, but why was she so tired? she wondered, remembering days she'd tramped over the Blue Ridge for hours without feeling as if she'd done a thing. Then she recalled the frightened, confused expressions on the young soldiers' faces as they were loaded into ambulances, and she understood. Why had

Daniel made the war a glorious fairy tale in his letters when it was nothing of the kind? Then, with a rush of understanding, she realized he wanted to keep her happy, protect her, preserve her innocence, for it was the Southern thing to do.

Seemingly reading her mind, Taggart brushed back her hair. "Don't let the things you've seen today make you sad," he advised, his eyes softening with sympathy. As he spoke she thought of the hungry-eyed children, the charred chimneys, and the wagon filled with coffins. "In their own way the mountains have shielded you from the war," he added, "and it will take a while for your mind to accept it all."

She gazed at him through her lashes, knowing he was far ahead of her in this respect. "It didn't bother me—the things I saw today," she lied, mouthing the words to make him feel better and ease her own shock.

"I hope they didn't," he replied, obviously not believing her, but accepting her attempt at bravery nonetheless.

He lowered his head and brushed his mouth against hers. As always, his lips stirred a passion within her, and she trembled, but she wasn't sure if it was from the thrill of being in his arms or the excitement of leaving the Blue Ridge for the first time. His lips were gentle and, as he caressed her back, she gave way to the peace unfolding within her. Tonight she would lie in the solace of his arms; then tomorrow she would see Daniel. She would see her brother, whom she hadn't laid eyes on since the beginning of the war.

Lord in heaven, she thought with a sudden shiver, nestling close to Taggart's comforting warmth. In what condition would she find him?

Chapter Ten

After Taggart and Silky arrived at the sprawling, white-washed complex that was Chimborazo Military Hospital, a woman looked up Daniel's location and jotted it down on a card. As the pair neared his ward, Silky clutched the card in her hand like a talisman, praying he wouldn't be as gravely injured as the majority of the men she'd already passed.

When they turned into Daniel's ward, she let her eyes stray over a sea of beds dappled by morning light. With a pounding heart, she walked down a narrow aisle that seemed to stretch to eternity, scanning the wounded soldiers, who met her gaze with hopeful eyes. Then she peered across the ward and saw light striking fire atop her brother's red hair as he sat on the side on his bed reading a newspaper. "Daniel . . . that's Daniel," she whispered, tightly clutching Taggart's arm. "I'd know that auburn hair anyplace."

He looked down, his eyes filled with understanding. "Go to him," he urged. "I'll catch up in a bit."

Brimming with happiness, she hurried toward the familiar figure, calling his name. Her brother dropped the newspaper and his gaze held her captive, a look of surprised delight flashing over his face. "Silky, honey," he said softly, tears welling in his wide green eyes as he struggled to stand, clutching to his headboard. "I can't believe what I'm seein'!"

It was then, as he crumpled upon the mattress, she realized his leg had been injured, making it impossible for him to rise completely. A heaviness in her bosom, she ran the distance between them and sank onto his bed, hungrily drinking in the sight of him as he held out his arms. Yes, his eyes snapped like always, and there was the same teasing grin on his lips, but he looked so much older and thinner it tore at her heart. Feeling as if she might burst into tears, she pressed her arms about him, and laid her head on his shoulder, remembering the boy he used to be, but was no more.

He clenched her in a great bear hug, and the warmth and power she detected in his big form cheered her a bit and told her he still had the strength to recover. Leaning back, he swept his astonished eyes over her. "Lord, when I heard you calling my name, I couldn't believe my ears," he muttered, still dumbstruck. He shook her gently, running his big hands over her arms. "You near scared me to death, girl! How in the world did you know I was here?"

She blinked, holding back tears. "I saw your name on a list of wounded, and it's a good thing I did, because you wouldn't have written me with the news, would you?"

He raked back his hair. "Well," he mumbled in an embarrassed tone, "I wouldn't want to worry you none." His gaze flowed from her head to her feet in disbelief. "How in thunderation did a little ol' gal like you make it all the way to Richmond?"

"It wasn't easy," she answered with a chuckle, "but I had help." She glanced at Taggart, who was now walking to the bed, viewing the proceedings with a smile. For a moment the two men silently measured one another; then, from the expression in their eyes, Silky was relieved to see they were going to be friends. "This is Lieutenant Taggart," she announced, proud to be introducing the man she loved to her brother. "He's from Norfolk, but we met back in the Blue Ridge and he escorted me here."

Daniel raised his brows, obviously impressed with Taggart's rank and fine civilian clothing. "I'm much obliged to you, sir, for seeing Silky here," he offered, leaning forward to shake hands. Half turning, he observed his sister approvingly. "She looks wonderful. You must have treated her real fine during the trip."

Taggart chuckled. "I'd be afraid to treat her any other way. You've done a fine job with that little sister of yours. She can outtalk and outshoot any man I ever met."

Daniel's eyes glinted with amusement. "You left one out, sir. She can outstubborn any human alive."

Silky let the men have their laugh, relieved that Daniel still had enough spirit to crack a joke. Then she slowly moved her eyes from their smiling faces and unwillingly focused them on Daniel's injured leg, searching for a way to open the delicate subject of his wound. "How long have you been here," she softly began, now braving a look at his face. "T-Tell me what happened."

He ran a hand over his leg. "My company took a lot of fire about three weeks ago, tryin' to hold off Sheridan. Some Yankee buzzard blasted me with a load of grapeshot and it cut up a lot of muscles. Dr. Cooke sewed them back, but they'll be a long time healin', maybe three or four months." He surveyed her with a thoughtful expression. "He told me I'd walk with a bad limp, but that don't bother me none." Resolve lit his clear green eyes. "Don't worry—I'll walk, all right. I've already laid it out in my mind."

Touched by his courage, Silky dropped her lashes so he wouldn't see her moist eyes. She understood what he meant, for she'd often used the phrase herself. When a mountain person laid something out in their mind, it meant they'd set their heart, will, and spirit on accomplishing a task and would not be defeated. For a moment Silky struggled to get control of her emotions, and glanced at Taggart.

Seeming to understand the situation, he looked around the ward; then his eyes returned to the pair, deepening with understanding. "Why don't you two catch up on things while I walk around and visit?" he proposed, excusing himself so they could share a private moment. Silky nodded, and as his large frame moved from the bed, other patients struggled up on their pillows, eager to talk with someone who might brighten their dull hours.

She took Daniel's hand, a lump of emotion swelling in her throat. "It's been a long breakfast spell, hasn't it?" she stated gently, remembering the day he'd left Sweet Gum Hollow, bursting with enthusiasm to whip the Yankees.

His eyes misted over. "Yep—it sure has. Longer than a rainy Sunday afternoon . . . longer than that view from Apple Hill." They smiled in understanding, and the smile bound them together, easing their pain a bit.

Daniel asked about all the folks in the hollow, and his eyes brightened as she described how, under Charlie's guidance, his hounds were treeing the biggest raccoons in the mountains and gaining quite a name for themselves. For a few moments they sat silently feasting their eyes on each other; then Daniel's gaze rippled over her in awe. "I declare. You look like a page out of a mail-order catalog, dressed up in those city clothes. Where in the world did you get them?"

The frank question made Silky realize she had a lot of explaining to do, so she began at the beginning, telling her brother how she and Charlie had captured Taggart at old man Johnson's pond. As the whole story poured out, only the lovemaking sessions left out in respect for her brother's sensibilities, his reactions went from amusement to concern.

"If he's a lieutenant in the Confederacy, how come he has the time to bring you to Richmond?" he asked, his voice rising with irritation. "That don't seem right to me."

Silky leaned close. "He's doing secret business for the Confederacy someplace nearby," she explained under her breath, "and although he can't talk about it, I get the impression he may be in the city a long time. That's why he could escort me here." She touched his face. "But you have to promise on your life you'll never tell a soul."

Daniel stole an inquiring glance at Taggart, who was now on the other side of the ward, talking to a patient. "You mean he's an agent?" he murmured in an incredulous tone.

"Yep—the finest ever," she answered with a smile, eager to see her brother's expression at the startling news she was about to relate. "And that isn't all. We're handfasted."

"Handfasted?"

"Yes," she replied excitedly, neglecting to mention she hadn't brought the subject up with Taggart yet. "When the war is over we'll be married."

Daniel stared at her wordlessly as the shock of her words hit him full force. Then, blinking in astonishment, he replied, "Are you sure? He looks a mite fancified for the likes of us."

She tightened her fingers about his. "Be happy for me, Daniel . . . be happy."

"I am," he responded with a heavy sigh, "but there are a lot of things I'm tryin' to piece together and some of them don't want to fit."

"I know . . . I know," she said in a rush, caressing his arm. "Sometimes I can hardly believe it myself, but our love is a natural fact. It's really true—true as sunup." She clutched his hand. "We're staying at the Spotswood and telling folks we're cousins, so you just got a new cousin, too."

When Silky noticed Taggart approaching the bed, she squeezed her brother's hand affectionately, signaling him that they should change the subject. They talked a bit longer; then, noticing lines of fatigue on his thin face, she told him good-bye, silently vowing to bring him something nourishing the very next day, and all the days after that. After she'd given her brother a last affectionate hug and a lingering backward glance, she and Taggart walked from the ward, all eyes upon them.

Once they were in the corridor her real emotions rushed forth, causing her to press a handkerchief against the corner of her eye. Taggart put his arm about her shoulder. "Give him some time. I think he'll be all right," he commented, sending her an encouraging smile that wrapped itself around her heart.

Silky nodded in agreement, realizing the Yankees might have shattered Daniel's leg, but they hadn't touched his spirit or his will to recover.

Occasionally they passed doctors murmuring in consultation, women volunteers walking in the other direction, and tired-eyed orderlies. Farther down the corridor they met a bearded doctor, and apparently seeing her distress, he stopped and introduced himself as Dr. Cooke, one of the directors of Chimborazo.

When Silky mentioned she had come all the way from the Blue Ridge to visit Daniel, she could see the doctor thinking, placing her brother in his mind. "A big lad with reddish hair—massive grapeshot injury to his right leg?" he asked, raising his bushy gray brows with a questioning expression.

"Why, yes," she replied, amazed that he could recall Daniel from all the other patients. Despite his position, the man reminded her of a grandfatherly country doctor, and she liked him immediately.

Taggart introduced himself and shook hands with the man, and the trio strolled down the corridor, chatting amiably.

"Shanahan is a fine soldier," the doctor stated, patting Silky's shoulder in consolation. "No complaint out of him." He bent his shaggy head and shoved his hands into the pockets of his long white surgeon's coat. "The Lord knows there are thousands of complaints these poor devils could make," he added, looking at her with eyes that glittered with angry frustration. Deep lines streaked across his brow. "We have almost no quinine, opium, or chloroform left, and damn little food to feed them."

They paused near the hospital's entrance and Silky put her hand on his arm. "Perhaps there is something I can do," she offered, noticing several ladies entering a ward carrying armfuls of newspapers to distribute. "I'll be here often visiting my brother."

The doctor surveyed her thoughtfully. "Yes, indeed," he said, adjusting his wire-rimmed spectacles. "I don't know where we'd be without our female volunteers." He turned, his gaze sliding over Taggart. "Where are you staying?"

"The Spotswood," Taggart informed him, also giving him their room numbers as he shook hands once more in farewell.

Dr. Cooke regarded Silky with compassionate eyes. "You did the right thing in coming, my dear. Your presence will be the best medicine your brother could ever receive."

* * *

"But I have four pairs of pantalets already," Silky told Taggart, sweeping her eyes about the dining room to make sure no one had heard her impulsive statement. She leaned across the table, and in a lower voice said, "No woman in her right mind needs more than four pairs of pantalets!"

Three days had passed since the two had first visited Chimborazo Hospital, and they now sat at a table in the American Hotel, one of the few places in the city that still served meals on a regular basis. They'd visited the hospital after breakfast as usual, this morning lingering as Silky discussed her new volunteer duties with Dr. Cooke; then they'd headed into downtown Richmond for another shopping expedition.

Silky found that many of the stores were closed, and those that were open were so empty of customers as to be almost abandoned, but it seemed that if a person had cash, new garments could still be purchased—albeit at a breathtakingly inflated price. Taggart had bought her several new gowns at what she considered ridiculous sums, and she was presently trying to convince him to return to the Spotswood where he'd ordered the merchandise sent. "I can never wear out all the things you've bought me," she explained earnestly. "Why, I've never had so many fancy-fine clothes in all my life."

He drew on his cheroot, passing a lazy gaze over her. "Don't you think it's about time you had them? All the pretty clothes, and hats, and shoes, and jewelry your heart could desire."

She glanced about the almost empty dining room, noticing two widows, veiled in black, leaving together. "Hush," she said softly. "Everywhere I look I see women in black. How can I think of buying pretty-colored gowns when half the women in Richmond are in widow's weeds?"

Taggart nodded, a faint smile on his lips as he considered her statement. "Well said, Fancy Pants," he acquiesced, placing his warm hand over hers. "If you're going to be conscience-stricken, I'll buy you no more gowns and we'll keep your pantalets down to four pairs even—with as few ribbons as possible." Amusement lighting his face, he signaled for the waiter, paid the bill, and they left the hotel and emerged onto the sidewalk.

Silky watched him hail a hackney, knowing that next week he would probably try to buy her another gown despite her protest. Frustrated, she smoothed her lace mitts and heaved a deep sigh. How did he come by all his money? she wondered yet again, thinking she wouldn't be surprised if he started lighting his cheroots with twenty-dollar bills. In the Blue Ridge there had been nothing to buy, but now that they were in a city, he was always purchasing something for her or Daniel—never himself. If she even glanced at a gown, or hinted that her brother might need something, it was theirs. Yes, his family was wealthy, but it troubled her deeply that he was always able to produce crisp new bills that looked as if they'd never been touched.

Once they were both seated in the carriage, Taggart surveyed Silky's soft face, thinking she was the lovliest woman he'd ever seen. As she twirled a pink parasol and rattled on about how much better her brother was looking, his thoughts drifted, and he recalled the day he'd spoken to the patients in Daniel's ward.

"When will it all end, Lieutenant?" one gaunt, hollow-eyed soldier had asked. "Do you think we can still whip the Yanks?" inquired another, the white bandage about his head contrasting sharply with his tanned skin. "I'd be willin' to give it another shot if they'd let me out of this hospital," vowed a man who looked no more than skin and bones. Taggart's conversations with the wounded Confederates had impressed him with the soldiers' bravery and lingered in his mind like a fever as he began to see the Southerners as likable individuals and not the collective enemy. Then the loss of Ned knifed through him for the thousandth time and he reminded himself that unfortunately they *were* still the enemy.

Silky laughed about something Daniel had said, stirring Taggart from his deep thoughts. With her fashionable garments, she was a stunning beauty and had charmed all the doctors at the hospital. It seemed everyone had believed their story, for most Southern women would be accompanied by a kinsman on a long journey, and Richmond's hotels and boardinghouses were bulging with families visiting wounded men in Chimborazo. Still, Taggart was relieved that his ruse of being a Confederate lieutenant on extended leave had been accepted unchallenged so far.

He regarded Silky's exquisite face, so young in the winter light—her smoky, long-lashed eyes, her full, pouting lips. With a twinge of concern, he tried to ignore the problems swirling inside his head: When would he be able to send her back to the Blue Ridge where she could be happy; how long could he keep her believing his story; and what would happen if she ever found out the truth about him?

He'd managed to get her settled and established a regular routine for her of visiting her brother—now it was time for him to make his first visit to Petersburg. But she was beginning to ask questions, troubling questions that he was hard-pressed to answer, questions that would interfere with his work: What were the details of his new assignment; how long would he be able to stay in Richmond; where did he go when he left her? Yes, since they'd arrived in the city she'd posed scores of questions, questions that kept him busy trying to come up with suitable answers.

Silky eyed Taggart as the slowing hackney rolled to a stop in front of the Spotswood. As he alighted and swung her to the ground she was well aware of his tremendous physical power and the feminine glances his dashing long hair and graceful strength attracted.

With the clatter of wheels and slamming carriage doors other guests arrived; then, from the corner of her eye, she spied a young girl approaching them, a shawl thrown over her head. The slender girl, who on closer inspection looked to be about sixteen, had a lovely face, her complexion a creamy café au lait, and when she smiled, as she did now, her dark eyes sparkled like diamonds. At first she thought the girl held out her thin hand to beg; then she could see her cheap calico dress was clean and freshly pressed and there was a sense of pride and assurance in her walk.

"Do you be needin' a maid for your lady, sir?" the girl inquired politely, touching Taggart's sleeve. "My name be Delcie, and I's worked for lots of fine ladies here at the hotel." She spoke in a soft, slurring voice, her liquid vowels as slow and sweet as molasses. The girl pulled a folded paper from her bodice and placed in it Taggart's hand. "I's a free person of color," she announced proudly. "You don't need to be worryin' about me none. I ain't no run-off slave. This here paper says I's free as a bird."

With a warm expression, Taggart scanned the paper and handed it back to her.

"If you hires me," she added, putting the document away, "I'll come in the mornin' to help the lady dress and do her hair real pretty like; then I'll come again in the evenin' and dress her 'fore supper. I does washin', too, real gentle like so's it won't hurt the lace. And I's fast, too. Why, I's so fast, when I stop it takes my shadow a whole minute just to catch up." She flashed him a big smile. "All I needs is three dollars a week."

Silky noticed how fragile the girl appeared and was touched that she wasn't too proud to ask for work when so many in Richmond, both black and white, were now begging. She knew she would be in Richmond many months while Daniel recovered, and the possibility of having a maid while she was here filled her with surprised delight. Even though she'd always done for herself, she secretly hoped Taggart would agree to the proposal just so the girl's courage would be rewarded.

Obviously amused, Taggart pushed back his hat, and with a smile, scooped into his pocket, then placed several Confederate bills in the girl's hand. "Come back to the Spotswood tomorrow morning, and if you can do all you say, you're hired at ten dollars a week." He studied Silky, an indulgent gleam in his eyes. "The lady you'll be taking care of is my cousin, Miss Shanahan."

Delcie widened her eyes in disbelief. "Ten dollars a week? Oh, sir, I'll sure enough be here!" Her face broke into an ecstatic smile, and she nervously curtsied not once but twice before turning and disappearing into the crowd.

Silky looped her arm in Taggart's as they entered the hotel, pleased with his generosity. " 'You'll be taking care of my cousin, Miss Shanahan'?" she echoed with a giggle, sending him a sideways glance.

He regarded her with twinkling eyes. "Not another word,

young lady. Not another word."

They strolled toward the sweeping staircase until the man at the registration desk called Taggart's name and held up a piece of mail. She watched him go to the desk, then walked over when she noticed him opening the creamy white envelope. "What is it?" she asked, seeing how his eyes raced over a large card with interest.

He handed it to her and grinned. "It seems you've swept Dr. Cooke completely off his feet. He's invited us to a dinner party at his home ten days from now. Evening clothes are required."

With a rush of excitement, she read the invitation as they walked up the stairs. "I've never been to a dinner party. What will it be like? Do you think the doctor lives in a mansion like the ones we pass on the way to the hospital?"

Taggart laughed richly. "Judging from his position, he probably does, and I'd venture to say half the aristocracy of Richmond will be at the dinner."

"Why do you think he invited us?" she continued, pleased and honored the doctor had thought of them. "You're an officer, but I'm no one special."

They entered her room, where all the dress-shop boxes had been brought and neatly stacked by a tall wardrobe, and he took her in his arms. "There you misjudge yourself, Fancy Pants. You're very special indeed—your face, your heart, but most of all your spirit. It seems the doctor is an excellent judge of character." He eyed her with amusement. "Why, as a mere lieutenant, I'll be riding on your coattails the evening through."

Suddenly realizing what the evening would entail, Silky pulled from his arms, worry assailing her. "But I won't know what to do," she wailed, putting a hand to her brow. She paced back and forth, her mind conjuring up all kinds of embarrassing situations she wouldn't know how to handle. "They'll probably have a jillion forks and spoons on the table and I won't know which one to use," she blurted, watching a smile break over his face. "And what if there's dancing after dinner? I don't know any more about waltzing than a pig knows about singing."

She hurried to him and, clutching his arms, scanned his

relaxed face, wondering how he could be so calm when the world was tumbling down about her ears. "I need some lady lessons, and you're the only one who can help me—you will help me, won't you?"

Taggart gave a crack of laughter. "Yes, of course," he answered, holding her lightly about her waist. He sent her a beaming smile of approval. "Don't worry. Before Dr. Cooke's party I can teach you everything you need to know. Why, I'll turn you into a real Southern belle, dripping *y'alls* and *why, thank you, sirs*, and fluttering your fan with the best of them."

"Lordamercy." She sighed, overcome with trembling emotion. "Just thinking about it makes me dizzy headed. I'm gonna be one of those ladies I've read about in the dime novels—the ones with the white skin who are always dropping their handkerchiefs and fainting."

A smile gathered in Taggart's eyes. "We may gloss over handkerchief-dropping and fainting. Personally I've always found fainting women dead bores."

Silky nodded. "Good. I put a bullet in a charging bear once, and if I didn't faint then, I doubt I ever will."

"Me too." He chuckled, tweaking the tip of her nose.

Her spirits high at the thought of being changed to a lady of fashion, she playfully slipped from his arms, then tossed her shawl and bonnet on a chair.

His gaze never leaving hers, he closed the room's shutters, so that only thin strips of light streaked through the louvers to play across the carpet. Knowing that he'd darkened the room so they could make love, she gazed at him with her heart pounding, unable to resist his dark charms. "Is this part of my lady lessons?" she asked, putting a soft purr into her voice.

He placed his hat on the bureau and divested himself of his jacket and tie. A roguish smile playing at the corner of his mouth, he gathered her into his arms and traced his hand over her back in sensuous circles. "I think you already have a good grasp of this material"—his eyes danced with merriment—"but every good teacher knows the importance of reviews."

She felt the warmth of his hands through her gown, and

as his lips met hers, she trembled with emotion. Yes, there it was again—a sweet, sumptuous feeling, rushing through her blood, delicious and overpowering. She looped her arms about his neck, returning the kiss, and shivered with excitement as he pulled the pins from her upswept hair and let it fall about her shoulders.

He deepened the kiss while his hand worked at the small buttons down the back of her dress, at last freeing them from their fabric loops. He pushed the gown over her shoulders, down to her waist, then gave it a firm tug so it slid over her puffed crinoline to pool at her feet. Slowly he raised his head and, his eyes gleaming like fiery jewels, helped her step from the gown and led her to the side of the bed. His nimble fingers removed more of her clothing until she stood in her corset and pantalets, the cool air bathing her skin.

"You should be ashamed of yourself," she teased throatily, excitement already streaking through her.

"I'm never ashamed of myself."

"I know," she whispered in amusement. "That's one of the things I like best about you."

He laughed and untied the drawstring on her ribboned pantalets, then slid his hands into the top of the garment and kneaded her bare hips. Moments later he brushed the pantalets down and they fell to the floor. At last she was nude except for her corset, silk stockings, and high-button shoes. Hungrily taking her mouth once more, he unlaced her corset halfway down the front, then turned its top down, so that her breasts spilled forth.

She moaned as he explored her mouth with his tongue and feathered his finger over her aching nipple, sending her blood pounding through her veins. With an exquisite touch, he rolled the sensitive crest between his fingers until she thought she would faint with pleasure. His lips never leaving hers, he unlaced the rest of the corset and tossed it aside. She sank to the bed with a deep sigh and relaxed into the mattress, wild sensations flaring within her.

After removing her shoes, he lay down beside her. His fingers lingered over the creamy flesh of her inner thighs before he stripped off her stockings, which made a whispery sound as they slid from her feet. Now he gathered her close and bent his head to draw on a taut nipple with loving lips. She clasped his shoulders, pulling him to her, and when his tongue flicked back and forth over her swollen crest in little butterfly strokes, a sweet, liquid fire surged through her, leaving her weak.

He stood, and she watched him undressing, the streaky light from the louvers playing over his huge frame. How much it would hurt her if she ever lost him, she thought, trembling at the possibility. Then the thought surfaced in her mind that until the war was over their time together was brief and unsure at best. At this precarious point in time, it seemed as if the future lay on a dim and distant horizon, covered with dark thunderclouds.

She was somewhat surprised that Taggart hadn't spoken to her about their future together himself, but she firmly shoved the fact aside, refusing to dwell on it. And how many times had she considered bringing up the subject of being handfasted? In her heart she promised herself she would—just as soon as her courage was high enough and she was absolutely sure of his love.

He sank down beside her, inching a thoughtful gaze over her. "I'll vow, Fancy Pants, I can hear wheels clicking in your pretty head. What are you thinking about?"

She traced her fingertips over his high cheekbones and the lines that fanned from his eyes. "I was thinking about the future—about what's going to happen to us," she answered, now smoothing her hands over his shoulders and clutching his corded arms. "When you get to thinking about it, life is so short, isn't it?"

He regarded her for a quiet moment; then a tender smile raced over his bronzed face. "Yes, life is short," he whispered huskily, his eyes dazzling her with passion that threatened to blaze out of control. "So let's start living it."

Pulling her to him, he reclaimed her mouth while his hand glided to the softness of her inner thigh, leaving a trail of fire in its wake. As his skilled fingers grazed over her intimate flesh, bringing her to sensuous heights of pleasure, she wondered how much longer she could endure the sweet torture. Quivering with need, she relinquished the last of her inhibitions as he stroked and teased her womanhood with delicate, erotic strokes.

She gasped as his lips left hers to trail to her breast. There he gently suckled and nibbled, lavishing moist attention on the sensitive crest until she ached to know the complete fulfillment of his lovemaking. With a tremulous sigh, she surrendered to the warm sensations clamoring within her, her heart hammering against her ribs.

Taggart continued his tender ministrations, making Silky light-headed with passion. He was driving her to distraction with the fiery kisses he fluttered over every inch of her skin, and a tremor of pleasure sailed down her spine, making her moan his name. At last a wild, budding ache asserted itself between her thighs, and she clutched his arms, whispering, "Love me, Taggart, love me as if there was no tomorrow."

His hungry lips descended on hers, and he covered the length of her with his muscled body. Her flesh ached with need, and as his hands flowed over her, bringing her to the point of reckless frenzy, she sighed with pent-up desire. Gently he parted her thighs, then slipped his hard manhood into her welcoming warmth. He moved within her, slowly at first, then faster, plunging so possessively she could scarcely catch her breath.

She arched to meet him, matching his rhythm as maddening desire spread through her veins like wildfire. Their breath intermingling, they moved in perfect harmony toward the pinnacle of ecstasy, and Silky accepted his driving thrusts with eagerness. Joy exploded within her like the sun as it rose over the mountains, bathing their peaks in fiery color. Then as she reached her crest, one trembling wave of pleasure after another crashed over her, consuming her with rapturous sensation.

As their bodies and spirits merged as one, Silky experienced a feeling of fulfillment that even her dreams had not been able to capture. Lost in a glorious realm that defied description, all the longing she felt for Taggart rushed forth, filling her with such intense emotion she thought her heart might burst with love.

After a long, breathless moment, she slowly drifted back to reality, nestled in his strong arms. Tenderly he trailed his fingers over her stomach and breasts and, lifting her hand, nuzzled his mouth over each of her fingertips. Content beneath his masterful touch, she felt as if she were floating on a fluffy cloud somewhere high above the world and all its troublesome problems.

He kissed her eyelids and the throbbing pulse in her neck, then sighed contentedly and relaxed against his pillow. "We'll have to schedule another lesson soon," he murmured sleepily. His voice was thick and dreamy and threaded with longing. "It seems I can never get enough of you." Murmuring words of love, he rolled toward her and cuddled her back against his chest, resting a protective arm over her waist.

Silky heaved a tremulous sigh, scarcely believing her present existence was not some fantastic dream. She could never remember feeling this happy, this wonderful, this contented. As she heard his regular breathing, she relaxed and her body melted into the soft mattress.

Yes, life was short, and who knew what lay on that dark horizon? she thought with a prickle of dread, not knowing when she and Taggart might be separated. But he'd escorted her to Richmond to see Daniel and always treated her like a princess. They would talk about handfasting soon—she just knew they would. Telling herself she'd deal with the future as it materialized, she decided to bide her time and be patient.

Taggart would never let her down—not a fine Southern gentleman like him.

Chapter Eleven

Delcie gave Silky's petticoat tapes a last tug, then tied them in a bow and turned her about in front of the cheval glass. "There you goes, missy," she announced, her large brown eyes dancing with life. "I'll be bringin' over your gown now, and afore you knows it you'll be ready for dinner."

Silky watched with awe as Delcie carried the gorgeous pink silk dress, trimmed with frothy lace, across the room. Delcie had been to the Spotswood several times now and Silky liked her more every time she saw her. This evening a red calico dress, frayed about the cuffs and flimsy from many washings, clung to Delcie's slight form. With her thick, curly eyelashes, delicately sculpted face, and ready smile, she was lovely indeed.

The girl had talked incessantly since she'd arrived, but Silky didn't care, for she was beginning her lady lessons tonight, and the chatter diverted her nervousness. After Delcie carefully lowered the billowing gown over Silky's head, she maneuvered her arms into the sleeves, feeling the cool silk against her skin. "Lawsy," Delcie said with a sigh, "you is sure lucky to have lots of money and fine clothes, and plenty of good food to eat. Mighty lucky indeed.''

When the gown had settled over Silky's body, she surveyed Delcie, noticing how slim she was. ''You don't get enough to eat, do you?'' she asked softly, her natural compassion stirred by the innocent remark.

The girl turned her about and started working on the tiny buttons on the back of the gown. ''Well, sometimes I does, and sometimes I don't,'' she answered thoughtfully. ''There's a passel of us free blacks livin' in a shantytown here in Richmond and we all share our victuals. Sometimes we gets a little chicken, but us ain't had any beef in a coon's age. Fact of bein', us just about lives on field peas and sweet 'taters. Sometimes Jim brings in some fish or a coon from the country; then us eats fine for a while.''

''Jim?'' Silky echoed, looking over her shoulder. ''Is he your brother?''

Delcie burst out with a high-pitched giggle. ''No, Jim's my man, missy! A few years back us was both slaves of old Master Talbet, who lived out on the Petersburg Road. He was a good master, but took no foolishness and worked us right smart.'' The girl smoothed the gown's waistline and, her tone as lilting as a melody, added, ''I was Miz Talbet's maid. 'Sides that I do other things for her like feedin' her cats. I always feeds them out on the back porch of the big house, and Jim, he was always messin' around that porch while I's feedin' them cats.''

Realizing Delcie had finished with the buttons, Silky turned and watched her animated face.

''One day I ask Jim if he be in love with one of them cats or he be in love with me.'' Delcie gave a crooked smile. ''Jim don't say nothin' but just grin like a possum; then I knows he's in love with me.''

Silky laughed in amusement.

Delcie's face softened with memories. ''Right after that, the old master died and Miz Talbet be left all alone with all them cats. When her eyes started gettin' real bad, she teached me to read 'cause she don't have no children or anybody else to read to her. I caught on to that readin' business real quick like. Miz Talbet always have me read her letters, and newspapers, and such like.''

Suddenly a worried look tightened her countenance. "Now don't be tellin' anybody that, missy," she softly advised, searching her new mistress's face. "Nobody's supposed to teach us blacks how to read, but sometimes they does when it suits them."

Shock rippled through Silky, for this was the first she'd heard of such a law, and it angered her that anyone should be forbidden to read.

The girl picked up some clothes from the bed. "Afore Miz Talbet went to her reward," she added, her gaze drifting over her shoulder as she hung the garments in a wardrobe, "she gave her other slaves to her sister, but she freed me and Jim. She give us writ-out papers to carry with us, so if the patrollers stopped us they'd know us was free."

She closed the creaking wardrobe door, then sauntered back to Silky. "But all me and Jim got for our freedom was a hungry belly. Us had no land, no mule, no cabin, no nothin' to set up housekeepin'. For a while us just simmered in our misery and scoured the woods for nuts and seined the river for fish. Then I thought of comin' up to Richmond for work. But us ain't found much. These be hard times, missy. And gettin' food seems to be the biggest problem for folks like us." She wagged her head. "Sometimes I gets real hungry for a little meat."

Silky sat down and raised her skirts so she could put on her shoes. "I can understand how you feel," she remarked, remembering the fine meat she'd hung in her smokehouse. "I'm partial to a good ham myself."

"Umm-umm," Delcie exclaimed, sinking down on the carpet and slipping shoes on Silky's feet. "I'd shore like a bite of ham now. All us folks in the shantytown are waitin' for spring so us can find a little wild greens and plant a garden. I reckon the folks in big houses will be plantin' gardens, too, food bein' as scarce as it is.

"You knows," the girl remarked thoughtfully, working on the buttons running up the side of the shoes, "I hears there's big warehouses of food right here in Richmond, filled with weevilly meal and lots of canned meat and such." She looked at Silky with soft brown eyes. "Story is some high-up gentlemens is savin' that food back. They's savin' it to sell to the white folks this spring when everybody will be hungry enough to eat one of old Miz Talbet's cats.''

Silky felt a prick of surprise. ''Is that so?'' she asked after a moment's hesitation. ''How did you find out about that?''

Delcie winked at her. ''Livin' where I does I hears plenty of big secrets,'' she answered in a conspiratorial tone. ''Most of the time the white gentlemens forget us black folks has eyes and ears, and us learns a lot by just watchin' and listenin'.''

The dusky girl stood, her slender hands on her hips. ''Jim and me are wantin' to get married, but things bein' what they is, we can't be rightly hitched like white folks,'' she explained, meandering to the vanity to straighten up the brushes and combs. She turned about, her face taking on a dreamy look. ''Soon as the money comes in, us will go north and get married proper like.''

Silky rose and walked toward her, compassion swelling in her heart. There were almost no slaves in the high Blue Ridge, and this conversation with Delcie had removed a veil from her eyes. Until this evening she had known little of the personal indignities and legal restrictions the blacks endured.

''Now don't be lookin' sad, missy,'' Delcie piped up. ''Me and Jim will make it up north all right.'' She widened her dark eyes. ''I'll do a little dab of work here, and he'll do a little dab of work there, and afore you knows it, us will be across that Mason-Dixon line, war or no war.''

Silky opened the vanity drawer and took out a few Confederate bills given to her by Taggart as pin money. When she placed the bills in Delcie's hand, the girl quickly gave them back. ''Oh, no, missy. Lieutenant Taggart already pays me for comin' here—ten whole dollars a week.''

Silky stuffed the money in the girl's apron pocket. ''Tonight when I'm eating dinner with him,'' she remarked with a smile, ''I want to picture you and Jim eating something good, too. I think it would make the food go down better.''

Delcie's eyes sparkled. ''Why, thank you kindly, missy,'' she offered cheerfully, her voice brimming with gratitude. ''This will be enough to buy a chicken and 'taters and such, and we'll cook us up the biggest, thickest pot of stew in Richmond.''

A lump rose in Silky's throat. Once again she pondered all the things she'd been taught, and began to realize how isolated her life had been in the Blue Ridge. With a sense of growing awareness, she reconsidered slavery, realizing that perhaps it wasn't the innocent, protective institution she'd been told it was.

Later that evening Silky clung to Taggart's hard-muscled arm as he escorted her into the dining room of the Spotswood. All about them elegant people conversed politely as they ate their meals. She'd been here before, but was still impressed with the room's peach-pink, silk-covered walls, and its mahogany tables set with china and silver that gleamed in the light of sparkling chandeliers.

Once seated, she listened to Taggart order dinner over the murmur of soft conversation and the tinkle and scrape of crystal and expensive flatware. A smile played over his face, and as always he looked magnificent, tonight wearing a blue jacket, an embroidered vest, and a white satin cravat that brought out his smooth tan.

The old waiter who was serving them looked at Taggart, a respectful expression in his dark eyes. "Will you be needin' anythin' else, sir?"

"If you have a white wine, serve it with the meal, will you?"

The old man ran a veined hand over his peppery gray-black hair. "I'll see what I has, sir."

They ate a wonderful meal of soup, roast chicken, buttery vegetables, and flaky rolls, with Taggart telling her which spoon and fork to use for each course. The waiter had found a bottle of white wine, and as he poured it, Taggart informed her about wines, spirits, and after-dinner liqueurs, making her wonder what he'd thought of the raw but powerful applejack she'd once served him in the Blue Ridge.

As she consumed the savory food, she scanned the sumptuous room, still amazed that a place like this even existed and that she was here. She also thought of Delcie and Jim eating their chicken stew by a campfire in their shantytown and all the meals she'd cooked over a grate in her own hearth. It seemed, she thought dryly, that where you ate your chicken all depended on who you knew and what color your skin was.

Enthusiastically, Silky helped herself to another roll and a third serving of chicken, cutting into it with relish. Taggart cast her a sidelong glance. "What's wrong?" she inquired softly. "Did I use the wrong fork?"

"Southern ladies eat only one helping of food, and usually not all of that."

"Now that really doesn't make sense at all," she answered, wondering if she wanted to be a lady after all. "Being cinched in a corset all day is one thing, but starving yourself just for manners' sake is something else all over again," she asserted as she looked at Taggart and finished every bit of her chicken.

When the waiter served creamy rice pudding for dessert, he brought out something Taggart called demitasse cups of what now passed for coffee in Virginia, then laid a small spoon beside each cup.

Silky picked up the tiny spoon, examining it. "What is this for?" she inquired, turning it over in her palm. "It looks like a toy."

Taggart's expression softened as if she were an inquisitive child. "It's a demitasse spoon," he answered, spilling a tiny bit of precious sugar into his cup.

Silky laughed, following his example. "Well, if that doesn't beat all. A little spoon just for these little cups," she exclaimed, sipping the bitter brew. Amusement shone in his eyes, and she wondered what she'd said that was so funny.

"Demitasse means half-cup in French."

"Lordamercy," she said wonderingly, setting down her tiny cup. "Why don't they give us a whole cup? This little taste is just enough to make a person mad!"

Taggart laughed and she studied his handsome face, amazed at his knowledge. If she'd ever had a doubt that he was an aristocrat, she had none now. He'd been raised to know the right fork to use and the right wine to order—and could even speak French. No telling what else he knew. He must have been brought up like a prince of the blood.

After she'd finished her coffee, she captured his eyes, yearning to know how he'd acquired all his social graces.

"Tell me about your days before West Point," she ventured. "What was it like growing up in Norfolk?"

Taggart's expression softened. "I grew up in one of those old Georgian mansions," he answered, his voice deep with emotion. "I can still remember how cool and shadowy it felt when I'd walk into the parlor as a boy, and how the study held the scent of leather-bound books." Pain darkened his eyes. "I scarcely have a memory of my mother—she died when I was very young. Sometimes I can almost recall the touch of her hand or the scent of her hair . . . then it's gone." Hard lines streaking his brow, he leaned back in his chair. "My father never remarried. For all practical purposes his brick factory is his life."

Unease rose in Silky as she considered the differences in their backgrounds. Like her, he'd grown up without a mother, but he'd been well educated and had all that money could buy. How simple and awkward she must appear to him. "You're wealthy, very wealthy, aren't you?" she asked, a blush stinging her cheeks.

Taggart rattled his cup down. "I suppose so," he conceded. He inclined his head, then stole a quick glance at her. "One day I'll inherit a great fortune, but I'd rather inherit my father's goodwill." He stared straight ahead for a moment before finally returning his attention to her. "You see, we never got along."

"But why?" she blurted out, honestly surprised.

Taggart tossed his napkin on the table. "He wants me to take his place when he's gone. He's told me that since I was a child." A humorless smile moved over his lips. "I postponed his wishes by going to West Point and starting a military career. Everything went well for a while; then like everyone else I got caught up in the war."

She said nothing, but just listened, remembering that on the way to Richmond he'd told her his dream was to own land, a confession that had astonished her mightily.

"Someday I hope my father and I can see eye to eye on something," he continued, his face hardening with frustration. "I'd like to change things . . . build a bridge between us." He drained his wineglass, then set it down solidly. "Sometimes I think all his money only gets in the way."

"There are many ways of being rich, you know," Silky remarked quietly, tracing the rim of her wineglass.

He ran his gaze over her. "Yes, and I'd say having a lot of money is one of the poorest."

Silky remembered her happy childhood, understanding what he meant. "Pa couldn't give Daniel and me much, but he gave us the will to fight. And he loved us with all his heart—and we loved him, too."

Taggart clasped her hand, making her skin glow with the warmth of his touch. His eyes glistened with understanding and his lips curved into a smile that melted her heart. "Then you're rich indeed—much richer than I," he remarked warmly.

"Step, slide, and step. Step, slide, and step," Taggart repeated as he danced Silky about her bedroom three evenings later. A late-night affair was being held in the ballroom below, and the strains of a lush waltz seeped through the floor, filling the chamber with soft, muffled music.

Overwhelmed that she was actually waltzing, Silky responded to his smooth, powerful moves, amazed that such a large man could be so graceful. Lost in the joy of the moment, she looked at his pleased face, stirred by his manly appearance. They'd been dancing a long time, and he looked sightly rumpled, his collar button undone, his black tie dangling loosely about his neck. He'd taken off his jacket, revealing his wine-colored embroidered vest, rolled-up sleeves, and muscled forearms. A cluster of damp curls clung to his forehead and a satisfied smile touched his lips as he gazed down at her with twinkling eyes.

"So this is all it is?" she asked, enjoying the feel of his warm hand spread over her back. "Why, it's just the same thing over and over again."

He nodded his head. "Yes, see how simple it is?"

How wonderful it was to feel his strong arm about her, to be swept smoothly about the floor as if she weighed no more than a flower. He pulled her closer, and gradually a deliciously sensual feeling swelled within her, prompting her to follow his lead until they danced as one. Just when she thought she knew all there was about waltzing, he negotiated a reverse and she made a misstep. "Oh, wait," she cried, embarrassed. "Show me that again."

Taggart whirled her about the bedroom again, demonstrating another reverse.

"Say, I like that move." She chuckled, thrilled to learn another step. "Let's do it again."

"We will later, but right now I'm going to show you something else," he responded, sweeping her into a low dip.

Silky thought the maneuver so amusing she started laughing and couldn't stop. "Do people really dance like that?" she gasped, trying to get her breath.

"All the time," he answered, leading her through another dip.

They waltzed for a while longer; then the music stopped, and from the ballroom below, Silky heard light applause and faint conversation. She eased away and, smiling, pushed back her damp hair. "Where in the world did you learn all these steps?"

"West Point. It's one of the requirements of an officer and a gentleman, ma'am," he replied, making a gallant bow that started her laughing all over again. They'd had a good meal, several drinks, and were both in a wonderful mood. It was one of those rare times in life when for a few hours everything seemed fine and troubles seemed far away.

Silky heard the orchestra striking up another piece and she slipped into the waltz position. "That was fun," she exclaimed, excited that she was easily catching on. "Let's waltz some more."

Taggart shook his head. "No, we can't waltz to this one."

"Why, for heaven's sake?"

"Because it's a polka. Just listen."

Silky cocked her head, liking the lively music even better than the waltz. Why, this sounded like one of the square dances she'd done back in Sweet Gum Hollow, she decided, her spirits soaring even higher. "This has some fire to it." She laughed. "Show me how to polka."

Taggart took her around the floor and she watched his swiftly moving feet, trying to follow his steps. "No, this one is too fast," she finally conceded, breaking away with a giggle. "I'll have to watch for a while."

"Fine, but who am I going to dance with?" No sooner were the words out of his mouth than he spotted one of her gowns draped over the back of a chair. With a devilish grin, he picked it up and started dancing to the polka, holding the gown in his arms. He danced with a solemn look, once even putting his hand over his heart as if he were in love. Silky knew he was doing it to amuse her, and he looked so funny swirling the gown about that laugh she did, until tears filled her eyes.

"Stop," she ordered, sinking to the bed. She lay back and covered her eyes with a spread hand. "You're too funny. I can't look at you anymore."

Laughing along with her, he tossed the gown aside, then fell on the bed beside her, his expression shining with mirth. "Thinnest girl I ever took around the floor. She couldn't weigh over five pounds," he remarked with a completely straight face. She giggled and he entwined his hand into her fanned-out hair, letting a lock slide between his fingers. "Having a good time?" he asked softly.

"The best," she murmured, her heart tripping a little faster.

Silky noticed his eyes becoming a deeper blue, smoldering with an erotic warmth that made her breath catch in her throat. Gently he cupped her face, and with a low groan he kissed her, crushing her against him with his free arm. At his touch, a sweetness rose within her and shot through her veins, promising a heady pleasure that was hard to resist. He kissed her with fiery urgency, and she clung to him, running her palms over the hard, corded muscles of his back. She could smell his musty scent wafting over her, and feel his thudding heart, and she went all soft and liquid inside, unable to deny him.

At last he released her to nuzzle her ear, his soft breath upon her cheek. "I think we'll go on to another lesson now," he murmured, fluttering kisses down her throat and working his way to the tops of her breasts, which swelled from her low-cut gown.

He lifted his head, casting her a playful look, and Silky trailed her fingers through his crisp black hair, reveling in the spark of fire in his eyes. "I have a feeling," she drawled softly, "that I've had this lesson several times before."

The next morning Silky sat up in bed and watched Taggart slip into his robin's-egg-blue watered-silk vest and button it. She loved the way they'd fallen asleep last night, the way he'd snuggled her back against his chest, and thrown his arm over her, cupping her breast. Even now a deep, languorous feeling coursed through her body, and there was a stirring warmth between her legs, reminding her of their passionate lovemaking. But he was leaving, she thought with a drowsy rush of depression, just when she wanted to be with him so much.

Getting out of the warm bed, she reached for her pink silk wrapper. "Where are you going today?" she asked, slipping into the garment. As she tied the wrapper about her, she noticed he'd already shrugged on a finely tailored jacket that made his powerful shoulders look wider than ever. She walked to him and studied his implacable face, wondering if there was any way to pry the information from him. "You're going to Petersburg, aren't you?" she inquired, tracing her fingers over his determined square jaw. "That's where you went day before yesterday, too, wasn't it?"

His eyes danced with amusement. "You're an insistent little thing, aren't you? Can't a man be about his business without a daily quizzing from you?" Interest flickering in his eyes, he surveyed her thoughtfully. "And just why do you think I'm going to Petersburg, anyway?"

She crossed her arms, very pleased with herself. "Oh, I have my ways," she answered, sashaying away, then turning and playfully gazing at him through her lashes.

He narrowed his eyes, but she was glad to see he'd tempered his stern look with a roguish smile. "Your ways?" he echoed, closing the distance between them and gathering her in his arms. He raised his brows inquiringly. "And just what do you mean by that, you sly minx?"

She pressed her lips together; then, so pleased with her cunning she couldn't keep it a secret, she confessed, "I asked one of the carriage drivers in front of the hotel where you might be going—what destination would take you away early in the morning, and not let you return until seven in the evening with red mud on the bottom of your boots."

Taggart's eyes focused intently on her.

"He said Petersburg—told me there was a heap of red mud down there."

He shot her a commanding look. "I can't confirm or deny your suspicions, Miss Pinkerton, but you must promise me, promise me with everything you hold sacred, you won't tell anyone this—not a soul."

"Yes, of course. How long will you be able to stay with me here in Richmond?" Silky asked, wondering why she could never completely pin him down on the length of time he would be in the area.

Taggart heaved a great sigh. "That's something you don't need to worry about. Probably as long as Daniel is in the hospital." His tone grew more serious by the second. "But if you value what I'm doing for the Confederacy, you must say nothing." He ran his hands over her shoulders and riveted his gaze on her as if to emphasize his words. "Do you understand? Not a word."

There was a moody look on his face, and Silky nodded. He really looked stern now. There wasn't a spark of playfulness about him; therefore she was sure she'd guessed where he was going. How wonderful it was not to worry about him suddenly traveling to another part of the South and leaving her longing for him. "Yes, I understand," she whispered, her fiery loyalty to the Confederacy making his mission a sacred cause to her as well.

"I'm glad that's settled," he replied. He smoothed his hands over her arms and released a ragged breath.

He walked away, but she followed after him, grasping his arm again. "Can't you stay longer this morning? You haven't eaten breakfast."

"I'm not hungry."

"You could visit Daniel with me." She laughed lightly. "After Dr. Cooke's dinner he has some special friend he wants me to meet. He won't tell me who it is. Says he wants it to be a surprise. Can you imagine that?" Determined to delay him, she smiled and suggested, "We could dance some more. We—"

"No," he interrupted. He stared down at her with a distinct hardening of his face, then swept his hat from a console and placed it on his head. "I must go now." He moved away, then turned and scanned her, a hint of annoyance in his gaze. "I have work to do—people depending on me." There was a suggestion of disapproval in his tone that aroused her anxiety, and a troubled silence stretched between them. "Surely you must understand," he added, giving her a last look of regret before he left the room.

Silky heard his footsteps fading away, and she ran to the window that overlooked an area where carriages waited for customers. Moments later she saw him stride to a hackney, speak with the driver, then duck into the carriage and slam the door.

How she missed him—longed to be near his side this very second. So many questions rattled about in her head. What was he really doing down at Petersburg, and just what did his mission for the Confederacy entail? If she only had a thinking place here, like the one in the mountains, she might be able to figure everything out, she decided, gnawing her bottom lip.

Brimming with questions, she ruefully watched the hackney leave the hotel and roll toward the railroad station. Vaguely disturbed, but not completely understanding why, she watched it with her heart as well as her eyes until she could see it no more.

The sound of clopping hooves penetrated the carriage as Taggart leaned against the seat, his mind troubled. He'd already made his first trip to the Petersburg line, presenting himself just as he had in Richmond. In one sense, things were going fine. He'd made friends with a few of the Reb officers and sergeants, all people who could help him and keep him informed. But there was still so much to do, so many places to see on the long line of trenches and fortifications. And things were piling up on him, weighing him down.

There was the problem of meeting Caroline Willmott. At this point, all he knew was that she was a dark-eyed beauty who lived by herself in a fashionable section of east Richmond known as Church Hill. Somehow he must make the acquaintance of this important lady in a way that would not reveal her loyalties to the Union or endanger her in any way.

Then there was that damn dream about Ned that kept disturbing his sleep. He'd had it again just last night, and woke up with the same feeling of despair and desperation. Would the dream never stop? Would the troubling fantasy never leave him in peace?

Most of all there was Silky. Somehow he had to find a way to make her understand he must keep his professional life separate from their intimate moments together. Since he would probably be with her until spring, when he hoped the war would end, that would be particularly difficult. Even now he thought of her inquisitive gaze and insightful questions and wondered if staying with her was hurting his mission more than helping it. How sharp she was, noticing a tiny bit of red mud on his boots. Now that she knew he was going to Petersburg, she would undoubtedly ask him even more questions—questions he must refuse to answer, for he was just beginning to ferret out what the Confederate command was planning for the months ahead.

As far as making love to her, he'd accepted the fact that she was so tempting, so fetching, there was no way he could resist her, even though he knew it would be best if he did. But what red-blooded man could? he wondered, remembering her soft auburn hair, those challenging black-lashed eyes, and those satiny lips always waiting to be kissed. Even now the memory of the night of love they'd just shared stirred his passion anew, making him anticipate the night to come.

The carriage stopped at the railroad station, and he got out and paid the driver. The sound of the chugging engines and shrieking whistles in his ears, he tried to clear his mind of everything but his work. His excitement built at the challenge before him. Surrounded by men in Confederate gray, he walked toward the Petersburg train, knowing one false step on his part could lead to tragedy.

Nine days after she'd begun her lady lessons, Silky awoke to the sound of rattling dishes. Still half asleep, she struggled for consciousness, thinking it was too early for Delcie to

arrive. Slowly pushing herself up in bed, she rubbed her eyes, and through a bleary gaze saw Taggart, tall, handsome, and freshly shaved, approaching her carrying a tray. His eyes danced with life. Even at this early hour, he was dressed in trim tobacco-brown trousers, a white shirt with rolled-up sleeves, and another beautifully embroidered vest, this one of cream-colored satin.

With a blink of surprise, she saw the tray contained cups and saucers, a silver pot of coffee, and a small cake free of icing but drizzled with syrup and decorated with pecans.

Taggart placed the tray on a bedside table, then sank down on the mattress to scoop her into his arms. "Good morning, Fancy Pants," he murmured, the scent of his spicy shaving cologne pouring over her. "Time to get up and eat a slice of your graduation cake."

"Graduation cake?" she rasped, her voice still thick with sleep. "What am I graduating from?"

"Your lady lessons," he announced, elevating a dark brow. "Tomorrow evening is Dr. Cooke's party, so for you this is graduation day."

Silky draped her arms about his neck, feeling his smooth, starched shirt beneath her fingertips. "Y-You're not going to"—she started to say Petersburg, but bit her lips and instead said—"that place today?"

He laughed low and soft in his throat. "Nope, I'm going to spend the whole day with you."

Pleased with the gesture, she hugged him tightly, then eyed the little cake that had undoubtedly cost him a pretty penny. Sugar being such a rare commodity in the South now, she knew it had been made with molasses and would be somewhat heavy, but to her it was the most beautiful cake in the world.

After kissing her lightly, Taggart stood so she could get out of bed and put on her slippers. She watched in amazement as he went to her wardrobe and retrieved the burgundy-colored velvet bonnet he'd bought her in Charlottesville. "Wear this today," he ordered, settling it on her head and tying the long taffeta sash under her chin. "I think it's the prettiest bonnet you have, and this is a day for a pretty bonnet if I ever saw one!"

Never missing a step, he began waltzing her about the bedroom in her nightgown and the plumed bonnet, humming the "Blue Danube Waltz" as she tried to keep up with him. "We're going to have a wonderful morning," he promised, taking her through a dramatic dip and making her giggle. "We'll visit Daniel; then we're going to the American Hotel for lunch. After we're finished there, we'll buy you a fan, the most gorgeous fan in Richmond."

"A fan? Whatever for? It isn't summer."

He threw her a look of mock surprise. "Why, my dear," he drawled, mimicking the voices of the fine ladies she'd seen in the lobby of the Spotswood, "carrying a fan has nothing to do with the weather. You simply cannot be a Southern belle without a fan. It would be shockingly improper to appear without one, don't you know."

Taggart looked down at the saucy little bundle he held in his arms, still warm from a night of sleep. Damn if the little heller hadn't done it, he thought with a glow of pride. In the space of nine days she'd quickly learned everything he'd presented. And what a pleasure it had been teaching her, he thought, recalling some of her wry comments about Richmond society and social conventions in general.

First he'd worked on her deportment. He'd taught her how to reply to greetings, tilt her head when they passed acquaintances, and give the slightest hint of a curtsy when meeting an elderly person or someone of rank. Second, he'd polished up her English, but he hadn't tried to eradicate all her mountain colloquialisms—and he didn't want to. Peppered through her speech, they gave it a tangy, refreshing character, and provided her with a strong sense of individuality.

Yes, the lady lessons had proved highly useful, for besides introducing Silky to city life, they'd kept her so busy she hadn't asked as many questions about Petersburg. Now that his work was just beginning, for her to know what was going on would be disastrous, and he had to keep her curiosity at bay at all costs.

They drank coffee and ate their cake; then when Delcie knocked on the door he disappeared into his room, only to reappear after a decent interval to escort a fully dressed Silky from the hotel.

After the morning he'd outlined, he hailed a hackney and asked the driver to take them to a city park, bisected with gravel paths overhung with giant trees whose last leaves boasted a final show of color. There, beneath bowers of gold and scarlet, in the deserted park, Silky walked down the paths, escorted by Taggart, who gave her humorous advice as they strolled along.

With warm satisfaction, he looked at her walking beside him, her taffeta skirts rustling crisply under her wool mantle. In essence, all his efforts had been to give her faith in her natural confidence and presence, so she could walk into Dr. Cooke's mansion and hold her own with the aristocratic guests. Looking at her today, he was sure he'd accomplished his mission.

"That's it, Fancy Pants, you look gorgeous, but hold your head a bit higher," he advised in a playful tone, firmly gripping her elbow. "Act like your blood is the bluest in the South."

Silky looked at his dancing eyes and raised her nose high in the air. "Blue, sir? Only creepy-crawly things have blue blood. My blood is red and I'm dang proud of it, too," she responded without missing a beat.

Taggart tilted his head back and laughed. "I can see," he said, "that I may have given you the manners of a plantation belle, but I haven't changed your rebellious heart one whit."

"No, and you never will."

Taggart walked backward in front of her, then stopped and, taking off his hat, bowed low. "Damn, I do believe you have it. The walk, the talk, the look. If I do say so myself, you're smashing. Everyone in Richmond will be at your feet."

Silky laughed, loving the look of pride she noticed in his gorgeous eyes. What a fantastic day she was having with him; how wonderful it was not to see that dark look on his face as he prepared to leave for Petersburg! A sense of accomplishment rose within her that she'd come this far, that she'd pleased him, and now had a minimum of the social graces. With a sense of elation, she realized she wouldn't embarrass him, and in her heart of hearts she had to admit she yearned to be a lady so she might have a chance of fitting into his elegant family after the war.

Later, when they were in the hotel, Taggart unwrapped the beautiful fan he'd bought her, and as she sat on the bench at the foot of her bed, laughing at him, he instructed her in its use.

"Fans are not simply for fanning," he advised her, snapping it open and gazing at her over its top. "Fans are for flirting, sending messages"—he folded it together—"and beating off overzealous beaux." He walked to her and, bowing low again, presented the gift. "Now you try it."

Silky paraded about the room, looking over the top of the fan, fluttering her eyelashes, but when he approached her for a kiss, she snapped it shut and smacked him on the arm, making them both laugh. "I do declare, sir, if you insist with this impertinence I shall ask my brother to call you out. He's a dead shot, and when you're lying on your funeral bier stiff and cold as marble, I shall not cry for you."

They talked the rest of the afternoon, Taggart giving her last-minute advice about subjects to be avoided in conversation, the treatment of older ladies, the leaving of calling cards, and the fine points of table etiquette. He touched on every aspect of being a Southern lady, even to the way she should arrange her hoops when she sat down, which confirmed her suspicions that he'd had bountiful experience with the fair sex and their complicated undergarments.

That evening they enjoyed a succulent dinner, once again in the dining room of the Spotswood. As they sat drinking their after-dinner coffee in the tiny demitasse cups, Silky felt Taggart's pleased gaze upon her.

It was all worth it, she thought with pride. All his lessons and lessons and more lessons had given her a confidence about people of consequence she didn't know she had. Of course, she wasn't really like one of the fine women she saw in the hotel who were true ladies, but she wasn't just a little mountain girl now, a little nobody who didn't have an idea how to act around fine folks.

At first she'd been embarrassed that she was so ignorant, but Taggart had persisted and made learning so much fun, she'd finally relaxed and realized being a lady was just about as easy as buttering a warm biscuit. He'd taught her how to dress, and speak, and dance, and even how to flirt, she thought, imagining how surprised the folks in Sweet Gum Hollow would be if they could see her spreading her gorgeous fan, then sinking into a low curtsy, her silken gown blossoming out about her like that of a princess.

Taggart extended his hand and she reached out and clasped it, feeling his strong fingers curl about hers. "Will I do?" she whispered, permitting her gaze to play over his bronzed face.

He gave her a look that spoke volumes, a look that sent her blood racing, a look that made her proud just to be sitting across the table from him.

"You bet," he answered quietly. "You bet you'll do."

Chapter Twelve

"You knows, missy," Delcie remarked, sweeping a brush through Silky's hair in long, relaxing strokes, "I's done decided you is about the prettiest little thing in Richmond whether your hair be up or down."

Silky laughed and looked at the girl's reflection in the vanity mirror. "I'm glad you think so," she replied, tying her wrapper closely about her. "I'm just wondering what Dr. Cooke's guests will think about me tonight."

"Oh, they's gonna like you real fine, especially the gentlemens," Delcie promised, a sly smile rolling over her face. "One look at you and they's all gonna fall out in the middle of the floor with big grins on their faces." She chatted on happily as she worked, talking about everything from the conditions in the shantytown to her and Jim's love life, leaving out few details about either subject. After she'd brushed Silky's hair until it glowed with red highlights, she pinned it back to cascade over her shoulders in loose waves, then teased little curls out about her hairline. When she'd secured the last hairpin, she stood back to admire her work, then softly commented, "Somethin' has been ridin' my mind, missy. Can I ask you about it?''

Silky turned, looking at Delcie's questioning face. ''Of course, what is it?''

''Well,'' the girl ventured, hanging her head, then gazing up once more, ''I knows you and Lieutenant Taggart ain't cousins, 'cause he don't look at you like no cousin. It's writ plain as day in his eyes when he looks at you. He's your man, ain't he?''

Silky felt blood sting her cheeks, then remembered she had nothing to be ashamed of. ''That's right,'' she began slowly, almost relieved the subject had been opened. ''He is and we're handfasted. As soon as the war is over we'll be married.''

Delcie studied her with soft eyes. ''That's fine, missy. I understands these things. Sometimes folks just have to do the best they can, just like me and Jim is doin' right now.''

With one secret out, Silky felt compelled to tell her another, not wanting to deceive her new friend, for whom she had a real affection. ''I'm not . . . not what you think I am,'' she confessed in an apprehensive tone. She leveled a gaze at the girl's understanding face. ''I'm not a lady like you thought I was when you first saw me with the lieutenant. He's been giving me lady lessons for the last couple of weeks. I-I guess you knew that already, though.''

Delcie gave a throaty chuckle. ''Well, I knows somethin' has been goin' on. And some of the things you says make me think you ain't been raised in no big house. But it don't make no difference where you comes from, or what you knows—you is a lady, a fine lady. One of the finest ladies I ever seed. Missy, you got real feelin's in your heart, and that's what makes you a lady''—she picked up a parasol and, twirling it over her shoulder, paraded about the bed—''not some fancy foolishness like this that don't amount to shucks.''

She looked so funny larking about with the parasol and fluttering her eyes that Silky had to laugh, and Delcie started laughing too. Making one last outrageous face, the girl tossed the parasol aside and surveyed her with a kindly gaze. ''Don't you worry, missy; everything you tell me be as safe as a babe in his mammy's arms.''

With a swish of her calico skirt, she put her hands on her hips and sashayed to the tall wardrobe. ''Now let's quit talkin' and decide what you's gonna wear to that fancy dinner tonight,'' she suggested, pulling out several silken gowns and placing them on the bed. ''I's gonna fix you up so pretty them gentlemen's eyeballs will pop right out of their heads.''

Thirty minutes later Silky stood in front of the mirror, amazed at what she saw. Delcie had dressed her in Taggart's latest purchase—a lovely lavender tulle-over-satin dinner gown. An off-the-shoulder shawl collar revealed the perfection of her throat and shoulders, its cotton lace flounce repeated in her short sleeves. A single pink silk rose nestled in her hair and was echoed by one pinned just beneath her creamy cleavage. Draped over a chair, a black taffeta cloak gleamed in the lamplight, ready for Taggart to settle it about her shoulders.

Was this refined young lady in the lavender gown with four ruffled petticoats the same girl who'd once raced through the leafy mountain hollows wearing buckskins? For an instant another reflection rippled before Silky's eyes, and she remembered looking into a pool of crystal-clear water as a girl. Even now she could smell the damp earth and grass and wildflowers, then quick as a shooting star the memory vanished. With a surge of relief, she sighed deeply, realizing she'd always be that same mountain girl whether she wore satin or buckskins. Nothing had ever turned her heart from the mountains and nothing ever would.

She walked in a circle, observing her reflection. ''Do you think Taggart will be pleased?'' she asked, a wave of unease surging through her now that it was almost time for him to arrive and dress for the party.

Chuckling deep in her throat, Delcie pranced across the room and fluffed up the gown's lacy flounce. ''Missy, if he ain't pleased, there's bound to be a few spokes missin' from that man's wheel.'' She pressed her lips together. ''Umm-umm, you be prettier than a princess in a book. Why, you be pretty enough for old Jeff Davis hisself!''

Silky tugged on her soft kidskin gloves; then her lashes swept up to meet Delcie's worried gaze. ''Now what's wrong, missy?'' Delcie asked. ''You looks kind of pale like.

Fact of bein', you is white as a catfish belly. Somethin' else 'sides lookin' fine is botherin' you, ain't it? Go on now, tell me what it is."

Experiencing a flash of heat, Silky snapped open her beautiful fan and waved it furiously. "I don't have any more idea than the man in the moon what those fancy folks are interested in," she answered, slowly walking about her bedroom to absorb her nervousness. Her hands trembling, she stared at Delcie's compassionate face. "I'm just a country girl, plain and simple. I don't know how to talk about anything but crops and horses and home cures. What will I say, Delcie? Lordamercy, what will I say?"

The girl's brows furrowed bemusedly. "Just say whatever come to your head. City folks bein' so set in their ways, you's bound to be refreshin' as a cool breeze." She tapped her foot. "They's gonna 'preciate a lady with firm opinions. I knows they will."

Silky studied her, fighting the doubt rising within her. "Are you sure about that?"

A smile lit Delcie's face. "No—I's not sure," she replied, saucily tilting her head to the side, "I's positively, absolutely, tee-totally certain."

Silky clutched Taggart's hand as their hackney inched its way about a semicircular drive filled with clattering carriages, then stopped in front of Dr. Cooke's mansion, whose windows sparkled with welcoming light. "Lordamercy," she breathed, gazing at the two-story edifice with white columns, wide verandas, and a high, sheltering portico, "that's the biggest house I've ever seen. Just thinking about going in there makes my bones feel all loose and wobbly."

Taggart blessed her with an encouraging smile. "Don't worry. You'll do fine."

He exited the carriage and helped her down, and, her heart beating a little faster, she let her gaze float over him. After receiving the invitation, he'd had a Confederate dress uniform tailored for him, and this evening she was privileged to see her hero in gray at last. His handsomeness tore at her heart, for he towered over the other men in the noisy driveway, and his air of command turned feminine heads, making the ladies whisper behind their fans as to the identity of the new arrival in Richmond.

Silky felt numb with apprehension as he escorted her up the mansion's steps and toward the open door, which shone like a rectangle of orange light. All about her rose the sound of heels on marble, the swish of satin, and the laughter of gorgeously dressed women. Once they were inside the large foyer, warmth and the strains of lilting music rushed over her. Tall, dignified, and radiating Southern hospitality, Dr. Cooke shook hands with Taggart, then smiled and bowed before her. "I'm so glad you could come to our little affair, my dear," he said, kissing her hand. "Your sweet face will brighten our evening."

She acknowledged his words, and after a servant had removed her cloak, Taggart escorted her into the drawing room filled with elegant couples, the men in gray uniforms trimmed with shining buttons and fanciful loops of soutache braid. And how beautiful the ladies looked in their crinolines, bright as tropical flowers. Their hair smoothed into sleek chignons, they wore gossamer shawls shot with golden threads, and lovely taffeta sashes, and from their wrists dangled spectacular fans of swan's down on velvet cords.

Silky moved her eyes over the elegant mahogany furniture, soft Oriental carpets glowing with color, and dazzling chandeliers. Before, she'd only seen pictures of mansions like this in her books, and now she was a guest in such a place, she thought with a thrill of excitement.

"Try this," Taggart suggested, lifting two glasses of champagne from a passing tray and handing one to her.

Tasting the bubbly wine, she looked at him with gratitude, but still felt weak and shaky, as if her legs might buckle beneath her. "I can hardly believe this is happening," she stated, permitting her gaze to circle and occasionally pause on the colorful group that to her comprised the aristocracy of the Confederacy.

Taggart clasped her elbow and began guiding her through the murmuring crowd. "Yes . . . actually it is happening," he allowed with a chuckle, "but you're going to enjoy it, so smile."

"I can't," she whispered hoarsely. "My lips are stiff."

"Well, nod, then."

"I wish I was in the mountains," she murmured, stiffly nodding at an elderly lady in passing. "I wish I was any-place but here."

Taggart put his hand on her back in a comforting gesture and, sipping champagne, they mingled with the laughing crowd, discovering most of the guests were connected with Chimborazo. Everywhere glorious frocks floated past them with a silken rustle: watered taffetas trimmed in rosebuds; cream-colored satins boasting a dozen flounces; velvets dripping with Chantilly lace.

Taggart escorted Silky to a quiet alcove and, cupping her chin, looked at her with sympathetic eyes. "How are you feeling now?"

"Do you want to know the truth?"

A faint smile catching the corner of his mouth, he nodded.

"My heart is thumping around like a frog under a pot."

Before she had time to collect herself, a captain approached and bent low over her hand, kissing it. After an introduction had been made, he gazed at her kindly and asked, "And how do you like Richmond, Miss Shanahan?"

Silky thought of Delcie's advice to say anything that came to her mind, but a great lump rose in her throat. "I—I like it just fine," she finally managed, feeling a blush rise to her hairline. The gentleman regarded her as if he expected her to elaborate on the comment, but it seemed she'd swallowed her tongue and couldn't think of a single thing to add.

Taggart placed her hand on his forearm and, in a protective gesture, covered it with his own. "My cousin is enjoying Richmond immensely, sir," he smoothly added, intervening and drawing the officer's attention to himself. "I'll vow she's visited most of the shops in the city, and we've scarcely been here a fortnight yet."

The captain smiled and moved on to another couple.

Silky held Taggart's gaze as if it were a lifeline. "Oh, I'll never be able to make it through the evening!" she whispered desperately.

He caressed her back. "Come on, Fancy Pants, you can do it," he urged, mimicking her mountain drawl. His eyes danced with merriment. "Remember, a shy dog don't get no biscuits."

The remark, made in an exaggerated accent, forced her to chuckle. From then on, she did feel a bit more relaxed, but much too soon it was time for dinner, and alarm rippled through her anew. Everyone started filing into the dining room, where Mrs. Cooke, a plump lady gowned in soft blue, greeted each guest with a smile.

Silky walked into the huge chamber, Taggart at her side. He lowered his head and softly prompted, "If you'll relax, before the evening is over you'll be a success." That smile she loved so well hovered on his lips, boosting her courage.

A twelve-candle chandelier sparkled over two of the longest tables Silky had ever seen. They were set with creamy china and gleaming silver, and above the tall arched windows, red silk drapes spilled to a glistening parquet floor. Servants dressed in frayed liveries were everyplace, already pulling out chairs and pouring water from silver pitchers. The scent of perfume and burning candles enveloped Silky as the guests closed in to find their place cards and take their seats. To her dismay she found she wasn't sitting beside Taggart, but across the table from him. Feeling that she might faint with excitement, she took her chair, then watched him sit down and nod encouragingly.

As she studied the ladies at both tables, she could see everything was not as it had first appeared. Many of their gowns showed signs of wear, and her sharp eyes saw where flowers and brooches had been pinned over soiled or damaged material. Why, I'm the only woman in the room with a new gown! she suddenly realized, astonished at the revelation. Underneath their veneer of casual elegance the great ladies of Richmond were barely holding on, no doubt all wearing garments that had been made before 1861. And beneath their smiles, she sensed a desperation they bravely tried to deny.

A tiny salad followed a clear soup, and with a sigh she looked about, hoping to start a conversation, but saw most of the guests were more interested in their pork-and-rice entree than in her. As she ate she glanced at an elderly physician on her right, who'd just experienced a coughing spell.

At first she said nothing; then as she became concerned for his welfare, she unconsciously relaxed. Forgetting her prior failures and determined to enjoy at least one conversation that evening, she patted him on the back, searching his reddened face. "If you'd treat that cough with goldenseal, it would be better before you knew it."

The man stared at her in astonishment, then blinked his eyes, his medical curiosity seemingly provoked. "Goldenseal? Why, that's some kind of herb, isn't it?"

Silky smiled, thinking she'd found someone she could converse with at last. "Yes, it is. Up in the Blue Ridge we can't get many bought medicines, so we use herbs like our great-grandfathers did. Granny Woodall uses goldenseal and she'll be ninety-eight this month." She chuckled knowingly. "I suspicion she's really older, but she shaved some years off her age when old man Ferris started courting her last year. They set up housekeeping about six months ago. That herb is a real invigorator. Granny has a rustle in her skirt, and old man Ferris still plays a frisky fiddle—if you know what I mean."

Several of the ladies tittered, and soon all those about them put down their knives and forks and listened attentively. An older woman across the table smiled at Silky and, blinking with sheer curiosity, asked, "What would you prescribe for arthritis, my dear?"

Silky tapped a finger over her lips. "Licorice root, motherwort, and mullein leaf," she answered thoughtfully. "That's what most folks in the Blue Ridge use. Some grind up a little grape root in that recipe, but those of us who've been doctoring a spell look askance at that." She sat back in her chair, seeing all eyes were upon her. "Ginseng is wonderful, too. The mountain folks call it 'sang, and it'll strengthen the body, calm the mind, and lift the spirits. If you take it regular it'll keep your hair dark, too."

At first dead silence hung in the room; then Dr. Cooke, who sat at the head of her table, rumbled with low laughter, making her wonder if she'd said something completely out of place. Placing his water glass aside, he laughed until he turned pink, and gradually everyone else joined in. "I knew the little mountain flower would stir up our blood with her forthright ways,'' he commented, leaning back in his high-backed chair. ''Most entertaining girl to come to this old city in years. She's working at the hospital twice a week now, you know. She'll be a tonic for us all.''

Surprise darted through Silky as everyone at the table shook their heads and smiled at her approvingly. Why, Taggart's advice about relaxing had made her a success, she thought with utter amazement. A warm glow rushing over her, she stole a look at his amused face. With a sigh of profound relief, she decided that the evening that had started out so badly might be fun after all.

A half hour later Taggart finished his dessert, very aware the Southern officers were eyeing him with keen interest. He had to silently admit he was ill at ease socializing with Dr. Cooke's guests. The Confederates in Bear Wallow had made him feel uncomfortable, but he sensed he could outwit them. These men would not be deceived so easily. What were they thinking? he wondered, watching their assessing eyes moving over him, sizing him up. Did they suspect he was a Yankee this very minute?

After dinner he took Silky's arm and escorted her back to the drawing room. ''What did I tell you?'' he murmured, scanning her pleased face. ''You have them eating out of your hand now.''

She blushed and he watched her blossom into the belle of the evening. It seemed that Richmond society had accepted her colorful personality and found it delightful. No doubt after tonight her social acceptance would be assured, and tomorrow morning they'd be deluged with invitations. With a spark of amusement, he wondered what the highbrows would think if they could have seen her spraying bullets at him in old man Johnson's pond.

She was besieged with bachelor officers who crowded about her, laughing at everything she said. Knowing his company wasn't at a premium at the moment, he wandered away from the group and mingled with some of the older officers. He shook hands with a captain who, to his surprise, was not a member of the medical service but assigned to Lee's Army of Northern Virginia. ''Yankees are a damn treacherous lot, something like rattlesnakes, if you ask me,'' the officer hotly declared, his eyes deepening with hostility.

Taggart, who was forced into listening to the man, could only guess how shocked he would be if he knew where his own allegiance lay. And how strange he felt wearing a Confederate uniform—the same type of uniform that Ned's murderers had worn.

''All Yankees are a hardheaded lot,'' the captain continued passionately, his voice dripping with contempt. ''They're plumb distracted on the idea the Union should not be divided.'' His lips thinned. ''If they'd act like gentlemen, they'd realize we're only asking to withdraw with honor. Now that's something every real gentleman should understand, don't you agree?''

A fire kindled within Taggart and he'd never wanted to speak his mind so badly, but he wisely reined in his emotions. From the corner of his eye he saw Dr. Cooke approaching with Silky on his arm, and, only too glad to leave the belligerent captain, he said his farewell and walked toward them.

''Let me introduce you to some of our late arrivals, Lieutenant,'' the doctor offered with a congenial smile. ''I think you'll find them very interesting.''

Escorting the pair across the room, he beamed at a lovely lady in powder blue, who sat by herself on a window seat, a pensive look in her large brown eyes. Taggart had noticed her during dinner, for she had a cool quality that set her off from everyone else at the table, but she'd been seated too far away for conversation.

''This,'' announced Dr. Cooke, taking the lady's smooth white hand and pressing it to his lips, ''is Miss Caroline Willmott, our hospital's lady bountiful. She heads the Chimborazo Benevolent Committee. I'll vow she has donated more funds to purchase medicine than anyone else in Richmond.''

Taggart's heart beat a little faster as he studied the woman, finding she did indeed fit the description he'd been given by the Information Bureau—a wealthy Southern heiress, out of her girlhood years, but still very desirable. To find her here of all places seemed an ironic, almost unbelievable stroke of good luck.

Dr. Cooke coughed discreetly. "You three get to know each other. Being Southerners, I'm sure you'll have something in common," he admonished before backing away to speak with some other guests standing by themselves.

Silky, feeling very out of place, watched Taggart take Caroline's hand and brush his lips over her satiny fingers. "So glad to meet you," he murmured, excitement dancing in his eyes.

A twinge of jealousy coursed through Silky. Who was this Caroline Willmott and why was Taggart so taken with her? Oh, she was beautiful, all right, beautiful in a way Silky could never hope to be, she thought dismally. A wonderful sight to behold, the lady's skin was as white as magnolia blossoms and her cheekbones high and finely sculpted. Her waist was small and dainty and her hands long and slender. Her exotic eyes glistened like jewels, her wide smile was enchanting, and every word she said sparkled with refinement. Why, she was perfect, absolutely perfect, and she smelled so wonderful, Silky thought, trying to identify the scent she wore.

"So nice to meet you," Caroline offered, gazing at Silky with large, sparkling eyes. "I hope you find Richmond to your liking. I can see you've already captured a host of hearts."

Silky's newly won confidence receded like an outgoing tide as she compared herself to the gorgeous creature on the window seat and found herself sorely lacking. This lady's tongue would never cleave to the roof of her mouth in a social situation the way hers was doing right now. "T-Thank you," she finally managed, almost overcome by the woman's powerful presence.

Her heart dipped as the breathtaking lady swung her gaze back to Taggart. Oh, he was smitten—anyone could tell that. His face virtually glowed as he scanned the lady's beautiful form. Why, he looked as if he'd found someone he'd been looking for all his life, she decided, feeling crushed and very insignificant.

With a little start, she felt Dr. Cooke's hand on her shoulder. Half-numb with dread, she heard him say that he wanted to introduce her to someone else. She surveyed Taggart and the lovely lady, hearing the interest in their voices, and catching the excitement in their glinting eyes. How she wanted to stay, but she knew she must go—go with the good doctor, while this magnificent creature cast her magic spell on the man she loved with all her heart and soul. Her twinge of jealousy growing to something resembling a sharp pang, she held Taggart's eyes in a hesitant farewell.

Taggart regarded Silky as Dr. Cooke led her away on his arm, noticing how pale and shaken she looked. He wondered what had happened to her budding self-confidence as he studied her thoughtfully for a moment; then, deciding he would speak with her later, he returned his attention to Caroline's expectant face. "May I sit with you a while?" he asked, anticipation bubbling through his veins like a heady wine.

"Yes, of course," she murmured softly.

She smoothed back her skirt to make a place for him on the window seat, and he sat down beside her, at once enveloped in her gardenia scent.

"Where do you call home?" she asked, gazing at him with patient eyes.

"Norfolk, miss, although I attended West Point and was stationed out West before the war," he answered, letting his voice be as natural as possible.

Her gaze clung to his. "Yes, you've lost most of your Virginia accent, I fear." She studied him long and hard. "If I were guessing, I'd say you'd been born somewhere in the Midwest."

Taggart knew he must let her know his true colors, but as he eyed the roomful of Confederates, he experienced a flash of concern. He noticed Silky stealing glances at him as she and Dr. Cooke talked to an older couple. How troubled she looked, he thought, making a mental note to come up with a believable excuse for his long talk with Caroline.

Then, pulling in a long, ragged breath, he looked back at the lady's finely sculpted face, deciding he must make a commitment and take his chances. "That's because I was really born in Ohio," he answered softly, his heart thudding against his ribs as he took her hand.

He held her startled gaze, noting a deep blush stealing over her creamy complexion. For several moments she only stared at him, her large eyes going liquid with speculation. Her fingers trembled ever so slightly in his, and a pulse fluttered at the base of her throat.

"I've been in the city several weeks," he plunged on, "and every day I've wondered when I was going to have the good fortune to meet you."

Her eyes glinted as his meaning flooded her mind.

Gently he turned over her long, slender hand and, in the open palm, traced the letters *U.S.*

Excitement flickered in her dark eyes, and she tightened her fingers about his in a sign of understanding. "They told me you were coming," she breathed in a soft, tremulous voice, her simple statement shot with deep feeling. "I've been waiting for you."

The next day Taggart leaned forward on Caroline Willmott's settee to accept a cup of deliciously scented coffee from her own white hands. Dressed in a rose-colored satin gown, she sat upon an ornate Victorian lady's chair, her glistening skirts spreading out about her. An expensive cameo edged in gold glittered at her neckline, and her hair was pulled back softly and caught at the nape of her neck in a finely knitted snood. Aided by afternoon light flooding into the room, he noticed a few strands of gray shining at her temples, but somehow they only enhanced her mature beauty.

After sipping the pungent coffee, he met her eyes and smiled. "This is a real treat, Miss Willmott. I haven't had a good cup of coffee for some time now."

From an impressive silver service, she poured a cup of the dark brew for herself. "Yes, indeed," she replied with an answering smile. "I'm saving some to serve to General Grant when he enters the city."

Taggart placed his delicate cup and saucer on the tea table that stood between them. "And when will that be?"

Caroline's eyes shone with happiness. "Sooner than you think, Major Taggart. The general has taken over a sleepy little town at the mouth of the James, just east of Petersburg, called City Point. He has Union barracks there, warehouses, tent hospitals, and a rail line to bring fresh troops right up to the trenches.''

To hear someone address him as Major once more sounded strange to Taggart's ears. But he trusted this lovely lady, trusted her so much that he'd revealed his real rank in the Union army as well as the details of his present mission. Although Caroline had no idea how emotionally involved he was with Silky, she did know something of the twisted path that had brought them to Richmond.

There were footsteps at the door, and, glancing that way, he saw a maid carrying a tray with plates and a small cake to the tea table. While the girl served them, he surveyed the opulent parlor, noticing red velvet drapes, an Oriental carpet, and an assortment of fine dark furniture, including a grandfather clock that towered in a corner, sounding deep Winchester chimes at fifteen-minute intervals.

When the maid left the room, Taggart turned back to Caroline, wondering how a lovely lady like herself could have escaped marriage. And more important, how could such a sheltered person become an intelligence agent, of all things? ''If I may ask you a personal question?'' he gently began, knowing no other way to broach the subject.

She sipped her coffee. ''Yes, of course, Major,'' she replied with a twinkle in her eyes. ''But you need not ask it. I can guess what you're thinking, for I've been asked the question before. I'm sure you're wondering why I'm helping General Grant.''

Taggart nodded and, forgetting his cake, watched her face take on a thoughtful expression. ''It's all my father's fault,'' she answered, a warm smile blooming on her satiny lips. ''He had more money than he could spend and made the mistake of sending me to a Boston ladies' academy.''

Taggart chuckled. ''I wasn't aware that a New England school could change a Virginia girl so much.''

A soft look flooded her eyes. ''In my case it did. I had a professor who changed my mind about many things. He was an abolitionist, and after a few weeks in his history class, ''I saw my whole upbringing in a new light.'' A blush stained her cheeks. "After I returned home, I simply didn't fit in," she continued, her voice roughening a bit with the memory. "My views were so different from those of the young men I met at the cotillions that I knew marriage with one of them was out of the question. And I must admit," she added with a wry smile, "I wasn't timid in expressing my views. Crazy Caroline, they called me. Crazy Caroline, who went north and became a bluestocking." She eased her cup into its saucer. "They still shun me, but it doesn't bother me anymore. My professor taught me the importance of expressing my opinions."

With a spurt of compassion, Taggart wondered if she'd fallen in love with the man, who, like most professors, would have been older than herself and probably married. How she must have struggled to maintain her integrity when she returned to a society that tried to force her into the mold of the traditional Southern belle.

He leaned forward to place his hand over hers, marveling at her courage. "Now I see why your loyalties remained with the Union, but for such a person as yourself to become an intelligence agent is remarkable."

She stood and walked behind the settee, her rustling skirts exuding the faint scent of gardenia. "I understand what you're saying," she returned, holding his gaze with smoldering eyes. "It's one thing to have opinions and hold loyalties, and yet another to risk imprisonment or death."

"Exactly," he replied, rising to his feet.

She tilted her head at one of the windows. "Come, let me show you something. Emma is really the one who put the steel in my spine," she explained, walking to the window and pulling back a lacy shadow panel.

Taggart joined her and looked out at a side yard and, next door, a two-story mansion, which was separated from the Willmott home by a wrought-iron fence.

Caroline turned around, a light burning in her eyes. "As a small child I played with a ball in this little yard. Once when my ball went over the fence, I spied a small black girl sitting on the Spencers' side steps, cleaning shoes. I called to her to bring me my ball and she did." Her face softened. "Her name was Emma and we became the best of friends.

Her mother was the Spencers' cook."

A gentle smile graced her lips. "I believe Emma and I talked to each other every day after that. We stood at that fence and told each other our secrets and our hopes, and when her mother was too busy to notice, I would open the back gate and we would play under the sheltering pecan trees." Her eyes misted over. "We were too young then to know the different paths our lives would take. When I was seven, Papa hired a governess to teach me to read and write, while Emma sat on the Spencers' steps and cleaned shoes."

They walked back to the tea table and she gracefully reclaimed her seat, spreading out her sweeping skirt. "Under the pecan trees I taught her everything I'd learned, and gave her books that she sneaked into the Spencers' attic, where she and her mother slept."

Taggart sat down and steepled his hands, realizing she was revealing her secret heart to him.

"When we became young ladies, we went shopping together, and of course everyone assumed she was my maid. One day when I was sixteen, we came home, and she opened the gate for me, then stepped back to let me enter the yard first. A few days later she started calling me *Miss* Caroline." A heavy sigh escaped her lips. "I tried to stop the spreading gulf between us, but soon after that I was sent to Boston. I wrote her letters, and received a few in return; then they suddenly stopped." She laughed a little. "My first Christmas holiday I think I was more eager to see Emma than Mama and Papa."

She tilted the silver teapot, warming her coffee. "But Emma wasn't here when I got back," she added, moisture glistening in her eyes. "The Spencers had sold her away while I was gone." She looked directly at Taggart. "Can you imagine that? They'd *sold away* my best friend. It made an indelible impression on me—one I'll never forget. I don't believe anyone should be allowed to sell another person like a piece of chattel, do you, Major?"

"No, indeed," he replied softly, now understanding what fired her amazing courage. "I'm of the opinion that we think alike in many ways."

"After Mama and Papa died I gave their slaves freedom

papers, then shocked all of Richmond by hiring them back.'' She shook her head. ''Crazy Caroline's foolishness was the talk of the town. I even financed several servants' college tuition in New England.'' She glanced at the door. ''Lucy, the girl who brought us this cake, is a graduate of a ladies' academy. I've trained her to work in any home in the city. Last night she served at the table of Jefferson Davis himself. She is invaluable to me.''

She sighed again. ''After Fort Sumter, everyone in Richmond was seized with secession fever. As soon as they ran up the first Confederate flag, I took a train to Washington and offered my services to the authorities. There was much confusion in those first days, so it was fairly easy to pass into Washington, especially for a lady.''

Taggart tugged his ear. ''One thing puzzles me, Miss Willmott. You send information to the Federals, but you also contribute heavily to Chimborazo Hospital.''

''Yes. Don't misunderstand my loyalties. I'm Southern born and Southern bred. I don't agree with the goals of the Confederacy, but I contribute money so that Dr. Cooke may purchase medicines to alleviate the suffering of my fellow Southerners. I also take food to Libby Prison to help feed the Union prisoners there.'' She smiled and a dimple played over her cheek, making her look young and almost girlish. ''Some people say I don't know whose side I'm on. They say I need a man to help me manage my father's great fortune, but I don't think so. Then I'd have the man *and* my money to manage.''

Taggart chuckled, then met her gaze, realizing that through the years she must have established an elaborate system for relaying the information she'd unearthed. ''The Rebs have been breaking a lot of our ciphers lately,'' he remarked thoughtfully. ''How do you manage to get your messages into the right hands?''

A sly smile played over her face. ''You're right about the ciphers. Telegraphing messages has become too dangerous, so I just walk them across to Washington or City Point or anywhere I want them to go.''

''Walk them across?'' he said, sitting back on the settee in surprise.

"Yes, I'll explain it to you sometime," she said with a laugh. "Meanwhile, just be assured that if you gather any information about the Petersburg line, I can relay it to the right sources."

The door opened once more and Lucy entered and began clearing away the elegant tea service. When she'd finished Taggart stood. "Perhaps it's time for me to go." He took Caroline's hand and bowed over it in a courtly gesture. "I believe we'll work well together."

She smiled, then rose as well. "Yes, I'm sure you're right." She arched her delicate brows. "How are you with numbers?"

"Good, actually," he answered, a little puzzled. "Why do you ask?"

"As you know, I head the Chimborazo Benevolent Committee, which presently needs an accountant to straighten our tangled financial affairs. I'll tell everyone you have volunteered for the job. Once you have a place on the committee we can meet without stirring anyone's suspicion. Since Miss Shanahan's brother is in the hospital and everyone supposes he's your cousin too, your interest in our group should be quite believable to the citizens of Richmond."

Taggart nodded, realizing just how clever she really was. "I'll see you in a few days, then."

"Fine. The next time you come I'll give you one of the new ciphers. I believe it's almost unbreakable."

The smile slid from her face and she looked directly into his eyes. "We have a lot of work ahead of us, Major Taggart. Both sides are suffering horribly in this war. It *must* be ended."

Chapter Thirteen

The same afternoon Taggart was meeting with Caroline Willmott, Silky walked into Daniel's ward at Chimborazo. All day her thoughts had dwelled on the beautiful lady she had met at Dr. Cooke's dinner party the night before. After she and Taggart had returned to the Spotswood, he'd told her that he and Caroline were discussing a mutual friend from Norfolk. But try as she might, she couldn't forget the glint of excitement in his eyes as he'd looked at the gorgeous creature. Still deeply upset, she'd thought of postponing her visit today, but she'd promised her brother she'd meet his special friend this afternoon, and she just couldn't let him down.

Her mind distracted, she was almost at Daniel's bed before she noticed a young girl sitting beside him in a straight chair, her face aglow as she spoke. With an inward smile, Silky coughed discreetly, thinking today's visit would be interesting indeed.

"Silky, honey," Daniel exclaimed when he saw her. Somewhat nervously, he nodded at the girl, who blushed prettily under his attention. "This is my . . . my friend, Abby Drumond."

A gracious smile touched Abby's rather plain face, making her genuinely pretty for a moment. Silky took her soft childlike hand in greeting, then sat down on the bed.

"This is my sister, Silky, all the way from the Blue Ridge," Daniel announced, patting the girl's arm affectionately.

Dressed in a modest gown and matching bonnet, Abby projected the innocent air of a well-brought-up Southern girl who'd been lovingly protected from the harsher side of life. She had a sweet, tender face, and large blue eyes that were fringed with long lashes. Her straight brown hair had been parted in the middle, brushed to a gloss, then smoothly coiled in a bun just above the nape of her slender neck. From her small person came the faint scents of soap and starch and rose water.

So this was her brother's special friend, Silky thought with amazement, eager to write Charlie about Abby as soon as possible. How surprised the folks in the hollow would be to know Daniel was courting a Richmond girl!

"I'm glad you can visit my brother," Silky offered, meeting her shy gaze. "He's used to being outside, and I know how bored he must get in here."

Abby laughed and looked at Daniel, her face becoming radiant. "Yes, he's told me many stories about the mountains—about some of his escapades—and yours, too."

"We were quite a pair, Daniel and me," Silky admitted with a dry chuckle. "I think we terrorized every coon and possum in the hills. They're probably relieved we're both gone."

Abby glanced at Daniel and a sudden blush tinted her creamy skin with soft color. "You told me you had a sister," she said, her quiet voice scarcely more than a whisper, "but not that she was so beautiful!"

"Beautiful?" Daniel echoed, pulling a face. "Why, she's just a freckle-faced kid." He ran his gaze over Silky in an exaggerated manner. "Say, you don't have freckles anymore. I hadn't noticed before. What happened to them? Did you bleach them off with buttermilk?"

Silky tilted her head, loving their teasing banter. "No, I had Granny Woodall hex them off," she replied, shaking his shoulder playfully, "and I told her to send them all to you!"

They visited for a half hour, talking about Richmond and the war; then Abby stood, her face wreathed in tenderness. "I must go now," she announced, moving gracefully to the bed. "I have some errands to run for Mama." She clasped Daniel's hand, love beaming from her clear eyes. "I'll see you soon."

Silky stood to say good-bye, and the girl respectfully inclined her head. "I hope we get to see each other again," she ventured. "I'm so glad we had a chance to meet."

Silky watched the girl walk away. She carried herself with a quiet dignity that was touching in someone who'd obviously been so sheltered. Then, with a spark of amusement, she surveyed Daniel, noticing that his eyes never left Abby's small figure until she'd disappeared from the ward.

After she'd gone, Silky tousled his hair. "Well, well. It's like that, is it?" She chuckled dryly. "Here I was feeling sorry for you being in the hospital and you're carrying on with some girl!" She sat down on the bed once more, thinking she'd never seen him look happier. "How in the world did an ornery rascal like you meet a delicate little thing like her?"

Daniel's eyes shone with happiness. "Every few weeks some of the nice girls from Richmond come to the wards to serve lemonade and a few sweets—but the rations are so scarce we call the get-togethers starvation parties." He shook his head, a big grin lighting his expression. "But that party was the best shindig I ever went to 'cause that's where I met Abby."

For a moment Silky put her own concerns aside and her heart softened as she listened to her brother rattle on about his sweetheart. Despite the glow on his face, she worried about his and Abby's future in these hard times. But pushing her concerns to the back of her mind, she gave him her wholehearted attention, praying providence would somehow bless the pair.

"Her father owns a lumberyard here in the city, and they're good solid folks," Daniel advised her proudly.

"Abby is just as kind as she can be and has a tender way about her I never noticed in a girl before."

"Lordamercy. Why haven't you mentioned her before?" Silky asked.

A thoughtful look rolled over his face. "I reckon I was kind of saving her for a surprise," he answered with an embarrassed smile. "And since you came to Richmond, things have sort of speeded up between me and Abby. I just wanted you to see her for yourself before I told you about her." His face flushed. "I-I wanted you to like her real bad."

Silky ran her hand over his. "I do . . . I really do. I can tell she's everything you say she is." She studied his pleased face, suddenly realizing that for the first time in his life her brother had fallen head over heels in love. Her throat tightened with emotion as she rejoiced in his newfound happiness. At the same time, she thought of her relationship with Taggart. If only it could be as simple and open as that of Daniel and Abby, she thought, remembering his many secrets and his new infatuation with Caroline Willmott.

Where would it all end? she wondered, trying to hide her worry from her brother. Where would it all end?

When the lilting waltz's last note melted into the air, Silky leaned back in Taggart's strong arms and met his amused gaze. "Let's get something to drink," she suggested over the hubbub of voices in the noisy ballroom. "I'm so dry I could spit cotton." Taggart placed her gloved hand on his arm and escorted her toward the punch bowl, maneuvering between beautiful ladies and Confederate officers wearing resplendent gray uniforms with gleaming gold sashes tied at their waists.

After Dr. Cooke's dinner, the invitations had arrived at the Spotswood in a flurry, requesting their presence at all the Richmond holiday festivities, such as this Christmas ball taking place in Colonel Lehman's mansion, one of the finest old Georgian houses in the city. Feeling all eyes upon her, Silky straightened her back and raised her chin a bit, excited to be at her first real cotillion.

Through the tall arched windows, she spied fluffy snowflakes drifting down, but inside the ballroom it was warm and inviting, and the evergreen boughs and ornamental fruit resting on the fireplace mantel gave the room a gay, festive air. At the refreshment table, Taggart poured her a cup of heated cider, spiced with cinnamon and cloves, but, just as she clasped the warm cup, Burton Harrison approached them, his wavy brown hair and finely tailored suit stirring her memory of their meeting on the train.

A smile wreathing his youthful face, he shook hands with Taggart.

"Oh, Mr. Harrison," Silky exclaimed, truly happy to make his acquaintance once more. "How are you? I haven't seen you since the day I arrived in the city."

Jefferson Davis's private secretary took Silky's hand and bowed over it in a courtly fashion. "No, miss," he answered, his kind brown eyes playing over her. "Actually this is my first social occasion since I returned to Richmond. I've been working with the president, usually until very late each evening." His face softened with concern. "I expect you've seen your brother by now. How is he faring?"

"He's getting better," she replied, somewhat surprised such a busy man would remember Daniel, "but it will be some time before he can walk again. His spirit is strong and I'm sure he'll soon be up and about." She transferred her gaze to Taggart, sensing he wanted to speak to Harrison.

Taggart studied the young man's tired face as he chatted with him, noticing how careworn he appeared. And well he should, he thought, for only last week John Bell Hood's troops had been decimated at Nashville. Although he hadn't seen Davis himself, word was floating about Richmond that he was extremely fatigued and on the verge of collapse. His secretary's appearance only corroborated the rumor. Putting on his best smile, he offered Harrison a cigar, then lit one up for himself.

"Judging from this wrap," the man said, examining the cigar as he rolled it in his fingertips, "I'd say it's Cuban." He breathed in the cigar's spicy aroma, then lit it with relish. "With the blockade on, I was under the impression only Yankees smoked cigars this fine."

Taggart glanced at Silky's curious face, then, making a

quick recovery, sent Harrison an affable grin. "Yes, I received several boxes of Cuban cigars in payment for a gambling debt recently. I believe," he added dryly, "that the gentleman had hoarded them as long as he could."

Harrison laughed and drew on the cigar. "It's fine, very fine indeed."

Taggart regretted his mistake with the cigar, but how was he to know that Harrison was a cigar afficionado? Silky had seemed to accept his line about the gambling debt with no trouble, so perhaps no great harm was done. He'd only talked another five minutes with Harrison when Colonel Lehman approached, a polished saber swinging at his side. The gray-haired officer wore a well-cut uniform, glittering with gold braid on the cuffs and collar and a red strip flashing down the trousers. "Sorry to intrude," he drawled in a grave tone, eyeing Taggart, then Silky, "but if possible, I must speak with Mr. Harrison. It's a matter of utmost importance."

The secretary shook hands with Taggart, then settled his gaze on Silky, an affectionate twinkle in his eyes. "So good to see you again, my dear. If I can be of assistance while you're in the city, please let me know."

Taggart watched Colonel Lehman walk away with Harrison, his hand on his shoulder. The two were in deep conversation, and as they moved into the entry, the colonel signaled a servant to bring the secretary his overcoat. No doubt the South had suffered another loss and Harrison was being summoned back to the Confederate White House. Taggart observed the pair thoughtfully, yearning to know the details of the affair.

At that moment the little orchestra in the corner struck up a waltz, and Silky looked up expectantly. Dressed in a white gown with gold embroidery, she resembled a Christmas angel, or, Taggart thought with a little tug of his heart, the most beautiful bride he'd ever seen. He took the cup from her hand and, placing it on the table, bowed formally. "It seems a shame to waste all that good music. May I have this dance, Miss Shanahan?"

Silky made a sweeping curtsy, her long white gloves outlining her lovely arms. "Why, of course, sir. I'd be delighted,'' she replied, a playful light twinkling in the depths of her green eyes, ''but if you dare say *step, slide, step,* I'll walk off and leave you standing where you are!''

He took her small hand and raised her from the curtsy. In moments they were whirling about on the glassy parquet, enveloped in a sea of swinging skirts and Confederate uniforms. He missed seeing Caroline here tonight, but Silky had asked him so many questions about her, he decided it was probably for the best. He'd temporarily stilled her doubts by telling her he was working with Caroline on the Chimborazo Benevolent Committee, but he knew one false step would provoke her curiosity afresh.

''You look gorgeous tonight,'' he informed her, studying her delicate features and creamy skin. She was no longer a mountain girl in buckskins, but the most ravishing creature he'd ever seen, he decided, his chest tightening with emotion. At the same time, he sensed every other man in the ballroom felt the same way. No doubt some of the officers might want to call on his beautiful cousin, he realized, knowing the possibility would pose a definite problem.

Silky considered Taggart, mulling over the incident about the Cuban cigar. It still troubled her when she thought of Harrison's comment that only Yankees smoked that kind of cigar, but Taggart's remark about the gambling debt had been acceptable, especially when every time she looked at him she experienced a great rush of love and affection. How glad she was that Caroline Willmott wasn't here tonight and she didn't have to compete with the gorgeous creature for his attention! It was bad enough that he had to attend meetings with her about raising funds for Chimborazo, but the committee did such good work for the hospital, it put her to shame to complain.

Looking over Taggart's shoulder, she let her gaze meander over the room and saw a dark-haired officer leaning with crossed arms against a column, watching her. She blinked at his fashionable Zouave-style uniform, for it was a sight to behold. Over a waistcoat of red he wore a jacket of black with red epaulets and rows of silver buttons. Red pantaloons covered his legs, and white gaiters rose almost to his knees. Despite his splendor, the first thought that came to her head was what a wonderful target he would make for some Union sharpshooter.

The man in the splendid uniform cast his sharp brown eyes up and down Silky, seemingly devouring her. At first she was flattered by his attention, but after a few minutes an uncomfortable blush rode her cheeks. Lordamercy, she thought, her heart beating a little faster. Who was this handsome man with the jet black hair, and why was he watching her so intently?

On Christmas Eve, Silky sat by Taggart's side in St. Paul's Church, a place she'd longed to visit since they'd arrived in Richmond. With the war going badly and severe shortages of commodities, a somber spirit pervaded the city; nevertheless, pine boughs and holly berries from the surrounding woods decorated the cold, drafty church. The ancient building was full of creaks and groans, and, from the balcony above her, she heard footsteps and coughing as the last of the parishioners slipped into place.

Wearing a new red wool mantle and fox-fur toque and muff, she glanced at Taggart, who, like the rest of the military men, sported Confederate gray. He was easily the best-looking man in the assembly, but how serious he looked, she thought, wondering what was running through his handsome head. Perhaps he was simply worrying about the war, for on the day of Colonel Lehman's ball, Sherman had taken Savannah, prompting Burton Harrison's early departure from the social gathering. To make matters worse, the flamboyant Union general was now rolling into the Carolinas, destroying everything before him.

Soft organ music began floating over the crowd, and she opened a musty hymnal in preparation for congregational singing. As the pastor claimed his place behind the carved pulpit, a murmur rippled through the worshipers and Taggart touched her arm, whispering, "Look to your left; it's Bobby Lee himself."

With a thrill, she saw Robert E. Lee walking down the aisle to claim a pew, reserved for himself and the group of junior officers who trailed his tall figure. Over six feet and soldierly in every way, Lee moved with purpose and assurance, his short steel-gray hair and whiskers adding to his manly appearance. An immaculate gray uniform, bearing gleaming general's stars, garbed his thick, hard-muscled body, while an elegant ceremonial sword glittered at his side. He radiated an air of gentlemanly dignity and quiet possession, but, with a pang of sadness, Silky noticed deep lines furrowing his bronzed face, undoubtedly carved by his great responsibilities. The stories she could now tell them in the Blue Ridge! she thought with pride. She'd seen the great General Lee himself, and he was as imposing as she'd always imagined.

Taggart studied Lee, thinking how much he'd aged since he'd known him at West Point. Possessing great strength and integrity, the general had borne his responsibilities gallantly, but one look at his tired, pensive eyes said it all. Like Jefferson Davis and his cabinet, Lee was living on hope, trusting that a stroke of fortune might give the beleaguered South another chance for victory.

With Lee and his entourage seated, the Christmas Eve service went on as expected, with singing and fiery exhortations from the pastor to hold to the faith and pray for the success and protection of the Confederate troops. Taggart realized that, ironically, churches in the Union would be filled tonight with weary families praying for the health and success of the Northern troops. So many prayers, he thought, covering Silky's hand with his. So many prayers when only one side could win, and the other must experience crushing defeat.

What would the New Year bring? He knew an old era was passing away. Would a spirit of reconciliation and hope sweep the land, or, after the hostilities, would there be continued strife and bitterness? He glanced at Silky's delicate profile as she studied her open hymnal, joining in with the parishioners who sang "O Holy Night." Where would they both be next Christmas Eve? he wondered with a flicker of sadness.

Would she be back in Sweet Gum Hollow while he was in Ohio, lounging in a paneled study, drinking expensive brandy and remembering this poignant evening in Richmond? Then, with a long, inward sigh, he realized he couldn't torture himself with possibilities. Like the rest of humanity all he had was this dark Christmas Eve of 1884, and he would have to make the best of it and trust the future to providence.

When the service was over, Taggart guided Silky from the church, passing officers in long Confederate overcoats and ladies in fur-trimmed mantles. After the pair had maneuvered their way through the murmuring crowd standing on St. Paul's steps, they walked down Ninth Street, gently falling snow icy against their faces. Illuminated by the glow of gas street lamps, silvery flakes came down in twirling showers, giving the moment a soft, magical quality. All about them were the sounds of the night: crunching footsteps in the snow, snatches of conversation from passing couples, their heads bent against the wind, and, in the distance, the sound of deeply tolling church bells.

Gradually Taggart heard singing, and from the darkness emerged a group of bundled-up children—carolers led by a minister wearing a thick coat, muffler, and a stocking cap. As they paused to listen to the children's pure voices he noted Silky's lovely form. Cold pinked her cheeks, and snowflakes clung to her fur toque and red wool mantle, glittering in the lamplight and giving her the appearance of a lovely Christmas doll. She was so special, so unique, he thought. He wondered what she'd do when the web of deception he'd woven came falling down about them, trapping them both. No, don't think about that! he sternly advised himself, putting his arm about her and drawing her close to protect her from the cold. *Think of tonight and tonight alone. Only by doing that can you survive.*

After another carol the children moved on, the sound of their sweet voices becoming softer and fainter. With a smile, Silky hooked her arm in his. "That was nice—really nice," she remarked thoughtfully, gazing at him with large, moist eyes. "One of the best Christmas gifts I ever received. I don't think a person could ever want anything more."

They strolled on, passing Capitol Square with its statue of George Washington, and the capitol building itself, its windows softly aglow with light. "Well then," Taggart commented airily, surveying her curious face, "I suppose I'll have to find someone else to accept the presents I have back at the Spotswood."

"You bought presents?" she asked, blinking the snowflakes from her long lashes. "You bought presents when half the shops in Richmond are closed?"

"Yes, of course," he answered matter-of-factly. "That's what most people do at Christmas, isn't it?"

The look of surprised delight on her face amply repaid him for bidding for goods on the black market and buying the blockade-run luxuries at a highly inflated price. What will she think of the rest of it? he wondered as they hurried through the snow, locking their arms about each other like joyous children.

After they entered the hotel, Silky rushed up the staircase, both thrilled and embarrassed that with people starving Taggart had bought her Christmas presents. Wasn't it enough that he'd found the wonderful ensemble she'd worn tonight? she thought, recalling the looks of admiration the garments had drawn at St. Paul's.

Just before they reached her room, Taggart beamed down upon her and, opening the door, said, "Merry Christmas, Fancy Pants."

With a small gasp she peered inside, the deliciously pungent aroma of the forest washing over her. A small Christmas tree stood on a table in the center of the room, glittering with decorations and white candles that flickered with light. Beneath the tree, several beautifully wrapped presents, their red bows full and lush, waited to be opened. And before the fire, on a serving table covered with a snowy cloth and set with the finest china and crystal, was a holiday feast crowned with the luxury of a ham, befrilled in paper and crusty with brown sugar and spices. Buttery vegetables, candied yams, biscuits, and a warm pecan pie with a bowl of thick whipped cream finished off the fragrant meal, which was complemented a bottle of champagne resting in a silver bucket filled with slushy ice.

With a flash of happiness she entered the room, removed her toque, and tossed it on a chair along with her muff and coat. What a wonderful medicine this surprise was for her lingering worries. Tonight she could forget about Petersburg, and Caroline Willmott, and everything else that was bothering her. Joy perking through her, she watched Taggart close the door behind him, a pleased grin on his face. She just couldn't figure him out. He could be so secretive and moody at times, then turn around and do wonderful things like this as if it were nothing. "What have you done?" she exclaimed, horrified at the expense of such a gesture, but loving it just the same.

"I thought you deserved a little cheering up. It *is* Christmas, you know," he answered, divesting himself of his hat and long Confederate overcoat.

She rushed to him and threw her arms about him. "How did you manage this? How in the world did you find a ham with all the butcher shops bare?"

A satisfied smile lit his face. "I had conspirators in the kitchen. When I mentioned what I wanted to do, some of the help told me about this enterprising farm wife who lives a few miles from the city. The ham came from her smokehouse and the vegetables from her garden." He nodded at the Christmas tree. "One of the porters put this up while we were at St. Paul's. The decorations belong to the hotel," he added with a dry cough. "They are more or less on loan."

She stood on her tiptoes and laced her fingers behind his neck, feeling the swell of his powerful shoulders. "Yes, I'm sure they are," she replied, kissing him lightly on the lips. "You paid the porter to cut a tree, then had him scrounge around in the hotel attic for spare decorations, hoping the manager wouldn't find out." She laughed with pure pleasure. "Few people would think of bribing a porter to take on such a mission, but I love it, you scoundrel."

He unlaced her fingers, then led her to the sofa, where she sat down, spreading out her huge green taffeta skirt. "I'm glad you approve," he remarked, snapping out a white linen napkin and placing it on her lap. "What use is there in being a scoundrel if a person can't do something outrageous now and then?" He opened the champagne, sending the cork bouncing off the mirror above the mantel and making Silky giggle. "Here, drink this," he ordered with mock severity, handing her a sparkling glass of the bubbly wine.

"Maybe it will calm you down some. You're having too much fun for a refined Southern belle."

She sipped the champagne, feeling its bubbles tickle her nose. "Now remember," she said, wagging her finger at him, "I'm just pretending to be a refined Southern belle. I'm a mountain girl, plain and simple, with hardly any upbringing at all." She directed a hard gaze at him. "If you think this little bit of sour plum juice is going sedate me, you have another think coming. To someone who's used to Uncle Dooley's special three-week-aged white lightning, this stuff isn't any more than a light belly wash."

Laugh lines crinkling his eyes, Taggart sat down beside her and served her plate with a slice of juicy ham and all the fixings that had been prepared to go along with it. The crackling logs sent out a glow that wrapped itself about them, and as they engaged in playful badinage, she surveyed his rakish face, thinking she had never loved him more. All this he'd done to give her one evening's pleasure. A warm, sweet feeling glowed within her heart, and she knew that if she lived to be ninety-nine, this would be the best Christmas Eve of her life.

"Ummm, this is wonderful," she remarked with a full mouth, and not even caring that she did. "Give me more yams and cut me a piece of pecan pie." She waved her hand excitedly. "And be sure to put lots of cream on it!" Laughing indulgently, Taggart obliged. "You know," she added, helping herself to another biscuit and reaching for the butter, "there's enough ham here for a dozen people. Who's going to eat it all?"

Taggart grinned. "The kitchen help. After all, they were the ones who told me where to get it in the first place." He glanced at his pocket watch. "Someone from the hotel kitchen will be up after a while to clear this away; then the scullery maids will eat like royalty tonight." He gave a warm laugh. "I've been told one of the waiters has managed to procure a bottle of whiskey. No doubt there will be quite a party below the stairs tonight."

Satisfaction hummed through Silky. Things couldn't be any better, it seemed. She knew Taggart had already given Delcie an enormous Christmas bonus that left her speechless, and Abby planned to bring Daniel a tasty home-cooked meal. The Confederacy might be in chaos, but everyone she cared about was amply provided for on this cold, blustery Christmas Eve.

After they'd eaten, Taggart lit up a cheroot and escorted her to the Christmas tree so she could open her gifts. She cast aside the red velvet ribbons and crackling wrapping paper to find a lovely silk shawl, a velvet reticule, and French perfume in a crystal atomizer, which she dabbed over her arms and neck. How expensive the gifts must be! she thought, guessing the luxuries had been brought into the Confederacy by blockade runners. A last package produced a book on California. With a cry of delight, she carried the slim volume to the settee, then sat down and ruffled pages that still smelled of printer's ink, discovering drawings of Spanish missions, vineyards, and a rugged coastline with crashing waves.

Taggart stood beside her, cigar smoke circling his head. "This book is less colorful than your dime novels, but more factual, I think," he advised with a nod of approval.

She rose and clasped her arms about his neck. "Oh, I love it. You couldn't have got me anything I'd love more!"

His eyes dancing with merriment, he reached into his pocket and produced a small jewelry box. "I almost forgot this," he apologized, placing the box into her hand. "Go ahead and open it."

For an instant her heart stopped, for she thought he might be giving her a ring; then she realized the box was too flat. Oh well, she told herself, lightly brushing her disappointment aside. *He will give me a ring one day; I know he will.* How could this night be less than perfect when he'd gone to such expense to make everything wonderful for her? She opened the box and a pair of golden filigree earrings, sporting diamond chips, twinkled up at her. "Oh, they're beautiful," she cried, her voice thick with emotion as she brushed back her hair to attach the jewelry to her earlobes. She gazed up at Taggart, noticing touches of humor on his pleased face. "Why, they're prettier than red shoelaces!" she exclaimed, raising herself to kiss his lips once more.

There was a soft knock at the door, and when Taggart

opened it, the kitchen crew entered to clear away the feast. There was laughter, flashing smiles, and "thank you, sirs" aplenty, when, after they'd completed the job, he tipped them generously for their efforts.

At last the pair were by themselves once more, and Silky twirled about, tilting her head to the side. "Santa Claus sure was good to me. Do you think he makes the rounds to those Yankee buzzards, too?"

Taggart laughed heartily. "Well, I imagine so," he answered, his mouth lifting with amusement. "I really don't know if Santa Claus holds Unionist or Confederate sympathies," he added, rubbing the back of his neck, "but considering his worldwide mission, I'll wager he's neutral—like the Swiss."

"Yes, I suppose so," she said vaguely, shaken by the dashing picture he made, standing before the fire in his elegant gray uniform with its gold sash and glittering buttons and trim. "Thank you so much for all my presents. I-I'm sorry. I don't have anything for you," she murmured, truly sad she had nothing to give him.

"Well actually, you might," he replied dryly, taking off his sash and jacket and draping them over the back of the settee. His starched white shirt contrasted starkly with his bronzed face and long black hair, and at that moment she couldn't think of anything she'd enjoy more than the feel of his lips upon hers.

As if reading her mind, he walked to her and took her in his arms, pulling her against his hard chest. She met his questioning gaze and, pulsing with desire, surrendered to the hot sensations clamoring within. For the time being, she pushed aside all her doubts and worries about him and their uncertain future. With the war raging about them, who knew what the future would bring? Absolutely no one. But tonight, she decided fiercely, she would be happy and luxuriate in the joy of the moment.

He lowered his head and brushed his mouth over hers, and she responded instantly to the warmth of his lips, lifted to the stars with a feeling so exquisite it almost took her breath away. Her whole body took on a sensual glow and, excitement swirling in the pit of her stomach, she felt her nipples tingle and strain against her blouse. Taggart gradually broke the kiss and rested his forehead against hers. "Speaking of Santa Claus, I think he has just arrived," he admitted with a sly grin.

Silky clutched his wide shoulders, meeting his amused gaze with a giggle. "Well, Lordamercy, don't stop what you were doing now," she ordered playfully, brushing her mouth against his once more. "I want everything he's going to bring me, and I want it right now!"

With a teasing growl, Taggart nimbly unbuttoned her blouse, slipped it from her arms, and tossed it aside, leaving her in her ribboned camisole. He pulled her to him again, then slid his big hand up her ribs to cup her breast while his lips moved over hers. Tenderly he massaged her flesh, and through the lacy material she felt the warmth of his fingertips at her nipple. With a contented sigh, she decided that dispensing with her corset this evening had been a good decision indeed. When he'd teased both nipples until they were pebbly hard, he eased back, holding her at arm's length. "Is that what you had in mind?" he murmured in a husky voice that was like a caress.

She surveyed his rugged features and, spurred by a hungry need, started unbuttoning his shirt. "Umm, I guess so, but I think we can make a few improvements." She ran her fingertips through the hair matting his chest, reveling in its crisp texture, the warmth of his skin, and, under her spread palm, the rapid thud of his heart. When she pushed the shirt from his muscled shoulders, he momentarily released her to shrug off the garment; then, before she knew what was happening, he tore her delicate camisole downward, splitting the front of it. "I think I'm getting the idea," he replied, a wry glint in his eyes as he removed the torn garment and hurled it across the room.

Pulling her close once more, he began rolling the nipple between his fingertips. Gently he tugged and flicked over the sensitive crest, bringing her to a frenzy of desire. The pleasure was so intense, so exquisite, she could scarcely bear it. Taggart feathered kisses over her face, then, seeking her mouth, kissed it, thrusting his tongue between her lips. He tasted of tobacco and champagne, and, as his plunging tongue continued its leisurely quest, a sweet, moist ache throbbed at the apex of her femininity, arousing her more than ever.

Gently breaking the kiss, he led her to the bed, where soft lamplight gleamed over the silken counterpane and wavered patterns over the wall. He pulled the bedding back, and together they sank upon the soft mattress, the crisp linen sheets cool against their skin. He trailed fiery kisses over her face and throat, and, with a deep sigh, she arched her head back, already slipping into the world of shimmering pleasure she knew so well. When he flicked his moist tongue over her breast, then firmly suckled her nipple with his warm lips, she gave a contented moan, burrowing her fingers into his long hair. His gentle tugging and pulling fanned the growing fires within her, building a hunger so great, moisture quickened between her legs in hot anticipation.

Taggart eased back to unbutton her skirt and untie the tapes on her petticoat. With one smooth movement he grasped the garments at her waist, then tugged downward, removing them over her hips and legs and depositing them on the floor. Next he took off her shoes, then slid his warm hands into the top of her drawers, whisked the cotton garment over her legs and feet, and tossed it on the carpet beside the other discarded clothing.

Silky blushed hotly to think she lay before him in nothing but her silk stockings, garters, and her new gold earrings. His dark head bent over her thighs and his lips touched her there, making her heart pound with such excitement she thought it might burst. Slowly and teasingly, he kissed the exposed flesh above the garters; then he rolled them down her legs, first one and then the other. After the garters had been cast aside, he peeled off her stockings, planting hot kisses down her legs as the silk slid away, revealing more flesh. At last his moist lips played over her bare arches.

He now stood to divest himself quickly of the rest of his clothing, then lay down beside her to take her mouth in a deep kiss. Encouraged by her response, he tightened his arms about her and the kiss grew more bold, sending a warm, tingling sensation skittering through her veins. A hot flush rose from her bosom as his fingers worked their way into the hair covering her woman's mound, then caressed her inner flesh.

Shivering with pleasure, Silky drew in her breath as he flicked over her bud of desire with an electrifying touch. As the juncture between her thighs throbbed sweetly, driving her near mad with need, she moaned softly. When he finally raised his mouth from hers, hot passion flared in his eyes, seemingly demanding a response.

"I want us to be together tonight," she whispered through trembling lips. "I want to feel your lips on mine, and the thud of your heart beating against my bosom," she breathed roughly, her body afire with an unquenchable ache she wondered if she could endure. "I want to remember this night forever."

He lowered himself over her body. At the touch of his warm flesh on hers, she sighed with pleasure, her heart racing out of control. He plunged his tongue into her mouth, and at the same time urged her thighs apart, cradling himself between them. Silky wrapped her legs about him, and, feeling the velvety tip of his hard manhood brushing against the entrance to her femininity, she trembled with longing and excitement.

He explored her mouth with his questing tongue, and rubbed the moist tip of his shaft against her, bringing her desire to a boiling point; then, with one powerful thrust, he groaned and sheathed himself inside her. Now their bodies moved in sweet rhythm, his thrusts met with her own natural upward movements, until their intensity stoked a raging inferno within her.

The shadowy room was filled with sounds—the sound of the snapping fire, the creak of the mattress, soft moans and labored breathing, the slap of flesh against flesh. There were scents, too—lush, rich scents to make one's blood run faster: the scent of the freshly washed bedding, the scent of burning logs, and the fresh scent of Taggart's shaving soap, mingled with Silky's spicy Oriental perfume.

Taggart thrust powerfully and relentlessly, burying himself in the folds of her soft body, until she thought she might faint with longing and desire. How she loved him, wanted him, couldn't get enough of him. A sweet, savage need built up inside her and she wanted to feel him plunging deeper and faster, deeper and faster. Light-headed with desire, she dug her fingers into his broad back, pulling him closer, glorying in the magnificent feeling building within her like a powerful storm.

Then, swept away on a golden crest of release, she cried out his name, her body throbbing with soul-drenching pleasure. On and on he strove, taking her higher and higher, prolonging her joy as long as possible; then when he could contain himself no longer, he spilled his hot seed within her, and she sobbed in release, experiencing heart-stopping tremors. Reveling in womanly fulfillment, she clutched him, luscious aftershocks rippling through her.

With a shuddering sigh, he sagged against her for a moment, then sank beside her, gently pulling her to him and murmuring endearments. Her spirit wrapped in shining bliss, she traced her fingertips over his back and, nuzzling against his neck, savored the dear warmth of him, the beloved scent of him. He kissed her gently, and his hands caressed her face, her hair, her arms, as if she were made of delicate porcelain. Outside the wind moaned and snow pecked against the windows, but inside she was warm and secure enfolded against him. He was so strong yet so tender, she thought, treasuring the glorious moment, and wanting to preserve it forever.

Her pounding heart slowing, she felt herself sinking into the mattress, her body and mind slipping into a hazy world of contentment. Then, as she looked into his soft eyes, a sudden thought caught in her mind like a skirt hem snagging on a bramble. This was the moment to tell him about being handfasted, she realized with a sense of profound relief. She could never choose a better time. Tonight they'd laughed and made love, and she felt so close to him, she was absolutely sure of his love. Yes, take your courage in your hands and tell him now, she told herself, something deep within her spurring her on—tell him now.

Chapter Fourteen

"I was just thinking about something," Silky murmured, idly running her fingers over his back as she nestled against him. She met his tender gaze. "Have you ever heard of someone being handfasted?"

He smoothed his warm hand over her arm. "No," he replied drowsily. "What does it mean?"

She looked into those sapphire eyes that could make her tremble with delight, and began to speak softly, still a little unsure of herself, still a little afraid. "Well, it's a mountain word," she explained, seeing she had his complete attention. "It has to do with an agreement—a commitment of the heart. Sometimes mountain people use it to mean that someone is married without the benefit of clergy."

He looked at her evenly, a little flare of surprise in his eyes, but she went on, trying to ignore her rapidly beating heart. "That's the way I like to think about us," she added, ruffling her hand through his dark hair. "In my mind, the first time we made love back in Jake's cabin, we became handfasted." She swallowed the rising lump in her throat, wondering if she'd made a mistake in broaching the subject.

"You're my man, and you'll always be my man, no matter what happens. A preacher can say words over us, but it won't make me love you any more than I do right now, at this very moment." She searched his eyes, waiting for him to respond in kind, but he remained silent, his face tense and unreadable. "I'll love you in the good times, and I'll love you in the bad times." She plunged on, deciding to say it all now that she'd started. She chuckled lightly. "I'll love you in the crazy times, and the upside-down times, and all kinds of times." She traced her fingers over his chiseled cheekbones, his brow, his firm lips. I'll love you forever and ever and ever."

He gazed at her, awe touching his features. "Is that how you think of us?" he asked quietly, his voice reverberating with puzzled emotion. "That we're married? You feel our bond is that deep?"

She gave a tremulous sigh. "Yes, and I always will—always and always till this old earth quits spinning and falls to pieces." Still she waited for him to make a similar commitment, but he remained silent, and a deep sadness rose within her. Perhaps it was just because he wasn't a mountain man, she thought desperately, fear clutching her heart. Yes, he didn't understand what handfasted meant, she decided at last. He just didn't understand.

His eyes deepened into such a deep sapphire, it almost took her breath away, and she sensed that he was about to speak, but instead he held her close, feathering his hand over her arm. "I've never met anyone like you. I've never had anyone make a declaration like that to me," he finally murmured, his tone soft and tender. "It's something I'll remember all my life."

"But—" she began, studying his face and hoping against hope that he might make some kind of commitment, even a small one.

He kissed her gently, cutting off her words, and even as he did so, she feared she'd made a mistake. He'd said he would remember the words all his life, but he hadn't responded in kind, hadn't said he loved her, too. Maybe he was ashamed of her mountain origins, she thought dejectedly, remembering how rich and well placed his family was.

Panic leaped within her, but Taggart was so gentle, so loving as he caressed her face, her throat, then moved his lips over hers in a kiss that promised love and security. Slowly she began to relax, and when he at last broke the stirring kiss, he looked deep into her eyes and whispered, "Go to sleep, Fancy Pants. Go to sleep, my sweet mountain girl. It's late, very late, and tomorrow is Christmas Day."

Her worries eased somewhat, she nestled in his arms, a drowsy contentment stealing over her. With a sense of relief, she gave thanks that she'd finally had the courage to broach the subject she'd carried in her heart so long. He hadn't said he loved her, hadn't said he considered them handfasted—but he *had* called her his sweet mountain girl. And in his eyes she'd seen something. Oh, she'd seen something, all right, and to her it looked like love.

He'd come around, she promised herself, feeling a little better already. He'd come to understand. It was just that he'd been raised in the city, and sometimes city folks could be a passel of trouble. They were different as they could be, and most of the time a person had to work awfully hard to understand them. She let out a long sigh. Wasn't it just her luck to be in love with one of them? Just before she drifted off to sleep she wondered what the new year would bring. Then she realized that as long as she could be with Taggart she didn't care. In his arms she would always be safe.

Taggart held Silky until he heard her deep breathing and was convinced she was asleep. He caressed her face and arms, wanting to comfort her as he would a lost child. Lord above, he thought, regret sweeping through him so profoundly it left him shaken. This gentle creature, this sweet bit of humanity, considered them handfasted, considered them married. It was almost too much to comprehend. When he'd first made love to her in Jake's cabin, it had been because he simply couldn't help himself. He'd continued making love to her for the same reason, never guessing what was going on in her lovely head. Never in his wildest imagination had he considered them married.

A suffocating feeling came over him as he lay there wide awake, the wonderful Christmas Eve ruined. Her words had suddenly forced him to face up to his deepest motives and desires. How could he go on with this charade, taking advantage of her, letting her trust him when he had no idea what the future would bring?

Bittersweet memories flooded his mind. He remembered how he'd felt when she'd ridden through a blizzard to rescue him; remembered how beautiful she'd looked in her first store-bought clothes; remembered how proud he'd been when she learned to dance and had charmed the aristocrats at Dr. Cooke's dinner party. Did this happiness and pride equal love? Did he actually love her? At this point, his life had been so rearranged by the war he didn't know. Even if he did love her, once she found out he was a Yankee, that he'd betrayed her constantly and repeatedly, she would despise him for sure.

In this war he'd killed men and committed other acts that in peacetime would have been unthinkable. But killing a man at a distance or firing a building was far different from making love to a woman who considered you her husband when you didn't share the same sentiment. The fact that Silky considered marriage so sacred and that she trusted him to do the right thing so fiercely only exacerbated the matter.

Silky's rosy lips were slightly parted and her breathing slow and regular. He reached down and gently brushed a soft tendril from her cheek, letting the shiny hair slip through his fingers. All at once, in that very moment, he suddenly understood what he must do. He would have to fulfill his vow to Ned and himself through another venue. Somehow he had to arrange things so he wouldn't be taking advantage of her trust any longer.

Somehow he had to get himself removed from his mission.

The day after Christmas, Taggart went to Caroline Willmott and told her that for personal reasons he could no longer continue his mission. He'd requested that a message be carried to Grant stating his wishes. He also requested that he be sent back into active duty, into a regiment that was seeing action. God knew he'd rather face a barrage of bullets than continue taking advantage of Silky's innocence. To know that she considered them handfasted, actually man and wife, made the situation intolerable. In his book, only a scoundrel would keep operating under such conditions.

Now, one week later, he sat in Caroline's library watching her rise from her desk chair, a worried look on her face. "I received a message from General Grant yesterday and I'm sorry to inform you that no agent is available to take your place," she explained, her eyes deep and troubled.

Taggart met her gaze, a leaden sensation claiming his stomach. He felt more trapped than ever, trapped and frustrated with a situation that was quickly becoming impossible. He slowly stood. "I know there are more agents available," he asserted defiantly, determined to press the matter. "Surely one of them can—"

"No—I'm afraid it's more than that. At this point it's too late to position another man in the valuable niche you have carved out for yourself." She gave a sympathetic sigh. "I'm afraid you've become a victim of your own success and must finish the mission you've so brilliantly begun." She handed him the message so he could read it himself.

After he'd scanned the paper, he shoved it away and stared from the library window, his mind dealing with a host of prickly questions.

"Considering your strong feelings about the matter, I know something would be arranged if it were possible, but it simply can't be done," Caroline said, walking to him and placing her hand on his shoulder. "You must continue with your mission. Information on the Petersburg line is of vital importance. The Union has enjoyed several great victories lately, but to win the war we must take Richmond. Surely you realize that."

Taggart turned and regarded her calmly. "Yes, I know," he admitted softly. "It's just that—"

"Major Taggart," she interrupted him, "I know you have strong feelings for Miss Shanahan, but men have died for one bit of information, and the possibilities that lie before you concerning Petersburg are staggering."

He studied her anxious face, knowing that in this case he could never make her understand just how intense the feelings of his heart really were. How could he explain such a complicated matter when he had trouble understanding it himself? Wordlessly he bowed over her hand, then turned and left her mansion.

As his carriage rattled down Church Hill he wondered how in God's name he could reconcile his conscience with his duty. He couldn't simply walk away from Silky. For until his mission was finished, until the end of the war, their lives were bound together in a fantastic charade he'd created out of necessity. And as much as he wanted to, he couldn't simply sit her down and explain his actions, for it would be too much of an intelligence risk. Like it or not, he was locked into their bittersweet relationship until it ultimately ended with the tangle of hurt feelings and unbelievable heartache he could foresee, but she could not.

As he reached the Spotswood, he decided he needed to gradually distance himself from Silky, so that when the time came to say good-bye her shock would not be as great. The heartache he would endure during the process was not to be considered. And to face the truth, he thought with fresh pain, he should probably cease physical relations with her. Perhaps in that way he could keep a piece of himself feeling honorable. He couldn't help what had happened in the past, the mistakes he'd made by letting his heart rule his head, but he could have some control over the future.

How he would resist the temptation of her lovely face and body, he had no idea.

In mid January, Silky approached Taggart as he paced about his room, scanning some papers he'd been working on. Smiling, she clasped his arms and sensuously ran her fingertips over them. "Do you have to finish that this afternoon?" she asked, her heart beating a little faster. "Let's talk for a while," she urged, hoping he would give her some attention and perhaps even take her in his arms.

He briefly regarded her, his expression veiled and a bit cool. "No, that's impossible, I have work to do," he bluntly answered. He walked away, sat down at his desk, and shuffled through the papers once more.

Tears stung her eyes. Since Christmas he'd seemed more secretive and evasive than ever—more emotionally remote from her, she decided, staring at his broad back. Deep in her heart she knew she'd made a mistake telling him that she considered them handfasted. Since her admission he'd retreated from her. He was gone so often, stayed out so late, always playing poker with a group of officers at the American Hotel. Something was wrong between them—dreadfully wrong, she thought with a feeling of helpless despair.

Summoning every ounce of her courage, she walked to his desk, determined to find out what it was. "I need to talk to you," she announced, actually taking the rustling papers from his hand and tossing them aside.

Dark hair falling over his forehead, he looked at her blankly. "Very well," he replied mechanically. "What do you want to say?"

Silky couldn't believe her ears. The man who'd always been so warm and caring, so passionate and full of life, now seemed coolly impersonal and remote. "D-Do you know we haven't made love since Christmas Eve?" she stammered, feeling a blush heat her cheeks even as she said the words. "That was three weeks ago."

He stared at her silently for a moment, then rose and combed a hand through his hair. Turning his back to her once more, he strode to the windows and stood there, golden light streaming over him.

What was wrong with him? she wondered frantically. Lately his reactions left her totally puzzled. A few days ago when the Richmond papers had printed the terrible news about the loss of Fort Fisher on the North Carolina coast, it didn't seem to phase him a lick. True, he expressed deep concern about the fall of the last Confederate port, but she sometimes sensed he really didn't care, and the thought chilled her more than the winter wind. If only she could break through this wall of reserve he'd built about himself and make him talk to her.

She moved to him, wanting to smooth her hands over his hard-muscled shoulders, but she feared he might walk away again. "What's wrong?" she suddenly asked, her voice raw with emotion. "Have I done something? Offended you in some way?" she inquired, her pride cut to the quick.

He continued to stare through the lacy curtains, the only sound the rattle of supply wagons from the street below; then at last he spoke in a deep but almost emotionless voice. "No," he answered quietly. "Nothing is wrong. You haven't offended me. You're usually asleep when I go to bed. I didn't want to wake you."

Silky felt a flicker of hope, and she tried to believe what he was saying, but in her heart of hearts she could not. "But we never talk anymore—never laugh like we used to."

"I've been busy," came the answer. "Certainly you know how busy I've been."

"I see," she replied softly, bravely accepting his excuse with a husky whisper. "I just hoped we might spend some time together."

In the mountains the girl she was might have reacted more aggressively, pursuing the subject further, but she was no longer that girl. She was a full-grown woman, changed and tempered by the things she'd passed through these last months. And although she sometimes made light of being a lady, she secretly wanted to be one very badly so she would be worthy of Taggart's upbringing. Surely a lady would handle this delicate situation with quiet dignity and do nothing that would lessen his opinion of her. Still, his sudden and mysterious rejection crushed her, and she longed desperately to make things right between them.

Taggart turned and considered Silky's dejected countenance, realizing how hungry she was for a bit of companionship. As planned, he'd spent less time with her lately, waiting until she'd gone to sleep before retiring so he wouldn't be tempted to make love to her. But noticing her dispirited expression, he asked himself if he'd gone too far. Perhaps he'd cut himself off from her too much in his attempt to put some space between them. And after all, who knew how long they still had with each other before Grant took possession of Richmond and put an end to the war? All this in his mind, he realized he owed her at least one day's outing to relieve the winter's tedium.

He'd already decided to take the train to Petersburg the next day, then rent a buggy and revisit some of the fortifications that made a southern loop about that city. Since she'd already guessed where his mission was and he hadn't planned to speak with anyone, no real harm would be done by bringing her along. Drawing in a deep breath, he rubbed the back of his neck. "Would you like to accompany me to Petersburg tomorrow?" he proposed thoughtfully, watching her face bloom with joy even as he spoke the words.

"So that *is* where you go," Silky remarked with glistening eyes, obviously thrilled that he'd invited her. She walked to him and circled her arms about his neck, forcing him to fight every natural impulse within him for kissing her.

A radiant expression lit her countenance. "Yes, of course, I'd love to come," she answered, her warm voice resonant with happiness.

The next afternoon Taggart pulled a buggy off the side of the dirt road that ran parallel to Petersburg's earthen breastworks. Feeling Silky clutch his arm, he turned to her, glad he'd asked her to come. He decided he needed to give her some companionship today, but still maintain a distance between them. Only, God knew how difficult that would be when he wanted to make love to her this very moment.

Dressed in her red wool mantle and sporting a fur muff, she looked the picture of fashion. A chilly wind whipped little strands of hair from beneath her toque and pinked her cheeks, making her look especially young and pretty. To a casual observer, she might appear nothing more than another lovely Southern belle, but from the sympathetic look in her eyes as she observed the soldiers, he knew she had weightier matters in mind.

He pointed at a group of soldiers standing atop a breastwork. "The men have been dug in, holding this line for nine months. Living in that maze of trenches they're exposed to the sun and rain as well as shell and mortar fire." He let his gaze travel over her, noting a frown knitting her smooth brow.

"Why are they standing out in the open?" she asked. "That looks mighty dangerous to me."

Taggart laughed. "It is. Some Yankee sharpshooter could pick them off in a heartbeat if he had a mind to. The poor devils are so bored they've become utterly reckless."

He snapped the reins and the team slowly pulled the creaking buggy back onto the road, billowing up little puffs of dust behind them. For another hour he and Silky rode about the Confederate battlements, and when the ragged soldiers shouted and waved their caps at her, she returned their greeting, raising her slim, black-gloved hand.

Pulling her mantle tightly about her against the icy wind, Silky scanned Taggart's face, shaded by a slouchy Confederate officer's hat. Just look at his expression, she told herself wearily. He's totally absorbed in those trenches and breastworks. Why, all he talks about or thinks about is the war, she thought sadly, snuggling against him just to make sure he knew she was there.

Once again she told herself that she'd made a mistake telling him that she considered them handfasted. Perhaps he was busy as he always said, but more likely he was just tired of her, she worried, desperation welling up within her. Her greatest fear, the possibility that some gorgeous woman like Caroline Willmott would steal him away from her, tied her stomach in knots every time she considered it.

She glanced at his clear-cut profile. Well, she'd just have to worm her way back into his affections, she thought with fresh determination. And today would be a good start. Why, it was the first afternoon she'd had him all to herself in weeks. Putting on a smile, she leaned against his shoulder, feeling steely muscles ripple under his overcoat. "Why are you always coming down here to Petersburg?" she quizzed. She was truly interested, but also trying simply to stir up some kind of conversation between them. "Why are you so interested in these old trenches?"

Taggart lit a cheroot and looked down at her. Narrowing his eyes against the cigar smoke, he met her searching gaze. "As I've told you so many times before, that's my business, Miss Pinkerton," he answered, not unkindly, but with a smidgen of irritation. He studied her inquisitive eyes. "You haven't told anyone about my visits here, have you?"

She laughed merrily. "No, of course not. Who would I tell? Delcie?"

"Good, see that you never do," he ordered, putting some authority into his voice. "The fact that I come here is our secret and our secret alone. Understand?"

She let out a frustrated sigh. "Yes, yes, I understand."

Taggart regarded her pleading expression, sensing how badly she wanted to talk. "The truth be told," he explained leisurely, "these old trenches, as you call them, are the only thing keeping the Yankees from taking Richmond at the moment." He pulled a teasing face. "What kind of impression would we make on good Queen Vic and those uppity Frenchmen if we couldn't hold our own capital?"

She laughed, her eyes shining. "Not a very good one, I'm afraid."

As the buggy rolled over the bumpy dirt road, they talked about the fortifications and laughed together for the first time in weeks. If he could only take her in his arms and explain everything, he thought wistfully. But it was not to be. How long things could go on this way, he had no idea, for he daily felt the ever-growing tension between them.

Yes, Caroline was right about his mission being vitally importantly, he thought, watching Silky's face brighten under the first real attention he'd given her in weeks. But what a terrible personal price he was paying to complete that mission.

January had flown past with a rash of bad news for the citizens of Richmond. Starved and broken of spirit, thousands of the South's finest soldiers had perished, their places taken by mere boys, while the well-fed Union forces increased with frequent drafts and an infusion of Irish immigrants. Still, the people of Richmond put on a brave face, indulging in glittering socials as they lived on hope, refusing to believe a cherished way of life was passing away before their very eyes.

Now in mid-February, as Taggart and Silky danced at a ball at Burton Harrison's home, everyone was abuzz with the sad news of Sherman taking Columbia and the evacuation of Charleston. "How can this be happening?" Silky demanded, staring up at Taggart with questioning eyes as he swept her about the crowded dance floor. "Wasn't there just a peace conference at Hampton Roads?" Her brow knitted with frustration. "How can the Yankees keep pillaging the South when they asked for a peace conference themselves?"

Taggart studied her tense face. He knew it would be almost impossible to explain to her that the South was losing the war—mainly because she refused to look at the facts. ''The peace conference failed,'' he offered indulgently, hoping he might make some headway this time, ''because Davis insisted on recognition of Southern independence, a proposal the Union couldn't accept.''

She looked at him as if he'd lost his mind. ''Well, Lordamercy, that's what it's all about, isn't it? We're a separate country and our independence should be recognized.'' Dressed in a low-cut gown of pink that displayed each swell and curve that lay so temptingly beneath it, she stared up at him, challenging him to defy her words.

Taggart negotiated a reverse, then, increasing the pressure of his gloved hand, brought her closer to him. ''Unfortunately the North doesn't see it that way, and they never will.''

She tilted her head, her gold earrings glittering in the light of the huge chandelier sparkling above them. ''Well, the North's opinion doesn't amount to a hill of beans anyway,'' she replied quickly, her creamy breasts rising and falling with each breath she took. ''Lee is sending Johnston to meet Sherman in the Carolinas and Uncle Joe will whip his pants off. I just know he will!''

It's no use, Taggart thought dully. Like most of the populace of the South, Silky failed to see the yawning chasm that lay just ahead for the Confederacy. With a deep inward sigh, he decided to close the subject for the evening. Since they were no longer sleeping together, an unspoken tension so thick it was almost palpable lay between them, and even small matters turned into disagreements. Why spoil the first good evening they'd enjoyed for weeks with further discussion about the war?

At one corner of the large room, he spied Burton Harrison smoking a cigar as officers with frowning faces surrounded him. Judging from their scowls and animated gestures, they were asking him to explain some of Davis's decisions, and the sight reminded him that he needed to spend more time with Caroline discussing possibilities that were opening up along the beleaguered Rebel line.

Taggart felt a tap on his shoulder and, turning about, noticed Captain Fouche, the young assistant provost marshal of Richmond. He'd met him at a poker game at the American Hotel and disliked him immediately because of his arrogance. From what the other Confederate officers said, he knew the man also abused his considerable power, and his first impulse was to ignore him totally. But realizing the slight would be taken as rudeness by the rest of the officers, he finally loosened his arms about Silky and stopped dancing.

Fouche bowed formally. "With your permission, I would like to waltz with your cousin," he stated in heavily accented English. "I saw her at a function in December. Since then, I've been out of the city, but all the while, I've thought of nothing but her lovely face."

Taggart resisted the urge to tell Fouche she was not his cousin. He resisted a stronger urge to escort her across the ballroom, out of the man's sight; then at the last moment his common sense asserted itself. Let him have the rest of the dance, he sternly advised himself, stepping back with a hardened jaw. Better that than cause an explosive scene. But he'd be damned if he'd give the perfumed fop the courtesy of an introduction. And he'd be watching—watching the suave captain's every movement. Noticing Silky's confused expression, he inclined his head and kissed her gloved hand. "I'll be waiting for the next dance," he announced meaningfully, shifting his eyes toward Fouche, then back to her. "So save it for me."

After Taggart walked away, Silky turned her attention to the officer standing before her and realized he was the same man who'd watched her so closely at Colonel Lehman's cotillion. At last she'd met the stranger who'd made such an impression on her weeks before. His eyes widened a bit and gleamed with speculation as he surveyed her in a sharp, assessing manner.

He bowed gallantly. "My name is Guy Fouche," he said warmly, extending a white-gloved hand. He gave her a smile, too intimate, she thought, for their first conversation. "Would you do me the honor of sharing the rest of this waltz?" he went on in a soft, purring voice.

Restrained by the rules of society, she could only nod and

accept his proffered hand. "Of course," she replied, already feeling his other hand at her waist.

Once they were dancing, he gazed down at her, his dark eyes alive with some indefinable emotion. "Your cousin is very protective, isn't he?"

Silky moistened her lips. "At times, sir. But I'm sure he's only trying to do his duty as a kinsman."

Fouche transferred his gaze to Taggart, who stood at the punch bowl, a scowl on his face. "His duty indeed. He never takes his eyes from you. He has the look of a suitor, not a kinsman."

Silky's heart jolted against her bosom and she laughed nervously. "Why, sir—what a thing to say. I don't agree at all!" Desperately wanting to change the subject, she put a pleasant note in her voice and commented, "I can't place your accent. You're not from Virginia, are you?"

Fouche's expression softened. "No, I'm not, *chérie,*" he replied, his tone shot with pride. "My home is just outside of New Orleans—Belle Carin plantation. My family raises sugarcane. My ancestors were some of the first settlers in Louisiana. We've preserved the old traditions, so I grew up speaking French, then learned English later."

All the while they moved about the ballroom, Silky sensed something slightly amiss about Fouche. It certainly wasn't his appearance. In fact, he was a good-looking, dark-haired Creole, who held himself ramrod straight. His manners were perfect and his actions bespoke his genteel upbringing, but there was something in his smile, she thought vaguely, something she couldn't quite put her finger on.

They chatted a while about Richmond, and as they discussed some of the generals, Silky found her partner had a biting wit and was a keen mimic. Appreciating his effort to put her at her ease, she became less distrustful of him, and when she relaxed a bit more, she had to admit he was truly a wonderful conversationalist. After he'd made a particularly funny remark and she'd laughed in spite of herself, he looked down at her with hopeful eyes. "I would like to call on you, Miss Shanahan," he declared, his voice threaded with longing. "Perhaps you would permit me to visit you in the lobby of the Spotswood?"

Silky's mind whirled with confusion. How could she tell him she was already in love with Taggart? If she refused him flatly, he might realize they were not cousins, and the story would be out all over the city. Best to be polite but cool, she thought, trying to come up with some acceptable answer. "Y-Yes, perhaps," she stammered, hoping she didn't sound too enthusiastic.

Two lukewarm words of encouragement were all Fouche needed. "Bravo," he exclaimed warmly. "Your answer has made my evening." His face glowed with pleasure. Holding her more closely, he whirled her about the ballroom, a broad smile on his lips that spurred her deepest apprehensions.

Lordamercy, she'd made a terrible mistake, she suddenly realized, wishing she'd given him a flat no. She'd only been polite, not eager, but the Creole hadn't taken it that way at all, almost trapping her into accepting his proposal with his confident enthusiasm. Over Fouche's shoulder, she glanced at Taggart and noted his dark glower. Although he continued to rebuff her advances, she still loved him with all her heart and hoped to rekindle the spark of passion, but matters were becoming more strained between them every day, with her seeing less and less of him. What would she tell him when the handsome captain in the dashing uniform started paying her court at the Spotswood? More important, she thought uneasily, what would Taggart tell her?

The next week, Taggart turned about in his desk chair and stared at Silky, astonishment touching his face. "You told him *what?*"

She heaved a great sigh, wishing there were some way to soften the news. The Lord knew it had taken her three days just to get up the courage to broach the subject with him. "I told him that he could visit me here— p-perhaps he could, that is."

Taggart stood, his eyes shimmering with amazement. "But why? Why did you do such a thing?" he asked in an irritated tone. "Don't you realize the problems that could cause?"

Silky turned, offended by his manner. With crossed arms she moved to the window, watching late-afternoon sun sparkle over a line of ambulances that rattled past Capitol Square. "I couldn't help it," she explained, clutching her arms tightly. "He penned me in a corner. I just told him yes, perhaps, and he jumped on it right away." She whirled about, widening her eyes. "I think he suspects we're not cousins, anyway. I think he knows we're . . . we're what we are. If I'd given him a hard no, he'd have known for sure."

Taggart lit a cheroot and tossed the match on a tray. "Do you know who the man is—what he is?" he inquired, a stern edge to his voice.

"He's an officer, of course . . . from New Orleans. He told me he came from a fine old Louisiana family," she answered with a spark of defiance.

"Fine Louisiana family, indeed," Taggart snorted, jamming the cigar in his mouth. "He works directly for General Winder, the provost Marshal of Richmond."

Silky stared at him, wishing there weren't so many military terms she didn't understand. "What does that mean?" she asked softly, her tense emotions barely in check.

He shot her a dark look. "That means a great deal indeed. Besides issuing passes and listening to the complaints of citizens, it means he has the power to make seizures without the benefit of habeas corpus. He can arrest civilians and military personnel alike without a warrant and imprison them without a charge preferred."

It crossed Silky's mind that if Taggart was a good Confederate as he claimed, that shouldn't bother him, but in the heat of their conversation she let the observation slide. With a toss of her hair, she shrugged her shoulders negligently. "I understand he has a lot of power, but I don't understand why you're so bothered about it."

"I'm bothered," Taggart stated, leisurely walking to her, "because Fouche isn't liked by his fellow officers." Distaste tightened his features. "Many of them feel he's not only a perfumed peacock but a bounder as well." He put his hands about her shoulders, his expression softening. "I don't like you associating with such a man."

Silky resented his proprietary air, especially since he'd given her so little attention himself lately. But the spark of jealousy in his eyes did provide her with the first measure of emotional comfort she'd felt in a long time. "I don't think I can totally avoid him," she admitted tentatively. "If he tells everyone what we really are it might hurt your work. People would suspect something was wrong and start to ask questions."

Taggart stared at her, grudgingly admitting to himself that she was right. He'd presented Silky as his cousin. For all of Richmond to know they were not would be disastrous for their social life and, more importantly raise doubts about his extended leave and pose the dangerous question of what he was doing here in the first place. He should have known, he thought, perturbed at himself for not planning ahead. He should have chosen some innocuous, calf-eyed swain to pay polite court to Silky, someone who would have presented no problem for either of them. There he had made a mistake, he decided. He'd also failed to tell Silky that one of Fouche's other duties was arresting Yankee spies. But that aside, her safety was utmost in his mind, and he had a bad feeling about the man. In fact, the thought of him touching her made his skin crawl.

Silky studied his troubled eyes, wondering what was going on in his head. From the look of things, she'd certainly touched a tender nerve with the subject of Fouche. She had known he wouldn't be pleased, but she hadn't expected this.

He walked to the windows, chomping on his cigar. "All right," he drawled in a flat, resigned tone. He turned about and looked at her sharply. "If he presses you, accept one invitation only—perhaps a buggy ride in the park in broad daylight, with Delcie along as a chaperon." His eyes flared. "If he does one thing out of line tell me immediately. And look for ways to discourage him. Tell him you're busy. Make up anything that comes to your head; just hold him at arm's length. And above all, don't encourage him."

Silky felt as if she were being lectured by a stern father or an elder brother. Maybe that was the way it should be, since Taggart had been treating her more like a sister lately than a lover. She considered telling him that she thought Fouche was amusing, much more entertaining than Taggart had been lately, but she had the grace to hold her tongue.

Taggart gave her a grave look. "I have serious doubts

about this man—serious indeed.'' The tension grew thicker by the second, and just then a mantel clock chimed the hour, claiming his reluctant attention. ''I'm sorry.'' He sighed, walking back to the desk and plucking his jacket from the back of the chair. ''I have an appointment, and I must go.''

Disappointment spiraled through Silky. He was leaving again, leaving her alone when they'd hardly spoken all day except for this depressing conversation about Fouche. He'd promised her dinner tonight; then he was going to take her dancing. She suddenly remembered how much fun she'd had when he'd first taught her to waltz. How they'd laughed and enjoyed each other's company. How wonderful it had felt to be held in his arms, knowing that feeling of warm security would later be replaced by heart-pounding passion. But the way he was treating her now wasn't fair—it just wasn't fair at all!

''We were going to dinner,'' she exclaimed, finally losing her temper, which after weeks of tension had snapped like a frazzled cord. ''Yesterday you said you'd take me dancing, too. You promised me.'' Her words hung heavily in the quiet room.

A deep frown streaked across his brow. ''Something has come up since then,'' he said, unfastening his hot eyes from her and glancing at the clock once more. He regarded her with a stormy countenance. ''I have important business to take care of. Can't you see that?''

Stung by his reply, she tossed back her hair. She'd tried to be a lady, tried to ignore her doubts and fears about their relationship, but she just couldn't do it any longer. ''I think I'm beginning to see a lot of things now,'' she exclaimed, her voice breaking miserably. She walked to him and clung to his arms, her vision blurring with tears. ''I'm beginning to see you have a reason for being so busy, and I think that reason wears a skirt.''

Surprise flooded his eyes, surprise that Silky read as incriminating guilt.

''I can't talk about this now,'' he replied with a stony expression.

Frantic, Silky blurted out, ''Do you realize how long its been since we made love?'' Her throat went dry with fear and desperation. "I-It's been more than six weeks now."

He looked at her coolly. "I see you've been keeping score. That only proves you have more time than I."

He walked to the threshold and she called after him, "Taggart, please tell me what's wrong." She trembled with emotion. "You've met another woman, haven't you?"

His hand on the doorknob, he threw her a keen glance that left her desolate. "Don't wait up, as it will be late when I return," he announced in an impersonal tone. With that, he strode out and closed the door behind him.

Silky stood quietly for a moment, then sat down in an easy chair, tortured by dozens of doubts and fears. Despite her efforts to return their relationship to the wonderful days they'd enjoyed in the mountains and when they'd first arrived in Richmond, Taggart was growing tired of her. Her worst fear had materialized, for every day since Burton Harrison's party he'd returned to the hotel smelling of gardenia perfume. At first she hadn't been able to place the scent because it was foreign to the Blue Ridge, but after visiting a Richmond florist, she'd finally been able to identify it. She'd noticed that scent on someone, too, but try as she might, she just couldn't remember who.

She laid her head on the soft chair and shut her eyes, overcome with depression. She was losing him, she thought, pain slicing through her. He was slipping through her fingers like water from a cupped hand. That was why he never made love to her anymore. That was why he looked for reasons to stay away from her. And that was why he'd made no commitment when she confessed her love for him. Deep in her soul, she already knew he was involved with another woman—a woman who wore gardenia perfume.

Chapter Fifteen

Captain Fouche flashed Silky a bright smile, his eyes gleaming with admiration. ''You look lovely, *chérie,* absolutely lovely. I do believe you rival the belles of Paris.'' She gave him her hand, then stepped back so he could get a better look at her new ensemble, a maroon day dress, worn with black mesh fingerless mitts, a saucy bonnet awash in black and maroon feathers, and a dainty ruffled parasol. ''No,'' he corrected himself, kissing her hand and drawing her to his side once more, ''On second thought, you put them to shame.''

With an inward flush of pleasure at his flowery compliment, she took his arm as they strolled through the park, their footsteps crunching over the twisting gravel path. March had finally come to the city, and with it the first burst of spring. The winter had been cold and dreary, but with a little sun the fertile Southern soil had produced early tulips, crocuses, and cowslips, whose blossoms nodded in the light breeze. Already a host of tender chartreuse leaves frosted the gnarled oaks, and soon there would be a glory of trailing jasmine along the iron fence and the heavy scent of magnolia blossoms on the air.

Fouche extended his white-gloved hand toward an old bench under an embowering tree. Behind the tree, in the center of the park, a huge three-tiered fountain splashed and splattered, making soft trickling sounds to soothe the nerves. "Perhaps you're getting tired. Shall we rest awhile?" he suggested gallantly. He whipped out a handkerchief and brushed off the bench, flicking away a few damp leaves that might stain her new gown.

With a sense of lingering guilt, Silky sat down, watching afternoon light dance over the brass buttons on the Creole's colorful uniform. A warm smile on his lips, he took off his military hat and claimed a place beside her, his face glowing with adoration.

How often she'd refused this man's invitations! she thought nervously. But today, when Fouche had arrived at the Spotswood, begging her to join him for a meal and a drive, she'd been so lonely, so depressed, so hungry for a bit of company, she'd finally accepted, even though Delcie was not there to act as a chaperon.

During lunch Fouche kept pouring wine into her glass despite her protests, and she had to admit she felt a little giddy, but it was so good to be out of the hotel with a companionable friend. Perhaps she'd acted foolishly, but how she reveled in the moist breeze upon her face and the sound of the warbling birds flitting through the trees. Why, the day was so light and fresh, she could almost pretend she was home.

Fouche's questioning eyes roamed over her. "What are you thinking about, *chérie?*"

She twirled her parasol, her spirits lifting. "I was thinking about the Blue Ridge and how I'd like to be there right now, with spring bursting loose over the mountains. The pussy willows will be out already," she told him, remembering the feel of the slick buds between her fingertips, "and pretty soon the dogwoods will billow out over the hollows like white clouds, perfuming the air with the sweetest scent God ever made."

Fouche offered her a look as soft as the air about them.

"You miss your home very much, don't you?"

"Oh yes, this is the prettiest time of the year in the mountains, except fall," she replied, recalling the season of scarlet leaves when she'd first met Taggart.

A tender smile gathered in the Creole's eyes. "New Orleans is gorgeous in the spring. I wish I could show you Belle Carin. By next month it will be a riot of color."

She noted his nostalgic expression, feeling more comfortable with him all the time. Taggart had said he was a dangerous man, that he abused his power, that he was disliked by his fellow officers—but today he'd sensed her nerves were frazzled with worry and he'd been kind and agreeable. In fact, he'd gone out of his way to entertain her, to amuse her, to make her laugh. He'd done all the things Taggart didn't seem to be interested in now. Could such a man be all bad?

Fouche fell silent for a while, and there was only the rustle of the breeze in the trees; then he took her hand in his. Rings glittered on his fingers, some set with rubies, others with garnets and sparkling diamonds. It amused her to see a man with so many rings, but somehow it made her like him even better, for she realized he loved pretty things. There was no harm in loving pretty things.

"There will be a ball next week at the American Hotel. Will you go with me?" he asked softly, his dark eyes gentle and pleading.

Regret surged through her that she must reject him yet again. Why should she hurt him when he'd always been kind and gracious toward her? "No, I'm afraid not," she demurred, trying to let him down as gently as possible. "My cousin and I have already made plans and—"

"This cousin of yours keeps you very busy, does he not?" Fouche interrupted, his face suddenly hardening. He glanced at the sparkling pond, then back at her. "*Mon Dieu,* every time I see the man he has a scowl on his face."

Silky turned her head, wondering how she might sidestep the delicate situation. "He has a lot on his mind. He's so busy and—"

"Busy doing what? He's on extended leave, is he not? How could a man with such leisure be so busy?" He turned her face to his, searching her eyes. "Is there anything you would like to tell me, anything about your friendship that I should know?"

Surprise leaped within her. She detected a spark of something besides concern in his expression, and a tremor, delicate as wind-ruffled water, passed through her. Desperately, she tried to compose an acceptable reply. "No, of course not. I—"

He trailed his warm fingers over her cheek. "It's just that your eyes are so sad, *chérie.* What has put that sadness in your eyes?"

For some reason she couldn't understand, Silky felt a tremendous urge to unburden herself to this charming young man. Perhaps it was because she'd had too much wine, perhaps it was because he was supplying in abundance what Taggart was not, perhaps it was because she was so utterly desperate, afraid of losing the man she loved to another woman. "I'm just lonely, I suppose," she finally answered, twisting the cords of her reticule between her fingers. "My cousin is away so much." She sighed thoughtfully. "We used to talk and laugh and play cards, and he used to go with me to visit Daniel."

Fouche's eyes glimmered with interest. "Where does he go now?"

"Various places," she murmured, gazing at the velvety park and remembering her graduation day, when she and Taggart had come here together. She felt a sudden loneliness and tears welled in her eyes. She grazed her fingertips over her temple. She was so light-headed, so trembly inside, she felt as if she might fly to pieces with nervousness.

"But where?" Fouche pressed, his voice rising and becoming insistent.

Silky regarded him, sensing he was a man used to getting what he wanted, including the answers to his questions. But his questions were becoming intrusive and personal, too personal to answer. "N-No, I can't tell you," she murmured, her hand trembling ever so slightly.

"But why?" He laughed, moving closer to her side, and putting one arm about her.

"I-I just can't," she replied. She noticed his eyes had taken on a hard, brittle sheen.

His jewels flashing, he clasped her arm, pressing his fingers into it. "You must tell me. Where does he go?" His strong face was set in cold resolve, demanding an answer. "Where does he go, leaving you alone and sad so much?"

Silky's depression over Taggart's rejection had drained her spirit to such a low ebb, she scarcely had the will to evade him. Suddenly all the hurt and resentment she'd ever felt toward him came rushing forth in a great tide of emotion, completely overpowering her and, not believing her ears, she heard herself whisper, "Petersburg. He goes to Petersburg."

As soon as the words were out of her mouth, a tear ran down her cheek, for she realized she'd betrayed Taggart by revealing their special secret. Why had she done such a thing? she berated herself. It was just that Fouche had been so pressing, so demanding, that somehow he'd forced the words from her lips.

Feeling so miserable she wanted to die, she pulled a handkerchief from the top of her reticule and dabbed at her eyes. If only she hadn't come, if only she hadn't let Fouche force all the wine on her!

The Creole studied her shrewdly. "Taggart is not your cousin, is he?" he prodded, not wanting to let up now that he'd broken down her defenses with his insistent questions. "He is your *cher ami, n'est-ce pas?*"

Silky rose, her heart hammering wildly. She didn't have to understand French to know what he was asking. She'd relaxed her guard and revealed one secret; now he was asking her the most personal question of all, trying to see into her very soul.

She walked away a few steps, trying to conceal her expression. If he didn't know the truth already, he surely would when he looked into her eyes. She pressed her lips together, vowing she'd never admit she and Taggart had been lovers, and if she had her way, would be again. But even then, she knew all was lost, for her silence was as good as an admission. If she could only shrug the question aside and lie stoutly, but somehow, about this important matter she could not lie.

Fouche turned her about, holding both of her arms. For a moment it was as if his mask of congeniality had slipped, revealing a flame of lust in his eyes. It was then she suddenly realized he was jealous of Taggart in the way only one animal could be jealous of another. And although she'd said not a word about their personal life, she was sure he understood their relationship. It was written plain and clear in his dark, envious eyes that now gleamed like onyx.

He lifted her hand to his lips. "*Chérie,* have no fear that I will judge you. In my heart I hold you guiltless, above bourgeois morality. Being French, I understand these things." He smiled, his face full of good humor once more. "No wonder the man glowers at me so, and I now appreciate why you have refused my invitations. Your sense of loyalty only makes you more desirable in my sight." He brushed his warm lips over her hand again. "Don't give the matter another thought. Your secret is safe with me. I hold the confidence absolutely sacred."

She felt as broken as a flower stem, so shaken she couldn't speak. Tears flooded her eyes. Fouche took her handkerchief and used the lacy bit of material to dab moisture from her cheek. "Shall we return to the carriage?" he suggested, his deceptively smooth voice edged with steel. He led her toward his smart carriage, waiting behind the iron fence edging of the park. Once through the gate, he handed her up to the leather seat with perfect courtesy, every aspect of his personality reflecting gentility.

He acted as if nothing had happened, but deep inside Silky realized a dreadful event had taken place. If she could only relive the last few hours, she thought miserably, wishing she'd had the strength to refuse his invitation this afternoon. Somehow the Creole had managed to wheedle information from her about Petersburg, then turn around and discover the true bond between her and Taggart without her even admitting it.

Heartsick and humiliated, she bowed her head, her throat aching with tears. She'd betrayed Taggart not once, but twice, she realized with piercing regret. And now, God help her, Fouche knew. He knew everything.

* * *

Garbed in a Confederate uniform, Taggart sat back in the carriage taking him to the railroad station the next morning, his mind swimming with thoughts and problems. Things were heating up along the line. Grant was bringing in yet more troops from the Union base at City Point and stretching his defenses even farther, forcing Lee to respond in kind. But Lee was so desperately short of men he simply couldn't keep up, and it appeared the thinning Confederate line would soon snap.

Taggart reviewed his personal life, thinking it was too bad it wasn't going as well. With a twinge of guilt he thought of the many hours he'd spent with Caroline, giving her bits of information for Grant, while Silky languished by herself at the Spotswood. Her association with Fouche concerned him greatly, and he desperately searched for a way to ostracize the man from her company. He recalled the afternoon Silky had accused him of seeing another woman. How pale and desperate she'd looked, and how he'd wanted to comfort her, but, not wanting to bring Caroline into the picture, he'd simply ignored the accusation and let the matter slide.

He knew Silky might confront him again, and in the back of his mind he realized he needed to come up with some believable explanation for his absences, but with the war moving along so quickly now, he temporarily put the thought aside. At this point, both his life and his emotions seemed more tangled and out of control than he would have ever believed possible.

A few minutes later his carriage creaked to a stop at the depot. He got out and, as he was paying the driver, he heard a hackney roll to a stop behind him. Turning, he saw a gentleman in civilian clothes step from the carriage and casually light a cigar. A burly man with gray hair and a bowler hat, he was apparently waiting for an arriving passenger, for he simply relaxed and took his time, puffing away on the cheroot.

But when the gentleman shifted his keen gaze over Taggart, a strange feeling flooded the pit of his stomach. For a moment, the man just stood there watching his every movement, his eyes glittering like knife blades—then at last he turned his head and looked away. Taggart wondered if the man was someone he'd met socially, perhaps at a holiday party, but he had a good memory for faces and to him the gentleman was a stranger.

He suddenly realized the man might have been following him, and wondered if he was a Confederate agent. He and Silky had been in Richmond several months now, and perhaps someone in intelligence had decided to take a look at his daily activities.

Then he reminded himself that for officers, three-month extended leaves were quite common in the Confederacy. He'd gone beyond that a bit, but he and Silky usually socialized with people attached to the medical service, a notoriously clannish group that paid little attention to what was going on in the rest of the army. On top of everything else, the Confederate command was so busy frantically fending off Grant's forces, they scarcely had time to notice one mere lieutenant who was chivalrously escorting a female cousin while she visited her brother.

Taggart finally decided the man was simply a stranger who'd felt some impulse to give him the once-over, possibly because of the new uniform he was wearing when so many Confederate uniforms were now tattered and worn. No, he was making too much of the incident—letting his imagination get the best of him because he was under such pressure.

Shaking off the eerie feeling that beset him, he strode away, deciding the man's lingering look meant nothing. He couldn't let himself get edgy now that he was making so much progress, now that a Union victory was so close. There was no doubt about it—change was in the wind, he told himself, walking toward the hissing train. The North was winning the war. Events were on the upturn. The question was—how long would they stay that way?

The next day Silky strolled down one of Chimborazo's corridors, carrying a stack of newspapers in her arms. Since her afternoon with Fouche, a kind of lingering guilt and depression had settled over her, seeming to sap the life from her very bones. Once or twice she'd thought of telling Taggart about her terrible mistake, but at the last moment her courage had always failed her. Trying to rationalize the horrible blunder, she told herself that if she had to reveal the secret, Fouche was the best person to tell. He was with the provost marshal's office and, as such, was used to keeping the secrets of the Confederacy. Still, the thought that she could have been so weak and careless filled her with a sharp guilt that stabbed repeatedly at her aching conscience.

She paused at the entrance to Daniel's ward, trying to calm herself. Then from the other side of the door she heard Rebel yells. Startled, she entered the huge chamber and noticed many of the men were out of their beds, all staring in the same direction. It was then she spied Daniel, walking on crutches for the first time. Inspired by his courage, his wounded comrades cheered him on and shared his victory. It was a sight to stir the heart, and she felt her depression slip away like a heavy cloak.

Abby was at Daniel's side, her slender arm about his waist, smiling and obviously encouraging him. Unaware that Silky was there, he hobbled to his bed and eased up on it, then handed the crutches to Abby, who sat down beside him, her face blazing with pride. Laughing, Silky walked to the foot of his bed, her heart soaring with happiness.

As soon as he saw her, he blurted out, "Did you see me walk? Did you see me? This was my first day, and I reckon I looked like a hobbled mule, but I'm bound to get better." A big grin shot across his face, making him look young and vital again. "I know I will."

Silky placed the newspapers on a little table next to Daniel's bed, then bent to hug him, still aglow at his fine progress. "You were wonderful, just wonderful!" She turned to smile at Abby and discovered tears glistening in her large eyes.

The girl rose and gave her a shy smile before returning her gaze to Daniel. "Well, I don't think you were wonderful," she remarked, her plain face beaming with love and making her beautiful. She took his big hand in hers. "I think you were magnificent." He blushed furiously, but, ignoring his embarrassment, she kissed him on the cheek. "I'll go so you can visit with your sister," she added, trailing her fingers over his face, "but I'll be back tomorrow to see you walk again."

Silky watched the pair say their farewells, a lump of emotion tightening her throat. After Abby had gone, Daniel attempted to walk for her, trying with all his might to take even steps while they both laughed at his efforts. Finally, exhausted, he put down the crutches and sprawled on the bed, his face pale with the strain.

Silky, who had told no one but Delcie that Taggart was seeing another woman, had intended to inform her brother today, but how could she mar his happiness with such depressing news? Let him have one day of pure joy, free from any worries or concerns, she thought with a rush of affection. They talked for a while longer, but knowing her work was waiting, she handed him the *Richmond Examiner* with a long sigh. "I brought you a paper, but I'm afraid you won't enjoy reading it."

Daniel propped himself up on one elbow, devouring a headline that reported another Confederate defeat. "Yeah . . . I know. Sherman is blazin' across Dixie like a roarin' fire," he responded in a flat, hollow voice. He threw the paper aside. "I'm satisfied we'll be gettin' precious little good news from now on."

Then a pleased look gradually gathered on his face as if he'd just realized something important. "But think about it," he suggested, his voice now vibrant with hope. "With all the fightin', and starvin', and sloggin' through the cold rain, and burnin' up in the heat—something good has come out of this old war." His eyes took on a soft, gentle look. "I met Abby. If that's all I get out of this war, I'll be satisfied, 'cause she's the best thing that ever happened to me."

Silky stared at Daniel, thrilled he'd taken his first steps, and delighted he'd fallen in love. Then, pain pouring through her, she asked herself if she could make the same comment about Taggart. For a moment dozens of conflicting emotions tumbled through her mind. Was meeting Taggart the best thing that ever happened to her? In her heart she desperately wanted to say yes, but at last, facing a painful truth impossible to deny, she secretly had to admit that, at this point, she just couldn't decide.

* * *

One day a week later, Silky looked through her bedroom window, watching Taggart talk to a carriage driver as he prepared to leave for an eight o'clock business appointment. Things had gone badly again this morning and her nerves felt as knotted and tangled as a snarl of embroidery thread. Would he come back late again, smelling of gardenia, and deflect all her questions with answers calculated to tell her nothing? Undoubtedly yes, she decided, her spirits sinking a little lower.

She started to walk away from the window when she heard Delcie coming through the door. A few moments later, the girl was at her side, breathing heavily as she tossed off her ragged shawl.

"Sorry I'm late, missy," she apologized, brushing back her tousled hair. "I overslept myself; then Jim had to have a bite to eat; then when I's comin' up to the room, Miz Wilson stopped me, askin' me if I had time to start fixin' her hair like I does yours."

"Don't worry," Silky replied affectionately. "As you can see, I managed to dress myself." Preoccupied with her worries, she returned her attention to the window, noticing Taggart's hackney had high red wheels.

Noticing what she was staring at, Delcie looked that way, too, her eyes growing large with interest. "That be Lieutenant Taggart gettin' in that carriage, ain't it?"

Silky nodded and watched the hackney pull away from the hotel and clatter to the end of the block, only to be stalled by a long procession of soldiers and supply wagons. She picked up the front of her skirt to walk away, but Delcie clasped her arm to detain her.

"Somethin' just flew into my head, missy," the girl confessed, mischief crackling in her eyes. "Them soldiers will keep that hackney there till us can get downstairs. Let's follow the lieutenant and see where he's goin'. Maybe us will get an answer to all them questions he don't answer."

"Well, just let that idea fly right out of your head," Silky scolded, surprised she'd bring up such a thing. "Sneaking around like that wouldn't be right."

With a frown, Delcie stiffly crossed her arms. "That don't make no never mind," she drawled, lifting her chin defiantly. "Us needs to see where that gentleman is doin' his work, comin' home smellin' sweet as gardenias every evenin'!"

Silky started to protest yet again, but Delcie tightly clasped her arm and pulled her toward the door. Before she knew it, they were on the stairs, then in the lobby, drawing the attention of several elegant ladies. "*No*," Silky whispered, "this isn't right."

Totally ignoring her, Delcie hustled her out of the hotel and into the fresh air. A hackney sat near the entrance waiting for a fare, and the girl opened the door, then shot a commanding gaze at the grizzled driver. "See that carriage with them red wheels? Well, follow it, but kinda hang back a little so's he won't know us is behind him."

Silky made a last stance at the open carriage door. "We can't do this. We can't—"

"Missy," Delcie declared, maneuvering her onto the seat, "you needs to find out about your man. You ain't eatin' right and you done almost worried yourself sick about all them secrets he's keepin'." She climbed in behind Silky and slammed the carriage door. "No need to be worryin' about doin' it," the girl informed her, flashing her eyes defiantly, "'cause us has done did it!"

Silky drew back and widened her eyes. "I've never spied on a person in all my life. I feel about as sneaky as an egg-sucking dog!"

Delcie slid her a sly glance. "You ain't doin' this 'cause you wants to," the girl replied, patting her hand consolingly. "You is doin' it 'cause you needs to. Them are two different things."

For fifteen minutes they wheeled through Richmond, the sound of the horses' hooves against the pavement resounding in their ears. Once Silky thought of banging on the carriage roof and ordering the driver to stop and return to the hotel, but at the last moment she held back, her growing curiosity winning out over her weakening pride. Delcie's insistence that they spy on Taggart, she thought guiltily, had provided her with a perfect excuse to salve her throbbing conscience.

Presently they entered a fine section of the city that

boasted many leafy estates and trees whose gnarled limbs arched together over the streets. As they slowed for a corner, Silky noticed Taggart's hackney rolling to a stop in front of a great mansion on a hill. Delcie, seeing the same thing, cranked down her window and called up to the driver, "Stop here, so's they can't see us." Then, moving close to Silky, she peered from that side of the carriage. "Us will just see what that gentleman is up to."

After Taggart spoke to the driver and entered the mansion, Delcie settled back and started talking. For the next half hour she rattled on constantly, and Silky's temples started to pound. When she thought she could stand it no longer, she started rolling down the window to call out to the driver herself. "I want to go," she blurted out, glancing at Delcie. "I feel like some common street woman, spying on her man."

Delcie grabbed her hand. "Just a little longer, missy. I reckon he be comin' out any minute now."

Silky sank back against the seat and closed her eyes. She longed desperately for the Blue Ridge, where everything was clean and sweet, and people were honest and a person didn't have to watch every word she said, afraid someone would use it against her. How low she'd sunk since she'd come to the flatlands, she thought with disgust. Here she was hiding around a corner like a sneak, spying on the man she loved.

"There! There!" Delcie cried, shaking Silky's arm. "Look, comin' out that big front door!"

Silky watched Taggart and a slender woman emerge from the mansion and pause on the porticoed porch. The dark-haired lady was fashionably dressed, but she stood at the threshold, shadows obscuring her face as Taggart talked, moving his hands in an emphatic manner. After the conversation was over, the lady handed him a white envelope, which he put in his pocket. Then he walked briskly down the steps to his waiting hackney.

When the woman moved into the sunlight, raising her slim hand in good-bye, Silky's heart lurched as she recognized Caroline Willmott. She suddenly recalled the evening at Dr. Cooke's, associating the scent of gardenia perfume with Caroline. Of course, could it be anyone else? she thought, a tight pain centering itself in her bosom and threatening to cut off her breath. What a great fool she was! Who else did she expect? Taggart had been coming here not several times a month to work on the Chimborazo Benevolent Committee, but nearly daily recently. Her vision blurred, and a great weakness came over her, making her tremble. For a moment she thought she might faint, and she clutched a hand strap for support.

Delcie narrowed her eyes, peering at Caroline. "That lady be painted up real good, but I reckon she be kinda old," she remarked skeptically. As the red-wheeled carriage drove away, she excitedly asked, "Want to follow the lieutenant some more?"

Silky waved her hand. "No, no. No more of this. Let's go back to the hotel," she answered, thinking she might be physically ill.

Delcie spoke to the driver, and as he turned the hackney about, she caressed Silky's arm. "Now don't you be worryin' about a thing, missy," she ordered in a solicitous tone. "That old woman could take a bath in perfume and she'd still be too old for Lieutenant Taggart. She's just too old!"

The words fell on deaf ears, for Caroline Willmott was still a gorgeous woman, and Silky had always been impressed with how regally she carried herself. A big lump lodged in her throat, for she remembered Taggart's privileged upbringing—an upbringing that included all the things Caroline was so familiar with and she was not.

By the time they'd reached the Spotswood, Delcie had calculated Caroline's age to be that of Methuselah, or Noah at least, in a vain attempt to right her mistake in insisting they follow Taggart. Heartsick, Silky tried to collect herself as she gave Delcie money to pay the driver, then rushed into the hotel, longing for the privacy of her room.

"Good morning, my beautiful one. What is your rush?"

Silky gasped as Fouche stepped in front of her, bowing his dark head in greeting. "I must make another short trip tomorrow, and I wanted to see you again before I left." His eyes filled with curiosity, he openly studied her face. "Whatever is the matter, *chérie?*"

After the shock she'd received, Fouche's appearance destroyed Silky's fragile composure and she fought back stinging tears. Of all the people she could meet this morning, he was the worst, she thought miserably, the very worst! The Creole suggested they sit down, and, noticing people were staring at her, she let him escort her to a quiet corner, hoping to say a few words, then leave.

"Now tell me what has happened," he advised, easing her into a chair. "It must have been something dreadful. I can see it in your face. Perhaps I can help."

"No, I can't—I . . ." Silky stammered, clutching the arms of her chair.

Fouche sat down beside her, his face tightening with impatience. "*Mon Dieu,* what has happened?" he insisted, his voice now tinged with restless irritation. "Must I beg you for an answer?"

Lordamercy, he was doing it again, Silky thought, feeling herself weakening under his persuasive manner. Then, pulling in a deep breath, she vowed she wouldn't make the same mistake twice. He might have tricked her once, she decided, strengthening her will against him, but she wouldn't let it happen again—ever!

Fouche clasped her hand, caressing it with his thumb. "You've had a terrible shock, *chérie.* You need a bit of cheering up. Let me take you out this morning. We'll ride in the park, then eat a fine meal." He held her shoulders lightly, sweeping an intimate gaze over her. "I insist we go out for a bit of fun. You should be with someone who cares about you."

Silky was so distraught about Caroline, she feared she might burst into tears right in the lobby of the Spotswood and disgrace herself forever. But she dredged up all her courage, finally managing to speak. "No . . . thank you. Not today, Captain. I don't feel like it."

With that, she rose and, briefly glancing at the Creole's stunned face, walked toward the staircase, her legs trembling beneath her. As she hurried up the steps, all she could think of was the envelope Caroline had given Taggart. What in heaven's name did it contain?

* * *

At eight o'clock that evening, Silky paced about her room, her pulse racing as she waited for Taggart to return so she could confront him about Caroline Willmott. All day the lovely lady's face had flashed before her, reminding her that she and Taggart had reached the point where they must resolve their problems. But how could they with so much tension between them? Anger and worry flickered inside her like smoldering kindling ready to burst into flame.

When she heard him enter his room her heart pounded, but, raising her chin, she walked across the floor. At the threshold, she saw him standing before an open wardrobe, his back toward her as he hung up his fine wool jacket. Hearing her footsteps, he turned and swept a speculative gaze over her. "Silky. What's wrong?" he asked, appraising her thoughtfully. Concern softened his eyes. "I've never seen you look so pale. Are you ill?"

She moved silently halfway across the room, pausing by a tall-backed Queen Anne chair. "No, I'm not ill," she answered, her voice hoarse with tension, "but I am sick—sick of all the secrets that stand between us." Guilt trickled through her as she realized she was keeping a secret herself, but Fouche had tricked her into giving him information, while Taggart was making a willful decision to be with Caroline. Feeling justified in her anger, she straightened her back and held her ground.

Taggart's eyes faltered over her, and in them she spied a spark of regret that gave her hope. "All right," he replied evenly, apparently realizing he'd have to discuss the situation. "Things have been building up between us for quite a while now. Come on. Out with it. Tell me what's on your mind."

Silky marshaled her courage. "If you really want to know," she slowly began, steeling her resolve with every word, "I will." Her mouth went dry, and for a moment she thought she might not be able to speak. "This morning, I saw you at . . . at Caroline Willmott's."

Surprise flashed over Taggart's face. "You followed me?" he asked incredulously.

Silky met his accusing eyes. "Yes, I did. It was Delcie's idea, but I could have stopped her if I'd really wanted to. I didn't want to. I wanted to see where you were going.''

Taggart blew out his breath, then, shoving his hands into his pockets, began pacing, a frown streaking his brow.

''Are you in love with her?'' Silky queried, letting her gaze follow him about the room.

He paused and stared at her, astonishment touching his face. ''No, of course not. I'm surprised you'd think so,'' he answered, his clipped tone slightly caustic.

Silky decided she might as well spill out all her anxious thoughts. Still, an unaccustomed pain squeezed about her heart and she clenched the chair back, steadying her trembling hand. ''What else could I think?'' she answered in a strained voice. ''You come in at all hours of the night, and it seems we have little to say to each other anymore.''

His eyes gleamed with troubled emotion. ''That's the nature of my work. You know I can't keep you informed of my every move. We've talked of this in the mountains and in Charlottesville.''

An unwelcome blush heated Silky's cheeks. ''I know it was wrong of me to follow you, but I had to know where you were spending so much time.'' She walked to him, her thoughts running together like wet paint as she struggled to express them. ''I know I'm not a Southern lady like Caroline Willmott,'' she admitted. She lightly clasped his arms, wishing she were more articulate. ''Why, she has social graces that put me to shame.'' A passionate sadness tightened her throat and she swallowed hard to steady her courage. ''Are you through with me? Do you want me to go back to the mountains?''

Taggart realized he'd hurt Silky yet again, for her misty eyes spoke with an eloquence he could not deny. Now that she knew about Caroline, he must soothe her feelings but somehow also preserve her innocence. He took her trembling body in his arms, trying to ignore its warmth and softness. ''No, I don't want you to go back to the mountains,'' he answered, noting tears sparkling on her lashes. ''I want you to stay right here.''

A wounded look came over her features. ''What about Caroline Willmott? Can you tell me you'll stop seeing her?''

Taggart groaned inwardly, wondering how he could ease

her mind without revealing his true relationship with the woman. Perhaps the truth—but not all of it—would be the best solution. "No, I can't tell you that." He eased Silky away a bit, holding her doubtful gaze. "Don't you remember I'm going over the books for the Chimborazo Benevolent Committee? Because of that, I frequently have business with her."

A frown knitted her smooth brow. "Yes, a lot of business, I'd say. I know you've been at her house, not once or twice this month for committee work, but almost every day this week. I noticed her perfume on your clothes—I can smell it this very minute!"

He eyed her stricken face, searching for words to extricate himself from the delicate situation. "Yes, we're planning a benefit dinner for the hospital," he countered, knowing the event actually was scheduled to happen. "Other members have been there, too. To coordinate such a large affair takes a great deal of work."

Silky stared at him, looking as if she only half believed him. "I saw her give you an envelope this morning," she commented in an accusing tone. "Is exchanging love letters part of your business with her?"

Taggart suddenly saw a way out of his troubles and smiled, trying to lighten the moment. Actually he and Caroline had been talking about new developments along the line—but these facts weren't for Silky's ears. Caroline's afterthought as he was leaving would provide his much needed excuse, he realized, wanting to settle this dispute before he left for Petersburg again.

"I'm glad you mentioned that," he answered in a comforting voice. Silky's eyes shone with curiosity. "Stand right where you are," he ordered, caressing her pale face. He went to his desk, then brought the envelope to her. "Here," he offered with a smile, placing it in her hand. "Go on—open it."

Silky stared at the creamy square resting in her hand, wanting to open it, yet afraid it would contain something that would destroy her life. She regarded him once more and his smile broadened, silently urging her to obey him. With quaking hands, she ripped into the envelope and pulled out a check for a thousand dollars signed by Caroline Willmott. The check was made out to Chimborazo Military Hospital. The notation on the bottom simply said *For medicine*.

Taggart retrieved the check, then took her in his arms, beaming down at her with those gorgeous eyes that always made her feel warm and flustered. "Caroline knew I would be stopping by the hospital soon, so she asked me if I would deliver the check to Dr. Cooke." He brushed back Silky's hair, his face glowing with goodwill. "As I said, my business with her concerns raising money for the hospital. I haven't mentioned everything we were doing, because as far as our relationship is concerned, it seemed of no real importance. Yes, she is an attractive lady," he admitted, nodding his head, "but no temptation to me in the least."

Silky blushed hotly. How embarrassed she was! She'd followed Taggart like a sneak and accused him of carrying on with another woman when he'd just been conducting business, as he so often said. And after all the bad thoughts she'd had about Caroline Willmott, the lady had donated money to the hospital where her brother was getting well.

She assessed Taggart and considered mentioning their absent lovemaking yet again, but her common sense told her this particular moment just wasn't appropriate. He'd already quelled her fears about Caroline, and it seemed things were getting better between them. Once everything else was straightened out between them, the problem of their love life would just naturally fall into place, she told herself, looping her arms about his neck.

Taggart looked down at her with twinkling eyes, caressing her tense shoulders as he spoke. "Now get your bonnet, Fancy Pants, and let me take you out to dinner."

Silky melted against his hard chest, convincing herself that her blunder with Fouche would cause no problems and simply dismissing it. How wonderful it was to be in Taggart's company once more! she thought, a thrill of joy surging though her. Just when she'd thought everything was the darkest, it seemed the sun had come out again.

Chapter Sixteen

Although he usually came to look at Confederate fortifications, a few days later Taggart rode one mile east of Petersburg to view Fort Stedman, a Union stronghold he'd heard rumblings about during his poker games with the officers in the American Hotel.

Now at ten o'clock in the morning he found himself in a Confederate trench, looking across a no-man's-land of rough ground and sharpened stakes at the earthwork fort, its embankments reinforced with sandbags and huge wicker baskets of stones. A big square box of a place, it stood out in the morning sun, bayonets glittering in the rifle pits before it.

A lanky Reb sergeant stood beside him explaining the fine points of trench warfare. "We don't really start fightin' so you'd know it till dark," the sergeant drawled in a heavy Georgia accent, pushing back his battered kepi cap. "Things get right interestin' then," he added with a toothy grin. "We yell out at the Yanks, 'Y'all take cover'; then we start shootin' mortar shells that light up the sky like broad daylight."

Taggart studied his lean, sunburned face. "Has it done any good?"

The sergeant laughed. "Not a bit. The Yanks and us have been here nine months shootin' at each other only two hundred yards apart and it ain't changed a damned thing."

Taggart smiled, then put binoculars to his eyes to get a closer look at Fort Stedman. It was surrounded on the front and sides by spiky entanglements of abatis, but he noticed the rear of the fort was completely unprotected. Not liking what he was seeing, he also noted the fort's walls were in poor repair, inviting a Reb attack. Undoubtedly he had to alert the Union that this Federal fort, so dangerously close to the Confederate forces, was the weakest spot in its line. "Let's walk to the west," Taggart ordered, moving on, so he could get a look at Fort Stedman from a different position.

As he and the sergeant made their way about the noisy Confederate soldiers, some talking, some playing cards, the scent of mud and closely packed bodies flowed over him. Here the men had scarcely enough food to keep body and soul together, while from City Point, the Union forces received everything they could want: endless ammunition, warm clothing, good rations, and even freshly baked bread. Sitting back in their plenty and lulled with a false sense of security, he guessed the Union had not reckoned with the Rebs' fighting spirit. That was definitely a mistake. Having lived among them for so long now, he realized it was their strongest weapon.

A half mile down the line, Taggart stopped and put the binoculars to his eyes once more to survey Fort Stedman's ragged walls from another perspective. "Looks like she's in damn poor repair," he commented gruffly, putting the binoculars away with a slap of his hand.

The sergeant spewed a stream of tobacco juice to the side, then grinned, displaying a mouthful of stained teeth. "She is," he snorted, taking off his cap, then clapping it back on again to emphasize the remark. "The Yanks can't work on her. During the day we don't worry 'em much, unless we see 'em buildin' on the walls—then we pick 'em off quick as lightnin'." His eyes kindled with satisfaction. "I think we got 'em half scared to death. I ain't seen nary a soul workin' on them walls for months."

An uneasy feeling claimed Taggart's heart. From his experience at Shiloh, he knew the toughness of the Rebel forces, and the ferocity with which they struck, splitting the air with shrieking battle cries that chilled a man's blood. With several Reb officers hinting that something might soon happen concerning Fort Stedman, he was sure this was the point where Confederate troops would try to break through the Union line. Somehow he had to get this vital information to Grant.

"We had us some party last night," the sergeant drawled on, breaking into his troubled thoughts. "We threw seventy-five shells at Fort Stedman, and they threw fifty-nine back at us."

"Any casualties?"

The sergeant shoved his hands on his hips and squinted toward the southwest. "Naw, but I heard they really got into it down the line. They climbed out of the trenches and got into some real fightin'." He swiped the back of his arm over his forehead. "Heard the Yanks cut us up real bad. They shipped a bunch of the wounded up to Chimborazo this mornin'."

With a sinking feeling, Taggart stared at the man's weather-beaten face, remembering this was the morning Silky went to Chimborazo for her volunteer work.

Taggart's train arrived in Richmond about seven o'clock. By the time he got back to the hotel it was almost eight, and as he strode up the stairs his thoughts centered on Silky, as they had during his long journey home. When he entered the room, lamplight illuminated scribbled papers littering his desk as well as the carpet around it. After taking off his hat and coat he smoothed out one of the crumpled sheets and found it to be part of a letter concerning a soldier's death.

Already guessing what had happened while he was gone, he walked into Silky's shadowy chamber and found her on the settee in front of the hearth, her face thrown into stark relief by the burning logs. By the fire's dull glow, he saw bloodstains on the skirt of her lovely gown and noticed tendrils of hair had slipped from her French roll and hung limply about her shoulders. The rosy blush had drained from her cheeks, leaving her with the blank expression of someone who'd witnessed a horrible tragedy.

He paused to light a lamp, and it was only then she turned, realizing he was there. She appeared so small and vulnerable, and projected such a forlorn air, he could have sworn she'd lost ten pounds since he'd seen her last. Yearning to see a spark of life in her empty eyes, he sat down beside her and searched her pale face. "You went to Chimborazo today, didn't you?" he asked, taking her cold hand and bringing it to his lips.

"Y-Yes . . . I did," she answered, her voice flat and thin. Her eyes clung to his as if trying to communicate something very important. "Dr. Cooke asked me to stay and help with the men who were brought up from Petersburg. Some of them were wounded so badly—I can't tell you how badly."

He took her into his arms, wanting to reassure and comfort her. For a while he caressed her back; then he brushed his lips over the top of her head and gently rocked her back and forth, wishing he could have shielded her from what she'd experienced today. If he could only take away her pain, he thought, remembering some of the horrific battle scenes he'd witnessed, and understanding how she felt. She relaxed her trembling body against him as he stroked her soft hair, a great tenderness welling up within him. "Don't think of it any more, my darling," he advised quietly. "Put it out of your mind."

She heaved a deep, shuddering sigh, and he moved back to wipe a tear from her cheek. She was so beautiful with the firelight washing over her auburn hair, and there was something sweet and defenseless about her that touched his deepest feelings. "You've had a terrible shock and you need something to soothe your nerves," he announced, rising and walking to a console on the other side of the room. He poured two brandies, then returned and sat down beside her. "Here," he said, putting a glass into her cold hand. "Drink this. It will do you good."

She sipped the brandy, glancing at him with a stricken expression. "I was trying to write a letter . . ."

"Yes, I saw."

Tears shone in her eyes. "A boy died today. I sat with him and he asked me to write his parents." She took a swallow of the brandy and placed it aside. "He was only a boy, not a man, just a boy," she insisted, her voice husky with emotion. "Why, he wasn't any older than Charlie." Frustration tightened her features. "I finally got something written, but I'm not happy with it. How do you tell someone their son has died a thousand miles away from home and among strangers?"

Taggart had written similar letters himself and could empathize with her feelings. "He wasn't alone—he had you," he reminded her, skimming a finger under her chin. "Don't discount that."

Her heavy lashes swept down. "He asked me to tell his folks that he died doing his duty. Did his duty include dying for the Confederacy before he'd even begun to live? Why, he'd probably never kissed a girl or owned a piece of good land, dark and rich and ready to be plowed." She looked up again, her lips trembling with anguish. "He was just a baby, but he's dead now—dead and cold as marble and ready for the grave. Is there no justice in the world at all? Why do things like this happen?"

Taggart swallowed a large gulp of whiskey, feeling it burn its way to his stomach. Lord, how many boys had he seen killed in the war, boys scarcely man enough to stand up to the recoil of their rifles? There was no way he could explain the unspeakable madness, he thought, his own heart aching that Ned had been slain when, as she'd put it, he'd only begun to live. Lacking the appropriate words, all he could do was comfort her.

He put his brandy aside and gathered her into his arms once more, the warm, sultry scent of her perfume flooding over him. "I'm sorry, I have no answers for your questions. Terrible, horrible things happen in war. People have pondered your questions for thousands of years and I don't think anyone has ever come up with an answer."

"I'm beginning to think," she said in a shaky voice, "that no cause is worth what I've seen today. Today has opened up a whole new field of questions I don't even want to think about. Today I learned that real war has nothing to do with colorful uniforms or brave speeches.''

He traced circles on her back, caressing her, trying to comfort her with his presence. Tenderly he brushed back the tangled hair from her pale forehead and placed a kiss there, and one on her temple, and one on her cheek. Lord, how he'd missed her! he thought, her vivid beauty bearing down on him like a spell. Before he knew what he was doing his lips found hers. When her moist mouth touched his, a warm glow ran through him, and all the old yearnings he'd ever felt for her came crashing back, a hundred times stronger than before. He hadn't meant to kiss her, but he had, and desire whipped through his bloodstream like fiery sparks, urging him to make love to her.

His arms slowly tightened about her, and his head reeled with the soft magic her presence always worked upon him. This can't go on, he told himself, remembering his vow not to touch her, but even as he spoke, ever-building desire raced through him, and he felt his discipline slipping, being pulled away from him by her overpowering desirability. Then, gradually, from somewhere within him, he called on the last of his self-control and, ignoring the passion in her luminous green eyes, gently eased her away.

Hurt and surprise touched her face and, looking like a crestfallen child, she clung to his arms. ''Kiss me again,'' she whispered, her tone low and throaty as she brought her lips to his once more. ''It's been so long. Please . . . kiss me again and make me forget.''

Silky studied his glittering eyes, her heart pounding violently. A hot sexual tension shimmered between them that took her breath away, but she sensed he was holding back, reining in his emotions, and for the hundredth time she wondered if he still cared for her. Then, beneath her fingertips, she felt muscles ripple across his back, and his strong arms encircled her more tightly, delighting her.

Now his mouth slanted across hers in a blazing kiss of passion and she moaned softly, totally surrendering to the moment. Banked fires began to smolder and burst into flame as she felt his searching hand at her breast. She relaxed against him, her mouth mingling with his, her tongue searching to conquer his. When he finally broke the savage kiss, she tilted her head back, looking into his stormy eyes. "Make love to me," she begged, craving the warmth and reassurance of his body against hers. "I want you so much . . . and you want me, too. I know you do. I can see it in your eyes."

Taggart needed no further invitation. Rising, he held out his hand, and together they moved to the bed. Silky took down her hair and, tossing her head back, let the tumbling locks fall about her shoulders. Taggart kissed her ears, her mouth, murmuring gentle words of love as his hands swept over her, thrilling and arousing her. When his lips crushed down on hers, she felt him tremble at the eager warmth of her response, and her tongue met his with a passionate fever of desire.

He unbuttoned the back of her dress, then, with a frustrated groan, held her away to tug it from her shoulders and over her hips. Within moments her gown and hoops and petticoat lay on the carpet. When he'd removed her corset and her breasts burst free, he drew in his breath at the sight, and his lips nuzzled over those pink-tipped mounds, teasing and nibbling them.

"Yes," she moaned, ruffling her hands in his glossy hair. "Yes, yes."

Now his warm hand slid into her pantalets to caress her buttocks and push down the light cotton garment that covered them. He sat her on the side of the bed and knelt to remove her shoes, garters, and stockings and, after he'd done so, she lay down, watching him undress. Her heart beat wildly as he slipped off his tall, polished boots, stripped away his white shirt and his military trousers. He was tall and powerful, with wide, muscled shoulders, lean hips, and corded thighs.

He leaned over her and mesmerized her with his skillful touch. Tenderly his lips played over her throat, her breasts, her stomach, leaving a trail of fire wherever they touched. With a will of their own, her arms encircled him and her fingers skimmed over his hard-muscled back, noticing a shudder rippling through him.

"Silky, my sweet Silky," he murmured, and, as he held

her in his arms, she sensed he was keeping his passion in check to prolong her pleasure. A profound tenderness shining in his eyes, he lowered his dark head and kissed her as he'd never kissed her before. His lips were eager and, as he explored her mouth, love's shining flame leaped within her, consuming her doubts and the haunting memories that plagued her mind.

He suckled her breasts until they ached with pleasure, at the same time caressing her stomach, thighs, and the silky triangle between them. She gasped as he stroked her fount of desire, relentlessly flicking over it until she throbbed with excitement. Tantalizingly, lingeringly, he brought her yearning to flower, and when she was moaning softly, aflame with desire, his lips met hers in a scorching kiss that sent fire skittering through her veins. Still pleasuring her inner flesh, his touch became gentle, then teasing in turn, taking her to heights of ecstasy she'd only imagined.

All her senses aglow, she felt his hard maleness brush against her, heard his ragged breathing, and was keenly aware of his warm, musky scent. Soft as the touch of his hand in her hair, his husky voice washed over her, murmuring words of endearment. He looked deeply into her eyes for a moment and, weak with love, she traced the outline of his cheek and ran her thumb over his firm, sensual lips.

Taggart gazed down at Silky's gorgeous face, her lustrous hair fanned out about her in a tangle of soft curls. Gently he brushed back a tress from her cheek, noticing the texture of her smooth, creamy skin, her tender pink lips. Lord, he hadn't meant to make love to her again and complicate the situation further, but it had been so long since he'd touched her, and his body, his very bones, ached with desire for her.

A pulse throbbed at the side of her neck, tempting him to kiss it as well as her sweetly turned ear, her smooth eyelids, and her glorious hair. How he wanted to plunge into her, to lose himself in her warm, velvety softness, and forget everything but this hour, this very moment. With a twinge of guilt, he realized he'd broken a vow to himself, totally failing in his plan to distance himself from her. Undoubtedly there would be repercussions to deal with and yet more problems to solve with the coming of the new day, but he put all that aside, concentrating only on Silky, determining to pleasure her as she'd never been pleasured before.

Silky surveyed Taggart's dark features in the dim light, and his gaze was almost tangible as it swept over her, caressing her, demanding her surrender. In response, she tenderly cradled his head and lowered it to her breast, her body arching to meet his lips. How she loved him, wanted him! She entwined her fingers in his hair, then with a thrill of excitement, realized his mouth was working its way lower, stirring dark, wanton feelings deep in her soul.

She drew in her breath as he nudged her legs apart and began kissing the inside of her parted legs, eliciting wild, blood-pounding sensations within her. Now he reached up with both hands to tease and tantalize her pebbly nipples, while his mouth inched closer and closer to the moist triangle between her trembling legs. His warm breath played over her femininity and, near mad to feel him within her, she feathered her fingers through his thick hair.

His mouth at last found her swollen bud of desire and she clutched his shoulders, moaning his name. Blushing hotly, she was overcome by modesty for a moment, then, losing herself in throbbing ecstasy, she released her inhibitions, dissolving in exquisite pleasure. Again and again his fluttering tongue teased her with loving persistence until she shuddered with a convulsive passion. Unable to help herself, she cried out in joy as intense pleasure swept through her, leaving her on the verge of swooning.

When every inch of her skin was pulsing with erotic sensation, he positioned himself over her, resting on his arms, his thickly haired chest brushing against her sensitive breasts. He lowered himself so that his manhood rubbed against her, and she quivered as she felt the moist tip of his shaft fitting itself into her welcoming folds of flesh. His long dark hair fell about his face, making him look like a highwayman of old as his lips traced a light pattern across her shoulders and between the cleft of her breasts.

"I never knew lovemaking could be so wonderful," she whispered, experiencing a soaring release as his lips suckled her breast once more. She moved her hips a bit to better accommodate him and, as his manhood plunged into her, she arched toward him. Each masterful stroke fired her excitement and she moaned and drew him closer yet. Pulsing need unfurled within her, growing and stoking a passion that threatened to blaze out of control. Now her hips twisted beneath him as she struggled to meet his faster pace. Hot pleasure rushed through her and she felt warm and glowing, as if she might burst at any moment.

In an ancient rhythm they climbed to magical heights, their very beings blended into one by the hypnotic cadence of their lovemaking. A wild, indescribable feeling claimed the core of Silky's being, and wave after wave of ecstasy crested over her. At last their love was expressed in the most elemental way known to man and woman, and she cried out in joy as they exploded in a starburst of sensual delight.

Afterward Taggart's body surged toward hers, and, lost in the glorious moment, they clung to each other until their racing hearts slowed. Sweet emotions overtook her as he moved to her side, holding her against him. Tenderly, he rained kisses over her face and hair, and love's drugging afterglow trickled through her, leaving a sense of deep security behind. Sighing with contentment, she relaxed, savoring the bliss of a union that still sent delicious sensations rippling through every muscle in her body.

On the verge of sleep, she felt Taggart's strong, protective arm about her and realized everything was wonderful again. Her body still tingling from his touch, she thought of the way he'd pleasured her tonight, taking her to the very pinnacle of joy. Although he'd never told her so, he must love her, he had to love her, she thought, her worries and doubts about Caroline Willmott melting away. Undoubtedly he would soon confess his love and make a commitment to her. Despite the war, despite their uncertain future, despite fate itself, everything would work out all right, she congratulated herself.

Yes, she thought with a tremulous sigh, everything would be just fine.

After lunch the next day Taggart noticed that Silky's eyes widened in surprise as he gave her a handful of Confederate bills to go shopping.

"All of this?" she asked, astonished. "I'm just going to buy a bonnet."

He laid a few more bills in her hand. "No—buy two bonnets, and a gown, and some new shoes as well. Buy anything else that strikes your fancy." He'd awakened thinking of Fort Stedman and, knowing he needed to express his concerns to City Point about the possibility of a Confederate attack, he'd hit upon the plan of sending her on a shopping expedition.

She gazed at the large bills, her brows arching questioningly. "Don't you have anything smaller?"

"No," he replied, trying to brush off the question with his best smile. "The bills will be fine. I'm sure the shops will be able to change them."

He surveyed her as she tied her bonnet sashes. How good it was to see her smile once more, he thought, his heart warming at the sight. Being with her last night had made him realize all over again how much she affected him, both physically and mentally. He regretted he'd let his discipline slide, but he'd been separated from her so long his desire had simply overpowered him. Their lovemaking had been passionate and magical, touched with a primal fire, but when he thought of their troubled, uncertain future a secret sadness passed through him.

Her eyes bright as sunbeams, Silky tugged on her black net gloves. "Now don't forget that Delcie is coming back to clean this afternoon," she reminded him cheerfully, picking up her reticule.

He took her elbow and escorted her to the door. "No, I won't," he answered, thinking she looked very desirable standing there caressed by golden light.

He drew her to him, holding her comfortably close. Cupping her breast, he pressed his lips on her forehead before capturing her mouth in a slow kiss. He could feel her heart pounding as his hand slid over her shoulder and along her hip in a familiar caress. When he drew back, a contented smile hovered on her lips, and her face was as soft and luminous as when they'd first made love in the mountains.

"Have a good time," he murmured, opening the door for her. He met her large, trusting eyes, experiencing a pang of compunction. Even now he sensed that their time together was almost over. Exactly what lay ahead for them he could only guess, but he knew it would not be good, and for a moment he felt like a man about to tumble into an abyss. He kissed her lightly once more, then watched her trim form move to the landing and disappear down the stairs.

He closed the door and returned to his desk. His mind churning, he retrieved a tiny key he always kept in his pocket and unlocked the bottom drawer. From its cluttered interior, he removed the cipher chart Caroline had given him and, placing it close by, started composing a paragraph about Fort Stedman.

A few minutes into his work he recalled the Reb officers would be congregating for another marathon poker game this afternoon at the American Hotel, and he had second thoughts. Why not wait until he'd seen the officers again to write a message? The men were beginning to trust him, and if he pressured them a bit, perhaps he could obtain more facts about the attack.

He tossed the half-composed message into an ashtray, struck a match, and touched it to the paper. The slip had just turned into cinders when he heard someone entering Silky's room and suddenly remembered he'd forgotten to lock the door. He realized it was Delcie and knew she would walk in on him at any minute. Quickly he pulled a cheroot from his vest and lit it to cover the scent of the burning paper.

"Lieutenant Taggart? Are you in there?" Delcie called from the connecting room. "I's gonna start cleanin'." Taggart heard her footsteps, and shoved the cipher chart under the large green blotter on his desk, not giving the action a second thought.

He'd just put the blotter in place when she appeared, carrying a basket of oils, rags, and dusting cloths. "There you is." She laughed, sweeping her open, friendly gaze over him. "I's beginnin' to think nobody was here." She eyed his littered desk and wagged her head. "You's the working-est man I ever saw," she exclaimed. She shook her finger at him. "You needs to get some fresh air. It be real pretty weather out there."

Taggart realized that she was going to stand there watching him until he left. "Out is just where I'm going, Delcie," he replied, standing and shrugging on his jacket. He picked up his hat and walked to the door.

Throwing her a smile of farewell, he left the room and jogged down the hotel steps. Outside in the soft spring air there was the creak of wagons as they rolled past, loaded with shot and shell to be conveyed to the rail depot and then on to Petersburg.

A hackney slowly rattled to the entrance of the hotel. Taggart hailed the driver and got in, his mind on the Confederate officers. From their excitement he knew an attack was planned, but he needed more details. He only hoped that tonight might be the evening some young lieutenant with too much alcohol in his bloodstream would give them to him.

He took a deep draw from the cheroot, only now remembering the cipher chart he'd automatically stowed under the blotter. For the time being it would be all right, he assured himself, relaxing against the seat. Tonight after Silky was asleep he would return it to the bottom drawer and lock it away. Lightly brushing the matter aside, he considered the evening ahead, believing things were about to come to a head.

Yes, somehow, deep in his gut, he sensed after this evening things would never be the same again.

Chapter Seventeen

Late that afternoon Silky entered her room, a porter by her side. After the man had deposited her boxes on a chair, she walked with him to the door and placed a coin in his hand. As soon as he'd left, she leaned against the closed panel, exhausted and still somewhat embarrassed. How surprised she'd been when, toward the end of her shopping trip, she'd gone into a bank to get some change to buy ribbons.

The bank teller had looked at the fifty-dollar note she'd given him, then, to her utter surprise, informed her it was counterfeit. Placing the bill by a real Confederate bill, he showed her a tiny line in the bogus note, scarcely discernible to the eye. The bill was an excellent forgery, the best he'd ever seen, but it was counterfeit nevertheless, and unfortunately the bank couldn't change it, in fact they would have to confiscate it. Wanting to escape the bank employees' curious eyes, she'd blushed and left the building, reminding herself she must tell Taggart someone had passed along some bad money.

Trying to forget the embarrassing incident, Silky took off her bonnet and tossed it aside. Then, hearing Delcie moving around in the next room, she walked to the open connecting door.

She was surprised to see the girl standing before Taggart's desk, looking at a folded piece of paper. Delcie glanced up with a start. "Oh, missy," she muttered, a hand flying to her throat. "I heard you come in, and I was just fixin' to bring this to you. I've never seen anythin' like it before."

Silky took the page and scanned it, seeing rows of seemingly meaningless words and numbers. At first she had no idea what it might be; then it dawned on her that she'd seen something like this before, and her insides went weak. A knot forming in her stomach, she recalled the paper looked like the information Taggart had been burning when she walked in on him from gathering eggs back in the mountains. "Where did you find this?" she asked, her voice none too steady.

"I was just polishin' Lieutenant Taggart's desk when I spied dust around the edge of the blotter," Delcie said in a troubled voice. "I was gonna give it a lick and a promise; then I reckoned I'd lift up the blotter and do it right." Her dark eyes widened with curiosity. "That thing sure looks strange. What's all that hen scratchin'?"

Silky tired to mask her anxiety with a light smile. "I'm really not sure . . . it's just something Taggart uses in his work."

Delcie shoved her dust rag in her apron pocket. "How could he use somethin' like that?" she demanded, her voice rising in disbelief. "And why did the man hide it like he don't want nobody to find it? Just tell me that."

Silky laid the rather stiff paper on the desk and escorted Delcie into her own room, tears burning at the back of her throat. "Let's just keep quiet about this until I talk to him," she advised Delcie, caressing her shoulder. She scanned Delcie's doubtful face, and in a kind, reassuring tone suggested, "Why don't you go ahead and leave now? I don't think I'm going out this evening, so I won't need you to fix my hair."

The girl threw a ragged shawl over her shoulders and walked to the door, where she paused. "I hopes I didn't do nothin' wrong. I didn't mean to be snoopin'."

Silky offered a smile of encouragement. "No, don't

worry. You didn't do anything wrong at all. Now go on home and I'll see you tomorrow."

Silky listened to the sound of Delcie's footsteps gradually disappearing as she closed the door; then, seething with apprehension, she returned to Taggart's room and sat down at his desk. For a few minutes she absorbed the shock of Delcie's discovery; then gradually her hand moved to a little cubbyhole drawer. With a prickle of dread, she pulled out cards and bits of paper, hastily reading them all. As far as she could tell, they were notes Taggart had written himself about Petersburg. Then she rearranged everything just as she'd found it.

Sick with fear, she picked up the paper with the strange writing and returned to her bedroom, then snatched up her reticule and sat down on the settee. She put the paper aside and opened the soft purse, feeling a hard pain in her breast that worked its way upward. Her fingers trembling, she took out all the bills Taggart had given her and studied them, comparing them in her mind to the note the bank had confiscated. Seeing that every bill contained the same barely visible thread as the false bill, she flushed hotly at the insult of her discovery. All the money Taggart had given her was counterfeit—not one or two bills, but all of it!

She picked up the paper, its numbers and words blurring before her, and suddenly realized it was some type of cipher. Drawing in a steadying breath, she tried to calm her nerves and reason things out. The cipher probably wasn't of Confederate origin. Since Confederate intelligence was located in Richmond, Taggart would be able to make reports orally. She studied the cipher, once again remembering the paper Taggart had burned in her cabin. It dawned on her that it wasn't notes on a mission to Maryland he'd destroyed, but a cipher similar to this, so Holt and his men wouldn't come back and discover it.

The counterfeit money and cipher were damning evidence, and coming together like two crushing blows, they couldn't be denied. It was then she recalled what Burton Harrison had said about the Cuban cigar Taggart had given him: *I thought only Yankees smoked fine cigars like this now.*

"He *is* a Yankee," she whispered to herself, tears stinging her eyes like liquid fire. He was exactly what she had thought he was the first time she'd laid eyes on him!

She felt as if she were two people at the same time—one watching, observing the situation with detachment, while the other trembled in shock and astonishment.

Shaking with rage, she realized she should have trusted her first impression of Taggart. He was a Yankee and he'd lied to her, over and over again without a thought for her emotions. He'd lied the first day he met her and had never stopped lying. He'd lied to get out of the smokehouse, he'd lied about his business in Charlottesville, and he'd lied about his new assignment. Her heart throbbing with pain, she now understood he hadn't accompanied her to Richmond to see Daniel out of compassion; he'd used her to spy on the Petersburg line!

What a little fool she'd been. He'd taken advantage of her ignorance about the world outside the Blue Ridge to deceive her, and he'd done it not once, but over and over again, becoming bolder each time. How could she ever have believed he was a Confederate agent after Zeb Clingerman had exposed him when the wounded soldiers returned to Bear Wallow? And how could she have discounted the look on his face when she'd caught him burning the chart? Why, even Charlie, child that he was, suspected Taggart wasn't what he claimed, but she'd been so blinded by her love, she wouldn't believe the boy.

Everything suddenly became crystal clear. No wonder Taggart had so much money—the counterfeit bills had been supplied to him in near endless abundance by the Union. No wonder he didn't have a Southern accent and was as secretive as a cat. No wonder he stayed out all hours of the night and never told her where he went. No wonder he'd never told her he loved her—he didn't—she was only a convenience for him!

Silky's heart constricted with anguish as she realized that he'd also lied about his reason for visiting Caroline Willmott. He'd just cleverly manipulated her as he had so often, this time using the coincidence of Caroline giving him the check for Chimborazo. All this, after she'd felt so cheap and embarrassed for following him, and so guilty for doubting him.

Then with a flush of shame, she realized that she'd believed all his lies because she wanted to believe them. Why, she'd given him her heart on a platter and even considered them handfasted. How he must have laughed at that idea. How he must have laughed at her passionate declarations when he'd so skillfully made love to her, thinking of her as only a willing body to assuage his lust. Totally humiliated, she drew in a trembling breath, her heart as torn and scarred as a battlefield.

Silky had been so distraught, it was only now that she remembered her careless words to Fouche. In one sense she regretted she'd innocently put Taggart in dire peril, but at the same time it seemed poetic justice, since he'd lied to her from the first day they'd met. Half of her wanted him to be apprehended, while the other feared it as intensely as her own death.

Tears spilling from her eyes, she fell across the settee and sobbed bitterly.

The mantel clock chimed two in the morning and Taggart had not returned to the Spotswood. Silky had been sitting quietly in the darkness since midnight, feeling as if her flesh had turned into cold marble. She'd cried until she couldn't cry anymore, and her temples pounded with a splitting headache. She must face him tonight, she thought, steeling her resolve against the distasteful task. She must face him and try to reclaim the shreds of her dignity, no matter how long she had to wait for his return. Over and over again she'd rehearsed what she would tell him, but she couldn't find words strong enough to express her anger, pain, and deep humiliation.

She could see everything so clearly now. How he must have rejoiced in her gullible, trusting mountain ways! All his sweet talk and all his kisses were only tools he'd used to charm her so he could get his precious information—information he'd sent North to be used against Southern soldiers such as her brother. When she'd given in to his charm and warmed his bed as well, he'd enjoyed another windfall that he'd maximized to the fullest.

She tormented herself with these thoughts until she finally heard him enter his room around three o'clock. She'd purposely left the connecting door open and light now pooled into the edge of her own room as he lit a lamp. Her heart jolting, she rose on trembly legs. She knew he was already at his desk, for she heard him opening and closing its drawers.

With a fluttering pulse, she picked up the cipher and walked toward the light. At the threshold of his room, she spied him standing before his desk, his chair shoved out behind him. His eyes wide, he held up the green blotter, staring at the polished wood beneath it.

At the sound of her footsteps, he turned about, a puzzled look darkening his countenance. "Silky. What are you doing up so late?" he asked, dropping the blotter back in place. "Can't you sleep?"

She neared him and as the light washed over her, his eyes flickered with concern. "You've been crying," he stated in a soft tone. "What's happened?"

"I know," she announced in a broken voice, trying to swallow the lump in her throat. "I know, and you can't fool me any longer. I know you're nothing but a lying, blue-bellied Yankee spy!"

The change on his face was incredible. For a moment it actually paled.

She let her condemning words sink in then held out the cipher. "I think this is what you're looking for," she stated, her voice quavering with hurt and anger. "Delcie stumbled onto it while she was dusting." Trembling, she walked closer. "There's no need to lie anymore. I tried to change one of those bills you gave me today, and the man at the bank told me it was counterfeit. Now I know all your money is false and counterfeit—just like you!" At last she'd done it, she thought, deep relief rushing over her. At last she'd confronted him with his deceitful lies!

He regarded her with glittering eyes, then took the cipher and slipped it into his vest. "I knew it was only a matter of time before this would happen," he answered, beginning to regain control of his emotions. "Understand one thing," he said in a stern voice. "This has nothing to do with us—with the way I feel about you."

Anger swept through her like a brushfire. "Lordamercy," she exclaimed incredulously, scarcely believing her ears. She paced about with crossed arms, purposefully dragging her gaze over him. "You're the coolest character I ever met. Why, lying is nothing more to you than breathing, isn't it? I trusted you, gave you my heart, and you made me the biggest fool in Virginia." She yearned to slap his handsome face so he would know a tiny bit of the pain she'd received. "Why did you lie to me—not a dozen times, but so many times I can't even count them?"

He appraised her with a bold gaze. "If you remember," he remarked dryly, "when you first ambushed me, I had to lie to save my life. If I'd announced I was a Yankee, you would have blown a hole right through me."

"I wish I had," she replied in a strangled voice, biting her lips to keep from crying. "There's something on my mind, something that keeps running through my head." She tried to steady her broken voice. "Why would you want to take up a life of spying, anyway? Why would you want to gain a person's trust and love only to lie to them, to use them and humiliate them? It's a low-down, sneaking business, enough to turn an honest person's stomach, if you ask me. Why in the name of God would you want to take up such a life?"

A hard look glazed his face, and at first he said nothing; then he began to speak slowly and deliberately. "There was a time I felt as you do myself; then the Rebs shot my little brother." His eyes snapped like flames. "He was only sixteen but so swept up in the Union cause he slipped off and lied about his age to enlist. "They didn't shoot him in battle," he added bitterly, "but in Andersonville where he was helpless, without a weapon to protect himself."

Shocked at the revelation, Silky stared at him, wondering what he would say next.

"They shot him and several other soldiers as a reprisal for a Union raid on a little Virginia town," he continued evenly, his voice hoarse with anger. "He never had a chance; he was slain like an animal." A bitter expression claimed his features. "On the day I heard the news I vowed to do everything possible to see that the Union won the war. When I discovered an agent could often be more effective than a whole regiment of men, I volunteered my services to the appropriate authorities."

Silky stared at him, feeling as if she'd been slapped in the face. All this he'd kept from her! He'd never mentioned a brother before. What else hadn't he told her about himself? How full of himself he was to want to punish the whole South because his brother had been killed by a few deranged men. Terrible things happened in war, as he'd told her himself. Hadn't Southern families lost sons and brothers, too? Hadn't families in the poor, beleaguered, starving South suffered more than the North could ever begin to understand?

"Other people have brothers besides you, Yankee! I have a brother who may have been wounded because of information you've sent North. Do you think you can play God, strike out at a whole army, simply because you've been hurt? Lord Almighty, we've all been hurt. Don't you know that? Can't you understand that?"

Silky was so disturbed she paced about the room, trying to calm her racing heart. On the verge of tears, she knew she must change the topic from his brother or lose her composure completely. She turned and, clenching her fists until her nails bit into her palms, she demanded, "Where are you really from, Yankee? I know it isn't Norfolk."

His hot gaze traveled over her. "I'm from Cleveland, Ohio. My father owns a brick factory just as I told you. I actually had an aunt who lived in Norfolk and I visited her many times as a boy and became familiar with the city. Everything I revealed about my childhood is true," he vowed, a restrained ferocity in his eyes. "I told you things I've never mentioned to anyone else before."

Furious, she walked to him. "I'm sure you have—and made them all up, I'll bet," she charged, a dry laugh slipping from her lips. "Why, you've lied about everything we've talked about but the color of your hair. And what's worse, you made me believe those lies!"

Taggart gazed at her milk-white face. Damnation! he thought. He knew this moment would arrive, but not on the same night he'd just wheedled a piece of unbelievable information from a captain in the American Hotel. He'd only returned to the Spotswood to lock away the code chart before rushing to Caroline Willmott's, so she could help him get the message to City Point. Never had time been as precious as it was now, when he was faced with explaining the unexplainable.

He scanned her willowy form, thinking she looked like a stricken child. A blue silk robe clung to her slight body, and even with her tousled hair and flashing eyes, which held a bright, hard gaze, she projected a wild beauty that struck him deeply. Wondering how he could begin to explain everything that had happened since they first met, he tried to take her in his arms. But she backed away, a pulse throbbing at the base of her throat.

He exhaled a deep breath, realizing her fiery pride would keep them apart. "Listen to what I have to tell you," he commanded, forcing back his own emotions and organizing his thoughts. "Yes, I lied to you! But I lied to protect you as well as to get my way. As God is my witness, I tried to leave you behind, to put you out of my heart and my mind," he went on harshly, wanting to break the fever-pitch tension between them. "I wanted to leave you in the mountains where you would be safe, but you followed after me in the blizzard. We shouldn't have made love. It shouldn't have happened, but it did, and with all the pain it may have caused, I'm happy that it did."

She stood silently, her green eyes blazing with suspicion and anger. He moved closer again, his speech fueled by a fierce need to express his tangled feelings. "When you asked me to escort you to Richmond, I refused, but you kept on until I agreed because I knew you'd come, and I knew you'd be taken advantage of and hurt."

All the color drained from her face. "And you didn't take advantage of me?" she asked coolly, her voice almost a whisper. "You didn't use me for your own purposes? What had you planned for the future? Were you going to lie to me for the rest of the war or the rest of our lives?" Her eyes were glassy with anger. "No, don't answer that. I suppose as soon as I'd served your purposes, you were going to scoot across that Mason-Dixon line and leave me behind with no explanation at all."

"This war is almost over," he said sharply, frustrated that her emotions made it impossible to deal with her. "The Confederacy is without funds and supplies and it can't last more than a few weeks at the most. Our lives can start again after the war. Don't you see that?" he lashed out, trying to play to her reason. "I must leave tonight, but I'll return and we'll work things out." Once again he tried to put his arms about her, but she twisted away, hair flying over her face.

Pushing back her disheveled locks, Silky gazed at Taggart. Something in his expression challenged her fighting spirit. "Do you expect me to believe that, you Yankee buzzard?" she asked. "Don't you think I know where you're going? You're going to see Caroline Willmott, aren't you? You lied about her just like you lied about everything else. Tell me that's not where you're going!"

Taggart's lips tightened and he made no reply.

She trembled under his overpowering gaze, and her heart thudded so hard she thought it might jump from her bosom. Tears brimmed in her eyes, but she held them back, not wanting him to see her cry, not wanting to give him that satisfaction.

Memories of all the times he'd lied fueled her with such anger she was nearly crazed and, her carefully guarded composure finally slipping, she picked up a china figurine and threw it at his head, missing it by only inches. The bric-a-brac crashed into the wall and smashed into smithereens. She gazed at his stony face through a sheen of tears. "Get out, you lying Yankee! Get out and never come back. I never want to lay eyes on you again. I hope you're caught and hung from the highest tree in Richmond!"

She watched him gather up his things and silently turn to go. Seconds later, he slammed the door behind him, and she sat down at his desk, trembling, desperately tired and weak. She pounded her fist on the blotter. "I hate that lying Yankee," she cried, her throat swelling with pent-up tears. "I hate him!"

Devastated, she suddenly realized she'd neglected to mention Fouche to Taggart. Had the trauma of the moment caused her to hold her tongue or had she purposefully withheld the information, hoping he would be captured? Painfully confused, but unable to deny she still harbored tender feelings for the Yankee she hated so much, she put her head on her crossed arms and cried deeply.

Taggart leaned back against the carriage seat as the vehicle traveled toward Church Hill, his mind filled with anguished thoughts. He'd dreaded this day since he'd first planned to deceive her, but the shocked, wounded look on her face had been worse than he'd expected. Lord, how could he make her believe he still harbored feelings for her after all his lies, especially when he hadn't sorted out the emotions in his own mind?

Dammit to hell, he thought miserably. What he would give to relive the last hour, to forestall their wretched argument. Why had he been so blunt, so harsh? he wondered bitterly, seeing her flashing eyes in his mind's eye. As difficult as it might be, he realized that somehow he must give her an explanation as to why he'd been forced to deceive her again and again.

It was all simple logic, he told himself, heaving a weary sigh. First he'd lied to save his skin—a good enough reason in any man's book. Then he had lied to aid his mission. As he became more emotionally involved with her, he'd lied to save her feelings. Later he'd lied to keep her ignorant of his business so she wouldn't be an accomplice if he was arrested by the Confederates. And so it had gone, with a valid reason for each lie. In effect, he'd rolled his sins forward, hoping they would be atoned at a later and more convenient time. In these wee morning hours, it seemed judgment day had arrived with no chance of atonement in sight.

Although he'd always lied to her for valid, logical reasons, he had to admit he'd never met a woman who thought logically about matters of the heart. Deep within himself he wondered if he could have forgiven *her* if she'd told him nothing but lies since the day they first met. It was almost more than the spirit could bear, he decided, imagining the brutal shock she'd received.

Then and there he promised himself that as soon as he'd

seen Caroline, he would find some way to reason with Silky if it was the last thing he ever did. No matter if it took three days and three million words, he wouldn't let her go until she understood what was in his heart.

Only when he'd considered all of this did he recall Silky's words: *I hope you're caught and hung from the highest tree in Richmond!* She was now a free agent with enough evidence to see that her wish came true. His heart pounded deeply as he pondered that fact, and he wondered if the woman who'd touched him more deeply than any before her would actually turn him in.

Taggart paced about Caroline's shadowy library, waiting for her to join him. Since her shocked butler had admitted him to her mansion ten minutes ago, he'd disciplined himself to think only of the matter at hand, knowing it was vitally important. The servant had lit a lamp for him and light now pooled from her desk, revealing papers and a creased map. After glancing at the ticking clock, he paced to the desk and, smoothing out the map, ran his finger along the Petersburg road, which he knew would be heavily guarded. A wave of anxiety sweeping through him, he'd just turned to stare at the clock again when Caroline walked into the room. Dressed in a red velvet robe, with loose hair falling about her shoulders, she looked surprisingly young.

"You must have stumbled onto something very important tonight," she remarked, a smile blooming on her lips as she gracefully crossed the carpet between them. She sat down at her desk and gestured at a second chair nearby. "Tell me your good news."

"I'm afraid the news is very bad," he answered, his voice raw with concern as he claimed his seat. "I have some astounding information about the line."

Caroline raised her delicately arched brows. "And what is that?" she asked, her eyes sparkling with curiosity.

"Generals Gordon and Early are going to launch a surprise attack against Fort Stedman day after tomorrow," he announced evenly. He paused for a moment, then slowly continued, noticing her eyes widen in astonishment. "Their force is estimated at five thousand."

As he'd expected, her face went pale with shock. "Five thousand?" she repeated softly, her bosom rising and falling with emotion. "Why, an assault like that could change the course of the war with one stroke. Any amount of forewarning we can give the Union will be of immeasurable help."

Taggart sighed deeply, remembering the shabby fortification. "I believe it's the Confederate's last desperate push," he observed darkly, "and having seen the poor condition of Fort Stedman, it's possible they may be successful."

Caroline put on her glasses and for the better part of an hour they studied the map and talked about the information he'd extracted from the Rebel officer. Then they put all the details he'd gleaned into cipher.

After they'd finished, Caroline was still pale and shaken. "Yes, indeed, we must get this news to General Grant as soon as possible. I don't think it would be putting it too strongly to say we hold the future of the Army of the Potomac in our hands this night."

Taggart rose and paced about the room. "Getting the message to City Point will be a devil of a problem," he stated, racking his brain for a plan as he spoke. "With this impending attack, the Rebs will have a sharp eye out for anyone who looks suspicious." He paused and studied Caroline sitting at the desk, distress stamped on her features. "I was just there and I know how tight their security is," he commented. He pulled out a cigar and lit it. "I doubt your usual couriers can get through."

He threaded a hand through his hair, thinking the task was almost impossible; then an idea suddenly coalesced in his mind. "We need something to distract the Rebs," he declared, waving his finger at her. A slow smile worked its way across his mouth. "We need something they want very much—something the courier can give them that will absorb their interest."

Caroline gazed at him over her little half-glasses. "Yes—but what? That's the question, Major."

Taggart braced his hands on the desk. "Outside of more troops, what do the Rebs need most right now?"

She sighed, her face blank.

"Food," Taggart responded. "I've seen them in the trenches—they're absolutely starving."

Caroline tapped a slender finger over her lips. "You know," she commented, "I think you're right. Ummm," she muttered thoughtfully, her eyes brightening a bit. "Tell me what you think about this idea."

She rose and walked about the desk, light flickering over her tense face. "I bought a large supply of canned goods before they became so scarce, and had my servants store the merchandise in the attic. Moses, one of my drivers, could take a dozen cases to the Confederate lines in an old wagon. I think after he delivered the food, he'd be able to drive a distance away, then simply abandon the wagon and slip through the forest to City Point. He knows the area well, and although he's still strong, he can feign a helpless appearance. Being occupied with the arrival of the food, I doubt the Rebs would take much notice of him, much less search him for a message."

Taggart puffed on his cigar. "But what if they did?" he asked.

She reclaimed her seat, her face lighting with mischief. "Don't worry. Moses will be wearing special shoes."

"Special shoes? What do you mean by that?"

She tossed her hair back, her eyes twinkling. "Remember you once asked me how I got messages to the North, and I said one of the servants walked them across?"

He nodded, wondering what that had to do with the problem at hand. "Yes, I remember."

"Well, the phrase has more meaning than you think," she said with a touch of humor. "Moses used to be a cobbler for a large plantation. He's made several pairs of shoes for my use with hollow heels. Whenever I want to send a message to the Union, I simply put it in one of the hollow heels, and a servant walks it to its destination.

Taggart smiled. "Clever," he said dryly, "very clever, indeed."

Caroline folded the message they'd coded and put it in her robe pocket. "I'll see that Moses is roused and the wagon is loaded with canned goods. He'll set out for the

Confederate line at dawn. When the Rebs see him, he can announce he's my servant. The officers know I purchase medicine for Chimborazo, so why shouldn't I send food to the trenches?'' Her eyes snapped with satisfaction. ''After all, everyone in Virginia thinks I'm crazy.'' Her lips turned upward as she put away the map. ''The soldiers will be so involved in opening the cans, they'll pay little attention to where Moses goes after he's unloaded the wagon.''

Smoothing back her hair, Caroline rose. ''I saw you looking at the clock when I entered the room, Major,'' she commented with a kind expression. ''And I can guess you're wanting to get back to the Spotswood. I suspect your haste concerns a matter of the heart. If you'll wait until one of my drivers gets dressed, I'll have him take you there.''

He smiled at her. ''I would appreciate that very much.''

They walked to the door, and at the threshold she paused, concern kindling in her dark eyes. ''Major Taggart, you must be extremely careful until General Grant takes Richmond,'' she warned, putting her hand on his sleeve. ''I just received word a few days ago that the Confederacy is launching an all-out search for Union agents.'' Her face tightened with anxiety. ''As you know, if you're caught, you'll be hanged.''

Taggart's carriage rolled toward the Spotswood, the horses' hooves sounding hollowly against the rough brick pavement. As the vehicle turned onto the street paralleling Capitol Square, he could see the tall hotel standing out dimly against the pink sky. His concerns about Fort Stedman still hovered in the back of his mind, but all the way from Caroline's mansion he'd thought of nothing but Silky and their quarrel. Now, pulling out a pocket watch, he noticed that it was almost six.

At last the carriage creaked to a stop in front of the Spotswood and he stepped to the ground, seeing a few people emerge from the building, whose roof was gilded with golden light. As the driver wheeled the carriage about and the horses clattered away, Taggart entered the hotel, strode through the quiet lobby, and bounded up the steps. A turn of the key let him into his shadowy room and he quickly walked to Silky's chamber, expecting to see her curled in the center of her bed, tangled in a nest of sheets.

Pausing to light a lamp, he could almost catch her sweet scent and feel her soft skin next to his. Then, as he moved the light over her bed, an aching hollowness almost cut off his breath. The bed was empty, the coverlet as smooth and untouched as it had been yesterday morning after it had been made. Frozen in disbelief, he stood silently. She'd left him. She was gone.

Quickly he set the lamp down and jerked open her wardrobe. It was still full. Hope perked through him. She hadn't taken her clothes, so perhaps she hadn't left after all. Then after examining her vanity, he found her brush and comb and a few other personal items missing. In his mind's eye he could see her sitting there brushing her hair, bits of loose face powder tracing the vanity. There were no signs of powder now. The vanity was perfectly clean and orderly, polished, in fact, and its cold perfection tore at his heart.

At the wardrobe once again, he pushed back the gowns on their hangers until he discovered only two were missing. A sick feeling flooded his stomach as he surmised what had happened. She'd left, but that wild mountain pride of hers had only permitted her to take the barest necessities and a change of clothes—the two simplest gowns she had. The girl who'd been the center of his life since that fateful day he'd heard *Freeze, stranger, or you'll be shaking hands with eternity* was gone, and the fact hit him like a kick in the guts.

Chapter Eighteen

''Missy, this place done gone downhill real fast,'' Delcie cried as she and Silky paused in front of a run-down boardinghouse at seven that morning. ''I wish to goodness I'd never told you about it!'' Trash and empty bottles littered the gutters along Murphy Street, and next door to the building there was a broken-down carriage with several ill-clad urchins playing over it.

Silky, assuming all the dignity she could muster, opened the creaking iron gate, but the plucky servant wrested the carpetbag from her hand and surveyed the building with disgust. ''I told you this was a bad place, but it's a heap worse than I 'membered. I sure wishes I'd known a better place to bring you,'' she added, circling her gaze back to Silky. ''Let's us go back to the hotel so's you can talk to Lieutenant Taggart. He'll be worried clean out of his mind when he finds you done jumped up and run off.''

Silky reclaimed her bag from Delcie. ''No, I'm going to take a room—at least for a while,'' she declared with firm resolve. She squared her shoulders and marched up the broken walk, hearing Delcie's clattering steps behind her.

"This be a real bad part of town, too," Delcie warned, clutching her arm.

Silky exhaled a long sigh and turned about. "Quit worrying. I'll be all right," she promised, trying to ignore the girl's troubled face.

With that, she smoothed down the skirt of the plain blue gown and walked up the porch steps. She hadn't slept the night before, but by the time Delcie had arrived at the hotel, she'd already packed a bag and decided to find a place of her own. She'd stay a little longer in Richmond, she thought, sharply knocking on the door. She'd stay until Daniel was recovered; then she'd go back to the Blue Ridge where she belonged, where she could be herself, where people were honest and didn't try to deceive her.

She knocked again and heard heavy footsteps, then a gruff call from inside. "Hold your horses. I'm a-comin'!" All at once the door flew open, and Silky found herself staring at a huge, slovenly woman with frowsy hair and a dirty apron. The harridan reeked of musky body odor, and as for her figure, she looked like an enormous sack of grain with a string tied about the middle. "Yeah . . . whatta ya want?" the landlady demanded, placing reddened hands on her hips.

Delcie tugged on Silky's sleeve. "Come on, let's just go," she whispered.

Silky shook off her hand. "I'm looking to rent a room," she said calmly to the woman. "The sign in the window says you have one."

The landlady opened the door a bit wider. "Room and board are five dollars a week," she announced, pushing her stringy hair from her eyes. "It's due every Monday mornin'. If you don't pay—you're out."

"A-All right," Silky stammered, doing some quick calculations and wondering if she could make her money last until Daniel was well.

The woman cast her gaze over Silky's face and figure, her eyes gleaming with suspicion. "This ain't no bawdy house—no menfolks in the room. I have my morals, you know."

The landlady let the pair into the shabby foyer, which held a fetid, unpleasant odor, then led them up the rickety stairs covered with threadbare carpet. At the top of the landing, she ushered them into a room with the same gaudy, faded wallpaper Silky had seen in the stairwell.

Her heart sank like a stone in a pond, for the room contained nothing but a little cot, an old chest, and a scarred table and chairs. A tiny fireplace, hardly big enough to hold a foot-long stick of wood, filled one corner, a black poker laying across the empty grate. Outside of that, the squalid cubicle was cold and bare, the antithesis of the lovely room she'd enjoyed at the Spotswood.

The woman glared at Silky. "Take it or leave it," she bluntly proposed, tapping her foot. "If you don't, somebody else will."

Silky stepped forward and laid a five-dollar bill on the woman's open palm. "I'll take it."

At the threshold, the landlady glanced over her shoulder. "Dinner's at six sharp," she announced roughly, "and don't be late. We're havin' corn bread and cabbage." She threw Silky a look of contempt. "Hope that's all right with your ladyship," she added before lumbering out and slamming the door behind her.

Silky eyed the room, fighting back her depression. She'd never been used to soft living, but her log cabin was clean and cozy and filled with mountain flowers, bright quilts, and other pretty things. This place was bleak and filled with dust and the scent of greasy cabbage drifting up from below. But like it or not, she *must* stay here until she could get back to the mountains, she thought, sternly pushing her aversion aside.

In a huff, Delcie unpacked the carpetbag, all the while mumbling under her breath. Afterward she came to Silky, her dark eyes troubled. "You can't stay here, missy." She sighed with exasperation. " 'Fore today, I's only seen the place from the outside. It's plumb filthy in here. 'Sides that, you didn't bring nothin' but two dresses. Why'd you come off with only two dresses?"

Silky flushed with anger as she thought of all the lovely clothes Taggart had bought her with counterfeit bills. "Two dresses are all I need," she replied crisply, wishing she had on her old buckskins this very minute. "It's all anybody needs."

The girl shook a slim finger at her. "You needs to go back to where you belongs," she informed her sternly. "Lieutenant Taggart been awful good to you and done bought you a heap of pretty things."

Silky raised her chin to a proud angle. "I don't want anything to do with Lieutenant Taggart or his money," she snapped, quickly crossing the room. "And I'd appreciate it if you'd never bring him up again."

Ignoring her request, Delcie pleaded Taggart's cause with all her might for twenty minutes. But at last she heaved a mighty sigh of defeat. "Reckon I'd better be goin' now," she finally said, her shoulders slumping in resignation. "But don't fret yourself none. I's comin' back and see how you's doin'."

"Wait," Silky called softly. "Go to Mrs. Wilson back at the Spotswood and tell her you're free to work for her now. She'll hire you in a minute. I know she will."

Delcie nodded. "I's gonna do just that. But I ain't worried about me; I's worried about you."

Silky smiled, touched by her loyalty. "You don't need to worry about me. I'll be just fine." She watched the girl move to the door, knowing she'd be gone in just moments. When she remembered the secret she'd spilled to Fouche, a strong impulse surged through her, and she blurted out, "Tell Lieutenant Taggart that—" Then, heaving a great sigh, she bit her tongue, asking herself if she was losing her mind.

Delcie gave her a questioning look. "Tell him what, missy?"

"N-Never mind," Silky replied nervously, thinking if Taggart hadn't left Richmond already, he soon would, now that she knew he was a spy. "It doesn't amount to anything." She moistened her lips, partially regaining her composure. "Remember now, if you do happen to see the lieutenant, don't be getting softhearted and tell him where I am," she ordered, putting some force into her voice. "Swear you won't."

Delcie pushed out her bottom lip in disapproval. "All right, if you be sayin' so," she answered, "but you be makin' a powerful big mistake, missy. A powerful mistake!"

After Delcie had gone, Silky sank to the lumpy mattress, untied a knotted handkerchief, and counted her meager funds. "Lord, what am I going to do?" she asked herself with a rush of panic, letting the folded bills slip through her fingers. She only had a little money, and Daniel had none. Well, somehow she'd just have to make her funds last until she could go home, she decided with a flash of spirit, tying up her money again.

An empty feeling crept through her as she stood and rubbed her aching temples. She tried to tell herself she hadn't told Delcie about Taggart's deceit because she didn't want to hurt the girl, but she secretly realized this might not be the case. And deep within her, she wondered if Delcie could be right about her making a mistake. Her heart whispered yes, but her wounded pride cried no, and she pressed her lips together, reminding herself of the many times Taggart had deceived her and made an outright fool of her.

She bowed her head and, as she did so, the diamond earrings he'd given her brushed her cheeks, reminding her she was still wearing them. She fingered the jewelry, knowing that if she hadn't been so distraught, she would have left them on her dresser at the Spotswood. How she wished she had, she thought, her heart swelling with pain as she recalled Christmas Eve—a night she'd been so foolishly happy, believing Taggart loved her.

She walked to the window, pushed back the dirty curtain, and watched a pair of skinny dogs roaming the street, sniffing in the gutters as they searched for scraps. Tears flooded her eyes, but she blinked them away, promising herself she'd cry no more. The first terrible shock of her discovery had lessened somewhat and a cool determination stole through her soul, chilling her with its intensity.

It was as if something warm and vital had died within her, leaving her incapable of love. But at the same time, a blessed numbness was spreading within her, easing her pain. She realized there was a new hardness in her, too—a hardness that had been forged by humiliation and disappointment. A shiver passing through her, she told herself she didn't care, for she had her pride and that was enough.

From this moment on, Silky Shanahan would lay her heart at no man's feet, she decided with steely resolve. And from now on Silky Shanahan would trust no man. Delcie was wrong, she decided, clenching the rough window casing to steady her trembling hand. She was as wrong as she could be.

It was almost dusk when Taggart returned to the Spotswood after a futile day spent searching for Silky. Besides combing the hotels, he'd gone to Chimborazo to see Daniel, and, after questioning him indirectly, he decided he knew nothing about her disappearance. With time Taggart was sure he could find her, but at this particular moment, it seemed the earth had swallowed her up. Tired and despondent, he paid the carriage driver, then made his way toward the people clustered at the hotel entrance.

His heart skipped a beat when he spied Delcie, dressed in a red calico blouse and skirt, talking to an elegant couple standing by the doors. When she saw him, she left the startled couple and darted across the street, dodging between wagons and carriages. He ran after her, and half a block later, clasped her slim arm. "Wait a minute, young lady. I need to talk to you!"

Delcie tried to squirm away. "I's in a hurry," she gasped, her bosom heaving deeply.

He looked into her frightened eyes. "Where's Silky? You're bound to know. Where is she?" he demanded tightly.

She let out a tremulous breath. "Yes, sir, fact of bein', I does know"—she looked at him apprehensively—"but I sweared I wouldn't tell!"

He pressed his fingers into her slim shoulders. "Can't you understand? I have to find her and explain things."

"Looks like you should have done a little explainin' a lot earlier. You hurt her somethin' awful."

"Come on, Delcie, you've got to help me," Taggart urged, searching her defiant face. "Won't you tell me if she's all right?"

Her expression gradually softened. "She has a place to

stay and somethin' to eat. You'll have to be satisfied with that."

A splutter of exasperation burst from Taggart's lips. "Does she have any money?" he asked, frustration flashing within him.

Delcie blinked her lashes. "S-She has a dab."

He reached into his pocket and pushed some bills into her hand. "Here, give her this."

"Oh, no sir," she replied frantically, shoving the money back at him. "She'd skin me alive for takin' that. I don't know what you all is fussin' about, but she done said she don't want none of your money!"

"Someone is going to take advantage of her. Don't you see that?" he said roughly. He wanted to physically shake the information from her, but forced himself to remain calm.

"Yes. I knows that. I done told her myself." She looked him straight in the eye. "Seems like folks is always takin' advantage of other folks, don't it?"

"Dammit," he snapped. "I care what happens to her."

The girl's dark eyes misted up. "I know you does, sir, but sometimes you don't show it very good."

Taggart looked down for a moment, and, in a heartbeat, Delcie twisted away and bolted down the street, her broken shoes clattering against the paving stones. He watched her bright skirt disappear around a corner and knew it would do no good to follow her. Someone with as much intelligence as Delcie wouldn't lead him to Silky. Doubtless she'd hide away until dark in some abandoned building, then slip away to the shantytown.

More frustrated than ever, he walked back to the Spotswood, a heaviness tightening his chest. Despair engulfed him as he considered Delcie's last comment before she ran away. Since he'd been gone so much lately, he could see how Silky would have felt that he'd abandoned her. If he could only relive the last months since they'd arrived in Richmond, perhaps things could be different. Then, with a painful shaft of insight, he realized their relationship had been star-crossed from the moment they'd met.

After entering the hotel lobby, he asked the clerk at the registration desk if he'd had any mail.

"Yes, sir, a servant brought a personal note for you," the man answered, offering him a white envelope addressed in a flourishing hand.

All the way up the stairs Taggart studied the florid script, wondering who the letter was from. When he entered his room and opened the envelope he had no doubt, for gardenia scent touched his nostrils. As he slipped out the heavy vellum sheet, he remembered Caroline's warning about the Confederates' all-out search for spies, and it once again crossed his mind that Silky had enough information to hang him three times over.

Questions and concerns clashing within him, he read the hastily written words: *Come immediately.*

An hour later, Taggart scanned the message Caroline handed him from Washington, then looked at her sympathetic face, scarcely believing what he'd just read. He could only stare at her for a moment as the full impact of the words swept over him, shaking him deeply. A fall from a new stallion had broken his father's neck. The man had lingered for days, but had been dead for over two weeks now.

"I'm sorry to be the bearer of such bad news," she offered, taking a seat behind her desk. "Evidently the Information Service had been trying to get word to you for days, but with no success." Her face tensed with concern. "When Moses delivered your information to City Point, he was given this message to bring back to Richmond."

Taggart looked at the neatly printed words once more. His throat tightened as he experienced the shock one always feels at the death of a parent. Memories swirled through his mind, and he recalled his father taking him when he was only nine on a tour of the factory that would one day be his. He remembered the man's scowls and sour moods, and the scent of his cigars—the same cigars Taggart now smoked himself.

He wished he could have been there to comfort his father before he passed away, but more important, he wished he could have worked out some type of peace between them. In his mind's eye he could see the elaborate funeral that had no doubt been arranged by his father's butler—the black hearse and black horses with black plumes atop their heads. Despite the grandeur of the service, he guessed only a handful of mourners had gone to the cemetery—out of social duty, for his father tended to make enemies rather than friends. At this moment he wished he could have been among that tiny knot of mourners.

"We were always different," he found himself saying to Caroline woodenly. "He was determined that I would live my life his way while I was determined to follow my own pursuits."

Tears gathered in her eyes. "I can empathize with you. My father and I were always at loggerheads, but I still felt a great loss when he died. I suppose it's only natural."

Taggart folded the note and put it in his vest pocket, strangely feeling as if he were neatly tucking away the first half of his life. "Tell me what happened at Fort Stedman," he asked in a strained voice, needing to stand back from the shocking personal news for a moment.

Caroline's expression brightened a bit. "At first the Confederates actually took the fort," she said, observing him thoughtfully. "For starving troops without shoes, it was an unbelievably gallant effort. They swung axes to smash their way through the wooden barricades, and their fury prevailed for a while; then the Ninth U.S. Army Corps counterattacked, capturing many prisoners." She sat silently for a moment, letting him absorb the important information. "The Rebels' last effort to drive the Union back and save Richmond has failed," she added pensively. "Surely Federal troops will occupy the city within a matter of days now, and the nation can be reunited." A gentle smile touched her lips. "It's good news, is it not?"

Taggart nodded, surprised to be agreeing that the death of so many men, despite the color of their uniforms, could be good news. At the same time relief rushed over him that his efforts had not been in vain. In the back of his mind, he kept recaling Silky's words that he was trying to strike back at the Confederacy for what had happened to his brother at Andersonville. But having spent so much time in the South getting to know the people, it was hard to think of them as enemies anymore. What a long, twisting path his emotions had traveled since Fort Sumter!

Caroline rose and walked to a sideboard that supported a cluster of crystal glasses and a decanter of brandy. "I think if a drink was ever in order, it is now, Major," she stated, glancing over her shoulder and capturing his eyes with hers. "Please let me pour one for you."

After he'd finished his drink, he said good-bye to Caroline and left Church Hill, his mind seething with the startling news she'd given him. On the way back to the Spotswood, he considered the practical impact of his father's death and suddenly realized he was now a rich man. But more important, he was a free man—free to live his life on his own terms. Then, a pulse throbbing in his temple, he saw Silky's face in his mind's eye. At this moment there was so much he wanted to tell her his heart was full to bursting. How he needed her. Lord, what he would give to find her.

When the carriage rolled to a stop in front of the hotel, he got out and took care of his fare. He was just walking toward the hotel entrance when the noise of clashing iron gates resounded from the park at Capitol Square and drew his attention. He noticed a soldier and his sweetheart entering the park hand in hand; then he blinked, and his heart lurched in his chest.

Standing under a gaslight, his face shadowed by a bowler hat, was the same gentleman he'd seen weeks earlier at the railroad station. The burly man's eyes briefly connected with Taggart's; then he turned his head and casually walked away as if he were only taking an evening constitutional.

With a shaft of fear Taggart stared at the man, realizing he'd been trailed by a Confederate agent for weeks now.

"What's on your mind?" Daniel inquired, fondly taking Silky's hand as she sat down beside him. "I know you've got somethin' to say. I could always tell by just lookin' at your eyes."

Silky had made an evening trip to the hospital to give her brother the terrible news about Taggart, but as she met his eyes, her courage failed her and she just couldn't do it. She knew he'd come to like and trust Taggart and she wanted to save him the horrible shock she'd received herself. Perhaps she could just tell him part of the truth—that she and Taggart had separated, and save him the hurt of knowing the rest. After all, the Yankee scoundrel would be leaving Richmond anyway.

"Taggart and I aren't together anymore," she whispered brokenly, slipping her hand away to brush back a straying lock of hair. "I-I've left him. I'm living in a boarding house on Murphy Street."

Daniel swept a shocked gaze over her. "Why, for God's sake?" he demanded, his stunned eyes full of unanswered questions.

"He cares for someone else," Silky confessed, thinking it was the easiest answer and believing it was also the truth. At the same time, she wondered why she was still protecting the rascal's reputation after what he'd done to her. It didn't make any sense—not a bit.

Her brother let out a soft whistle. "I figured there was trouble brewin'. He came by here this mornin' askin' me all kinds of strange questions, but not tellin' me why," he said, his face still blank with amazement. "I knew he was hidin' somethin', but I had no idea what."

"Well, now you know," she whispered sadly.

Daniel's eyes glinted with rage. "Lord, I wish he'd come here again," he snapped, his face suddenly becoming rock hard. He clenched his fist until the knuckles turned white. "Why, you two were supposed to be handfasted. What I'd give to be well enough to beat him into the ground," he declared hotly. "Officer or no officer, I'd give him a thrashin' he'd never forget!"

Tears pricked Silky's eyes. Oh, if it was all that simple, she thought miserably, trying to hide her crushed spirit behind a faint smile. "If he does come here, promise me you won't tell him where I am," she begged, taking a deep breath to steady her nerves.

Daniel patted her arm. "No, of course not," he promised, his voice raw with distress. He gazed at her with sad and compassionate eyes. "Are you all right? I might be able to borrow some money."

"No—I don't need it," she lied brightly. "I'm fine."

Then all the pain she felt suddenly rushed forth, and she

angrily flicked away a tear. "No—I'm not all right," she confessed, an awful emptiness engulfing her. "That's why I want to go back home." She clutched his hand, her heart near to breaking. "Oh, Daniel, I'm so homesick. I want to go back to the Blue Ridge. As soon as you're well let's go back to Sweet Gum Hollow, back to the old home place." She laughed a little, trying to cheer up for his sake. "No telling how Charlie has kept it up, but we can make things right again."

Daniel squeezed her hand. "No, honey," he said gently. "There's somethin' I've been needin' to talk to you about, and I might as well do it now. I ain't going back to the mountains to live. That's a part of my life that's passed."

Silky's heart started beating faster. "What do you mean?" she murmured, her body stiffening. "What kind of foolishness are you talking about?"

A thoughtful look flickered over her brother's face. "I've asked Abby to marry me, and her father has offered me a job in his lumberyard. She says she reckons I'll be runnin' it someday. I've been wantin' to talk to you about it for weeks and just couldn't find the words." He floated a soft gaze over her. "Sweet Gum Hollow is the prettiest place in the world, but if we both stayed there all our lives, we'd just eke out a bare livin', and it ain't no place for a city-raised girl like Abby."

Speechless with surprise, Silky listened to him go on, knowing she couldn't spoil his joy. She'd often wondered how the pair could find their happiness, but had never considered Daniel leaving the mountains. Never that. Why, the mountains were in his blood, just as they were in her blood. Never in a million years had she dreamed this might happen!

"You know old man Johnson has been after us to buy the place ever since Pa died," he continued, his voice now full of hope. "We could sell it and put the money on a place here where there are more opportunities." He paused, looking deep into her eyes. "I reckon if it's all right with you, when I'm well enough, I'll go back and talk to him. We'll sell out and halve everythin' up."

Silky tried to hide her shock. Why, their piece of the Blue Ridge had been in the family for over a hundred years, and their parents and grandparents were buried there, making the land sacred. But if she didn't agree to the proposition, Daniel couldn't marry Abby and work in her father's lumberyard. And he loved her so, and she loved him. She could see it in their faces.

"I'll see that you always have a place to live," Daniel promised, searching her face with his kind eyes.

Too hurt to speak, she swallowed back her tears and only nodded. She glanced downward so he couldn't see her eyes, silently rejecting his well-meant charity. "Sure," she finally answered. Mastering her emotions a bit, she looked up, trying to put just the right amount of lightness in her voice. "If that's what you think is best, sell it to old man Johnson."

Silky sat in stunned silence, holding back her tears as Daniel related his plans for the future. She'd counted on going back home with all her heart and soul, and now the welcoming refuge that had nurtured her all her life would be gone. Lord above, she thought, desperately trying to mask her true feelings from her brother. What in God's name would she do now?

The next evening Taggart entered his room and, after locking the door behind him, lit a lamp, then took off his jacket and hung it on the back of the desk chair. The room was chill and the hour was late, the clatter of a few carriages leaving the Spotswood the only sound to be heard. He'd just returned from searching a group of modest hotels for Silky and decided that tomorrow he'd begin the mammoth task of visiting the boardinghouses.

Walking to the window facing Capitol Square, he pushed back the lace curtain and noticed gaslights wavering in the night mist. He'd already sent a message to Caroline that he was being followed, advising her to be extremely careful. Everything in him told him he should get out of Richmond as soon as possible, but he just couldn't force himself to go as long as a chance remained that he might find Silky. Lord, where had the little spitfire gone? he wondered, dropping the lacy panel and moving to the console to pour himself a drink.

He'd just taken a sip of the fiery liquid and placed the

glass aside when he heard creaking footsteps on the stairs. The murmurs of low, masculine tones caught his attention, and, as he recognized the desk clerk's voice, shock flew through him. He immediately understood what was happening, and raced for the pistol in his discarded coat.

Before he reached the desk, a key turned in a lock and, led by Fouche, a score of Confederate soldiers burst into the room. Three of the soldiers leaped upon him as one man as he grappled for the pistol and knocked him to the floor. Calling upon all his strength, he managed to rise and shake them off, but when he'd loosed himself of one man, two more rushed in to take his place. Shouts and curses rent the air as he fought them fiercely, but the struggling soldiers finally overcame him by sheer force of numbers and pinned his arms behind him.

After they'd snapped handcuffs on his wrists, he let his gaze move over the embarrassed desk clerk, who stood by the door, his mouth agape in surprise. "S-Sorry, Lieutenant Taggart or—or whoever you are," the man spluttered, his eyes wide with astonishment. "I felt bad about using the passkey, but Captain Fouche said he needed to get into the room—he said you were a Yankee agent."

Fouche, his face twisted in disgust, waved the man away.

A dozen possibilities raced through his head as Taggart battled a sense of crushing regret. If he hadn't been so occupied with his personal problems, if he'd only kept his jacket on—he might have got away. With a pistol he would have had a fighting chance to blast his way through the Rebs and escape into the night. Thank God he'd burned the cipher, he thought with deep relief. And even as the soldiers' fingers bit into his arms he realized that somehow, some way, he would try to escape.

He scanned Fouche, a study in arrogance and pride. The man's eyes blazed and his face glowed with the triumph of his personal victory. Clasping his hands behind his back, the captain paced back and forth in front of Taggart, light glinting over the brass buttons decorating his colorful uniform.

"I'm arresting you," he announced in a rough, excited voice, "and taking you in for questioning." He paused to jab a finger at Taggart. "I believe you are a Federal agent''—a smirk played across his dark face—''and your attempt to flee only confirms this.''

Taggart wiped blood from the corner of his mouth, but remained silent, denying Fouche the response he obviously craved.

The Creole swept a contemptuous gaze over him. ''Not a word to say, hey monsieur?'' He laughed low in his throat, then tilted his head at the open door, signaling the soldiers to escort Taggart from the room. ''Very well, then. We'll see if confinement in Libby Prison will make you more talkative.''

Chapter Nineteen

The next afternoon Taggart strode about the third floor of Libby Prison, trying to find some way he might escape. Murky light, speckled with dust motes, poured through the barred windows of the huge chamber, and, all about him, scores of listless men coughed convulsively. The scent of dirt and urine permeated the air, cobwebs hung from the open rafters, and rats scuttled over the planked floor, vying for morsels of food with the hungry prisoners. He could see that the men who'd been confined here for months suffered from infection and malnutrition, but, more importantly, a desperate hopelessness, a sickness of the soul.

Taggart recalled the night before, when Fouche had brought him here and he'd seen the prison looming up like a derelict fortress against the night sky. After the Creole had escorted him to the first-floor office, the prison commandant, Major Turner, registered him in a large book bound in red leather. Moments later his clothing was searched, and he was taken here to begin his incarceration, which would last the rest of the war.

Taggart now watched the prisoners trade small possessions and go about their daily routines, his mind far away from this wretched place. A pang of doubt assailing him, he remembered Silky's angry face the last time he'd seen her. Although a rational part of his mind told him she was so angry she might have reported him to Fouche, his heart simply didn't want to accept it, for the betrayal would be too much to bear.

After a lunch that consisted of a piece of moldy bread and a cup of foul-tasting water, two guards escorted Taggart to Major Turner's office, whose walls were covered with Confederate battle flags. Illuminated by shafts of light streaming through the barred windows, Fouche sat behind the commandant's desk, a smug smile riding his lips. "You may sit down," he intoned coldly, indicating a straight chair in front of the desk. Affecting a casual air, Taggart claimed a seat and stared at Fouche, bracing himself for what he knew would be another interrogation.

The Creole rose and rounded his desk, a lock of jet black hair falling over his forehead. "I want you to tell me about your accomplices," he demanded in a superior tone. "I want names—the names of everyone who aided you in Richmond."

"You already know what you ask is impossible," Taggart scoffed, somewhat surprised the officer would think he might answer the question.

"We'll see if that is the case," Fouche returned, leveling a hot glare at him. He opened a folder on the desk and began rifling through a mass of tattered, dog-eared documents. "I see here that you have visited Caroline Willmott many times. I have the date and hour of every visit listed in black and white before me."

Surprise flared within Taggart, but he was careful to keep his face void of expression.

A crooked smile played over Fouche's lips. "Perhaps you were not aware that while others were singing her praises as a beneficent saint, I posted men to watch her house." He impatiently drummed his fingers on the blotter. "I have been surveying the lady for months, and I believe with all my heart that she is betraying the Confederacy."

His diamonds glittering, he crossed his arms. "Your association with her makes me doubt her that much more.'' Stroking his chin, he walked to Taggart's side. ''What brings you and the lovely Caroline together? Why are you such good friends?''

''We're both members of the Chimborazo Benevolent Committee,'' Taggart snapped, firing his spirit for the battle ahead.

Fouche threw him a condemning frown. ''A convenient cover, indeed—but one I do not believe,'' he stated, his voice heavily laden with sarcasm. His gaze glimmered with speculation. ''If you cooperate in this matter, your stay here will be considerably more pleasant.''

It rankled Taggart that Fouche thought he would implicate Caroline to save his own skin. At the same time, he knew the wily officer would keep hammering at him, asking him questions about Caroline and, in the end, bring her to the provost marshal's office for questioning. Women agents had been arrested on both sides, and if Fouche decided to arrest Caroline, no one could save her, not even Dr. Cooke. The taint of spying on her own kind would so contaminate her, the good citizens of Richmond would forget her charitable activities and clamor for her execution.

Making a quick decision, he looked into Fouche's piercing eyes. ''Surely as a man of the world, you can understand. Must I put the situation into words?''

Fouche eyed him coolly. ''Are you trying to make me believe you and Miss Willmott are lovers?''

''Will you leave me no room to protect the lady's reputation?'' Taggart asked sharply. He dragged his gaze over Fouche. ''Yes,'' he finally answered with a sigh, ''if you must know—we are.''

''Many believe she has harbored Union sympathies for years,'' the Creole prodded, his face glowing with vengeance. ''Is this correct?''

Taggart shrugged negligently. ''I don't know her mind on that subject. I went to her mansion because I enjoyed her company.'' He hid his true emotions behind a bland smile. ''We didn't talk of the war.''

Fouche sat down behind the desk and scratched out a paragraph on a clean sheet of paper. He put an ordinance book behind the statement and brought it to Taggart, along with a pen. "Read this," he ordered bluntly.

Taggart saw the paragraph claiming that he and Caroline had been lovers—that their relationship was purely physical and, to the best of his knowledge, she had not conspired against the Confederacy.

Fouche focused narrowed eyes on him. "Will you swear this is correct? Will you sign the statement?"

Realizing it was better that she be thought a loose woman than forfeit her life, he wordlessly signed the paper, then handed both it and the pen back to Fouche.

The Creole strode back to the desk and sat down. "Along with me, most of Richmond knows the lovely Miss Shanahan is not your cousin, but your *cher amie,*" he commented, slipping the document into the folder. He laughed lightly. "Oh, that all men had such cousins." His gaze raked Taggart mockingly. "Surely you won't mind if I relate your feelings concerning Miss Willmott to Silky so she may find another protector."

Taggart rose to his feet, wanting to snap Fouche's aristocratic neck. He'd only taken a step forward when the soldiers grabbed his arms, holding him back. "You won't be able to find her," he answered, seething with a growing rage he could barely contain. "She's left Richmond."

Fouche rose. "My dear sir," he replied, his manner cool and correct. "You're sorely mistaken." He walked about the desk once more, his hands on his hips. "In fact I suspect she will be visiting me any day now, seeking my protection."

"You're wrong, you insufferable fop!"

Fouche's eyes dazzled with anger. "Didn't you know we are very close?" he asked, obviously savoring the moment. "How do you think I confirmed my suspicions that you were a Union agent? The lady told me you were visiting Petersburg early in March. I ordered a man to begin following you immediately."

Fouche's words cut into Taggart's heart like thorns; and he felt the sharp stab of betrayal. But all this he hid from his inquisitor and stood stoically, waiting for what might happen next.

The Creole's delighted expression said he'd found a tender nerve he might work upon. "You have great discipline, monsieur. I admire that in a man. But I assure you, before our talks are over I will break you down."

He signaled the soldiers to take him away. "Put the prisoner in the special security cell at the end of the corridor," he commanded, planting his booted feet well apart. "We shall give him the best Libby has to offer." He studied Taggart. "I think we have made some progress already. My last revelation should give you something to think about for several days."

As Taggart was escorted from the office, he realized the prison's main entrance was not too far ahead and, making a quick decision, he scrambled toward it. Moments later, one of the guards yelled and slammed the stock of his rifle against his head, knocking him to the floor. His head splitting with pain, he rolled to his back just as Fouche emerged from the office, a pistol in hand. "Watch him well, you fools, or he will escape!" he ordered with blazing eyes.

Taggart gazed up at the Creole's animalistic face. What a cold, twisted piece of humanity he really was, he thought, realizing his dandified airs were quite deceiving. No doubt, after first suspecting him, the officer had played the gallant lover to wheedle information from Silky and she had succumbed to his charms.

"Get up," Fouche ordered, waving the pistol at him. "Get up before I kill you now!"

With three weapons trained on him, Taggart could only crawl to his feet and rise. Within a few moments he'd been shoved in the security cell, which had one window that looked out to the prison exercise yard while the other was fixed into the door. The heavy panel slammed shut, a key turned in the lock, and the guards strode away, leaving Taggart to his own devices.

As the sound of the men's ringing footsteps faded away he considered Silky's betrayal, the fact paining him like a twisting knife in his back. Why had she given Fouche the news about Petersburg after he'd repeatedly told her to keep it a secret? What had possessed her to do such a thing at a time when she still thought he was a Confederate officer?

He clenched the bars of the window overlooking the exercise yard and yanked them to test their strength. It was a difficult question for which he presently had no answer. But he told himself he would know the truth the day he saw Silky's face—if that day ever came.

Sharp raps on Silky's door caused her to turn about with a start. Her heart pumping, she hoped it wasn't the slovenly landlady, who was always hounding her for payment. On the other side of the door, she heard Delcie calling her name and, with a rush of relief she let her in, noticing she was in a state of agitation.

"Oh, missy, I have some news to tell you," Delcie exclaimed, so excited she could scarcely speak. She closed the door and leaned against it. "Let me get my breath," she pleaded, placing a hand over her heaving bosom. "I's been runnin' nearly all the way over here."

Silky clasped her trembling arm and led her to the bed, where they both sat down. "You're shaking like a leaf," she murmured, afraid someone had tried to hurt her. What's wrong?" She held her quaking hand and noted that it was icy cold. "Calm down and tell me."

Delcie's eyes glinted with fear. "Missy, Lieutenant Taggart done got hisself arrested as a Yankee spy!"

Silky's heart lurched crazily. She heard the words, but rejected them so violently they scarcely registered. She searched the girl's panic-stricken face. "How did you find out about this?" she whispered, shocked that Taggart had stayed in Richmond instead of leaving as she'd expected.

"I went to the Spotswood today to start working for Miz Wilson," Delcie gasped, still trying to catch her breath. "All the cooks and dishwashers was talkin' about it, askin' me if I hadn't worked for Lieutenant Taggart. They asked me what he was like, and if I knowed he was a spy. They asked me if he was good to me, and—"

"Slow down, slow down," Silky ordered, clutching the girl's shoulders. "Tell me just what happened. Who arrested him?"

"Why, that Captain Fouche who was always hangin' around like a starved dog, beggin' to take you on buggy rides. He came bustin' into the Spotswood late one night with a bunch of soldiers and made the desk clerk open the room."

Lord above, Silky thought, panic rioting within her. Why hadn't she acted on her gut instinct and warned Taggart about Fouche? A hot sickness swept through her when she realized it was because she'd been so angry and confused. Because she'd hesitated, trying to sort out her feelings, he was now in danger of losing his life.

"You knowed Lieutenant Taggart was a spy, didn't you?" Delcie asked frantically. "That's why you jumped up and ran off. Somethin' about that paper told you, didn't it?"

"Yes . . . it did," Silky nodded, retreating into her own thoughts. Her mind churning, she realized that although Taggart's arrest might not be reported in the newspaper, shocking gossip such as this would spread like wildfire and they would both be the talk of the city. All of Richmond society would know about the scandal, including Burton Harrison and Jefferson Davis himself.

Silky clutched Delcie's arm. "Did you find out where Taggart is?" she inquired, fearing the answer she was about to hear.

Delcie's gaze clung to hers. "I sure did. They carried him to Libby Prison. That be a bad place, missy."

Silky shuddered inwardly at the news. Fouche seemed so cold and unnatural at times, almost as if his emotions were deadened to the feelings of others. Gnawing the inside of her lip, she tried to analyze all she'd heard.

Delcie took her hand and stroked it gently. "Lieutenant Taggart may be a Yankee, missy, but that man be crazy in love with you. I knows he is. He talked to me one day—chased me down, tryin' to give me money for you."

"You took money from him?"

The girl scowled. "You knows I got better sense than that!" she replied in a disgusted tone. "I knows you don't want none of his money, so I throwed it back at him." She began stroking Silky's hand again. "But that shows he be thinkin' on you. That he wanted to find you and take care of you."

Silky rose, clutching the back of her neck with one hand.

"He may have been looking for me," she responded dryly, "but not because he cares about me—it's because I know too much about him."

Delcie stood, her face set in angry lines. "Now why you be talkin' like that, makin' it sound like he be some kind of bad man?" she asked, her voice full of reproach.

Silky turned her head, trying to ignore Delcie's words, but even as she did a pair of sapphire blue eyes materialized in the recesses of her mind, and all the feelings Taggart had ever evoked moved softly through her heart.

Not letting up, Delcie squeezed her hands. "You's got to get him out of that place," she pleaded. "They'll hang him for sure in there!"

Silky walked to the window, guilt stealing through her. In one sense it was her fault that Taggart was in prison; then she reminded herself he was the one who had provoked his arrest when he'd first set out to deceive her. Even if she could forgive him, what good was a one-sided love that constantly ripped her heart apart?

She turned and looked Delcie square in the eyes. "Don't you understand? He lied to me—lied so many times that I can't even count the lies," she explained, tightly crossing her arms. "And you know he's been carrying on with Caroline Willmott for months now. The last night we were together, I asked him if he was going there and he didn't deny it. That's what hurts me the most."

Delcie laughed, then walked to Silky and lightly held her shoulders. "There ain't nobody that ain't lied sometimes," she rasped, her fingers moving in caressing circles. "And if you thinks he'd rather sleep with that old woman instead of you, you done lost ever' grain of sense you ever had. You's just got to forgive him for those lies and what you thinks he *might* have been doin' with Miss Caroline. This war done made everybody a little bit crazy."

Silky considered her friend's words. She realized she must still have feelings for Taggart, or the news of his capture wouldn't have affected her so strongly. But were those feelings strong enough to permit her to forgive his lies and unfaithfulness? Part of her heart wanted to do just that, but her common sense told her that such forgiveness would take the soul of a saint—something she didn't possess.

Delcie's eyes sparked fire. "Missy, if you deserts your man now in the hour of his need," she said evenly, "you'll regret it the rest of your born days. I just knows you will."

Silky fought against the girl's prediction, mixed feelings surging through her. She'd given Taggart her honest love, her very heart and soul. She'd committed to him unconditionally, and he'd returned her love with treachery and unfaithfulness. She couldn't feel more betrayed. . . . Still, there was something that pulled at her heart.

That afternoon Silky gazed at Daniel, thinking he looked as if she'd slapped him in the face. "Taggart's a Yankee agent?" he said softly, firing her a sharp glance of disbelief. "Why, that's the most damn fool thing I ever heard," he whispered, his face going paper-white with astonishment.

They were sitting on one of the hospital's screened sun porches, where she'd taken him for privacy, and she clutched his arm to emphasize her point. "But it's true," she answered, feeling herself blush with embarrassment at what her brother must be thinking. She bolstered her courage, knowing she must tell him the worst before he heard it from someone else. "Not only that, but Captain Fouche has arrested Taggart and locked him away in Libby Prison."

Visibly shaken, Daniel leaned back against the little wicker settee. "I-I can hardly believe it," he stammered brokenly. "What you just told me is wilder than one of them dime novels you used to read!"

"Yes . . . it is," she replied roughly. "It takes a while for it all to sink in."

Daniel's stunned gaze riveted on her as she related how she'd discovered Taggart's real allegiance and how she'd left him not only because he preferred another woman, but because he was spying on the Confederacy. When she'd finished her story, she sat silently, watching her brother's eyes blaze like emeralds. What a fool he must think she was for being taken in by the Yankee's smooth ways, she decided, her emotions still raw with indignity.

Daniel searched her face. "Why didn't you tell me this when you said you'd left him?"

Silky gazed downward, struggling for words. "I-I don't know," she finally managed. Getting a tight grip on her composure, she met her brother's puzzled gaze, wondering why he was looking at her so intently. "But I knew I had to tell you now, before someone else did." She slumped back dejectedly. "I'm sure the scandal is the talk of Richmond."

They discussed everything until there was no more to say; then she stared wordlessly at sunlight glittering on the James River.

"Have you talked to Fouche?" Daniel suddenly asked.

Silky swiveled her head toward him. "No, of course not!"

"Well, maybe you should," he advised matter-of-factly. "It might be good for you to know the details of Taggart's arrest so you can clear your own name. After all, you were seen with him all over Richmond."

She considered the idea, totally shocked, for outside of Taggart the last person she wanted to see was Fouche.

"No, I can't do it," she answered, scarcely believing her brother had brought up the subject. But even then, in her heart of hearts she knew she would.

The next morning, Silky rose, dressed, and pinned her thick locks atop her head, with little stray curls softening her hairline. She still wondered if seeing Fouche was the right thing to do, but for the first time since she'd left the Spotswood, she powdered and rouged her face and glossed her lips with a bit of color. When she'd finished she put on her earrings, realizing she'd soon be forced to pawn them and indirectly accept Taggart's charity whether she wanted to or not.

On her way down the creaking staircase she heard a noise and, at the bottom of the steps, the fat landlady stepped into the little foyer and glared up at her. "I ain't had no payment for this week yet," the frowsy woman snapped, shaking an accusing finger in her direction. "You better pay up or I'll put you out on the street!" she added, her gaze hard and unforgiving.

"Yes, I'll take care of that matter soon," Silky promised,

and caught a whiff of rancid body odor as she squeezed past the woman.

"Well, see that you do!" the harridan called after her.

Silky breathed a sigh of relief once she was on the street. The weather was wonderful: the wind cool and fresh on her face, and the sun warm on her body as it slanted through the trees. Her spirits a bit higher, she walked four blocks to a better section of town, where she could catch a hackney to the provost marshal's office, which was situated all the way across Richmond.

After placing several of her hoarded coins into the driver's cracked palm, she entered the carriage and leaned back for the ride across the heart of the city. Wagons piled high with mattresses and odds and ends of furniture rattled down the streets, while hollow-eyed pedestrians jostled past each other with grim determination. It seemed an air of confused desperation had settled upon Richmond, and by the time she reached the city's eastern quarter she'd noticed many vacant businesses, broken windows, and FOR SALE signs.

At last she saw the two-story brick provost marshal's office and, after leaving the hackney, entered the building and asked to be directed to Fouche's office.

Upon seeing her he rose to his feet, his face alight with surprise. "I'm delighted you've come, *chérie,*" he crooned, handing her into a chair near his littered desk. His expression briefly darkened. "I can guess why you're here, and I'm afraid the answer is no. No one may see Taggart."

Silky hadn't seen Fouche in weeks, but she noticed he was still dressed in the best of uniforms and wore new boots, glassy with polish. And if she wasn't mistaken, he'd added another ring to his collection. Judging from his sleek, polished appearance, no one would suspect most of the starving South was living on rice, bacon drippings, and dried apples sweetened with sorghum. "I didn't come for permission to see your prisoner," she replied lightly, trying to sound casual as she reined in her nervousness. "I came to talk to you."

He smiled broadly. "Oh, well. That's a horse of a different color." Briefly glancing at the door, he slapped his hands and a young soldier appeared, offering a starched military salute. ''Bring a pot of coffee and some cakes,'' he ordered, ''and be quick about it.''

Fouche sat on the corner of his desk and gazed at Silky with smug amusement, looking, she thought, like a cat watching a mouse. ''What shall we talk about, *chérie?* Is there an upcoming ball I may escort you to? Perhaps you need a bolt of contraband silk for a new gown.''

''No. Nothing as pleasant as that,'' she began tentatively, idly arranging her skirt as she searched for a way to open the delicate subject. She looked up and took a deep breath. ''When I heard you'd captured the Yankee, I assumed he told you that''—she moistened her lips, searching for the right phrase—''that . . . I was no longer staying at the Spotswood.''

He offered her a patronizing smile. ''No—actually he told me you'd left town, but I correctly assumed he was lying.''

Fear fluttered through Silky, for she knew it would be difficult to pry any information from the officer that he didn't want to give. ''Since I wasn't there when he was arrested,'' she stumbled on, her voice breaking under the strain, ''I've only received secondhand news about the affair. I was wondering if you could give me more details?''

Fouche rose and went to his chair. ''If your heart is set on discussing this depressing subject,'' he said tiredly, ''then we shall, but only briefly.'' He sat down, holding her gaze. ''First let me say that your name is clear in the affair. Taggart has not implicated you, and it is my opinion that he duped you along with the rest of Richmond.''

A hot blush captured Silky's cheeks. ''When did you first suspect him?''

Fouche pursed his lips. ''I first met him at the American Hotel during a poker game. He was very evasive about his past, and my instincts told me I should start digging into the matter.''

Silky's pulse raced. Undoubtedly Fouche had been eager to court her so he could pump her for information on Taggart, she thought, recalling his pressing questions. It was then she understood she hadn't come here to clear her own name, but to find out if her admission about Petersburg had been the reason for Taggart's arrest. ''Did you start investigating him after . . . after that day in the park?'' she asked, her keen interest absorbing some of her nervousness.

''Yes,'' he continued in oily tones. ''One of my agents followed him to Petersburg and talked with the soldiers he'd quizzed, finding out what he was about.'' He tilted his brows in amusement. ''You made quite an impression in your lovely red ensemble. Many of the soldiers remembered seeing you with Taggart last January on an extended buggy ride around the trenches.''

Silky's heart thudded with the realization that it was her inability to keep a secret that had been responsible for Taggart's arrest.

Fouche steepled his fingers, his rings glittering. ''Taggart was wise to claim he was attached to a regiment in the western theater,'' he remarked thoughtfully. ''We rarely see those officers in Richmond, so there was no one I could speak with to check his story. Then one day I managed to get a letter through to his supposed regiment commander, and his reply told me the Yankee's name wasn't on their roster. After considerable work I found he wasn't on the roster of any Confederate regiment.''

Fouche leaned back and spread his hands. ''Voilà, it was as simple as that.''

The young soldier entered and placed a tray on his commander's desk. As the lad poured coffee, Silky tried to collect her nerves, realizing how clever the Creole really was.

After the soldier had left the room, Fouche handed her a cup of the dark liquid and served her a little cake. ''Taggart's frequent visits to Caroline Willmott also made me suspicious of him,'' he added, a brittle tone entering his voice.

Silky bristled inwardly at the mention of the woman's name. She tried to compose her features, but was sure she'd failed.

''I've felt that Caroline Willmott was a Federal agent for some time and had her house watched. Soon after meeting her, Taggart became a frequent visitor.''

Silky stiffened at the news that Caroline might also be a Yankee sympathizer. At the same time it provided a scrap of hope that the pair's relationship pivoted around politics instead of romance.

"I can see by your reaction that you're surprised," the officer remarked with wicked satisfaction.

Silky took a sip of coffee, realizing he was playing tug-of-war with her emotions, and anticipating with dread what he might say next.

Fouche rattled his cup into a saucer, then moved to her side, his strong French cologne nauseating her a bit. When, ever so gently, he placed his hand on her arm, she felt strangely violated by his soft touch. "I recently questioned Taggart about his frequent visits to her mansion, and he insists they were making love, not conspiring against the Confederacy."

Silky shuddered with humiliation at the brutally effective words, and she wondered how much longer she could keep sitting there, pretending everything was all right.

The officer returned to his desk, and from its drawer produced a signed document. He approached and handed it to her. "I know you were very fond of him, but here is a sworn document he signed avowing to the fact they were lovers."

Silky looked at the signature that blurred before her eyes. Just what I expected, she thought bitterly, despair overwhelming her once again. Taggart had openly confessed to making love with Caroline. Of course, she knew Fouche was advancing his own cause, but now the facts were out in the open—in a sworn statement, no less—and she could no longer salve her feelings with the hope she'd clung to so tenaciously.

Fouche regarded her solicitously. "Are you all right, *chérie?* You look quite ill."

Silky sat emotionally naked before him, only her fiery pride holding back her tears. How skillfully he'd led her into this trap! Surely he knew how much the statement had devastated her, but his expression said he didn't care. "I'm fine," she answered brightly, silently vowing she'd never let him glimpse her pain and embarrassment.

She tossed the document aside as if it were nothing, then took a taste of her cake, her throat so tight she could scarcely swallow. "These cakes are very good," she added, pasting a smile on her trembling lips. "I haven't had anything sweet in weeks."

Fouche sighed deeply, as over a problem of great magnitude. "Yes. The lack of luxuries in the South is quite appalling, is it not?" Then he took her hand and pressed it to his lips. "But there are ways of obtaining these luxuries." He ran his warm gaze over her, making her blush at the message she read in his eyes. "Stay with me, *chérie.* Let me protect you from the harsher side of life. My family has great wealth. I swear you'll lack for nothing."

Silky felt a prick of surprise. After wheedling information from her and assaulting her with words calculated to break her heart, could he now be proposing marriage? She detected something perverse in his nature that set her nerves on edge, and as his hand slid over her arm once again, her skin crawled beneath its warmth.

Her pulse fluttering, she put her coffee on the tray and rose to go. "I-I'm too confused to consider anything more today," she stammered, her mind seething with questions and fears. She put a hand to her temple. "In fact, I feel a headache coming on, and think I should go."

Fouche bowed his head in acquiescence. "I understand," he commented softly, "but please come again." He kissed her hand, then looked up, his eyes brimming with passion. "If there is anything you need, you have only to ask." He raised a questioning brow. "Shall I have a soldier drive you back to your dwelling?"

"No, I'm fine," she replied, and made up a quick excuse so he wouldn't know where she was staying. "I want to walk a while before I hail a hackney. The fresh air will help my headache." She made her way to the door and left the building without even a look back in farewell.

Once outside, she blinked tears from her eyes. What a ninny she'd been to think that Taggart might have been faithful to her. She should have trusted her inner feelings instead of listening to Delcie's advice. She walked briskly for a few blocks, looking back to see if Fouche had sent someone to follow her, then hailed a passing hackney. She got in and slammed the door behind her. Would she wear her heart on her sleeve the rest of her life? she berated herself, angrily grasping the swinging hand strap. Yes, Fouche might have been lying to her, but there was a good chance that he wasn't.

Still, some elusive emotion nagged at her mind and urged her to delve into the matter further. Then, with a bolt of insight, she realized the one person who might tell her the truth about the affair was Caroline Willmott. But just thinking of the lovely aristocrat and the fine mansion in which she lived made her confidence sink to a low ebb.

It would take a heap of courage to confront Caroline Willmott, Silky thought, clenching the hand strap until her knuckles were white. Did she have that kind of courage?

Chapter Twenty

Silky stared at Caroline Willmott's door, simmering with nervousness. A huge brass knocker, depicting a lion's head, decorated the door, and she wondered if the animal's snarling mouth represented the welcome she would receive inside. She'd changed her mind thirty times about seeing Caroline, but finally decided she must make the visit, if only to satisfy her raging curiosity.

Her fingers trembled as she reached for the knocker; then she dropped her hand, her courage suddenly failing her. Angry with her own foolishness, she pulled in a long, steadying breath. "Lordamercy, I can't stand here all morning like a scared goat," she muttered, finally slamming the knocker down hard several times.

All at once the door flew open, making her gasp in surprise. A neatly dressed butler peered from the shadowy foyer, his dark eyes roaming over her. "Yes, miss?" he drawled patiently.

"I'm here to see Miss Willmott," Silky stammered, her throat so dry she could scarcely speak. "I mean, may I see Miss Willmott?"

''And who might you be?'' he inquired, a frown tightening his inquisitive features.

''M-Miss Shanahan.''

With a look of surprise, the old man nodded. After casting her a discreet glance, he ushered her into a cool foyer filled with treasures, then led her into a library, carpeted with thick rugs and furnished with graceful mahogany furniture. ''Miss Caroline will be down directly,'' the butler assured her, bowing his gray head once more before leaving the room.

Silky surveyed the book-filled walls and lavish furnishings: the French chests, carved writing tables, soft, velvet-covered chairs and sofas. The chamber had an immaculate, well-cared-for look and smelled of fragrant flowers. No wonder Taggart was drawn to Caroline, she thought with a flash of embarrassment. He'd been raised in a mansion, in a wonderful place like this, and was used to the finer things in life.

Here he could feel at home and be with a real lady who'd also been born and raised in gentility; here he could talk about places Silky had never been, and places she'd never seen, and people she could never hope to meet. And here he could relax in gorgeous surroundings, she thought with a twinge of jealousy, wondering if the pair had shared a kiss before the marble fireplace.

Noticing a sparkling chandelier overhead, she tilted her head backward and walked in a circle, thinking it was even more beautiful than the ones at the Spotswood.

''Do you like it, my dear? Papa had it shipped from Italy after one of our trips abroad.''

With a start, Silky looked at Caroline, who'd just walked into the room, dressed beautifully in a low-cut gown of pale green silk trimmed in creamy lace. With her dark hair sleeked back and tumbling over her shoulders, she looked like spring itself. A smile softened her face as she extended a slender hand at a grouping of furniture near a sunny bay window. ''Please have a seat. I'm happy you've come.''

Silky, battling her nervousness, claimed a seat on a red-striped settee with a thick velvet cushion. How foolish she must have looked staring upward at the chandelier, like a little hillbilly who'd never been out of the backwoods.

For a moment the pair sat in awkward silence, Silky trying

to put her thoughts into words; then Caroline spoke up, gently saying, "I can guess why you've come, my dear—to ask me about Major Taggart."

Silky tried to collect her scattered composure. "Yes . . . that's right," she answered, stunned that Taggart was really a major.

Caroline lifted her finely arched brows. "I've heard that he's been arrested"—a frown gathered on her face—"and I suspect Captain Fouche will be here shortly to also take me in for questioning."

Silky just stared at her, astounded she would be so candid with her comments. At the same time she was surprised to find herself warming to the woman, relaxing in her charming presence.

Caroline's dark eyes swept over her kindly. "In case you've heard something else, I must be truthful with you—Major Taggart and I have been working together for the Union cause."

Shock rippled through Silky that this elegant lady would utter such words in her presence. She stiffened at the thought that this woman had worked for the downfall of her beloved Confederacy. And to think of her sleek head bent low by Taggart's as they examined some map pained her so it almost took her breath away. Still, she had to admire her courage, for her manner was so cool she might be talking about attending a ball, not committing an offense punishable by death. In effect, by making the confession, this lovely creature had just put her life in Silky's hands. "W-why are you telling me such things?" she murmured, highly uncomfortable in being privy to the explosive secret.

Caroline rose and walked behind her chair, the swish of her petticoats cutting through the strained silence. "I'm telling you this," she began, "because I feel that I must. Decency demands it." Morning sunlight splashed over her creamy complexion as she regarded Silky thoughtfully. "I'm placing my trust in you, believing you will not reveal me."

Silky's heart beat faster, for she'd come to confront Caroline about this very matter. She'd been prepared to pry the truth from her any way she could, match wits and words with her, but she'd never expected this disarming graciousness. In her heart she knew she would keep her silence, and she once again felt herself changing inside. It seemed it was very difficult to wound an enemy when, in her eyes, she saw nothing but friendship and concern for Silky's own welfare.

"I visited Captain Fouche," Silky said haltingly, deciding to plunge on and have everything on the table. "He showed me a document that Taggart had signed"—she pressed her lips together—"that said that his visits here had nothing to do with the war." Her head spun with nervousness, and she wondered if she could finish her statement. "It said you were . . ."

"Lovers?" Caroline asked, her face shining with compassion.

"Yes," Silky whispered throatily.

Caroline ran her hands over the back of the velvety chair. "I can assure you from the bottom of my heart that this is not true. No doubt Major Taggart is claiming this to explain his presence here, to protect me."

"To protect you?" Silky blurted out without thinking.

A hint of a smile grazed Caroline's pink lips. "Yes, all agents know they must be prepared to sacrifice their reputations as well as their lives. Now the question is whether he will be able to make the Confederates believe him—especially Captain Fouche."

Her expression sympathetic, she walked to Silky and sat down beside her. "I assure you, my dear, I have great respect for the major, and I do have some tender feelings for him," she confessed, glancing down at the admission, "but we were never lovers." She lifted glistening eyes and considered Silky with slow deliberation. "You're the one who loves him, aren't you?"

The lady's frank question was almost too much for Silky to bear. The words *no, I don't love him!* were on the tip of her tongue. How could she love a slick-tongued, blue-bellied Yankee who'd lied to her since the first day they'd met? Didn't the woman have any grasp of the situation at all; didn't she understand she'd been used in the worst sense of the word? She wanted to tell Caroline all these things, but instead she simply said, "I'm all mixed up inside right now. I don't know how I feel."

Caroline clasped her soft hands over Silky's. "You should be proud of Major Taggart," she offered enthusiastically. "He's a real hero. He's risked his life many times to bring the war to a close."

"He's risked his life, all right," Silky answered impulsively, her words sounding harsh even to herself. "He's risked it to bring down the South."

"But he has sympathy for both sides, my dear," Caroline responded. "He has respect for the South, just as I do. He loves all that is good and fine here. Surely you cannot blame him for fighting for what he believes is right." She caressed Silky's shoulder. "I'm sure he loves you," she gently ventured.

A laugh burst from Silky's lips. "He couldn't love me. We're as different as night and day. He's from the city; I'm from the country. He's had a fine education and been everywhere; I'm a nobody. Our meeting was just an accident. It shouldn't have happened." She waved her hand at the gorgeous room. "He's used to a place like this"—she glanced down in embarrassment—"and someone like you." Her lashes fluttered up and she scanned Caroline once more. "And he deserves someone like you."

The lady looked deeply into her eyes. "You don't understand him. I saw how anxious he was to get back to you the evening he brought the information about Fort Stedman."

Silky sat in silence trying to digest her startling words. Fort Stedman? So that was why Taggart had rushed off that horrible night.

"And besides that," Caroline continued, "he tried to have himself removed from his mission. I have known for some time that you were lovers, and it's for this very reason the major asked for another assignment. Unfortunately it was impossible for Washington to honor his request."

Hope rose in Silky as she considered the situation with a fresh perspective. There was so much she didn't know, so much she didn't understand about Taggart, she suddenly realized, thoughtfully smoothing back a wisp of hair.

"If there was anything I could do to free Major Taggart, I would," Caroline explained, "but General Grant is on the move from City Point. Everything is in a state of confusion and flux. At the moment I'm afraid my hands are tied. I cannot get help from outside, and my active interference in his arrest would doom us both. If you can do anything to save him, you must."

She took Silky's hand once more, pressing it with hers. "And if you need a place of refuge, come here." She hesitated for a moment, then continued, her voice faltering a bit. "You must believe we were never lovers," she vowed earnestly, "for we were not. He loves you."

Silky's mind tumbled with questions and doubts—so many doubts. The memory of Taggart's signature on the document came swimming back, and she reminded herself that he'd never committed himself to her in any way—never told her he loved her. She'd yearned desperately to hear those words, but they'd not passed his lips even once, only a string of lies he'd used to manipulate her.

"If I only knew what to believe," she murmured, closing her eyes for a moment in concentration. "If I could only grab on to some fact, some certainty." She let out a tremulous breath and gazed at the older woman through misty eyes. "You say you and Taggart weren't lovers, while Fouche swears that you were. What would you believe if you were in my place?"

Compassion flickered over Caroline's features. "I'm not sure. The decision is yours alone," she answered, letting her hand fall away. "No one can tell you what to do. And, in the end, I think your decision must be based on faith and love—not facts."

In the midst of her turmoil, Silky regarded the woman's lovely face, knowing she was right. Surely the only place she would find the answer for her troublesome decision was in her own heart.

Taggart restlessly paced about the security cell as, for the fiftieth time, he searched for a way to escape. His stomach rumbled with hunger, for he hadn't been fed since moving here, having only received a cup of brackish water each day. In one corner, a thin, torn mattress served as a bed, and in the other, a chamber pot sent its nauseating reek over the filthy cubicle. I have to get out, he told himself, his mind reeling with concern about Silky and what might be happening to her. He paused at the window facing the exercise yard, clenched the bars, and tried to get a breath of fresh air. A dank breeze from the river touched his face as he watched hundreds of prisoners mill about, taking their exercise while Confederate guards, rifles in hand, monitored their steps.

He studied the slow-moving prisoners, who seemed to him as if they were moving in a dream. Last night he'd had a dream himself—but a new dream, not the old one that had plagued his mind since his brother had been executed. During the small, wee hours Ned had smiled and told him everything was all right, then asked him to let go of the striving that had held him captive for so long.

His heart full of love, Taggart had agreed, and almost immediately felt a new sense of peace. It seemed this new dream had enabled him to rid himself of the driving need to achieve justice for his brother's death. That need had been replaced with a thankfulness for the years they'd had together, and he'd suddenly understood that in his memories he would have his brother with him forever, as long as he himself drew breath.

He wondered why he should have such a dream, and realized it was because of the people he'd met all over the Confederacy—decent people whose goodness had wiped out the evil of a few men at Andersonville. But most important, it was because Silky had opened his eyes to the healing power of love. His dream had changed because he himself had been transformed inside, he saw, understanding that forgiveness had finally released him from the dark fantasy.

His thoughts drifted back to the day they'd first met, and he smiled at the picture of her waving the long-barreled rifle at him. Then he recalled their glorious days in the woods: the brilliant foliage, the sound of breaking twigs underfoot, the mellow scent of dried vegetation. With a twinge of awe, he recalled a perfect autumn day, Silky's exquisite form outlined against the bowers of scarlet leaves that surrounded them on all sides, effectively shutting out a world that had gone mad with war. Would he ever see that perfect face again?

Still deep in thought, he heard the sound of footsteps and jangling keys and, turning about, spied Fouche and two armed guards approaching the cell. The Creole, a muscle flicking angrily in his jaw, ordered the cell door unlocked, then walked toward Taggart while the guards stood at the ready, their weapons pointed at his chest.

"Perhaps you would like to recant your statement about Caroline Willmott," Fouche proposed, his simple comment loaded with threatening overtones.

Taggart studied his arrogant face, noticing his clenched jaw and narrowed eyes. "Why should I do that?" he remarked in a relaxed tone, realizing the man was reaching the end of his tether.

Fouche's mouth thinned with displeasure. "I've questioned some of her neighbors," he commented, his footsteps taking him the length of the cell and back again as he clasped his gloved hands behind his back. He paused to fix a sharp gaze on Taggart. "Even loyal neighbors occasionally leak a family scandal," he remarked, beginning his pacing once more. A cynical smile played over his lips. "It seems the lady lost her heart to a professor at some Boston college years ago. The neighbors assure me that while Miss Willmott may be a trifle strange, she isn't one to indulge her carnal desires."

Taggart stared at him, outraged that Caroline should have been discussed by Fouche and her neighbors like some scarlet woman. "I can only tell you what happened in my case," he replied, watching the officer's face harden with cold fury. "I stand by my story." With a sense of relief he knew that Fouche didn't have enough evidence to arrest Caroline or he would have already done so. Undoubtedly that was why he was here.

His face marked with contempt, the Creole stripped off his fine gloves, shoved them under his belt and began yet another half hour of questions about Caroline, all of which Taggart refused to answer. At last Fouche strode away from him, then turned, his mouth set in a stony line. "Do not be so proud, monsieur. The Union has not broken through Lee's line yet. And it is doubtful if that event will ever take place."

The officer swaggered about, a spiteful smile pursing his

lips. "You might like to know that Miss Shanahan did visit me recently, just as I knew she would. She was quite interested in your statement about Caroline Willmott." He stared at Taggart, his eyes chips of stone. "I'm sure I'm correct in my assessment, for she went quite pale upon reading it."

A curse falling from his mouth, Taggart gazed at him, rage pouring through him at what Fouche had done. He knew that although the Creole might have started seeing Silky to gather information, he now wanted her with an almost insane lust and would do anything to have her.

Fouche paused to let his next barb penetrate Taggart's brain. "Don't worry about the lovely lady, for I plan on seeing that *all* of her physical needs are met. I'm sure you understand my meaning," he growled contemptuously.

Something snapped within Taggart and he lunged at Fouche, managing to shove him against the cell wall. Filled with scalding fury, he was clenching his hands about Fouche's neck when the guards lit into him, slamming their rifle butts into his ribs and forcing him away.

Taggart clutched his stomach and gasped for breath as Fouche and the guards hurried from the cell, their eyes wide with surprise. "Lock the door!" the officer cried, slamming it shut as Taggart rushed toward it. Only a moment too late he yanked against the bars just as one of the frightened guards scraped a key from the lock and backed away, his face pale with shock.

Fouche glared at Taggart through the bars, his gaze blazing with anger. "Do not think you will be freed if Grant is lucky enough to reach Richmond," he promised, vindictiveness cutting fresh lines over his stony features. He rubbed his neck, which bore the marks of Taggart's fingers. "Before that happens you will receive my personal attention. In the confusion, no one will take me to task for an unfortunate event that might have taken place while you were trying to escape!" he threatened, jerking on his gloves. He threw Taggart a look of festering hatred before striding away.

Taggart, still trying to get his breath, watched Fouche and the guards pace down the corridor and disappear out of sight. For a moment a terrible emptiness spread through him, but he pushed it back, determined to keep a part of himself untouchable from the Creole's reach.

Pain streaked through his side as he walked to the exercise yard window and braced his arm against its rough facing. Grant would be taking Richmond soon, he told himself, shoring up his faith. Soon this nightmare would be over, and he'd be released from this hellhole called Libby Prison. Afterward he would find Silky and discover why she'd given Fouche the secret that had put him here in the first place.

Breathing easier now, he held on to this thought with all his might.

Shocked at what he'd told her, Silky stared at Daniel as they moved down one of Chimborazo's corridors side by side. "You're leaving the hospital? But where will you go?"

He paused, resting his weight on his crutches. "Abby's family has asked me to come and stay with them," he announced proudly, a grin sweeping over his features. "They have a spare bedroom and are willin' to put me up till I can go back and sell our place in the Blue Ridge. Then as soon as I build up a little nest egg from workin' in the lumberyard, me and Abby can get married."

Silky considered what he'd said, somewhat surprised things were moving along this fast with him and Abby, but happy nonetheless. She knew the situation was not unusual, for many of Richmond's citizens had opened their homes to the wounded soldiers who were now billeted all over the city. Being with Abby would make Daniel recover faster, and in her heart she knew he would receive better care and food than in Chimborazo. Of course, the Drumond home was located on the edge of the city, making visits difficult, but knowing the change was for the best, she quickly adjusted her emotions.

Having rested a bit, Daniel limped ahead. "Are you doin' any better?" he asked.

"A little," she answered, striving for a casual tone as they turned into his ward. "But I'm still confused." She looked at his sympathetic face. "My feelings are so tangled up I hardly know what to think anymore."

Her brother hobbled to his bed, eased upon it, and cast his crutches aside. "Are you sure Taggart was seeing another woman?" he suddenly asked, startling her with his blunt words.

With a prickle of humiliation, she glanced away. "I-I was wrong about that," she admitted. "He was seeing one, but not for the reason I thought."

"Why didn't you tell me Taggart was a Yankee when you first split with him?" he continued, his inquiring eyes weighing and assessing her reaction.

Momentarily abashed, she realized he'd asked her the same thing once before. "I-I don't know," she answered, trembling inwardly at the question.

A frown wrinkled Daniel's brow. "I do. I think you're still in love with him."

"That's impossible!"

"Maybe not," he replied thoughtfully. "I've been layin' here thinkin' it all over, wonderin' why you didn't tell me he was Yankee the moment you knew it." A satisfied smile moved over his lips. "I think it's because you still love him and were tryin' to protect him."

"That's crazy," she declared in an exasperated voice. "I knew Fouche was onto him, but I didn't take the trouble to warn him, did I?"

"No—but I think you wanted to. Besides that, you thought he'd already left Richmond." His face softened with understanding. "You had plenty of chances but you never turned him in to the authorities, did you?"

Silky realized she'd once considered doing just that—but, in the end, she simply couldn't. She bit her tongue, refusing to admit this embarrassing fact to her brother.

His gaze fastened on her, forcing her to face a truth she wanted to ignore. "You didn't let on a peep to me about him bein' a Yankee till he'd been arrested and you had to tell me."

"Lordamercy, I can't believe what you're saying," she stated. "Have you lost your mind? When you found out he was a Yankee it hurt you as much as me!"

Daniel raised his brows. "Yeah, what you told me gave me a turn, all right, and for a while I wanted to kill him." His voice became soft and intimate. "But people are people.

Scratch them, and they ain't Yankees or Rebs, they're just people."

"W-What do you mean?" she muttered, her voice hoarse with surprise. She recalled Taggart had once said something very similar back in the mountains.

"When I signed up," her brother continued, putting his hand over hers, "I thought the Yankees were devils just like everybody else in the hollow did; then my company took some prisoners. While I was takin' care of them, I found out they were pretty much like us. They just talked different and lived in another part of the country."

"But Taggart lied to me!" she cried, pulling her hand away. "What kind of life could we have together, with all his lies standing between us?"

Daniel sat forward, demanding her complete attention. "Whatever kind you wanted to make it."

Dumbstruck, she stared at him, detecting a certain wisdom in the depths of his clear green eyes. He'd always had a firm grasp of what was really important in life.

"Don't you understand why he stayed here in Richmond instead of hightailin' it to the north like he should have done?" he asked, his gaze drifting over her. "He stayed here to find you. If he can do that much, it seems you might at least consider talkin' to him."

Silky sat quietly, too stunned to utter a word.

"You were hurt because he lied to you," Daniel explained, "but you were hurt worse because he was workin' against the Cause—against your dream."

She took a deep breath, realizing he was right. "But we still have a chance," she exclaimed hotly, her passion for the Confederacy whipping through her veins like a living fire.

Daniel chuckled. "You're a Reb all right, the biggest I ever saw—but it's all over, honey. We fought and we fought like wildcats, but there wasn't enough of us, and we didn't have enough to fight with."

"Could you forgive Taggart?" Silky whispered.

He expelled a long sigh. "I reckon I could. This whole nation will have to do a lot of forgettin' and forgivin', so I'll have plenty of company." He considered her gently.

"The question is—can you forgive him?"

She couldn't have answered him even if she'd wanted to.

"The war is over, honey. It's time to latch onto a new dream. Latch onto it hard and fast and never let go."

A sick feeling coiled in the pit of Silky's stomach like poison. "You're leaving the city tonight?" she asked Delcie as they walked along Murphy Street in the cool dusk. "Can't you wait until morning?"

The girl clasped her hand. "No—the Yankees are almost here, missy," she answered. "They done captured Petersburg, and folks is gettin' out of Richmond fast as they can. Everybody that's able is sellin' their house or just leavin' it standin' and takin' off."

Crushed by the news Silky stared at her, not knowing what to say. It was April second and almost dark when Delcie had knocked on her door, suggesting they take a walk. Now, as the pair strolled along the broken sidewalk discussing the situation, rumbling wagons rolled past them, riffling up dust in the gutters.

"Everythin' sure is a big mess," Delcie continued, her eyes misting with emotion. "See them wagons?" she asked, glancing at the shadowy street that was filled with riders and conveyances of every kind. "Me and Jim is goin' west like them, then circle back to Baltimore." Tears trembled on her thick lashes. "I just came so's I could tell you good-bye."

Silky paused, catching her elbow, not wanting her to go. "But the Yankees are coming to free the slaves," she blurted out before she thought.

Delcie widened her eyes. "You forgets me and Jim is already free." She tightened her shawl against the twilight chill. "Us is leavin' 'cause of the fires."

"Fires? What are you talking about?"

"Missy, when the Yankees come bustin' into Atlanta half the city burned down and a lot of folks got killed. Our shantytown bein' so flimsy, it'll burn for sure." An uneasy look settled on the girl's face. "Come mornin' Richmond will be a real dangerous place to be!"

As Silky considered what lay ahead for the couple, a tremor skittered across her skin. "Do you have any money to help you along?'' she asked, looking into Delcie's concerned eyes.

Delcie hung her head, then looked up, her face etched with worry. ''Just a speck. Us figured on gettin' work along the way.''

Silky surveyed her dejected posture, suddenly realizing she'd been the best friend she ever had. Spurred by a strong impulse she didn't completely understand, she slipped off Taggart's earrings and gazed at them, a host of poignant memories rushing over her. Then, very slowly, she opened Delcie's hand and dropped the them into her cupped palm. ''Here—take these with you,'' she ordered hoarsely, knowing Taggart would approve of the action.

Delcie shook her head. ''Oh, missy, I can't take them earrings. What'll you do when your money runs out? Why, it's nearly runned out already.''

''Daniel is getting some back pay,'' Silky lied. ''He'll loan me a little till I get a job.''

''I knows the Confederate army don't pay nothin' no more,'' Delcie replied, trying to thrust the jewelry back into Silky's hand. ''Lieutenant Taggart done give you them earrings for Christmas. You needs to keep them to remember him by.''

Silky bit back her tears. ''No,'' she whispered, knowing she'd recall every second she'd spent with him for the rest of her life. ''I can remember him just fine without them.'' She forced a smile, still holding Delcie's disbelieving gaze. ''Everybody needs a wedding gift. This is my wedding gift to you and Jim. When you get north, sell them and have a real wedding like you've always wanted.''

By now, tears welled in Delcie's eyes and, clutching the earrings in her fist, she wiped them away. ''Missy, my heart feels like it's about to bust. I thanks you. The money from these earrings will give us a whole new start.''

Unable to speak, Silky watched Delcie slide the jewelry into her apron pocket, then blow her nose on a ragged handkerchief. ''You's just got to forgive Lieutenant Taggart,'' she said, trying to collect her emotions. ''I knows that man loves you, even if he ain't told you so.'' She narrowed her eyes. ''Some men just be hardheaded that way. And maybe he lied to you, but I reckon he lied to keep you from carryin' on so.'' She trembled and chaffed her thin arms. ''Don't matter what he lied about now. This war be just about over now anyway.''

As if by mutual consent they walked on, and Silky realized Delcie was virtually echoing her brother's advice. ''Even if I decided to forgive him,'' she said, ''there's no way I could tell him—not with him locked up in prison.''

Delcie clasped her arm. ''I's done told you, you's got to get him out of that place. Some of them guards might shoot him out of meanness 'fore Gener'l Grant gets here. 'Sides that, the lieutenant be locked up and can't help hisself. He'll suffocate for sure when the fires start.''

Silky scanned the girl's tense face. She knew she was right. Fouche was so vindictive there was to telling what he might do, and the area about Libby was full of old warehouses, just waiting to explode with fire when the first wind-driven spark hit their roofs.

Delcie wiped back her tears and pointed a slim finger at the next corner. ''I's got to go now, missy. Jim be bundlin' up our stuff, and he's supposed to meet me 'cross the street over there.'' Her face a welter of emotion, she caught Silky's hand once more. ''I knows how you want things to be,'' she allowed with glassy eyes, ''but sometimes life don't work that way. Most folks just have to take what life hands 'em and do the best they can. If you looks hard enough, you'll see you can make somethin' good out of what you's got. Once you understands that, you's gonna feel a heap better.''

Delcie transferred her attention to the corner and, following her lead, Silky saw a huge black man emerge from the milling crowd waiting to cross the street. Dressed in ragged clothes and a floppy hat, he wore two bedrolls tied to his back and carried a bulging sack over his wide shoulder. His anxious gaze traveled the length of the street, then circled back and paused on Delcie, prompting a relieved smile on his face.

Delcie looked at Silky, tears rolling down her cheeks. ''I's gonna remember you always,'' she murmured, backing up and letting her hand slowly slide away. ''I's never gonna forget you!''

Silky stepped forward and hugged her friend's slight frame tightly against her. "Don't worry about me. I'll be all right," she whispered, holding back her own tears.

Delcie eased away, her eyes glistening with emotion. "I prays to God you will be." With that, she picked up her ragged skirt, and wove her way through the traffic to Jim, who enveloped her in his big arms. Bathed in sunset colors, the girl raised her slim arm in farewell; then the pair clasped hands and swiftly disappeared into the throng moving westward.

Misery cutting through her, Silky started walking back to the boardinghouse. Her life was changing so quickly, almost as quickly as the glowing sky, she thought, noticing lamplight blooming in the windows along the way. Delcie had been an integral part of her days since she'd come to Richmond, and now she was gone—gone forever. Desperately lonely, Silky realized she would never know if the girl made it north, never know if she had her wedding, if she had children. All she'd have would be a collection of memories and suppositions about her future.

As the sound of creaking wheels broke into her dark reverie, she scanned Murphy Street once more. Riders with bundles tied over their mounts' rumps hurried westward, making their way around wagons piled high with furniture. With a dull sense of foreboding, she saw that all Delcie had predicted was coming to pass. The Union would be in Richmond in a matter of hours, and soon after that the South would taste defeat.

A great ball of tangled emotion in her bosom, she saw her boardinghouse, and a few moments later sat down on its steps. How she'd wanted the South to win; how she'd wanted to see the Stars and Bars flying proudly over every building in Virginia. Lord, how desperately she'd wanted all of this. But with tears sliding from her eyes, she realized with the fullness of her heart and soul that it was not to be. The realization filled her with unspeakable pain, but after it had abated a bit, she sensed a new sense of peace welling up within her.

Yes, her blood would always course hot at the sound of "Dixie." Never had the world seen an army that had fought with such valor as the Confederacy, she thought with fierce pride. With a third of the men and a quarter of the supplies of the Union, the South had nearly achieved the impossible—but in the end it was simply not enough. With burning eyes, she knew she had to produce the strength to accept this fact and keep on living.

Pulling in a steadying breath, she turned her thoughts to Taggart. She had to grudgingly admit that in his own way he possessed an integrity that made her proud, for she knew he'd tried to have himself removed from his assignment because of her. And it would take a fool not to see that Caroline Willmott was a person of honor.

At the same time, her most basic instincts told her Fouche was a cheat and a liar, and he lied not as Taggart had lied to foster a cause or protect a person's feelings; he lied because he was cruel and perverse. Relief washed over her as she accepted the fact that Taggart and Caroline weren't lovers. There was no way she could prove this, she thought, but as the lady had suggested, she'd looked into her heart and found her answer.

The South had lost the war. In that area her dreams had been smashed. Taggart would never be her hero in gray—but he was a hero in his own way, and she could make something good out of that, she decided, remembering Delcie's advice. With a little sob, she admitted to herself that she loved him even if he was a Yankee, and the admission shook her world.

With a long sigh, she felt the strength of that admission empower her. It was all so clear now: what was a war compared to a lifetime of love? Surely their love was more important than any cause, even a beloved cause. And because of that love she'd found the strength to forgive him. She suddenly understood love was the key—it was the only thing worth living for and dying for—nothing else could even come close. Because of love, Daniel and Abby were on the cusp of a new life, and Delcie and Jim were on their way north to be married. Yes, happiness was possible if she was strong enough to swallow her pride and go back to Taggart.

Her spirit aglow with a new purpose, she slowly stood and straightened her back. Trembling, she stared at the traffic rattling down the dark street. Somehow she had to free Taggart, she decided, resolve steeling her spirit. Then, with a shaft of despair, she remembered she'd betrayed him. If by the wildest chance she could manage to get him out of Libby, would he forgive her?

It didn't matter. Even if he wouldn't have her, she still had to do her best to save him. Her heart aglow, she finally understood what love was all about.

Chapter Twenty-one

After pacing about for hours trying to come up with some plan to free Taggart, Silky tossed a shawl about her shoulders and left her room, praying that Burton Harrison might help her. Aided by light from a dim gasolier attached to the stairwell wall, she saw the shadowy outline of a man entering the foyer and drew in her breath. It was Fouche. As she'd expected, he must have sent someone to follow her the day she'd returned from the provost marshal's office. How else would he know where she lived? she thought, shock momentarily rooting her to the landing.

"What are you doing here at this hour?" she asked harshly, hoping she could send him away with a show of courage.

Looking at her with a peculiar stare, he started walking up the stairs, weak light flickering over him. How different he looks, she thought, offended he'd chosen this very inopportune time to invade her privacy. For the first time since she'd met him he wore civilian clothes—an expensive suit and fine boots. His hair, usually so well groomed, was windblown, and a string tie hung loosely about his neck, giving him a hastily dressed appearance.

When he paused by her side, she detected the scent of whiskey on his breath and noticed his eyes were clouded with drink. She'd always known he was overfond of expensive wines and French brandies, but had never seen him like this, his fine discipline ruined by overindulgence. He clasped her arm, his fingers pinching into her skin. "We must talk," he said, wrenching the key from her hand.

Terror threatened to engulf her, but she silently vowed she'd never let him know how scared she was. After turning the lock, he shoved her into the room, then closed the door and tossed the key on the table.

"What do you want?" she demanded, raising her voice to cover her desperate fear. "I'm in a hurry."

"Doubtless," he replied coldly. "As you must know the Yankees will soon be invading Richmond. I've come to escort you out of the city before they arrive. Pack a few things and I'll take you to Danville, then on to New Orleans."

So that was why he was drunk and dressed in civilian clothes! she thought, disgusted with his cowardly behavior. He'd shed his uniform because he'd abandoned his post and was fleeing the city. Her nerves taut, she presented her back to him and crossed the room. "I'll manage fine," she replied briskly, deeply relieved her voice still held steady. "I don't care to go with you."

"You're making a grave mistake," he exclaimed reproachfully. "Don't you understand? The South has lost and the Yankees will have their retribution if it means burning the whole city."

She turned and noticed his eyes gleaming with a sick light. Squaring her shoulders in defiance, she boldly met his gaze. Instinctively she knew she couldn't let him intimidate her; at the same time, she felt her courage curling up like a dry leaf.

When he came to her, his manner became overly polite, as it had been when she first met him. "I'll be your protector," he offered, his mouth slack with lust. "You'll need one now that Taggart can no longer look after you."

Panic swept through her like swift flames. "What do you mean by that?" she asked, stiffening.

Fouche assessed her sharply. "I wanted to save your feelings, but you're forcing me to be blunt." She caught her breath as his dilated eyes revealed all the cruelty and ugliness within him. "He has met his expected end. He was hanged this afternoon."

Silky's heart lurched crazily. Feeling as if she'd been kicked in the stomach, she braced her hand on a chair. "No, you're lying," she cried. "You're making it up. It's nothing but another of your lies!"

He reached for her, but she stumbled backward, her shawl slipping to the floor. He clenched her arms roughly. "It's true. He's dead and you're better off without him." He shook her as if she were a rag doll. "Listen to me. I'm offering you my protection. I have money, more money than you ever dreamed of."

Feeling totally exposed and helpless, she knew she had to keep him talking until the landlady came to check on her male caller. "And where did you get all your money?" she breathed, trembling with fear. "How could your family afford to spare such funds? Everyone in the South is ruined now, even the rich," she rushed on, saying whatever came to her mind. "Why, the only people who really have money are speculators."

A sheepish smile surfaced on Fouche's mouth and, her stomach turning, she realized she'd accidentally put her finger on his source of wealth. "Why, that's what you are, isn't it?" she rasped, suddenly understanding why he made so many trips out of town. "You intimidated the warehouse and railroad workers here in Richmond, then shipped the merchandise to other parts of the Confederacy, didn't you?"

"I only did what others have done," he answered with annoyance, his tongue loosened by drink and the excitement of the moment. "It doesn't matter how I got my money—the point is I have plenty and I'll take care of you."

Silky tried to wrench away from him. "I wouldn't marry you if you were the last man in the world!" she vowed, her spirit surging back and sending fresh strength to her limbs.

Fouche's mouth fell open. "Marry you?" he laughed, his eyes brightening with contempt. "Do you think me a fool? I would never marry another man's leavings. My name is the oldest in New Orleans, my blood the finest in the state. I said I would take care of you—make you my mistress. As white trash, that's the best you can hope for.''

She struggled violently to free her arms. No one had ever called her white trash before, and the words struck rage within her. White trash, indeed! Why, her family had been among the first settlers in Virginia, and her forefathers had fought valiantly in the American Revolution. ''I don't *think* you a fool, I *know* you a fool!'' she cried, finally freeing her arms and soundly slapping his face. ''I'd never leave Richmond with you. I'm going to get Taggart out of prison!''

His eyes flickered with such malice her blood ran cold. ''I'd rather see you dead first.''

''So he is alive?'' she exclaimed, her intuition verified.

Ignoring her question, Fouche brutally grabbed her waist and jerked her against him. ''I'll show you, you little spitfire. I'll take what I want, then be on my way without you.'' She tried to escape, but his fingers cut into the flesh over her ribs. ''I've wanted you for so long,'' he muttered, his eyes gleaming with hot longing. ''Wanted you all the time you were sleeping with that Yankee, and I promised myself I would have you—and I shall.'' He lowered his head and pushed his lips against hers. His hot, fetid breath washed over her face, his mouth bruised hers, and his hand groped at her breast.

Silky hit out at him again and again, her only thought to protect herself. I'm almost away from him, she thought, her heart palpitating wildly. Just one more blow and I'll be free. Then, as his fingers dug into her arms once more, she realized that with his greater strength she was at his mercy. Knowing she had to do something to even the odds, she suddenly shifted her weight to one side and, taking advantage of his surprise, shoved at his chest with all the strength she possessed.

Instantly he released her and, tangling his feet in the discarded shawl, tumbled against the table, hitting his head on its sharp corner. His eyes rolled up in stunned shock for a second; then he crumpled to the floor and remained perfectly still.

Silky stood frozen, her gaze riveted on his motionless body. Lord in heaven, have I killed him? she wondered, her breath coming in rough gasps. With a churning stomach, she inched closer and dragged her gaze over him, searching for signs of life. Tears stinging her eyes, she finally saw his chest rising and falling and heard him moan softly. Thank God, she hadn't committed murder trying to protect herself, she thought with a relief that left her shaking. Then to her horror she heard Fouche mumbling as he flickered in and out of consciousness: "You little vixen . . . I'll get you . . . get you for this."

At that moment she heard the heavy landlady treading up the stairs. "What's goin' on up there? What's all the racket about? I told you I run a decent house!" the irate woman bawled out angrily.

Silky glanced at Fouche's limp form on the floor, then at the door, which would soon be opened by the landlady. Her mind focusing, she realized she had to get out of the room. She had to discover if Fouche was lying about Taggart's execution as she thought, or if the worst had happened. Frantic with fear, she also knew the Creole might regain full consciousness at any second. The time for thinking and planning was over. She had to act now, and act fast.

She opened the door and hurled herself past the landlady, who was still struggling up the stairs. The woman held her fist in the air. "Come back here! Come back!" she shouted threateningly.

With the desperation of a frightened animal, Silky ran from the boardinghouse into the darkness, wondering where she might find a mount. Hastily scanning the dimly lit street, she saw a young man holding the reins of Fouche's horse. Because of the panic taking the city he'd evidentially hired the adolescent to watch the animal so it wouldn't be stolen.

That mattered little now. The Creole wouldn't be doing any riding for a while, she thought with a rush of hope—not with his head feeling like it had been hit with a cannonball. She only hoped when he did regain consciousness that he had enough sense left to remember he'd been bested by the girl he'd called white trash. She'd leave him in the care of the shrewish landlady—like a scorpion and a venomous snake, they'd make a matched pair.

She gave the surprised lad a coin, then hitched up her skirt and hoisted herself into the saddle. The skittish mare danced about for a minute but, using her mountain skills, Silky managed to turn the horse in the direction she wanted to go. Then, slapping it on the rump, she bolted down the street, dodging some other riders, her only thought to get away from the boardinghouse as fast as possible.

Silky rode for fifteen minutes, then spotted Burton Harrison's mansion from half a block away. No one could miss it. Illuminated by the passing refugees' torches, a Confederate flag snapped from its big front porch, and every window glowed with light.

She urged her horse to the side of the house, dismounted, and tied her reins to an overhanging limb hidden in the shadows. All about her everything was in utter chaos. From the neighboring streets she heard the shouts of mobs, sounds of rumbling wagons, and the beating of drums, all mixed up together. With a prickle of fear she hurried up the mansion's steps, thinking Richmond had gone completely mad.

A soldier carrying a box of documents rushed from the house and passed her on the steps, in such a hurry he didn't even notice her. Like the rest of Richmond, he seemed to have one thought: getting out of the city. The mansion's front door stood wide open, and with a sense of dark wonder she walked into its foyer, noticing there wasn't a servant in sight. In the parlor, papers protruded from half-open drawers, and other documents littered the floor.

At the end of the wide hall she spotted a packed carpetbag with a light overcoat draped over it. A top hat rested on a nearby console. The sound of shuffling papers reached her ears and, turning right, she spied Burton Harrison hunched over a table in his book-lined library. Papers covered the table, and boxes of documents sat on the floor, their contents spilling onto the scarlet carpet. Flames crackled in a fireplace behind the table, racing over thick stacks of folders and scenting the air with the odor of burning paper.

Harrison looked up, utter astonishment marking his youthful face. "Silky," he said, raising his brows in surprise.

"What in God's name are you doing here? You should be getting out of Richmond. I'm afraid the South is on her knees." Fatigue dulled his soft brown eyes. "There is nothing left . . . nothing at all."

Wordless, Silky neared the overflowing table.

Harrison stood to pitch another bundle of documents on the snapping flames. "I'm leaving as well, as soon as I dispose of some personal papers," he confessed, throwing a weary gaze over his shoulder. "I'm escorting Mrs. Davis and her children to Danville where they'll be safe. The president will follow behind us."

"Where is our army now? Where is Lee?" she whispered, scarcely believing a whole nation could fall as easily as a house of cards.

A look of sadness passed over Harrison's tired features. "His forces are travelling west, toward Lynchburg, looking for food. The general is trying to join Johnston in the Carolinas for a last effort." His shoulders slumped with fatigue. "But all is lost—utterly lost. The move comes too late. Perhaps if Lee had joined Johnston earlier the ploy would have worked, but the powers that be didn't want to give up the capitol. Now we're losing it anyway."

Silky stared at him, still shaken from her confrontation with Fouche.

"Why, you're trembling, my dear," Harrison observed, gazing at her kindly. "Don't worry, there is still time to escape. Come with me and Mrs. Jefferson and the children." He reached over the table to cup her chin. "I'll see that you're safe—that you get on a southbound train before Grant enters the city."

"No, I can't go," she answered swiftly, blinking back her tears. She rounded the table and clutched the fine fabric of his sleeve. "I have to see Taggart—make sure he's all right."

"Taggart?" Harrison echoed, his gentle expression evaporating into a blank stare. "You've come on the eve of Armageddon to talk about a Yankee scoundrel who used you to enter Richmond society and spy upon us?"

"Y-yes, I suppose I have." She studied his shocked face, wondering if she'd made a mistake in approaching him.

"Fouche says he's been executed. Is this true? You'll tell me the truth, won't you?" she pleaded, her voice hoarse with tension.

Harrison appraised her with incredulous eyes. "Why should you care about him? Let the matter be," he advised, disapproval gathering in the shadows of his face. "He deceived you along with the rest of us, but you're now free of him. Count your lucky stars and forget he ever existed."

"But that's just it," Silky confessed, feeling a little ridiculous at the admission. "I can't." She let her hand fall from his arm. "Haven't you ever loved someone no matter what they've done? Loved them with all your heart and soul, no matter what you had to forgive them?" She pulled in a deep breath. "Haven't you ever loved someone like that?" She noticed shock glinting in his eyes as he struggled to camouflage his emotions.

"No, thank God, I have not," he answered with disbelief. His gaze crept to a large register bound in red leather, then slowly moved back to her. "But, for your friendship, for the time we enjoyed together in this once great city," he stated, his voice now tinged with compassion, "I'll give you the information you want."

Picking up the book, he opened it and traced his finger over Taggart's name, which in her state of unease blurred before her eyes. "There have been a few executions during the last week, but Taggart was not one of them. This register was brought to me from Libby Prison only a few hours ago, so I can vouch for the veracity of its contents."

Silky's heart leaped with hope. Fouche had lied, just as she'd expected. She felt as if she herself had been reprieved from the gallows. Exhilaration lifting her spirits, she observed Harrison's frowning face. "But where is he?" she queried in a rush of relief. "What part of the prison is he in?"

The secretary ran his eyes over the book once more, then swung his attention back to her. "He's in a special security cell, but I have no idea where it's located." He laid the register aside, concern darkening his expression. "Surely you aren't thinking of going to Libby? The government ordered several tobacco warehouses torched to delay the Yankees' progress in the eastern part of the city, and the fire is spreading. I suspect that whole quarter will soon be aflame," he warned, his voice scarcely more than a stunned whisper.

"Yes . . . I am," she answered, fresh determination reviving her.

He clasped her shoulders, and gazed at her as if she'd lost her mind. "No one can help you get there, and it would be folly to try," he advised her. "Come to Danville with me."

"No . . . I'm going to Libby," she asserted, her voice reflecting a calmness she didn't feel. She realized that although the brick prison itself wouldn't burn, its shake roof would catch fire and collapse, pouring flames and smoke into the interior of the building. She had to get started and she didn't have a moment to spare. Energized by her fear she suddenly pulled away from Harrison's grip and ran from the library before he could stop her. Ignoring his cry for her to return she raced from the mansion, her footsteps ringing over the parquet floor.

On the porch she paused to catch her breath and saw that the clamoring parade of westbound civilian refugees had thickened. A babble of wild, excited voices reached her ears, and the scent of smoking torches touched her nostrils. Wagons and buggies creaked and groaned, heavily loaded with men and boys clinging on where they might. The more fortunate rode double on horses and mules, while the dispossessed plodded along on foot, bedrolls strapped to their backs.

She hurried to the side of the mansion to get her mount, and with a dart of alarm noticed a man yanking at the mare's reins. Frantically she ran to the bounder and beat at his back with her balled fists. "No, get away! That horse is mine!" she cried, trying to pull his foot from the stirrup.

With a mighty grunt, the no-account turned and cuffed Silky on the ear, knocking her to the ground. He swung into the saddle, galloped across the shadowy yard, and rode away. Dazed by the blow, she watched him melt into the crowd through a sheen of tears. She felt as if she might break down right then and there, but bit back her tears. She was now on foot with the whole city to cross.

Spurred by fierce determination, she slowly rose, her face

stinging from the sharp blow. Still a bit dizzy, she crossed the yard, then started walking eastward, jostled about in the flow of traffic moving against her. Lord above, she thought, a strangling sob almost choking her. How would she ever get to Libby Prison in time to save Taggart without a horse?

Silky walked eastward toward the prison, smoke burning her eyes. From the tobacco warehouse fires, others had started, and a lurid glow hovered above the city's spires and towers, painting the streets with a nightmarish light. The last of the troops and ambulances and artillery wagons rumbled past with a semblance of order—but the civilians were another story. All about her there was a frantic trampling of feet, and furniture and household goods lay in the streets to be pawed over by a populace gone mad with fear and avarice.

The frightened cries of women and children rent the smoky air as everyone pushed against her on their westward exit, and she felt like a fish swimming upstream. She would have given anything for a hackney, but that was impossible, for those that were not engaged had been commandeered by the army. Like herself, here in the heart of Richmond, nearly everyone was on foot. When she did see a carriage, it was so loaded with people and goods the horses could scarcely pull it.

Out of breath, she leaned against a shop, her heart hammering against her ribs like a bird in a trap. For a moment she recalled Fouche's sick, crazed eyes. Had he recovered enough to track her down? Was he searching for her this very minute? Then, shivering at the possibility, she shoved it aside, knowing she had to save her dwindling emotional strength to get through the night. At least Daniel was safe, she thought, giving a silent prayer of thanks he was on the fringe of Richmond with Abby's family, out of the range of the fires.

But here things were different, and the scenes she saw could have come from hell itself. With a long, quavering sigh, she surveyed the destruction about her. Stores had been broken into, ransacked, and looted. The frenzied crowds had snatched merchandise from burning factories and places of business and were toting it off in sheets and shawls. With some amazement she noticed the looting was not confined to the lower classes, as gently reared ladies pushed past each other carrying boxes of food. People were white faced with fear and dread, and those who were not hurrying westward milled about like lost souls with hollow, vacant looks in their eyes.

A brick whizzed by Silky's head and crashed into a nearby window, filling her ears with the sound of tinkling glass. She merely trudged ahead, locks of damp hair falling before her eyes. The last Confederate pickets now came through, their ranks broken and mixed. Apparently an officer had given them an order to destroy all liquor supplies to keep it away from the rabble, for the soldiers noisily rolled whiskey barrels into the streets and pried off their lids.

With loud thumps, the men turned over the barrels, and gallon upon gallon of whiskey poured into the gutters, its strong scent permeating the air. Other soldiers threw cases of bottled wine and brandy from third-story windows to destroy it, and the sound of crashing glass grated against her ears.

The purpose of the order was soon defeated, for riffraff scooped up the whiskey in cups and pans and anything that would hold liquid and started guzzling it down. Wild-eyed men and painted women tried to drag away the half-filled whiskey barrels with their own hands. A large portion of the crowd became drunk and staggered off, laughing hysterically.

Everything possible was being done to keep anything of value from the Yankees, and other soldiers burst open barrels of molasses, which spilled out and ran into the gutters, mingling with the whiskey.

The stockpiled warehouses that Delcie had mentioned so long ago had been opened, and the food was carried off by rich and poor alike, some people getting into scuffles over barrels of flour that were now worth five hundred Confederate dollars each. Why hadn't these supplies been issued to the hungry soldiers before men like Fouche could get at them? Silky wondered angrily. Why had they been hoarded away by greedy speculators when the boys in gray were starving?

Her strength almost gone, she plodded on, often dodging aside to escape being run down by some desperate teamster cracking a whip above his horses' backs. Longingly she gazed at the overloaded wagons, but there was no chance of getting a ride, for they were all going in the wrong direction. How many miles had she come? she wondered, looking around for some landmark that she recognized from her earlier trip across Richmond to the provost marshal's office. She paused to wipe her wet brow, then limped ahead, sweat trickling between her breasts and her gown sticking to her back.

Later, a sharp pain in her side forced her to stop, and for a moment she almost yielded to a powerful urge to sink to the pavement and just give up. The Lord knew her throat was dry and parched and her feet were so tender she could scarcely put them against the paving stones. Who would know? Who would care? she thought, her head swimming with fatigue. Libby Prison might already be aflame. Taggart might already be dead. If he was, she didn't care to live anyway.

In this dark hour all the demons of doubt and fear she'd ever known assailed her, telling her it was no use. *Give up, give up,* they ordered. *It's useless to go on. Foolish to go on. You can't stop a building from burning. Listen to your better judgment. There is nothing you can do. Nothing.*

Then from deep inside her she felt a spurt of anger. Anger such as she'd known when Sergeant Holt came to her cabin to confront Taggart. Anger such as she'd experienced when Fouche had called her white trash. Now she knew this raging anger because she'd come this far and was ready to give up. She'd thought that discovering Taggart was a Yankee was the worst thing that had ever happened to her, but nothing could be worse than him dying without knowing that she'd forgiven him. Giving up now would be like giving up on her dreams—giving up on love itself.

She realized her whole life had come down to this test of strength and will. What she needed now was that flinty will that had brought her ancestors from Ireland and across Virginia to the Blue Ridge. The same will that Daniel had used to determine that he would walk again. He'd laid it out in his mind, and she could do the same thing. Somewhere within her she caught on to a slender cord of courage, and in the midst of her pain and despair it glimmered like gold. Hold on. Hold on, she ordered herself, mentally grasping the cord.

She'd guided Taggart to Charlottesville through a blizzard. Made it to Richmond to see Daniel in the midst of a war. And dammit to hell, she could keep on walking, putting one foot in front of the other until she reached Libby Prison. Somehow she would make her strength last. If it ran out she'd just will herself some more. Her body might be exhausted but her mind wasn't. As long as she could keep on thinking, keep on believing in herself, she could keep on manufacturing courage.

Taking a deep breath, she started walking eastward once more.

Chapter Twenty-two

Later that night, Silky peered through the predawn darkness, dazed and confused. A man had given her wrong directions to Libby, costing her much valuable time, and at this point she feared she'd lost her bearings. Guided by raw instinct, she walked for another twenty minutes, then rounded a corner. What she saw made her heart pump with joy. Through the acrid smoke she caught her first glimpse of the prison and its fenced yards.

Behind the dark mass, huge orange clouds speckled with fiery sparks boiled into the inky sky, and she saw the edge of the prison roof was on fire. She noticed Dribrell's Warehouse and Mayo's Warehouse, both on Cary Street, were also aflame, and with amazement she watched men throwing sacks from one side of the Gallego Flour Mill, even as fire licked up its other side.

A fresh breeze whipped from the south, and all about her one incandescent glare spiraled up after the other. Flames leaped across the shake roofs, sparkling like long, greedy fingers against the darkness, setting whole blocks afire. And on the James, the high-arched bridges were in flames, the rushing water beneath them sparkling with reflected light. How ill advised the order had been to fire the tobacco warehouses, she thought with mounting alarm. The Yankees wouldn't need to burn Richmond, for it would be destroyed before they got here!

Covering her mouth with a handkerchief against the suffocating smoke, she raced toward the prison. From the next street she heard roaring flames and the crack of timbers as a roof collapsed and crashed into the building it had once sheltered. Then through the curling smoke, she spied men running toward her—men clad in tattered blue uniforms. Yankee prisoners. Somehow they'd got free, but how was that possible? Had General Grant already entered Richmond?

Within earshot, one man whooped and raised his cap in the air. "They've left the prison. Richmond is ours!"

Silky realized the frightened Confederate guards must have abandoned their posts as Fouche had, and the prisoners had managed to escape. Surrounding fires cast light on the building, and she could see the Yankees through the open third-story windows as they scrambled toward the stairs that would lead them to freedom. She wondered if the soldiers had released Taggart from his security cell or, in their hysteria, forgotten him. Perhaps they didn't even know he was there. In her darkest hour she'd thought there was nothing she could do to save him, and she now realized she might be the only one who could.

The heat of the flames warm on her back, she rushed toward Libby as soldiers streamed past her. She noticed a small door standing open, and, once inside the prison, she frantically hurried through the first-floor corridors, searching for the security cell. As she threaded her way through the maze, she heard explosions from outside and knew the Confederates were blowing up arsenals to deny them to the Yankees. There was a roar and a great crash as another wooden building fell. Without a doubt, the prison roof would soon fall, too

She moved ahead, half blinded by the smoke, then heard running feet, and through the shadowy haze saw two prisoners, their eyes wide with fear. Her stomach fluttering with emotion, she rushed to the first, but he shoved past her in his haste to escape. Gasping for breath, she clutched the other soldier's arm. "Where's the security cell?" she cried, going into a coughing fit. "Tell me where it is!"

The Yankee grabbed her shoulders and wheeled her about. "You must have come in the side exit," he wheezed, tears streaming down his grimy face. "Go to the end of the corridor"—he pointed, giving her a little shove—"then turn right." Then he sprinted away, disappearing the way she'd just come.

Silky followed the soldier's directions, moving through thick smoke. She knew she was reaching her destination, and at last spied a windowed door and saw a pair of man's hands clutching the bars, and behind them a soot-streaked face. Taggart! she thought, racing toward the end of the corridor.

"Here, Silky, unlock the cell!" he shouted between coughs, slamming his shoulder against the door as he tried to break it down.

Desperately she tried to twist the knob, but it wouldn't move. "I've come to get you out of here before the prison burns down, you Yankee buzzard!" she informed him over the din outside the building.

"The keys are in the main office," he shouted with flashing eyes. "Turn around—you just passed it. Hurry, the Rebs will be blowing up the powder magazine any time now!"

Silky stumbled back down the corridor, trailing her hand along the wall until she found the office. Once inside, she swung her gaze about the smoke-filled room, then opened desk drawers, picking up papers with both hands and wildly dumping them on the floor. When she did not find the keys there, she trembled with sheer panic. Now absolutely frantic, she surveyed the office again, and finally spotted a fancy uniform jacket hanging on a peg.

She flew to the jacket, and with trembling hands slid her fingers into first one pocket, then the other, at last touching metal. Sobbing with relief, she pulled out a ring of jangling keys, careened from the office, and ran for the security cell. There, she jammed one key into the lock, then another, afraid none of them would fit.

From his place behind the bars, Taggart watched Silky fumble with the keys. Lord Almighty, what she must have come through to get to the prison. Soot speckled her finely molded face, and her bodice was drenched with perspiration. Her lovely auburn hair was tangled and hung in damp strands over her tired eyes. At last a key turned in the lock, and when the door swung open he clasped an arm about her, running for the main entrance.

Once they were free of the building, Taggart paused and clutched Silky in his arms, nothing else in the world mattering to him. How he regretted that he'd never told her that he loved her, loved her more than the moon and stars, loved her more than life itself. What a woman she was—this hard-headed little Reb! As he looked into her teary green eyes, he knew that although Fouche might have slyly wheedled the information about Petersburg from her, she hadn't purposely betrayed him. Lord, she'd come through the fires of hell to free him, and that act had to be prompted by a heart brimming with sheer love.

"I'm sorry," she sobbed, her face tight with anguish. "I told Fouche about Petersburg, but I didn't mean to. Will you forgive me? I—"

"Yes, I know—hush now," he said in a soothing voice, brushing back her long hair, which glinted like copper in the orange light. "It's forgotten already."

He enfolded her more tightly in his arms, memorizing the feel of her warm body and sweet curves beneath his hands. "Don't you ever take off again, you little minx!" he rasped just before his mouth moved over hers for a long, breathless moment.

When he withdrew, her eyes sparkled up through her tears like diamonds. "Don't worry, you'll never get rid of me now."

He held her against his chest, and over the top of her head saw the surrounding warehouses go up in flames. All about them was shouting and confusion as the last of the soldiers escaped from the prison. "Come on, we've got to get out of here," he cried, sliding an arm about her as he decided what might be the best route for their escape.

Silky huddled against Taggart's side; then, looking about,

her heart jolted, for she saw Fouche gallop up across the street and yank his skittish mount to a halt. Lord above, she thought with a rush of panic; somehow he'd managed to commandeer a horse! A crude bandage circled his head, and his fine jacket was torn and dirty. Even at this distance his eyes glinted with a hot, crazed look, and she realized that his fierce jealousy and lust for revenge had brought him here. As he dismounted, the wind whipped back his jacket, and she spied a pistol glinting at his side.

Evidently Taggart saw the same thing, for, clasping his arm about her, he started running. Seconds later a stupendous explosion shook the earth, knocking them to the ground. Light blazed up, followed by a gigantic mushroom of smoke. Taggart covered her body with his, and as debris pelted down like rain, she realized the Confederates had set off the huge powder magazine housed in the city arsenal. All about them buildings trembled as if an earthquake had taken place, and windows shattered from their casings and crashed to the street.

Once vibrations from the blast had passed and they'd regained their breath, Taggart rose and helped Silky to her feet. Quickly she glanced across the street and saw Fouche's mount cantering about wildly—then, putting a hand to her mouth to stifle a sob, she noticed a building had collapsed, its heavy rubble covering the place where the officer had stood.

Feeling a warm hand on her shoulder, she turned and fell against Taggart's broad chest. "Lord, how terrible," she breathed, clutching her arms about him and thinking no one should have to experience such a death. "That could have been us," she added hoarsely, shivers skittering down her spine.

Taggart's fingers pressed into her back. "Don't think about that now," he ordered, pulling her closer and kissing the top of her head. "It wasn't, and we're safe." He ran his fingers over her arms and hands and scanned her face for cuts. "Are you in one piece? Are you all right?"

She tossed her tangled hair back. "Yes . . . I'm fine," she whispered weakly.

Taggart studied her pale face, knowing she couldn't go

on much longer. Lord, what if they'd been killed instead of Fouche? he thought, squeezing her soft body against him in a protective gesture. Now that they'd been reunited he never wanted to let her go. Not when he had so much to make up for.

A large section of Libby's fiery roof crashed into the prison with a terrible splintering sound, and toward the center of town another arsenal exploded. After the initial blast, loose cartridges ignited with an earsplitting rattle, their noise mingling with the roar of the fire.

Her face smudged with soot, Silky gazed up at him with quivering eyelids, then sagged against him, her body limp and heavy. "They're going to blow up all of Richmond," she muttered against his shoulder, her voice raw with fatigue. "Where can we go to be safe?"

He put a protective arm about her and led her away from the area of destruction. "I know a place," he answered as they paused at the corner of Cary Street to stare back at the smoldering debris scattered about the prison.

He smoothed back a lock of shining auburn hair, then looked into her eyes that were glassy with fear and exhaustion. "Don't worry, my darling, I know a place."

Caroline Willmott rose from the breakfast table and placed her napkin aside. "Please excuse me now. I must see how Moses is coming along with his work." She moved to the door, her skirt swinging, then glanced back over her shoulder gracefully. "He's raising Old Glory from the top of the mansion," she announced with pride. "I believe it will be the first flag hoisted today."

Silky regarded the lovely lady, honored that she knew her, and glad that she lived here on Church Hill, far from the devastation around Capitol Square and the Libby Prison area.

Taggart pushed back his chair as a rakish grin settled on his lips. "While you're at it," he advised, "don't forget to make a fresh pot of coffee."

Caroline's eyes glistened like the sun in water. "Yes . . . don't worry, Major," she replied, a hint of laughter in her voice. "I'd never forget General Grant's coffee."

After she'd left Taggart stood and, wrapping his big hand about Silky's, helped her to her feet. "Let's watch the sun rise," he suggested with an underlying tone of tenderness that made her heart turn over in her breast. "I think we have some unfinished business."

"All right," she responded softly, feeling much better after a little rest and a nourishing breakfast. She'd already given him the news about Delcie and her brother, but they had so much more to talk about, she thought, her pulse racing a little faster.

Clad in a tattered white shirt and snug-fitting breeches, Taggart slipped his arm about her waist as they walked to a bay window that overlooked Richmond. It seemed they'd been separated forever, and when he drew her to him, pressing her bosom against his hard chest and folding her in his arms, all the wonderful feelings he'd ever stirred came blazing back stronger than ever.

Her head resting against his shoulder, they looked at the city. Below Church Hill half of Richmond lay in smoldering ruins against a rosy dawn sky streaked with scarlet. Occasionally a small arsenal exploded, billowing up a white cloud, and in the smoky shadows glimmers of fire could still be seen. But on the whole, the masses of vehicles and people had abandoned the streets, leaving an eerie pall over the capital of the Confederacy.

"What a waste," Taggart muttered softly. "What a terrible waste this insanity was."

Silky turned, engulfed in warmth as his hands glided over her back, molding her to his body. She looked into his eyes, feeling a little quiver of excitement. "Yes, nothing will ever be the same again. Everything has changed, but change always brings a chance for a fresh start."

"Silky," he began slowly, "I took advantage of you, and I know I've hurt you more than words can say." The rising sun tinged his rugged features with golden light. "But I hope to God that you can forgive me for being the biggest fool who ever lived, because I don't think I can live without you."

She placed a finger over his firm lips. "You don't have to say anything," she breathed, a soft tenderness blossoming within her. "I learned something on that long road from the Blue Ridge to Charlottesville to Richmond. I learned that the best war is the one that's never fought."

She threaded her fingers through his tousled hair. "And I learned that love doesn't hold any loyalties." She trembled, and he placed a kiss on her forehead. "But most of all, I learned you're more important than any cause."

A tear slid over her cheek, but he flicked it away. She nestled against him and in a stronger voice added, "I was holding on to an old worn-out dream with all my might. Holding on to it so hard I couldn't let go to latch onto something more important." She clasped her hands over his broad shoulders. "I've been thinking it over, and I finally decided the war was about a lot of things, but it wasn't about us."

With a feeling of gratitude, Taggart sloughed off the tension he'd been carrying for weeks. They'd passed through treacherous waters, but somehow they'd survived, he thought, pulling in a deep breath of relief. Thank God she understood how he'd felt since he'd first met her. While in Libby, he'd mentally composed one speech after the other, trying to explain his feelings. But it seemed that in her innocent wisdom, she'd already known what was in his heart.

"That's right," he murmured, sliding his hand up her neck to cradle the back of her head. "Where my mission was concerned, my allegiance was to the United States, but what I felt for you had nothing to do with the war."

Her gaze fell for a moment; then she looked up again. "It took a long time, but I understand that now," she replied softly.

"Lord Almighty, how I love you," he vowed, speaking the words he had wanted to tell her every day he was in prison.

Silky's breath caught in her throat. He said it, she thought, scarcely believing she'd heard the confession from his mouth. He'd actually said he loved her—not that he needed her—but that he loved her. How warm and witty and full of honor he was. What a good man he was! she decided in a moment of perfect, intense happiness.

Cupping her face, he murmured, "I loved you all along, but wouldn't let myself believe it because I didn't think we could work out our differences.'' His gorgeous eyes mellowed with tenderness. ''Lord, how glad I am this war is over.''

Taggart bent his dark head and kissed her eyes, her cheeks, and her neck, where a pulse was beating wildly; then his mouth was on hers. As his moist lips played over hers, she felt banked fires smolder and burst into flame inside of her. And that old languorous feeling began stealing through her once again, leaving her yearning for the fiery sensations only he could provide.

Gradually the sound of clattering horses and martial music came to Silky's ears, and Taggart loosened his embrace as they gazed at the colorful spectacle before them.

The United States Ninth Corps, a glittering stream of blue and gold, was passing down the street as the first of the Union forces wound their way into the beleaguered city. At their point, in front of the colonel, and the adjutant, and the bugler, and the three hundred men, and two hundred horses, and sixteen caissons, and the gleaming regimental band, rode a lone color guard on a prancing black stallion. From the standard the young soldier proudly held aloft, a banner rippled in the morning breeze—not the Stars and Bars, not a Union battle standard, but a spanking-new American flag.

The sight of the fresh-faced Union soldier pricked Silky's heart and reminded her of Taggart's brother. Tears gathered on her lashes, but she blinked them away. ''I understand how you feel about your brother,'' she said, painfully recalling all the young men that had been killed in the war, ''and I'm truly sorry about his death.''

Taggart tilted her face to his. ''Somehow I've managed to let that go, thank God.'' He sighed deeply, stroking his thumb along her jawline. ''I've finally understood it takes a wise man to see whether he's fighting for a principle or simply indulging his anger. Ned's death will always be a great tragedy, but I can live with it now.''

''Well,'' she whispered, swallowing back her emotions and managing a little smile, ''it seems there's just one thing left for us to decide.''

''What's that?'' he asked, fluttering a kiss over her lips.

She glanced at him through her wet lashes. ''Are you

going to surrender to me, or should I surrender to you?" she asked playfully. "The North may have taken Richmond, but our association is a different thing altogether. Personally I think you should surrender to me—you know, give me your sword and all. Being a high-ranking Union officer with yellow striped pants, I'm sure you have one."

Taggart laughed heartily, relishing her irrepressible spirit. He might have striven for happiness in the past, but at last he'd found the joy he'd been searching for all his life in this feisty bundle of mountain mischief. And the very thought that he was planning on spending every candlelight with her for the rest of his life filled him with heart-quickening joy. "Very well. I surrender—unconditionally," he offered, his lips lingering on each of her slender fingers and finally her soft palm.

After a moment of hesitation, he considered her tender face. "There's something I need to tell you—something important," he said, faltering a little over the words as sun struck fiery lights in her hair. "While we've been apart," he added, feathering his fingertips over her cheek as he spoke, "I received word that my father has passed away. His death changes circumstances completely for me."

Silky regarded his tense face and trembled. How much she'd wanted him to have a chance to straighten out affairs with his father. She remembered the warm feeling she carried for her own—but unfortunately this was not to be and there was nothing she could do to change the matter. "I'm sorry," she uttered in a whispery sigh, smoothing her hands over his corded arms in a comforting gesture, "sorry that you two could never be friends."

Silently he gazed down at her, his appreciative eyes expressing what his lips could not say.

"What will you do now?" she whispered, knowing his answer would alter her life forever.

She could tell he was mastering his emotions, and after a moment he straightened his back and added, "I have it in my mind to resign from the army."

Alarm poured through her, for she knew the people in Ohio wouldn't accept her, just as the people in the Blue Ridge would never accept him because he'd fought for the

Union. ''I-I see,'' she replied quietly, trying to make her voice sound normal. ''Then you'll be taking over your father's factory.''

Taggart's expression lightened. ''No—actually I'll be selling it,'' he answered, laugh lines streaking from his amused eyes. ''I'm going to put that fortune to another use. I have my heart set on buying land, like I've always dreamed about.'' He ran his finger down her nose, then over her lips, searching her eyes. ''What do you say, Fancy Pants? Will you marry me and strike out for California? We'll buy land there and start over. We'll forget this war ever happened.''

Silky drew in her breath, thinking she would die from happiness. Wildly throwing her arms about him, she stood on her toes to rain kisses over his face. ''Oh yes, a million times yes,'' she cried, the words coming not only from her lips, but her heart and soul as well. Tilting back her head, she laughed with pure, unadulterated joy, feeling as if she'd scooped the sun from the sky and it was now shining in her heart. He hadn't mentioned being handfasted—he'd done better. He'd actually asked her to marry him and to go to California, that wondrous realm she'd always dreamed about, that golden shore where dreams came true!

Taggart chortled lightly at her unrestrained enthusiasm.

''Are you sure you mean what you're saying?'' she asked, her bosom heaving with emotion. ''A rich man like you could marry anyone he wanted,'' she insisted, almost out of breath, ''one of those fancy Yankee girls you met at those West Point balls, anyone, why—''

He shook her gently, halting her runaway words. ''I don't love you for what you're not; I love you for what you are—and what you are is something glorious to behold.'' He studied her with sparkling eyes. ''Don't you believe what I'm saying?''

She giggled merrily. ''Well, yes—I'm beginning to. It's just that I've always had a hard time believing anyone who doesn't like okra and buttermilk. And now that I know you're a Yankee, I'm sure you really don't like either one.''

He gave a throaty chuckle. ''That's right, and I never will, but I love *you,* you sassy little Reb.''

She looked up at his roguish face, thinking she was the

happiest woman in the world. California was a long way off, and the future was full of uncertainty, but their love would protect and sustain them. Together they could face anything. "And I love *you*—you low-down, blue-bellied, Yankee buzzard!"

Taggart's brows shot up in surprise; then he laughed richly.

"You won't be sorry you're marrying me," she promised, intentionally using the heavy mountain drawl that had colored her voice when they had first met. She tossed her hair back and tilted her head to the side. "My love is just like my applejack," she teased with a little chuckle. "It'll make your ears ring, your eyes water, and sweat pop out on your brow. Why, you'll feel so good, you'll have to walk sideways to keep from flying!"

He flashed her a devilishly wicked smile. "Ummm, don't I know it." He pulled her closer, moving his hands in tender circles over her shoulders. "I don't think our peace negotiations are over yet, ma'am. There's one more item on the agenda."

"Very well, sir," she said crisply. "The prisoner has permission to speak."

He lowered his lips to hers, his hands sliding from her shoulders to her waist and leaving a tingling warmth in their wake. "I think we should seal this bargain not with a peck on the lips, but with a proper kiss," he murmured, his voice threaded with fiery passion. He flashed her a provocative grin, moving his strong hands over the hollows of her back. "Don't you?"

Before she had a chance to answer, his mouth captured hers with ravishing insistence, and she circled her arms about his neck, responding to the magic of his touch. As his lips burned over hers, searching, demanding, making her his, happiness sparkled through her like dazzling fireworks. Enveloped in warm glory, she melted against his hard chest, thinking that from this day forward their love would last for eternity—well, maybe not eternity, she decided with an inner smile—but a jillion years at least.

And it was then, during this moment of wild ecstasy, that Silky Shanahan realized that while the Confederacy might have been defeated, *she* had won the war.